DARK
WATERS

Also by G. R. Halliday

From the Shadows

DARK WATERS

G. R. HALLIDAY

Harvill *Secker*

LONDON

1 3 5 7 9 10 8 6 4 2

Harvill Secker, an imprint of Vintage,
20 Vauxhall Bridge Road,
London SW1V 2SA

Harvill Secker is part of the Penguin Random House group of companies
whose addresses can be found at global.penguinrandomhouse.com

Penguin
Random House
UK

First published by Harvill Secker in 2020

A CIP catalogue record for this book is available from the British Library

penguin.co.uk/vintage

ISBN 9781787301436 (hardback)
ISBN 9781787301443 (trade paperback)

Typeset in 12.5/17.5pt Adobe Garamond Pro by Jouve (UK), Milton Keynes
Printed and bound in Great Britain by Clays Ltd, Elcograf S.p.A.

Penguin Random House is committed to a sustainable future for
our business, our readers and our planet. This book is made
from Forest Stewardship Council® certified paper.

For Alisa

Chapter 1

When she still had all of her arms and legs, Annabelle liked to drive. And it was while she was on one of her drives that she made the first mistake.

Her iPhone. She'd left it on the passenger seat of her BMW, instead of taking the time to slide it properly into its little holder on the dashboard. It lay beside the copy of *Heat* magazine and the touring map of northern Scotland she'd bought at the services outside Stirling. She'd stopped for petrol and a fast-food breakfast, an indifferent ham sandwich and a coffee in a paper cup. Afterwards she'd folded the cardboard packaging and the cup and slid them carefully into the recycling bin, rather than leaving them on the table for the tired-looking waitress to clean away. Annabelle was twenty-two years old and tried her best to be a nice girl.

Before she got back in the car she thought about calling Miss Albright, who lived in the flat on the other side of the landing from her in London. She was ninety but in truth it wasn't really Miss Albright she was concerned about. It was Mr Pepper, Miss Albright's dog. A Pomeranian. Black with a pink tongue. Because Miss Albright couldn't leave her flat often Mr Pepper spent much of his time inside. Most days Annabelle would cross the corridor to take him out for a walk. Usually he'd be waiting for her at the door, growling slightly with anticipation. Stupid as it sounded, she thought Mr Pepper might be less anxious if Miss

Albright could reassure him somehow that Annabelle would be back soon. Everything with her divorced parents felt broken and complicated, the exact opposite to how she felt around Miss Albright and Mr Pepper, who both always seemed so pleased to see her.

She looked at the time on her iPhone. 7.05 a.m. Miss Albright would still be in bed. Annabelle resolved to call her that afternoon and decided instead to take a first selfie in Scotland. Fifteen selfies, actually. A selection to get the right feel. Head at the right angle, the correct pout on her red-painted lips, brown hair framing her face in the right way. Taking in the word BRAT printed in red on her white T-shirt (long-sleeved, as always). The blue BMW M4 her dad had given her as a very late twenty-first birthday present behind her. In the distance the first mountains of the Highlands, dusted with spring snow.

After a quarter of an hour fiddling with the photo filters, she decided the image was as good as it would get. She typed, 'Look ugly today but who cares! Heading beyond the wall!! Road trip to the frozen north xx.' It sounded spontaneous enough when she read it back. She posted it to Instagram, the only social media app she used regularly, then flicked through some of the pictures. People smiling, looking beautiful and having fun. She had hardly met any of her Instagram friends in real life, but maybe they would see her picture, maybe they would notice her like she was noticing them?

Maybe he'll notice too and feel jealous you've come to Scotland without him knowing? Annabelle dismissed the ridiculous thought. *He* was in the police and acted like he was forty. Probably didn't even know what Instagram was. The last thing she wanted was to hear from him anyway. After what happened. This trip had nothing to do with him. There was no doubt it felt scary coming

2

all this way on her own. But when did she need an excuse to drive? Driving fast was the only time she felt OK.

An hour later she could still taste the salt and grease from the ham, stuck to her lips. But at least the coffee kept her sharp as she drove north on the A9. It had been six hours overnight on various motorways from London to Stirling. Not bad going. In the end it took another two and a half to Inverness. This was good too.

It was still morning when the road dropped down off the moor and she could take in the city of Inverness for the first time, tucked in at the edge of the water – the Moray Firth, according to the satnav. Straight ahead a large bridge spanned the water; Annabelle wanted to drive on over it. Instead the satnav told her to turn left at the first roundabout she came to. Reluctantly she did as she was told and drove through the outskirts of the city. A grim industrial estate that didn't fit with her image of what the Highlands should look like at all. Nothing tartan, nothing like *Outlander*.

Her disappointment abated ten minutes later when she exited the other side of the city and rejoined the water. The wide river was directly beside the road, and in the distance she saw a row of dark mountains and felt a flutter of excitement. *The wild mountains of the west, Glen Affric, the most beautiful glen in Scotland.* She'd read about the famous drive down Glen Affric online, but she was heading for a lesser-known road. And the satnav told her it was only twenty-five miles to her destination. Half an hour later the mountains were so close they seemed to loom over her. She passed through a run-down village and finally stopped when she saw the sign: GLEN TURRIT.

It was here, at the start of this lonely glen, that she made her second mistake.

The gate that blocked the road was closed but not properly

secured. The last person through had draped the chain loosely around the wooden post but not clicked the padlock shut. Annabelle held the lock in one hand and glanced around at the steep wooded slopes rising on either side of the road. According to a sign by the gate this road was STRICTLY PRIVATE. She knew from online forums it had been built to service a huge hydroelectric dam constructed in the 1950s. The single-track road hugged the river that wound down the glen for miles and eventually ran across the top of the dam. Then continued on, for over twenty miles, to another locked gate near Strathcarron. Close to the Isle of Skye on the west coast.

When Annabelle was making the hasty plans for her trip she'd stumbled on a post that said it was sometimes possible to pay the keyholders at each end of the road to open the gate. 'Twenty quid each should do it,' the post had read. 'And it would be cheap at twenty times that price. When else are you getting your own private racetrack through a Highland glen?'

A single-track road with towering dark mountains on either side, and not another vehicle within thirty miles. It was like being in the perfect car advert – she pictured a disciplined driver, dressed in a suit, piloting his vehicle across miles of empty tarmac in an otherworldly vision of car perfection. She could feel the sweat standing out on her palms at the idea. Rural driving was amazing when you watched the lads on *Top Gear* bantering, but the reality was always different. She recalled the trip to Cornwall for Dad's wedding a few months back, stuck behind caravans and people carriers.

This was going to be different. She glanced around again at the thick forest by the side of the road. Still holding the padlock in her hand. The place seemed completely deserted, the scale and loneliness intimidating compared to the bustle of her usual city life. Patches of snow were still visible high up on the mountains, but the sun was warm enough for Annabelle to stand there in just her long-sleeved T-shirt and black leggings. She hadn't fully believed the road actually existed until now, and what were the chances of finding the gate open? It was like she was meant to race down that road.

The drive was perfect. The open road, the wide blue sky overhead and the mountains topped with snow. Those delicate tight bends through the woodland beside the river. For once Annabelle could really push the car. Blast through the turns, hammer down on the throttle and hear the engine blaring, then stand on the brakes before the next turn. She wasn't aware of the nervous smile that kept breaking through the tight expression of concentration on her face, nor the feeling that everything else, everything she didn't want to think about, could be left behind her. Like the dust rising up off the road and drifting in the morning sunlight.

Finally, after long twisting miles, the road straightened out as the valley widened. The mountains retreated from the road. As she sped over a slight hump, feeling the car momentarily rise then fall as the speedometer crept close to a hundred, the grey wall of the dam became visible in the distance.

The perfect morning sunlight fell on the road, lit the heather on the open moorlands to a muted mustard colour.

Annabelle took a deep breath and smiled again. She slowed the car a little. It was like being at the centre of a vast amphitheatre, the mountains the walls around the arena, the skies above the spectators.

It occurred to her that she really should take a photo. She glanced at the holder on the dashboard, saw it was empty and remembered she'd dropped the phone onto the passenger seat.

She looked up at the open road ahead. It was needle-straight for at least the next mile, nothing coming in the opposite direction. She eased her foot off the throttle a little more, then reached across to the passenger seat and felt around for the phone. Her hands found glossy paper instead. She glanced at the seat. The phone had worked its way under the magazine.

She looked up again. Ahead there was a huge tree by the side of the road, virtually the only one in the open moorland of the valley. The road was still empty though, still straight. Reassured, she reached again to push the magazine aside. Glanced at the passenger seat, saw the phone and made a grab for it.

'Gotcha!' Annabelle straightened up and turned back to the windscreen.

The little girl was standing in the middle of the single-track road.

Time slowed. Annabelle took the girl in with almost freeze-framed clarity. Her white T-shirt and cut-off jean shorts, her skinny arms and legs sticking out. Bare feet on the tarmac. Blonde hair, pale skin and blue eyes locked onto Annabelle's with a strange kind of certainty.

Annabelle didn't have time to touch the brake. Instinctively she jerked the steering wheel down hard to the left.

The BMW rocketed off the road at seventy miles an hour. Annabelle stared at the thick tree with its rough folded bark. The half-second before the impact stretched into infinity; it seemed she even had the chance to ask herself, *Why did the girl have to step out here? Why right beside the only tree in the valley?*

Annabelle didn't know it until much later, but she had made her biggest mistake a long time before. By choosing that model of car in that particular shade of blue.

Time sped up, the car met solid wood, and everything was black.

6

Chapter 2

DI Monica Kennedy was watching the opposite side of the busy Burger King restaurant in a retail park in Inverness. A young woman sitting alone at a table was staring hard at a boy, her son presumably, who was strapped into a buggy beside her. His little fists clenched across his green T-shirt, his head down. As she observed the interaction Monica felt a familiar sense of disquiet rising from the pit of her stomach. The feeling that something wasn't right, that somehow it was her responsibility to step in. The kind of notion that had drawn her to the police. It had got her into trouble more than once.

'Can I have more sauce for my chips?' She turned at the sound of her four-year-old daughter's voice cutting through the babble of the other diners. She realised she'd been staring across the room for the better part of a minute. She blinked and took Lucy in – curly blonde hair, blue eyes.

'Of course, honey.' Monica reached for a sachet of tomato ketchup and handed it to her, trying hard to resist glancing back at the mother and her son. The boy, aged about three, had looked well dressed, well cared for. No obvious signs of violence or neglect. *You're so edgy these days. Can't stop yourself sniffing out trouble, can you? Even when you're supposed to be spending time with Lucy.* This had been her daughter's Sunday treat, a trip to the cinema (*The Secret Life of Pets*) then Burger King.

At least I didn't immediately return Hately's call, Monica argued in her defence. Her boss, Detective Superintendent Fred Hately, had left a message while she was in the cinema asking her to call back as soon as possible. This wouldn't have been unusual, except Monica had been off the Major Investigation Team for almost half a year. Taking a break to spend more time with her daughter after an investigation had nearly ended in tragedy for both of them. Hately had agreed to her request for a secondment and she had been placed in the traffic department. This was the first time he had contacted her outside office hours in months, and she felt the knot tighten in her stomach. The call could only mean bad news.

'They said at the nursery we shouldn't eat too much ketchup or salt,' Lucy piped up as she squeezed the sauce out onto her chips.

'That sounds like good advice.'

'Why are salt and ketchup bad?' Lucy asked, screwing her face up with puzzled interest, a characteristic expression.

When Monica glanced back over, the woman was still staring hard at the child in the buggy, whispering something to him. Monica realised that he was holding a small toy tight between his hands. A teddy bear. She noticed he was twisting it by the neck, apparently unconsciously. Monica noted that the woman was smartly dressed in boots, jeans and a grey sweater. No obvious signs that she was under major psychological pressure.

'Did that boy do something naughty?' Lucy had noticed her mum's interest.

'I don't know, sweetheart.'

Lucy pushed her tray away. 'I'm finished.'

Monica nodded and stood up. A couple of diners turned to look at her. She was over six feet tall in her flattest shoes and had the pallid complexion of a corpse. Her face framed by shoulder-length dark hair, she was wearing a long grey tweed coat, threadbare in places. She rarely went unnoticed.

She stepped round the table, helped Lucy into her jacket and zipped it up. On their way out of the restaurant Monica couldn't stop herself from having a final glance at the mother and son. The boy was staring straight ahead, his cute round face set in a scowl. His mum was scrolling through her phone, now seemingly oblivious to the child beside her. *You see, it was nothing, just a little family argument. It's your paranoia making things much worse than they are.* As the thoughts rose, Monica looked down at Lucy. To check that her daughter was there beside her, even as she felt that small hand tight in her own.

When they were safely back out in the Volvo, Monica finally returned Hately's call.

'Kennedy?' His normally assertive Glaswegian voice sounded almost rattled when he answered after two rings. Monica glanced in the rear-view mirror at Lucy; her head was down and she was staring at a book open on her lap. Outside, a family ran laughing from their car through the open doors of the cinema, feeling the first spits of the cold May rain that was now hitting the Volvo's windscreen. Her mind served up a distant fragment of childhood memory: her, her mum and dad, running together from a storm. And somehow that family under those grey skies carried a sense of what was coming Monica's way. 'A male body's come in. A bad one. DI Simpson is down south on a case. You're my best investigator. I can't hand something like this to DC Crawford, he's too inexperienced. Do you think you're ready?'

She stared out of the windscreen. 'I'll be right there.'

9

Chapter 3

The pathologist raised his head and smiled up at the sound of the door as Monica pushed it open. It was the first time she'd seen Dr Dolohov since the case at the start of the winter.

'DI Monica Kennedy.' His unusual accent rose in greeting – Russian that somehow sounded closer to southern English than anything. He ran a hand over his shaved grey hair and adjusted his glasses. 'The best investigator in the north! Back to fight more of this world's monsters! Has she still got it though?' He smirked then tilted his head to look up at her with genuine curiosity. 'You look sad though; I expected you to be excited.'

Monica shook her head at Dolohov's facetiousness, though she couldn't help but like the man. There was something refreshing about his naked curiosity. Better than being lauded as a hero, better than the dark whispers about her past.

'Just my daughter, everything that happened in the last case . . .' she heard herself say. Though why she was opening up to him of all people, Monica had no idea. 'I think it makes me overprotective . . .'

'Children can be little devils,' Dolohov said, as if delivering a piece of sage advice for the ages. 'I'm sure a lot of people would be happier without them. Before she met my grandfather and moved to St Petersburg my grandmother was a child in the Ukraine. During the famine in the 1930s she said her little friends would go missing from the street. People sold their children as food. Can you imagine?'

'I'd rather not think about it.'

'Yes,' Dolohov said. 'Well, maybe those people wouldn't either. But then they had to. Maybe it's better to have some hate in your heart for your children. Just in case.'

Monica frowned at the doctor's curious philosophy. Even after six months away, a few minutes of conversation with him was more than enough. She glanced back at the morgue door. She had messaged two of her colleagues from the Major Investigation Team to meet her here.

DC Connor Crawford was about to turn thirty. Monica had first worked with him on the case six months before. She had initially been wary of his taste for bars and women, before growing to trust and even like him. His sometimes barely contained wildness meant it wasn't exactly a surprise he was running late. He might well have been out drinking or in someone's bed, even on a Sunday evening.

DC Ben Fisher's absence was more puzzling. He was the younger of the pair, in his mid-twenties. He was a university graduate, academic and precise. More openly ambitious than Crawford, who he seemed to irritate perpetually. Fisher's hair was dark and he wore it short with a conservative side parting. Sometimes Monica couldn't help thinking of the pair as opposites: Crawford a lively jack of hearts, Fisher a quiet, calculating jack of clubs. The three of them had worked closely together on the previous case, and each had paid a price. In one way or another.

Monica shook her head to dislodge the nagging memory of the case. It was in the past; best it stayed there.

Fisher was annoyingly keen and determined to make a good

impression, and she'd been a little surprised to find the corridor outside the morgue empty. No DC dressed in a well-cut suit, already fiddling over his laptop, setting up a decision log for the case. Had he changed that much in half a year?

'Anyway,' Monica said finally, determined to change the subject. She trusted Crawford and Fisher enough to know they would both get there as soon as they could; she would fill them in on the details of the case later. 'Why was Hately so keen to have me come back early for this?'

Dolohov's face lit up. 'Over here.' He pulled on a fresh pair of surgical gloves then walked over to one of the refrigerated storage units at the back of the mortuary. 'Some fishermen spotted him – he was caught up before one of the hydroelectric dams, near Beauly.' Monica nodded. She knew the area from scenic drives out to the west of Inverness to visit the glens.

Dolohov paused then pulled the drawer open. What was left of the body was bloated, swollen and badly decomposed. Blanched skin that had begun to break down into its constituent fats and proteins. The face was barely recognisable as human, spread out wide so the features were indistinct. Monica swallowed her instinctive disgust and forced herself to lean in a little closer until she could see the black facial hair on the chin and above the lips. She ran her eyes over the rest of the body. The left leg missing from the calf down. The right arm gone at the shoulder, the left arm at the elbow.

'What happened to him?'

'He drowned,' Dolohov said. 'Water and plant material in his lungs. Before that he . . . had a bad time.' He cleared his throat, pointed to the mess of flesh at the shoulder where the right arm should have been. 'Removed at the joint, the whole thing torn out,' he said with a flourish. Then he gestured to where the lower left arm should have been. 'Removed at the joint, the whole thing torn out,' he repeated, pausing for dramatic effect. 'It's *possible* these two injuries could have occurred naturally in powerful, fast-flowing water. If his arms were caught up in a weir, for example.'

Monica nodded, although this scenario sounded highly improbable to her.

'But look.' Dolohov pointed to the remains of the left leg. A visible section of white bone stuck out from the bloated flesh. 'Here the bone was torn. Chewed through by a cutting implement.'

'A cutting implement?'

'Probably a saw,' Dolohov said. And his eyes flickered up to meet Monica's.

'For Christ's sake.' Her softly spoken words echoed in the white-tiled silence of the morgue. 'You said he drowned. So this was done to him pre-mortem?' She understood now why even Hately had sounded rattled.

'Someone cut him up while he was still alive.' Dolohov said, nodding slowly. 'Piece by piece.'

Chapter 4

Monica stood on the bank of the River Beauly and watched the eerie lights of the dive team as they moved out into the deep black water behind the Aigas power station dam. It was almost 10 p.m. now and completely dark apart from the industrial lights on the dam and the headlights from the Volvo, two marked police cars and a police van. Cutting through the cold night. The divers were beginning their search for the missing body parts. For clues that might help answer the questions the body presented. Who was the victim? Why was he in the water? And, most importantly, who did it?

'Feels really remote out here. Only twenty miles from Inverness but it's a different world once you're in among the mountains.'

Monica glanced down at the sound of DC Connor Crawford's voice. He was almost a foot shorter than her. She took in his high cheekbones and narrow face, his wiry but muscled body lit by the headlights. Inevitably his red hair was carefully combed up into its sculpted quiff. He was wearing a slightly shabby brown wool suit under a tan leather jacket, a contrast with the crisp white collar and cuffs of his shirt and the strong smell of expensive aftershave that drifted off him into the cold night air. Almost as if he'd planned his outfit for effect. The ruffled but attractive detective dragged away from his exciting extracurricular activities.

Crawford had turned up just as she was leaving the morgue, carrying three cardboard coffee cups. A convenient explanation for why he'd missed the delights of a close look at a dismembered and decomposing corpse.

'That's the Highlands,' Monica said finally in reply. She knew that Crawford had grown up on the remote west coast, but he seemed to have developed a mix of fear and disgust for any non-urban area. She'd wondered more than once why he hadn't just transferred down to London or the Scottish Central Belt. It would have suited him much better.

He stared into the black water, shrugged. 'My grandad used to say that they had to re-convert parts of the Highlands to Christianity. That they had gone back to paganism in the remote areas. *The dangers of superstition*, he called it. Always gave me the creeps.' He folded his thin arms across his chest, a barrier against the idea and the crawling cold.

Monica pulled her own coat tighter and took a sip of luke-warm coffee, DC Fisher's cup. *Well, your second young protégé still hasn't turned up so you might as well have it.* The thought reminded her. 'Did Ben Fisher call you?'

Crawford stared straight ahead at the water. 'Why would he call me? You know what he's like. He's probably tucked up in bed with a bit of light reading from the *Senior Investigating Officers' Handbook*. Thinking of ways to impress you,' he said over his shoulder. For a moment Monica couldn't help but imagine Fisher sitting in bed, dark hair in a precise side parting, glasses on the end of his nose, a neat pair of pyjamas instead of his well-cut suit, studying theoretical cases while missing the messages on his phone about an actual case. Monica almost smiled at the picture, but she continued to stare at Crawford. She sensed he knew more than he was letting on. He had a knack for ferreting out information after all. 'Wouldn't want to be in there at night, that peaty water, can't see your hand in front of your face.' Crawford nodded at the water. She watched the sinister white ripples of the divers' lights deep under the surface. Unnatural, like fairy lights crossing over from a different world. Monica imagined the claustrophobic dark waters, shivered and wondered for a second whether Crawford was speaking from experience. She seemed to have a dim recollection of overhearing him describe a diving trip he'd taken. Exploring ancient shipwrecks? In the Mediterranean?

'We have to be seen to at least look,' she said finally. If Crawford did know anything about Fisher's absence he wasn't about to share.

'You think it could be organised crime?'

'It's the first thing that comes to mind. Given what little we know of the victim's profile. Middle-aged male, physically large.' Some of the most disturbing cases Monica had worked on were gangland crimes in London and Glasgow. Brutal tortures, sadistic dismemberment. But for some reason her instincts told her it didn't quite fit here.

'Why not get rid of the body properly? Bury it somewhere?' Crawford gestured vaguely into the darkness further up the glen. He was jogging up and down now to keep warm, his jacket and suit inappropriate for the icy spring weather it turned out.

'Maybe they wanted him to be found? Maybe—' Before Monica could finish the thought she felt her phone vibrate in her pocket. The number was unknown but when she answered with a curt 'DI Kennedy' the voice on the other end of the line was strangely familiar. An unexpected echo from the past.

Chapter 5

Annabelle could feel the blackness all around her. She opened her eyes, blinked and blinked. Panic rising with every second that the darkness failed to clear. Something was very, very wrong.

For half a second she hoped she might be home in her flat with the shutters closed. *It's the middle of the night; you're still mostly asleep.* The thought made sense. But as she tried to force this idea into reality an image entered her head: a map with a picture of mountains and lakes on its cover. The other memories quickly followed. The gate. The road. The little girl. The crash.

You've been blinded, that's why you can't see! Your eyes are gone!

The thoughts sent adrenaline surging through her body. She tried to sit up and the first wave of screaming agony came on. Searing up from her right leg.

'Help me! Someone help me!' she screamed, trying desperately to sink back away from the pain. But it stayed remorselessly with her until the tears were running down her face.

For a long time there was only the pain. Gradually it faded until Annabelle realised that although her head ached like the worst migraine, there was actually no pain from her eyes. She stayed very still and tried blinking again. Still no pain. Reaching up with both hands she felt the balls of her eyes through their lids. They seemed normal. Slowly she opened her eyes and peered into impenetrable blackness.

It was the darkest hour of the night – that was why she

couldn't see. She was trapped in the car and her leg had been horribly broken in the crash. It was obvious. If she was in the car her phone must be nearby. She replayed the moment: stretching for her iPhone. How could she have been so stupid? She took a deep breath and slowly moved her left arm. Feeling for the steering wheel, for any familiar object. But her hand grasped nothing but cold air.

Annabelle resisted the new panic that was gathering and tried again. Stretched her hand out to the right this time. If she was still in the car then surely her fingers would touch the door. She could find the handle and begin to orientate herself from there.

Her outstretched fingers brushed something for just half a second. But she recognised immediately what she had touched. Carpet. A deep shagpile carpet that felt almost identical to the one in her old family home. The one in her bedroom all those years ago. It wasn't possible. The inside of the BMW was leather and plastic, and the carpet on the floor completely different. When Annabelle brought her shaking fingers back to her nose they carried a musty smell. Absolutely nothing like the freshly serviced citric interior of her car.

At the same time her overstressed mind registered an obvious fact for the first time: *You're lying flat on your back.* Why wasn't she in a car seat? The terrifying truth that had been circling rose up into her conscious mind with absolute clarity. She couldn't feel the steering wheel or the door handle because she wasn't in the BMW. She was somewhere else, somewhere dark. It meant someone had moved her from the wreck of the car. It meant someone had put her here.

Chapter 6

'Monica? Monica Kennedy? Is that you?' She stared into the black water at the divers' spooky lights. Tried to place the voice on the other end of the line.

'Who is this?'

'It's Bill, Bill Macdonald.'

Monica squeezed her brain, searching through the hundreds, thousands of names that she'd encountered over the years in her work. Criminals she'd arrested, colleagues she'd worked with, victims, witnesses. The voice was familiar though, with a strong Inverness accent. 'Give me a clue,' she said finally.

'You know,' the man said, sounding almost insulted that she hadn't recognised him, 'Bill, Big Bill, from the Marsh.'

The Marsh was Rapinch, an unfashionable part of Inverness. The part Monica had grown up in, the part her mother still lived in. And as he said the words, Monica was taken back thirty years to school. The micro-hell of the Scottish country dancing classes that all pupils were forced to attend. She was almost always one of the last picks. Her unusual size intimidating to the adolescent boys. But on the rare occasions that Big Bill Macdonald attended he would often raise his head of thick blond hair in her direction. Monica could still remember the feeling of bliss at not having to bend her back and half crouch to hold hands. The feeling of being the smaller of the pair. As his nickname suggested, he was already six feet tall and weighing over two hundred pounds by his third year of high school. He rode his dad's old Triumph motorcycle from the age of fourteen and wore scuffed leather biker trousers to class, his hands permanently stained black with oil. An aspiring Hell's Angel, like his father, who was rumoured to have been a member of a notorious biker gang. His family lived just round the corner from Monica's. Sometimes she used to sit on his driveway and chat to him when he was working on his motorcycle. She could still remember the heat of the afternoon sun on her back in the summer. The way he would glance over, his eyes seeming to linger on her long legs and the shape of her hips.

'I got your number from your mother, I didn't even know you were back up here. It must be . . . what? At least ten years?'

Ten years and the rest, Monica thought. *But not long enough.* If it hadn't been for needing her mum's support with Lucy, she would have stayed away for a lot longer. Unbidden her mind ran back down all those years to the scene with her father. Eyes meeting in horrified understanding, cold rain on both of their faces. The year 2000, the millennium. She'd got into her car, started driving and hadn't seen or spoken to him again until his deathbed, twelve years later. By then, mercifully, he'd been too far gone to talk. *Dad again.* Ever since the last case it felt like he was haunting her thoughts, her dreams. The streets in Inverness she used to love walking down with him when she was a child, the same ones she walked down with Lucy now. All those memories rising up like living things.

She glanced down at Crawford to break the chain of thought. He was fiddling with an iPad in the passenger seat of the Volvo. Flicking through images of the unidentified body, taken before it was pulled from the water. She could see the bloated corpse snagged in low branches that hung into the water. Right beside the small fisherman's shelter, just waiting to be found. It occurred to her that someone could even have hooked it up there purposefully.

'Can I help you with something, Bill?' She was keen to put the call, and the haunting memories it triggered, behind her and get back to the case. Usually when an old acquaintance contacted her unexpectedly it was because they were in some kind of trouble they thought a detective could magically make go away. Dimly she recalled her mum filling her in on gossip about Bill's family. Did he have a son? Some trouble with drugs?

But when Bill started talking again what he said had nothing to do with his family. 'There's a lad here, causing trouble . . . He mentioned your name. Told me he knew you, that I should call you to come and get him.'

The centre of Inverness was Sunday-night quiet when Monica pulled the Volvo over beside Ness Bridge on Huntly Street. Almost directly opposite the red-stone mass of Inverness Castle, floodlit against the black sky. The lights of the street lamps reflected back off the black river. Monica found herself staring down at it for a moment and wondering if the dead man's arms could have made it past the dam and be floating below her. Grasping at cold nothingness on their way out to the sea. She shivered at the image, reminded herself that the Ness wasn't even connected to the Beauly.

'Always trouble in this pub.' Crawford's voice cut into her thoughts. He gestured across to the dark exterior of the bar Bill Macdonald had directed them to. The Clach. Monica crossed to the door and tried the handle. Locked up tight. A faint glow of yellow was visible through the blurred glass above. She hammered on the door.

A buzzer sounded and the door clicked open. She caught the

familiar pub smells: faded perfume, stale beer and body odour. She stepped inside and took in the row of bottles behind the bar, the shadowy room. A fruit machine flashing remorselessly in the far corner. Close to the machine a man was sitting on a bench. Hunched forward with his head in his hands. Monica moved closer. He had dark hair and was wearing a blue shirt, torn at the collar.

'Fisher?' Monica didn't try to hide the shock in her voice as her younger colleague glanced up at her. His normally pristine hair scuffed into a mess. A red mark standing out on his cheek. The glasses he usually wore nowhere to be seen.

Monica had assumed Bill Macdonald's call was about some petty criminal from the Marsh. Someone who'd given her information somewhere down the line. Hoping a detective's name would be a get-out-of-jail- or get-out-of-a-kicking-free card. Despite Ben Fisher's no-show at the morgue, the idea that it could have been about the young detective constable, so uptight it seemed a physical impossibility he'd ever make it past the door of a pub, let alone consume a mouthful of alcohol, hadn't even edged into Monica's mind. The image of him in bed nursing a copy of the *SIO Handbook* still seemed so much more believable that she had to double-take to check it was really him. She glanced behind her at Crawford, caught the shock on his face as one of his hands went up to his red hair.

'I heard he'd been going out drinking a lot . . . I didn't know he was out tonight,' Crawford said defensively. Monica turned back to Fisher and swore under her breath. The last thing she needed was one of her most thorough investigators having some kind of character transformation at the start of a murder case. Especially when she was only just back on the team after half a year away herself, and not exactly at her most robust.

'What the fuck happened, Fisher?' Monica's surprise at seeing him here overloaded any sense of discretion.

'He started on one of the MacFarlanes.' Monica turned at the deep voice from behind the bar. Big Bill's wide face remained boyish, over a decade since Monica had last seen him. Still framed by thick blond hair. 'Punched him, then said he was going to kill the boy.'

'The MacFarlanes?' Monica repeated dumbly. They were well known to the police, a problem family. One of the relics of the clan system that somehow still existed in fragments across the Scottish Highlands, even 250 years after Culloden. Representatives of a lingering tribal morality and the Celtic urge to pass a bottle and share in the wildness.

Bill nodded. He was dressed in a leather jacket that made his thick frame somehow more intimidating. She noticed now that two other men, friends of Bill presumably, dressed similarly in dark jackets, were sitting together further down the bar. They had been hidden around the corner when she first walked in.

'They were set on kicking his head in and throwing him in the firth at Ferry Point.'

Monica shook her head slowly. Momentarily forgetting her anger with DC Fisher and feeling pure relief that it had happened in this pub, with Bill around. Fisher was lucky to be in here and not in the hospital or the morgue. But relief was tempered by the knowledge that if he'd crossed the MacFarlanes his card was marked. They wouldn't be interested in involving the police, but Fisher could expect retribution somewhere down the line. Maybe not for years, when he'd forgotten all about it.

'What a mess,' Monica whispered, crouching to check on Fisher properly. The knuckles on his right hand were swollen and bleeding. A mark on his right cheekbone was coming up as a purple bruise already. Most likely a left-handed assailant, she noted almost subliminally. The young detective stared down at the dirty floor, refusing eye contact. 'What happened?' she asked again, still staring at Fisher but addressing Bill.

'The usual. Your man there had been in drinking all afternoon. Started mouthing off at people. Threatening to have them arrested.'

Monica glanced over to Crawford. What Bill was describing was enough to get anyone kicked off the force. She couldn't shake the illogical sense that it was all connected somehow: her paranoia earlier at Burger King, the body in the morgue and now this. A final cap on the shittiest of Sunday evenings. And it made absolutely no sense. Fisher seemed to value his work above almost everything else in his life. Almost like the police was a surrogate family. On the surface he had come out of the difficult case the year before with the least damage, and with his reputation as a promising detective established. Why would he, of all people, have done something this stupid?

Chapter 7

Despite the pain from her leg, Annabelle must have fallen into another concussed sleep, because in her dream she was back in London. Walking across London Bridge on her way to a party in a strange old Victorian dance hall. The kind of place that was deliberately shabby with upturned beer crates instead of tables and bean bags instead of chairs. She was supposed to meet someone there, maybe her mum or her dad.

She looked around. There were groups of people, all looking perfectly at home in the trendy environment. As if there was nothing more natural to them than to look perfect, posed like an Instagram image that had been hearted a million times. But there was a shadow moving slowly from the corner of the room. Across the dirty wooden floor, over those bean bags and beer-crate tables. It carried a hint of something that could taint and destroy.

Annabelle adjusted the way she was standing. Tried to adopt the pose of nonchalance she'd practised for when she was waiting outside a lecture hall at university, her hip a little off to the side, her phone held almost at arm's length as if she were just glancing down at it, rather than compulsively checking it for notifications.

The shadow drew near and her leg began to throb. Hotter and hotter until Annabelle couldn't help but look down. She saw that somehow a small black tent had been erected around her right leg. With horror she realised that something was moving about inside it. The pain pulsed harder, and Annabelle screamed. She looked around desperately for help, praying her mum or dad might have appeared, but the people had all turned away. Anyway, she realised now, they were waxwork models. Standing frozen under the eerie orange light.

She woke soaked in sweat, agony coursing through her body from her broken leg. *Try taking deep breaths*, the voice inside her head suggested, *like the therapist told you to do when you start panicking*. It was a laughable defence against the all-encompassing cocktail of pain and terror, but she didn't have many options. She kept her eyes screwed tight shut and tried to breathe slowly and deeply. After a minute she found that the voice in her head had been correct: the pain had receded slightly.

But fear spread slowly to take its place. The memory of the carpet on her fingertips. Like the one in her childhood bedroom, but old and rotting. Where was she? Who had put her here? Clearly it couldn't be the same carpet. She hadn't lived in that house for over a decade. It was hundreds of miles from the Scottish Highlands, and Mum and Dad had acrimoniously divorced years ago. But in some strange way it felt like she'd been transported back to that quiet room where she would sit on her own with the toys. Back to that house and all the simple strangeness it had taught her about the world.

A sound cut through her fevered thoughts. A body shifting slightly on a wooden chair, which creaked in response. Annabelle froze; the breath stopped in her chest. Then she heard the hiss of breathing. Someone was in the room with her. Surely the person who had taken her from her car and brought her here.

Horror washed through her body like a rapidly rising tide.

Slowly she opened her eyes. Instead of the impenetrable dark there was a grey half-light this time. Above her there was a smooth concrete ceiling. Her mind couldn't quite comprehend that this was really happening, and a whimper must have escaped from her lips because the chair creaked again.

'Shhhh . . . You're safe here.' The person stood up and moved closer, their voice almost a whisper. 'Just think of this place as your new home.'

Chapter 8

Monica's mum leaned across the worktop, her handsome face alive with excitement.

'I thought it must have been an emergency – he said it was *business.*' Angela Kennedy shook her head of thick grey hair as she recounted the story of Bill Macdonald's late-night call to the house, asking for Monica's mobile number. She'd repeated a similar phrase at least three times already since her daughter had come out of the shower.

The night before, Monica had decided it would be better to sleep on the sofa at her mum's house in the Marsh than go back to her own flat. Sleeping fully clothed on the sofa was a habit she'd developed in the last six months. She slept more lightly there, which seemed to lessen the nightmares, and keeping her clothes on helped too: ready for the monster coming in through the window or the door.

Monica rubbed a hand over the painful crick in her neck. If anything her mum's sofa was even more uncomfortable than the one at her own flat. But at least she'd be around while Lucy had breakfast – her daughter was already asleep when Monica arrived the night before. She hadn't wanted to wake her to take her home. Since Monica returned to Inverness when Lucy was born she had tried to limit her visits to Rapinch. Bad memories of her early days as a detective, when things had gone seriously wrong with her dad, too many faces from the past. This morning she was regretting her visit for a different reason as her mum began asking uncomfortable questions. 'I thought it might be to do with *the case* you were called back for, maybe he had some *intel*?'

If only, Monica thought. She chose her words carefully, aware that there was a chance they would be repeated in the local shop. Or anonymously on one of the online forums her mum visited to discuss her favourite topics: true crime, TV crime dramas and crime fiction.

'It was nothing serious, a little bit of trouble at the bar he manages.' Monica could already picture her mum conducting her own *investigation*. Digging into this nugget of information with her friends at the salon next time she had her hair done.

What the hell was Fisher thinking? She remembered his fixed expression in the car outside his house after she'd asked him just that question. She had turned to face him as Crawford sat beside her, staring straight ahead to save his colleague's embarrassment.

'I forgot to eat ... I've been having a bit of a hard time. Since the case last year.' He snorted a strange little laugh. 'A bit of women trouble too actually.'

Monica had stared back at him, still struggling to fit all this with the bespectacled, geeky version of DC Ben Fisher she'd first worked with and eventually come to respect as a detective. She knew how badly the case he was referring to had affected the whole unit and the wider Highland community, but on the surface Fisher had seemed unscathed in comparison to herself and Crawford. *Maybe you're being naive?* Monica had challenged herself. In truth she hadn't given much thought to how the case had impacted the young detective. While she and DC Crawford had been recovering, Fisher had been drawn deeper into the hideousness of the follow-up investigation. Maybe this had rocked his world more profoundly than anyone realised? Clearly he respected hierarchy, the sense of safety that authority could provide. Aspects of the case had challenged these comforting ideas. Maybe it was this that Fisher was struggling to cope with? She sighed and let some warmth creep into her voice. 'Look, do you need something, Fisher? Time off? Counselling?'

'I'm fine. It was just a really bad night, boss.' His face was twisted in discomfort. She could see how mortified he was to be sitting here like this, and that gave her a moment of reassurance, that he still clearly cared about the job. 'Things got on top of me . . . It'll never happen again. I promise.'

She had continued to stare at him for a long time. Watched his eyes stay locked to the back of the headrest in front. Everyone had their secrets, everyone made their mistakes. She knew that as well as anyone. The MacFarlanes were never going to make a complaint against him. Technically she and Crawford hadn't witnessed any crime. Monica trusted Fisher as an investigator, knew from experience how thorough he was in his work. She really needed him on the case that had just come her way, she would be working closely with him, could keep an eye on him.

Cutting through Monica's thoughts, Angela said, 'I thought because of his boy? You remember? Andrew? I told you, he'd been caught with those drugs. Dealing them? What a worry it is for Bill and Bill's mum.' Angela went to stir something on the hob. 'Do you want special eggs? That's what Lucy's having? Aren't you?' Her mum's 'special eggs' were a fat-laden mix of cheese, butter, eggs and salt. Lucy nodded from where she was sitting on the sofa, already at work on the arduous task of lacing up her little trainers.

'I'm fine, thanks.' Although the smells from the hob were

appealing, Monica didn't feel like eating. 'What happened with Bill's son?' A welcome change of subject.

'He got in with a bad lot. Started using that cocaine, and selling it. A silly boy, only nineteen and he's looking at jail.' Angela laid the plate on the small table in front of Lucy. 'A very silly boy, taking drugs. If anyone ever tries to make you take them you say no! Don't you, Lucy?'

The Major Incident Room was already busy when Monica pushed the door open and stepped inside. Catching the familiar mix of smells – machine-brewed coffee and freshly applied deodorant. A thrum of orderliness and control. Almost six months away and it felt like nothing had changed.

She had already heard from the desk sergeant on her way into the station about Fisher's unfortunate first trip to a boxing gym with Crawford. An overzealous sparring partner who had bruised his face up. A good story; it seemed like the kind of thing that would happen to Fisher, Monica decided. Probably a few of the older detectives, who DC Fisher's references to proper procedure and best practice rankled, had even been cheered by the news.

She glanced between her two young detectives, who were sitting together at a desk. Fisher was neat again now in a blue suit and with his dark hair with its careful side parting. He was wearing a replacement pair of black-framed glasses, the angry purple bruise on his cheek partially obscured by concealer. Crawford beside him in the same brown suit from the night before, his quiff of red hair looking slightly damp from whatever product he put on it, a smattering of stubble across his narrow face. Monica had decided he must use some kind of beard trimmer rather than a wet razor to keep it permanently at that length. Despite how different the two detectives were in looks and character, together they exuded a collegiate competence, their foibles currently hidden by their formal dress.

If only they knew, Monica thought, glancing around the office as she remembered the scene in the pub the night before.

They were joined by a third detective. DC Maria Khan, a woman in her early thirties. She was wearing a grey trouser suit, albeit a badly cut and ill-fitting one in comparison to those of her two male colleagues. Monica had met the new detective in passing but not yet worked with her. She had been brought onboard to assist with the investigation and handle media interest in the case, which Monica had no doubt was going to be considerable. Crawford had mentioned that Khan had left a career in the media several years previously to become a detective after some 'major shitshow in her personal life'. 'She's clever, good at the job, closed book though. Keeps herself to herself,' he had added, which in Crawford's parlance probably just meant she didn't respond to his attempts at flirtation. Monica introduced herself, shook Khan's hand then looked her quickly up and down. Noted her attempts to disguise her prettiness by tying her dark hair back in a severe ponytail and wearing thick-framed glasses. Which wasn't a bad idea, Monica thought, when you spend your days around criminals. Khan sat down at the table with Fisher and Crawford. Thankfully her presence meant the other three could act like their visit to The Clach had never happened.

'What have we got from the missing persons?' Monica asked, pleased that they could actually focus on the investigation. She already knew that the search of the river had failed to turn up anything so far.

Crawford cleared his throat. 'A couple about the right

age – forties and fifties,' he said, pointing to the files on the table. 'Would tie in with what Dolohov estimated.'

'What do we know about them?'

'The first one's interesting. Sebastian Sinclair, aged fifty-three. Declared missing two weeks ago by his wife, Karen Sinclair—'

'Wait,' Monica cut in, '*The* Sinclairs, who own half of the Highlands?' Sinclair Enterprises was the biggest company in the north of Scotland, responsible for dozens of major engineering and building projects.

'That's right. One of them.'

'He went missing two weeks ago? Why wasn't it in the press?'

'Maybe the family wanted to keep it low-key,' Khan suggested. She had an archetypal Lowland Scottish accent, from somewhere like Stirling, with just a hint of Glaswegian. Harsher than the soft Highland tones Monica was used to hearing in Inverness. 'They're connected. They would probably be able to keep it out of the local press for a while if they wanted to.'

Monica nodded. It sounded plausible but also begged a lot of questions. Principally, why weren't the rest of his family desperate to find him? If they were, then surely a media appeal would have been close to the top of their priorities.

'Here.' Crawford slid a photo out of the file. It was a corporate image, the kind that might appear on a business website. A slim man in a blue suit in his fifties with dark hair, smiling slightly. An authoritative pose with his hands locked together in front of him. She held the photo at arm's length and mentally compared it to the decomposing corpse in the morgue. 'It could be him, although the body seemed heavier.'

'Might have put weight on since?' Crawford said.

'We're going to need DNA from his family.'

'I'll get in touch with his wife,' Fisher said, sounding more eager than ever. Another good sign that last night was a one-off, Monica noted hopefully. His phone buzzed on the desk as he was speaking. He glanced down at it, then frowned.

'What?'

'Just someone being an idiot,' he said sniffily, holding the phone up. Khan leaned in beside him to read the message out.

' "Looking for training tips. Are you free to demonstrate some boxing this evening?" ' As she read it a huddle of detectives in the corner of the room working on another case let out cackles of laughter.

'Just ignore them, Fisher,' Monica said, pointedly turning her back to them, but thinking, *At least the boxing story's sticking.* 'Do we know anything else about Sebastian Sinclair?'

Fisher switched his phone to silent as Khan opened a copy of a local lifestyle magazine. A feature was spread over several pages with a picture of Sebastian Sinclair and a woman standing together outside a large office block.

'I recognised the name and remembered reading this a few months back,' she said, pointing to the headline, BROTHER & SISTER TEAM PUSH COMPANY FORWARD. 'Sebastian Sinclair and his sister Heather took over the running of the company after their father passed away. Apparently they're expanding the business, doing well with it.'

'Would seem to make the organised crime angle less likely,' Monica said, wondering again why the family would report Sebastian Sinclair missing but not want it covered in the local press. Some kind of corporate embarrassment? 'What about the other one? You said there were two.'

Fisher held up a photo of a smiling man wearing jeans and a T-shirt. Dark hair splattered with grey. Monica squinted at the image. 'What's his name?'

'Theo Gall. He's a bit younger,' Fisher said. 'Declared missing by his wife Pauline Gall almost three weeks ago.'

'What do we know about him?'

Fisher scanned down a printed sheet. 'Born in Inverness. Convictions for theft of an automobile, falsely claiming benefits, tax fraud, assault, driving while under the influence . . .'

'Career petty criminal. He sounds the more likely, especially from the organised crime angle. We should still have his DNA on file,' Monica said as she stood up. 'Khan, if you can draft something for the press, an appeal for witnesses in the area. Fisher, you start going through the house-to-house information from locations around the river. There's a chance someone saw whoever dumped the body.' She thought about it for a second. 'Find out if there's an anglers' club, birdwatchers, walkers visiting the area. They might have noticed something out of the ordinary up in the glen.'

'What about the hydro workers?' Fisher piped up.

'Hydro workers?'

'You know the hydro dams up in the glens, for generating electricity. When they were building them they dug huge tunnels under the mountains, dammed whole glens. They're major engineering projects – need regular maintenance,' he said, speaking authoritatively. 'Workers actually have to drive down into the tunnels, check the pressure and so on. One of them might have seen something.' Despite his slightly patronising tone Monica was encouraged again by the re-emergence of his geekiness.

She nodded. 'Look into it. Is there anything else?'

Khan seemed to hesitate. 'A call came in this morning, ma'am. A woman out in a place called . . .' She picked up a piece of paper from the desk and Monica noticed her chapped hands and chipped fingernails. Clearly manicures weren't high on her list of priorities. For a second Monica's curiosity kicked in and she found herself wondering about Khan's transition from media to police. Maybe the new detective would tell her herself somewhere down the line if they became close. Maybe not; some things were best left unsaid. 'A place called Little Arklow?' Khan continued finally. Monica nodded. She knew the village – out in one of the glens, notorious for troublemakers and dropouts.

'What is it?'

'I don't think she was very well. Apparently she calls the station a lot, was shouting down the phone.'

Monica sensed the new detective was concerned she might be wasting her boss's time with a pointless lead. 'What did she say?'

'She said that she knew what had happened to our victim. That –' Khan hesitated again '– that the people who killed him had killed before. Lots of times.'

Chapter 9

Annabelle struggled desperately to bring her heart rate back under control as she tried to process what she'd just heard: *Just think of this place as your new home.*

'No!' the shout ripped involuntarily from her throat as she turned to face the speaker, her whole body shaking uncontrollably. 'Where am I? Why did you bring me here?' The flood of adrenaline had even overwhelmed the pain in her leg. The person was standing in the corner of the room, just a shadow in the poor light. 'Why did you bring me here?' But the moment of righteous indignation faded as the figure stared back without reply. 'I'm going to get up, and I'm going to go.' Annabelle's tongue was a lump of lead in her mouth. Still the person didn't reply. She began edging to the side of the low bed, her leg singing with pain.

'I wouldn't do that.' The person moved a half step towards her. Annabelle couldn't judge the age or sex of the speaker from their voice. 'Your leg was very badly broken. The Doctor attempted to save it, but it was touch and go.'

'I don't care. Just let me go.'

'The Doctor said this might happen.' The voice was flat and dead in the same way that the room was dead. An unearthly relic from a half-forgotten nightmare. 'I don't want to do this, but he said I might have no choice.'

Annabelle watched, frozen, throat like clay, body clamped

tight, as the figure reached to the ground and picked something up. It was some kind of face. For a moment her frantic brain assumed it to be a living thing. A head hanging separate from its body. She sank back in horror. The figure lifted the head closer so Annabelle could better see it. She shrank further back on the bed. It was a kind of mask. It looked to have been made from a metal can with holes roughly cut for the eyes and mouth.

'He said I should strap this on to you if you didn't stay calm. Once it's on any noise you make will just come echoing back into your ears, so there'll be no point shouting.' The person gave a strange little laugh. 'Now, are you going to stop being silly and do as you're told, or do I have to put this on you?'

Chapter 10

It was still morning as Monica followed the road west down the glen beside the River Beauly until it became Strath Glass. A wide, flat valley with mountains rising on either side. She pulled into a lay-by on a rise in the road when she spotted the mobile control-room van. When Monica banged on the door there was no response. After a minute she noticed the volunteer searchers in the distance working their way slowly up the river; probably the team leader had gone down to work with them.

Monica watched for a moment as some picked their way among the silver birch and Caledonian pine trees by the water's edge. Others waded in the shallows. The spring sun had broken through the clouds; the lines of snow on the mountains in the hazy distance stood out as sharp white edges against the sky. She took a deep breath of the mountain air and allowed herself a moment to appreciate the silence and being alone in the wide-open space. It was almost funny. She lived close to one of the most beautiful landscapes in the world but only ever seemed to visit it for the darkest reasons. Like searching for the person or persons who had killed and dismembered the still unidentified corpse in Raigmore Hospital's morgue. The corpse of Sebastian Sinclair? Theo Gall? Or someone else, someone they didn't know yet?

Under the gentle light the searchers in the distance put Monica vaguely in mind of children guddling in the water for minnows. She remembered a camping holiday with her parents – Glen Coe, south of Fort William on the west coast of the Highlands – back in the mid-1980s when she was becoming an awkward teenager. When the weather was good there was nowhere more beautiful, and if there was enough of a breeze even the biting midges were stilled. She recalled lying beside a slow-moving river. The smell of dried heather and the sun's heat on her skin, watching some younger kids wading in the shallows. Those cheap fishing poles bought from the campsite shop. Just a bamboo stick with a wire and plastic net on the end, fulfilling some primal urge to chase and catch and contain. They would take the little fish from the river and keep them in claustrophobic jars and buckets, taking ownership of them. Monica remembered watching, trying to understand the impulse, why people needed that control. Her father was the same. His need to be in control seemed to grow as she became a teenager and began to assert her independence. He started to *check* the books she brought home from the library in central Inverness before she was allowed to read them – she had to hide the Stephen Kings and Clive Barkers under the ancient history texts. To *check* where she was after school, who she'd been speaking to on the way home. For some reason she never felt able to discuss these things with the few school friends she trusted, to ask if this was *normal*. It had felt like a betrayal to her dad, who she had still loved then. She always felt safe around him as a teenager, a contrast to school, where she faced casual taunts about her height and the way she looked on a daily basis, even though he was so controlling, as if he thought she was still about eight.

Things had been easier when she really was that age. *Daddy's girl.* She remembered his prison officer's uniform – maybe it had fired her interest in joining the police. One Sunday, as a child, she had gone with him to see where he worked out at Carselang Prison. In the middle of nowhere, framed by mountains. She was allowed into the entrance office, even though Monica's mum had explicitly told him not to take her inside the brooding Gothic pile. *Please, Dad! All right, but just don't tell Mum!* She remembered the smells, an enclosed mustiness mixed with the scent of far-off cooking, distant shouts echoing down corridors. How thick the walls were, how proud she'd felt at sharing that moment with him. The way the other officers gathered round and spoke so respectfully to *her* dad, the men laughing at his jokes.

And she couldn't help remembering another time, twenty years later, when she made the same drive across the prison's entrance bridge for a very different reason. This time as a junior detective investigating the death of one of the prisoners, a case that her dad became embroiled in. One that had coloured all her memories of him and finally ended everything between them.

Monica caught herself thinking of him again. Why now, when she had barely thought about him or why she had left Inverness in years? *It's because of Lucy.* The answer came straight back from her subconscious. Everything that happened last year, and now watching her getting older, almost to school age. It's taking you back to your own childhood. Monica shook her head. Her upbringing hadn't been perfect, her parents had their faults, but they never physically hurt her, they always loved her. It wasn't until she was an adult that things went really wrong with her dad. This time Monica felt a moment of panic rising from her stomach with the thought, and she glanced around the wide landscape. Suddenly feeling horribly vulnerable beneath the open sky. She took a deep breath and got back into the

Volvo, forced the illogical feelings down into her stomach, then checked the time to take her mind off them.

Only 11.30 a.m. Little Arklow was a twenty-minute drive.

'Most likely a waste of time,' she whispered. But when a call came in claiming to know the identity of a murderer someone had to check it out. She was here anyway, so it might as well be her. Besides, keeping busy seemed like a good idea when her mind seemed determined to dredge up every uncomfortable memory it could.

Just before the village of Cannich the road split in three directions. One went on towards Glen Affric, a second to Glen Mullardoch; Monica took the third. A hard right that led along a single-track road in the direction of Glen Turrit. She knew that further up the valley the road was private. But the dead-end town of Little Arklow was situated a couple of miles before the public road ended. What was left of the town anyway.

Monica remembered hearing a late-night radio documentary, BBC Scotland probably, during a long drive back from a case she'd worked in the far north-west Highlands. It had been about the building projects that Fisher had mentioned. The thousands of workers who were brought into these remote Highland glens to carry out the dangerous work. The presenter had mentioned the history of Little Arklow. Originally a camp for Lowland Scots and Irish workers, it was a permanent village from the 1940s to the 1970s while several dams were built in the area. At its height there had been five pubs and over two thousand residents, but when the work ended, those who could moved on.

After fifteen minutes Monica came to the painted sign: LITTLE ARKLOW. Half of the cheap prefab houses were without their roofs now. A stray dog stared back at her from a narrow alleyway.

Visible behind it the ever-encroaching forest of silver birches. What remained of the place was a magnet for troublemakers and misfits, drawn by low rents and free squats. Monica glanced at the single battered-looking pub that remained halfway along the main street. The Turrit Arms.

Not the kind of place we'd bring Gran for lunch on a Sunday drive, Monica thought, looking in at the grimy windows. As the idea occurred to her she remembered a recent trip they'd taken with a complaining great-aunt. Every time they'd stopped she had made a fuss about the child lock on the back door of the car, which prevented her from getting out, until Monica had spent a frustrating ten minutes in a rainy lay-by disabling the thing. She shook her head at the irritating memory and slowed to check the house numbers, stencilled in fading black paint on the whitewashed doors. Fifty yards further up the street she pulled over at number 76, killed the engine and got out.

Down a side street a group of four men were sitting on plastic chairs. Beyond them in the distance dark mountains were visible: Glen Turrit. And beyond that Glen Mullardoch and Glen Affric. The body could have been flushed out from a river in any one of those long valleys. How many hundreds of square miles to search? A lot. As if hearing her thoughts the four men raised their heads in unison, turning to watch her. They were dressed in an assortment of shabby tracksuits, jeans and jackets. Faces hollowed out by the long winter past.

She turned away to the house and double-checked the number on the gate matched the one she'd written in her notebook because the place looked abandoned. It was a traditional Highland croft house – an ideal holiday home except for the harling peeling from the walls, the holes in the roof and the advancing birch forest on either side which seemed to be about to swallow it.

The door was opened before Monica even knocked. A woman wearing a faded Oakland Raiders baseball cap over greasy grey hair looked out at her. Her face was dirty and weather-beaten. She glowered up at Monica from under the brim of her hat.

'You on your own?' the woman said, peering beyond Monica. 'Proof they're not serious.'

'I'm looking for Gillian Keegan?' Monica held out her warrant card. The woman barely glanced at it.

'Won't do any good anyway.'

'Why not?' But the woman had already turned and gone inside.

Medieval was the word that came to Monica's mind when she followed her in. The floor in the kitchen was compacted dirt, and a birch branch poked through a hole in the broken window. Gillian was perched on a chair by the fireplace, attempting to light a roll-up from the embers. With the smoke rising around her face in the shadowy room she made Monica think of the stories her mum used to tell her about the Cailleach, a Gaelic witch.

'You never answered my question.'

'No one wants to listen.'

'Try me,' Monica said, glancing around for somewhere to sit. She realised that Gillian was already using the only chair and instead stayed standing.

'No one listened when it happened to my friend Euston Miller either, that's why.'

'What happened to him?'

'He was murdered four years ago. Same as the one in the river.'

'Who murdered him?' Monica asked. Watching Gillian's face under the shadow of her cap.

'Shouldn't you be the one telling me that? They weren't inter- ested when I went to your lot about him. They said he'd done it to himself but he wouldn't have. Not when he was so close.'

44

'Close to what?'

'Someone got him drunk.' Despite Gillian's distracted air, Monica could hear the genuine distress in her voice now. 'They drove his car into Dog Falls in Glen Affric. He didn't do it himself. He wouldn't have just left me.'

Monica wiped the back of her hand across her face. 'I'm sorry for your loss,' she said mechanically.

Gillian stared up at her with something close to malevolence in her eyes. 'As if any of your lot care when some drunk from out in the sticks turns up dead.' Her voice dripped contempt.

Monica was about to reply when she felt her phone vibrate in her pocket. She dug it out, went to switch it to silent then realised it was actually an alarm. A reminder that if she didn't leave now she would be late collecting Lucy from nursery. She swore under her breath and hit the snooze button.

'I'm here now,' Monica said. 'Who do you think killed him?'

Unexpectedly Gillian pulled the baseball cap off to reveal her head of matted hair. She threw the hat hard across the room and spat on the floor. 'I told them years ago. It was the Affric Men who did it to him. He told me they would and they did.'

'The Affric Men?' Monica repeated back. Whatever she had expected Gillian to say – the name of some local ne'er-do-well probably – this wasn't it. 'Who are the Affric Men?'

Chapter 11

Annabelle stared at the mask with horror. She was beginning to realise that she was in trouble. The worst possible trouble. She lay frozen, as if the person, just feet away across the room, might somehow forget she was there.

'I take it we're in agreement then? You'll do as you're told?'

If you don't the mask will be strapped tight around your head, probably you'll be tied to the bed too.

She realised her head was nodding slightly.

'Good. I could tell you were sensible.' The person laid the mask on the floor and sat back down. 'I'll bring you something to eat soon. The Doctor said it's important you build your strength, help the leg to heal as best it can.' Then stood again almost immediately. 'I'd better go. I shouldn't really be here.'

'My phone,' she heard herself whisper. 'I need my phone.'

'Your phone?' The person made a snorting sound, something like a laugh. 'You won't have to look far. It's right beside your bed.'

Annabelle turned her head to the left. She realised that the room was lit by a dim lamp standing on a table close to the bed. Right there beside it was her iPhone. She made an impulsive grab for it, as if it might be snatched away. The feeling of relief was immense as she squeezed it tight in her hand, like spotting an old friend in a distant lonely city.

'I'll leave you to make your calls.' A moment later the door clanked shut and Annabelle heard a bolt being drawn closed.

She stared down at the phone. Her elation faltered when she saw the web of cracks across the black screen. It broke in the crash, of course it did. The tears stung her eyes as she heard the distant sound of a second heavy door slamming shut. It seemed to come from above her, as if she were deep underground.

For a moment she couldn't even remember how to switch the iPhone on. She gulped the tears away. *Please, please work, please.* Finally she remembered that she had to hold the button on the side and the button on the front down at the same time to start it. With shaking finger and thumb she pushed them in and watched as, incredibly, the phone responded. The white apple logo appeared on the screen and relief blossomed in her chest.

'Thank you, thank you, thank you,' she whispered. Still staring at the screen, phone cupped in her hands like a sacred object. Her mum's face came into Annabelle's head. How long had it been since she'd spoken to her? More than a year. Annabelle had tried to talk about her childhood, about her parents' divorce. Her mum had got annoyed, asked why Annabelle always had to make a fuss, told her that not everything was about her. Annabelle hadn't tried to see her or even speak to her since. But she would give anything for a five-minute call with her now, with anyone.

She typed her passcode in. The screen opened with its gloriously efficient movement, revealing the familiar little lozenges of her apps. Her thumb landed on the green phone icon at the bottom right. She hit the Keypad option and quickly typed in 999, then the Call icon. She held the phone to her ear, praying for a voice on the other end of the line.

There was only silence though.

Slowly she moved the phone from her ear and looked down

at the screen again. 'No Network Connection'. The space at the top left that normally read 'O2-UK' now showed 'No Service'.

Of course it did, why else would they have let you have your phone? They were keeping her here. Maybe she'd even die here and no one would ever know.

For a long time she sat there on that bed, in that musty darkened room, praying for the return of 'O2-UK'. But no matter how hard she willed it the screen never changed. The deep blackness piled down on her, and as the adrenaline ebbed from her body the pain edged back in a chill tide.

Chapter 12

Despite being late leaving Little Arklow, Monica was actually among the first of the mothers waiting outside the nursery to collect their children. She completed the drive to Inverness in under forty minutes. A record time, probably. Aided by the caffeine from one of Crawford's cans of Red Bull she found in the passenger seat pocket. The spring day had turned gloomy and spits of rain were hitting the windscreen as she pulled up. She reached into the rear of the car for her umbrella before she climbed out and went to wait for Lucy by the wall.

The black umbrella flicked satisfyingly open, and she glanced at the time on her phone: ten minutes early. She should chat to some of the other parents, like a normal person would. Instead she found herself dialling Crawford for an update.

'Fisher and Khan haven't come up with anything obvious from the house-to-house so far.' Crawford sounded frustrated at the lack of progress. 'No abandoned cars down the glens, nothing suspicious. It's like the body just appeared there, out of thin air.'

Monica glanced along the street to the other mothers congregating at the nursery entrance. A few curious faces were already turning to glance at the solitary detective. Feeling a moment of paranoia, she allowed herself to imagine what they might be saying about her. What they might know about her. Monica forced an awkward smile back at them. Who didn't have things from their past they were uncomfortable about? Who hadn't made mistakes? It would be easier if she were friends with some of them. But unlike her mum, who seemed able to strike up conversations wherever she went, Monica couldn't do small talk.

'What about the organised-crime angle?'

'I've spoken to a few contacts, but if they know anything they're not saying. Could mean there's something big, could be nothing . . . I've been asking about Theo Gall, to see if anyone knows what he's been up to recently. Nothing so far.'

'What about Sebastian Sinclair?'

'Sinclair?' Crawford sounded surprised she'd even mentioned the name. 'You're talking about Inverness royalty, practically. You saw that spread about him and his sister, property magnates. Not one of my contacts, I'm afraid. You'd be better asking Hately. He's in with that crowd.' Monica nodded – she hadn't thought of talking to her boss about it. 'Seems less likely than Gall though? Don't you think?'

Monica tended to agree. But the fact Sinclair's disappearance hadn't been reported in the local press niggled her. 'Probably. We should have the DNA back on the body tomorrow, we'll know if it matches what we have on file for Gall.'

'I've requested DNA from Sinclair's family too.'

'We'll speak to his wife about his disappearance tomorrow.' A thought occurred to her then. 'Do "the Affric Men" mean anything to you?'

'The Affric Men?' he repeated back to her. 'I don't think so, why?'

But before she could expand on her conversation with Gillian Keegan the nursery doors were opening and the children were pouring out.

Monica turned the shower down a little and stuck her hand under the running water to check it was at a child-friendly temperature. Then called Lucy through from the living room where she was watching *Horrible Histories* on Netflix. A naggingly inappropriate programme for a four-year-old, but Lucy loved it.

Monica undressed and in the bathroom mirror caught a glimpse of the scar. The thick white mark was six inches long and ran from just above her dark pubic hair to close to her belly button. A permanent physical reminder of the night at that house the previous autumn, of the case that almost made her quit the force. Like she needed one, like the guilt could ever recede. She laid a hand over it, as if blocking it from her sight might somehow hide it from memory too. She shook her head at the notion as Lucy came wandering through and Monica waited dutifully for her daughter's small, slow fingers to take off the T-shirt and jeans she was wearing.

Monica resisted the urge to ruffle that thick mass of blonde curls, something that Lucy had recently taken to protesting against. Instead she watched her daughter in the mirror. She was still cherubic with those curls. Still relatively unselfconscious about her naked body. Monica had tried hard to stop her own bouts of physical self-hatred from being passed on to her daughter. The kid stepped carefully into the shower and Monica reached for the special anti-tangle shampoo she used on Lucy's hair. So different from her own straight black hair, lined with grey now. She worked the shampoo through the curls, trying hard not to pull at them.

'Did you get to see Grandad's bones at his funeral?'

'His bones?' Monica repeated, taken aback. The question was strange even by Lucy's standards.

'Granny said that lots of people came to his funeral. But it was before I was born so I wasn't there except in your tummy.'

'You don't see someone's bones at their funeral, honey,' Monica said gently. Her mind was drawn back five years to the scene at Tomnahurich Cemetery. Rows of mourners in black, faces grey. Her mum was correct, there had been lots of people there. Barely one who Monica had felt connected to. She wondered for a moment where Lucy had got the idea you might see someone's bones at a funeral.

'What was on *Horrible Histories*?' Monica asked, sensing this might provide the answer.

'Just "Stupid Deaths",' Lucy replied after a moment, referring to a section of the programme that celebrated the unusual ends of historical figures. 'A king got his leg infected by someone's head that he cut off and he died from it.'

'Right.' Monica wondered again if the programme was in any way suitable for a four-year-old. 'Was there anything else good on it?' She was keen to steer the conversation away from another reference to her father. But Lucy never replied and stood staring down at the plug hole instead, watching the frothy water spin. Monica tried again, 'You never told me what you did today at nursery?' Lucy glanced up at her, shook her head quickly and looked back down, her mind clearly elsewhere now. For a moment Monica pictured herself crouching to glower at the kid, putting the pressure on her to talk. If only getting inside her daughter's head was as straightforward as forcing evidence from a criminal.

After the shower she towelled that small body dry then took Lucy through to the bedroom to help her into her pyjamas. Once Lucy had climbed into bed, Monica sighed internally as her daughter's eyes remained fixed on the ceiling in a preoccupied stare. It was only when Monica leaned in to kiss her goodnight that Lucy finally seemed to realise she was even present.

'Do you think that dreams can be real?' Lucy asked, her face expressionless as if it were the most everyday question.

'Why do you ask that?' Monica replied slowly. 'Did you have another scary one?'

'I dreamed that a lady was trapped in a room,' Lucy said. 'I dreamed that she was frightened. A monster wanted to eat her.'

Chapter 13

An odd chill ran up Monica's spine at Lucy's description of her dream, but she tried to keep her voice light. 'Why did the monster want to eat her?'

'I don't know.' Lucy shrugged, suddenly wide awake again, turned away and grabbed the book of cats that was inevitably lying on her bedside table. 'What colour of cat do you like the best? I like ginger ones, especially if they have white patches.'

After another long conversation about what colour and size of cat she would most like to befriend, Lucy finally drifted off to sleep. Monica went to double-check the front door was locked and bolted, then sat on the sofa. She considered opening one of the bottles of wine in the rack her mum had bought and filled for her, but remembering the stink of booze on Fisher's breath the night before, she made herself camomile tea instead. She flicked through the collection of records she had inherited from her dad, selected a yellow-and-red LP, slid the record from its sleeve and set it on the turntable without checking the artist. She dragged the headphones over her ears, volume low in case Lucy called. A voice crooned out and Monica checked the sleeve. 'Indian Love Call' by someone called Slim Whitman.

She considered turning the TV on to check what coverage their body had generated in the evening news, but remembered DC Khan had been tasked with keeping track of the media and would inform her of anything significant. Instead she picked up her laptop and typed 'Affric Men' into the search engine. Gillian Keegan had refused to elaborate any further earlier that afternoon, insisting Euston Miller had put all the information online somewhere before his death. At the recollection of the name, Monica slid her phone out and typed a message: 'Could you look into Euston Miller's death? Suicide in Dog Falls, Glen Affric, four years ago.' She sent it to Fisher, sensing it might be helpful for him to stay busy.

She turned back to the laptop. The search had returned ten pages of results. Five minutes of clicking through revealed that most of the sites provided information or services for tourists visiting 'Scotland's most beautiful glen', as Affric was billed. This seemed to confirm her suspicion that the Affric Men only existed in Gillian Keegan's slightly addled mind. Monica continued scrolling hypnotically down the screen anyway, engrossed by random stories of hillwalkers rescued from the winter mountains or the latest advocate for releasing packs of wolves back into the Highland wilderness.

Then her eyes caught the words and for the second time that night a chill ran up her spine. Blue letters stood out against a bright background: 'The Truth about the Affric Men and the Glen Affric Triangle by Euston Miller'.

'Gillian was telling the truth,' Monica whispered. And involuntarily she glanced out through the gap between the blinds at the dark night sky, the glow of lights from the city. She clicked the link.

The page that slowly loaded looked not to have been updated since the 1990s. On the left-hand side there was a column of fuzzy images. Under the header was a map of Glen Affric, Glen Mullardoch and Glen Turrit with a lopsided red triangle sketched over the top of it. She hit the first image, the entrance to what looked like a huge tunnel. It opened a gallery featuring a series of black-and-white images of men excavating the tunnel. She scrolled down to read the paragraph beneath: 'The earliest of the recorded incidents took place in 1954 when the first six-mile-long tunnels were being sunk through the Turrit massif to feed the great loch that was to be dammed up behind the planned Turrit dam . . .'

Monica scanned further down the page, impatient to read about the actual incidents Euston Miller was referring to. Her eyes landed on a photograph of the front page of a newspaper dated 10 December 1954. The headline read: BUTCHER RUNS AMOK IN HYDRO TUNNELS. Monica sucked in a breath. She wasn't sure what she had expected, but it certainly wasn't this. She zoomed in to read the faded words.

It is reported that up to ten men have been killed and a number more trapped after a disgruntled tunnel worker is said to have detonated explosives at the entrance to one of the access tunnels, trapping a significant portion of the day shift within the mountain. Subsequently the man, named locally as former Scottish Hydro employee William McBride, is said to have attacked surviving members of the works gang armed with a shotgun, before turning the weapon on himself. Rescuers were met with scenes of devastation. A number of tunnel workers are still unaccounted for and there are fears that without light they may have become lost among the maze of small exploratory tunnels in the lower reaches of the mountain.

Monica took a sip of the tea and reflected for a moment on the horror of being lost in a maze of dark tunnels. Somewhere she'd visited in her nightmares recently, more than once.

She opened a fresh tab and typed: 'Turrit tunnel collapse William McBride', expecting a string of results. Surprisingly only a handful came back. Surely such a major event would have a slew of pieces written about it. She tapped on the first result, a short Wikipedia entry which described the incident in less dramatic terms than the newspaper article.

Early reports on the Turrit Tunnel Tragedy suggested that explosive charges had been deliberately set off by a disgruntled former employee, drilling engineer William McBride, something that his family vigorously denied. A subsequent investigation found that the integrity of the entrance tunnel had been compromised by a lack of adequate bracing to hold the roof in place, and the repeated use of explosives within the tunnel caused the entrance to fail. In all a dozen workers were killed in the accident, making it one of the worst single incidents in the history of Scottish Hydro dam building. Which stands out even in the early years of the hydro projects in the Highlands, when health and safety was notoriously lax.

Monica set her laptop down on the coffee table and stood up to stretch her back. So was the investigation report nonsense? Or was the newspaper story sensationalised bullshit? Maybe somewhere in between. Either way she still couldn't see what bearing it had on a murder investigation over sixty years later, regardless of Euston Miller's theories and his potentially suspicious death.

Unless, the idea fluttered into her mind, *unless there really is something bad about those mountains. The way there's something bad about Little Arklow.* Monica took a mouthful of tea and gazed out at the black skies again.

Chapter 14

Scott MacConnell turned his head each way, flicking his shoulder-length blond hair out of his face as the panic washed over him. His blood was on fire, and the dark mountains of Glen Turrit loomed over him from all sides.

He bit his lip, wished he was anywhere but here. *And to think . . .*

To think that for all his life he'd wanted to go travelling, to visit the Scottish Highlands in particular. Ever since he was a little boy growing up in the ass end of nowhere. Or Botha, Alberta, Canada, to give it its proper title. Since he was eight years old he'd known he wanted to travel. During those long hot summers when the prairie was brown with mud, the bitterly cold winters where it was virgin white. Staring at that map of the world on his bedroom wall. Dreaming of the Amazon rainforest, the heat coming off the Sahara Desert. But like most dreams, life had got in the way. Somehow he'd ended up thirty years old with a job and a mortgage. More recently a failed marriage to boot and maybe a broken heart, because it had been her more than him. He'd wanted a family, she didn't. He'd pushed the point and it was a deal-breaker.

'Every cloud though . . .' He'd said it with a fixed smile more times than he could remember. Because with Laura gone and the house sold he could finally chase the dream. He'd spent so many days working as a carpenter listening to audiobooks about epic journeys, so many nights in front of the TV watching adventure shows. Finally he'd actually done it, quit his job and gone. Australia, Thailand, Morocco, Spain, France, England, finally on to Scotland. The Scottish Highlands, ancestral home of his family at some point in the distant past. It was a kind of homecoming, the final part of his journey. His transformation. Because over the course of the year he'd been away Scott felt like he'd gone from being a thirty-year-old boy to being a man. He'd been through testing times: robbed at knife point in Bangkok, a freezing night huddled alone in the Atlas Mountains. Difficult things, but they'd made him stronger, and he hadn't regretted a minute of it.

Until that morning.

He glanced around the mountains and then at the forest again. Over to where his green one-man tent was still pitched close to a small river, surrounded by a copse of Scots pines. Last night it had been the most picturesque camping spot imaginable. This morning Scott realised he'd made a huge mistake coming here. There was something wrong with this place.

The people had come in the early hours of the morning. After Scott crawled into his sleeping bag, zipped up the tent and switched off the light on his head torch, he'd drifted into a deep sleep. Bone-weary after the long day of hiking through the rough country around Loch Mullardoch then down into the valley of Glen Turrit, where he planned eventually to meet the road he knew ran through to the west coast. He'd woken in the darkest hours of the night when the noises started, little more than a whispering among the trees at first. A sound that could easily have been dismissed as a breeze coming down off the mountains.

But as he lay with the smell of tent fabric and the cold spring air in his nostrils the sounds persisted. Growing louder until Scott couldn't deny what he was hearing. Voices from the woods around the tent. He'd sat up slowly in his sleeping bag. Hardly daring to breathe as the voices, two or three of them, had continued. Surely they weren't meant for him. Surely they were for someone else. But who else could they be for? Out here in the middle of nowhere. Miles from the road. As he tilted his head to hear better, his sleeping bag rustled against the fabric of the tent.

The voices stopped and Scott froze.

He imagined someone edging through the darkness, closer to the tent. Desperately he tried to remember where he'd packed his folding knife. It had to be kids – teenagers looking to play freak the dumb tourist – he told himself as he patted blindly around, searching for the knife. But would they really come all the way out here? And there was something about those voices. Something so creepy about the raspy sounds, persistent but always just on the verge of comprehension. The way they seemed to carry a message: Here we are beyond civilisation. Here wildness reigns. With mad eyes and hair like snakes.

Scott tried hard to ignore such notions and finally his fingers closed reassuringly around the heavy knife. He grabbed it tight and carefully teased the blade out with the nail of his thumb. Straightened it until he felt the locking mechanism click into place in his shaking hand. He sat hunched forward with the knife gripped tight in his fist. Head cocked to the side for further noises. There was nothing though. Just the trees shifting slightly in the breeze and the sound of his own breath in his ears.

By the time dawn began to break Scott had almost convinced himself that his fears had been unjustified. The sounds had

been a trick played by his imagination, a kind of aural hallu-
cination, nothing more. He'd heard about that kind of thing.
People who'd gone for several days without talking to another
human beginning to hear voices. There was even a theory that
this was what Jesus Christ experienced when he was alone in
the wilderness for those forty days and nights.

Finally, when it was almost completely light outside, Scott
felt safe enough to unzip the tent inner. Whatever it was, hallu-
cination or real, it had gone now. And it would be another
story to add to the rest of them when he was home in Canada.
He moved to open the tent's outer flap.

The thing was hanging about three metres away. It took Scott
a moment to realise what it was because it was dressed in human
clothes, and his first instinct was to think that a dummy had
been suspended in front of the tent in a strange practical joke.

Up until he saw the blood. Caught its deep iron smell.

He blinked and took in the orange waterproof jacket, the
black trousers, ill-fittingly forced on over the stag's hind legs.
The blood was dripping from its antlers and making a dark
pool on the ground. The four legs were each attached by rope
to the trees so it made an X shape. The head hung loosely down
so its antlers were pointing towards Scott. In a state of near
panic he looked around at the forest, the gloomy mountains
beyond. Expecting someone, a figure, to be standing there
among the trees, staring back at him. There was no one though,
just the trees, seeming closer now, denser than the night before.

'Hello?!' he shouted without thinking. Out of some desperate
need to feel a human connection, to know that things were OK.
Immediately he slapped a hand over his mouth. Whoever had
strung the stag up like that was not someone he wanted to
speak to. But they were here now, hiding among the trees.

The thought sent a fresh bolt of adrenaline through Scott's body. He swallowed and squeezed the knife tighter in his hand then looked back at the stag. It was only now that he recognised the clothes. They were his. From the backpack he'd left in the outer section of the tent. Someone had crept in, had been mere inches from him in the night, without him knowing.

For some reason this seemed the most terrifying thing of all, and Scott realised that he was shaking all over. He forced himself to swallow and tried hard to understand what was happening.

'They left the stag to scare you. If they actually wanted to hurt you they would have done it by now,' he murmured. 'They could have killed you while you were asleep.' Clearly they wanted to frighten him. A not so subtle message to get the fuck out of here, that this wasn't his place. 'Message received loud and clear,' Scott said under his breath. Still scanning those dense trees. He crouched by the tent and quickly deconstructed it, then stuffed his few possessions into his backpack. In less than five minutes he was ready to get the fuck out of this valley, out of Scotland.

Stupidly he'd decided against buying a map for the trip; it had seemed more adventurous that way. And the trek from the Mullardoch Hills down to meet the road through Glen Turrit was relatively straightforward. He had no idea how far it was to the road or what the best route was. He glanced around desperately, and his eyes landed on the river. If he followed it downstream it would take him to the valley floor, eventually to the road. He shouldered his pack, glanced up at the stag for one last time, shook his head and turned to go.

Then the screaming started. Off to the side in the thickets of silver birch. A sound of primal terror, of rage, that made him freeze. He forced himself to move, then he was running over the uneven ground, the rocks and heather by the side of the river. The madness he could hear in that disinhibited scream pushed him on. Scott was good at running. He'd played soccer all the way through elementary and high school, always out on the wing. He'd even done a handful of marathons, spending his evenings during the long Canadian winters running laps in a local sports hall. In a straight race he could beat ninety-nine out of a hundred people. Especially with a head start like this.

Without even thinking about it, he shrugged the backpack off and quickened his pace. Glancing around constantly to make sure he didn't trip on one of the protruding roots or turn his ankle on a loose boulder. The blood pumped hard in his ears so he couldn't tell if the screams were following or not. Up ahead the landscape flattened out. For a moment he thought it might be a road. He slowed and looked around. Took a deep breath, tried to calm his breathing.

The little girl was standing at the opposite end of the clearing. She had straight blonde hair and was wearing a dirty white T-shirt with a character from Pokémon Go on it. She was looking directly at him, as if she had expected him to appear at that exact moment at that exact place. She was holding something in one hand. There was something about the fixed expression on her little face, a look that Scott had never seen before. As if she was somehow connected with the nature that surrounded them. The trees and the river. The things that had seemed so beautiful just the day before, but now seemed frightful, to claw at the fringes of his sanity.

He took a deep breath and stepped closer. 'I wonder can you help me? I'm looking for the road?'

The girl stared straight back at him without replying and slowly held her hand out towards him. At first he thought she was indicating a direction, then he realised what she was holding, pointing towards him.

It was a hand, dried black. Fresh horror bubbled in his mind because he knew those darkened fingers somehow touched on a fate that was already set down. He stopped dead. There were footsteps coming closer through the heather behind him. The knife was tight in his hand. *Do something! Move!* But his arms stayed locked by his sides. Shaking so hard they no longer seemed to belong to him. The world rocked and his vision blurred.

When the fingers tightened around his neck from behind, Scott screwed his eyes tight shut and let the knife fall from his hand. In his head he repeated the words over and over: *This is a dream. This is a nightmare.*

But Scott wasn't asleep. And his nightmare was only just beginning.

Chapter 15

The next morning Crawford took the turn-off for the newbuild estate high on the hill above Inverness. He glanced again at Monica beside him. Although it was almost six months since they had last worked together, she could still read his body language. The way he was sitting slightly forward in his seat told her there was something he wanted to say but was uncomfortable about. She took a breath and felt the tension in her neck from another night sleeping on the couch. It took her a moment to realise that she was actually irked she could read Crawford so easily. Maybe he could read her in the same way. The idea troubled her. The closeness that it implied.

'Spit it out, Crawford.' Bad news about Fisher, drinking again? She knew it was unlikely to be anything about the case. The corpse's DNA result had come back that morning. It didn't match with the DNA they had on file for Gall. They had already spent half an hour discussing the implications back at the office. How having career criminal Theo Gall out of the picture undermined their organised-crime theory. 'What is it you've got to tell me?'

Crawford glanced over at her, green eyes widening slightly. Caught out. 'It's just . . .'

Monica stared impatiently out the window at the rows of detached sandstone houses, the uniformly perfect gardens. The heartland of upper-middle-class Inverness. Doctors, lawyers, business people, accountants.

'Well, I was chatting to your mum the other day—'

'My mum?!' This wasn't what Monica had expected, although actually she shouldn't have been surprised. When Monica and Crawford had both been laid up in Raigmore Hospital after the previous investigation had gone catastrophically wrong, he had struck up an unlikely friendship with Angela Kennedy. Monica had assumed this was a short-lived response to the trauma of the situation, but more than once she'd turned up at her mum's house to find them sitting at the kitchen table, chatting over tea and biscuits. Irritatingly, her mum had even taken to citing Crawford's opinion on matters of police procedure.

'She said about Lucy wanting a cat?'

'Right,' Monica said slowly, wondering just what direction this strange conversation was going to take.

'You remember the social worker? Michael Bach?'

How could she forget. She'd worked with him on that same case, but despite their shared experience – maybe because of it – they weren't close. Probably they both wanted to put the experience behind them. Seeing each other more often than they needed to could only be a reminder of everything that had happened.

'He called the other day – something about one of his clients . . .' Crawford turned his hand over to show the details were unimportant. 'We were chatting, and he said a new cat's started coming round to his house.' Monica had visited his remote croft with Lucy the month before after a child psychologist suggested seeing Michael again might help lessen the traumatic memories from the previous case for Lucy. Monica remembered how her daughter had been enchanted by the cats there. With a little flicker of irritation she also remembered how Crawford had ended up coming on the trip after Lucy had insisted.

'It's quite lazy,' Crawford went on. 'Just wants to be inside in the warm, but it doesn't get on with the other cats. The ginger one, Colonel Mustard, he's been picking on it. We thought . . . well . . . maybe Lucy would like it?'

Monica felt a second flare of irritation – at Crawford, Michael, her mum. As if they knew what was best for her daughter. Just because she was a single mother everyone thought they had a right to interfere. She sighed though, because actually it might not be a bad idea. The child psychologist had even suggested an animal companion might help bring Lucy out of herself.

'I'll think about it,' she said finally. Crawford nodded, looking visibly relieved. He took a right turn. The buildings on this street were more widely spaced than the ones they'd passed below. Better described as mansions than detached houses. With metal railings surrounding the gardens, gates across the driveways.

Crawford pulled over outside a house with SINCLAIR carved into a large piece of slate on the gatepost.

They got out of the car. The house faced out towards the Moray Firth, the tree-covered Black Isle beyond it. To the far west Monica could see the Beauly Firth fading into the mountains. Glen Affric, Glen Mullardoch, Glen Turrit, Glen Strathfarrar, Strathconon, and the bulk of Ben Wyvis further north with the last runnels of winter snow still clinging to it, visible through the spring haze.

'Did you find anything else about Sebastian Sinclair?' Monica asked, remembering their conversations the day before. 'I haven't had a chance to speak to Hately yet.'

'More or less what was in that article,' Crawford replied. 'Sinclair Enterprises is the biggest company based in the north of Scotland. The founder, Innes Sinclair, died a few years ago, left it to his two kids, Sebastian and Heather.' Crawford reached to hit the intercom button and after a few seconds the gate swung open. 'One thing I didn't realise: Innes Sinclair had a ton of small businesses. Shops, garages, hairdressers, taxi companies, you name it. Fingers in a million pies. A lot of them are still owned by the Sinclairs, apparently.'

Monica nodded, stored this piece of information away. So far her picture of Sebastian Sinclair remained frustratingly two-dimensional. Little more than a cardboard cutout of a conventional Highland businessman. *Hopefully his wife can flesh him out a little for us*, she thought as they walked down the driveway and saw a figure appear as a dark shadow through the glass of the front door. The woman who opened the door looked to be in her forties. She was wearing pink lipstick, and had shortish blonde hair. Styled, Monica realised, like Princess Diana's iconic look. She was wearing a white blouse with red polka dots and a matching skirt. More glamorous than Monica had imagined the wife of her 2D version of Sebastian Sinclair to be, but in a curiously outdated way, as if she genuinely hadn't changed her hair or wardrobe since the 1980s.

'Karen Sinclair?' Crawford asked. She nodded, face set firm but with the hint of a smile. Monica had the strange sense that the woman had spent her life honing this expression. Crawford held out his ID and introduced himself then gestured to Monica. 'And this is DI Kennedy.'

'Do you mind if we come inside?' Monica watched the moment of alarm pass across Karen's face: bad news on your doorstep in human form. She took a fluttery step back and gestured them in. The open-plan hall and the grand staircase overlooked by a gallery made Monica think of American TV shows she landed on when she was unable to sleep and channel-hopped. An Invernessian version of *The Real Housewives of*

Orange County. So far from the Inverness she'd grown up in, where pretty much everyone she had known lived in a council-built house or flat. Karen Sinclair led them through into a sitting room. Monica took a seat on a corner sofa and admired the high ceilings, the huge windows and the views out over the firth. Crawford sat down heavily beside her and crouched forward, hands on his knees.

'It's him, isn't it?' Karen blurted, her thin arms folded across her chest. 'The one on the television.'

'We don't know that,' Monica said, doing her best to sound reassuring. 'We won't know for sure until the DNA results are back. But we're very concerned for Sebastian. He's been missing for three weeks now?'

Karen nodded. Monica watched the way her hands were now clasped anxiously in front of her.

'Will . . .' Karen's voice died away then came back. 'What happens to me? If it's him?'

'Sorry, how do you mean exactly?'

'Do . . . Will I still be able to live here? They won't try to make me leave, will they?'

'Who would make you leave?'

'The Sinclairs, Sebastian's sister. They never liked me because of my family. Because we didn't have money. Now they'll take the house from me, won't they?' She sounded like a panicked child.

'I'm sorry, I'm not the person to speak to about that,' Monica said. Karen stared back at her, nodding, eyes wide. But Monica could tell she wasn't really taking the words in.

'We just want to ask you a few questions about Sebastian. You reported him missing two weeks ago?'

'I just thought that he could have been in trouble,' Karen said finally.

'How long exactly was he gone, before you reported him missing?' Crawford asked, chipping in for the first time.

'I'm not sure.' Karen's eyes went to the thick carpet between her feet.

'You're not sure?' Monica replied, trying to keep her voice soft. 'That's unusual, not to know when you last saw your husband.'

'Sebastian . . . Sometimes he goes on business trips for days at a time. I thought he'd forgotten to tell me. He's a very busy man.'

'Who was the last person to see him?'

'His last appointment was at head office, a meeting there with his sister.'

'When was that?'

'Friday the nineteenth of April. It's marked on the calendar.'

Monica nodded. She knew that Sinclair's credit card had last been used at a petrol station on the way out of Inverness, the morning of 19 April. Seven days before Karen formally reported him missing. Taking a week to report your husband missing? It was a red flag for Monica. But Karen did seem vulnerable. Maybe she had genuinely thought he was away on business?

'Did he text or call after that?' Monica asked.

'Text?' Karen repeated the word as if it were some new curiosity. 'Oh, no. I don't . . . have a phone.'

'Why not?'

'I just don't like them. If anyone needed me they could always pass a message through Sebastian. Or come to the house.'

Monica nodded slowly because this was another red flag of a different kind. Did Sebastian Sinclair coercively control his wife? Prevent her from contacting friends and family?

'Sebastian didn't want you to have a phone?' Monica asked, probing a little further.

'I just never needed one,' Karen snapped back, arms folded

tight now. Monica could see that there was no point pushing the question for now.

'There was nothing about Sebastian going missing in the local press?' Monica asked, changing tack. 'Why's that?'

'I don't know about any of that,' Karen said. 'Heather told me she'd handle it.'

Monica thought about it for a second. Was Sebastian Sinclair a workaholic? Controlling but distant from his wife? Closer to his sister? Clearly they now needed to speak to Heather Sinclair. Currently the last person known to have seen Sebastian and who possibly kept his disappearance out of the press. Even if the body turned out not to be Sinclair's, Monica's experience told her that something wasn't right here. And if the body was Sebastian Sinclair then where had he been for those missing three weeks? Dolohov estimated the body had been dead and in the water for only a few days. Had Sinclair been hiding from someone? Or was he being kept somewhere?

'Does Sebastian have any enemies? Anyone who has a grudge against him? He must have rubbed up against a lot of people in his business,' Crawford asked, seeming to echo Monica's thoughts.

'I don't know about enemies, any of that side of things . . .'

'I know you don't work for the company, but did he ever mention anything. Any difficult relationships? Any troubles with business? Difficult clients?'

'That's not my area. I've always been a homemaker.'

'And you send your son to boarding school, is that right?' Monica said, catching a sense of another little fracture in the woman's life. A *homemaker*, a mother whose only son was elsewhere.

'It's better. To get the best start in life. A lot of people would kill to have that opportunity for their children.'

Monica heard Crawford's phone go off in his pocket. His ringtone was now the song 'Tainted Love' by Gloria Jones. Monica glanced at him in irritation. He searched his jacket, mumbling an apology. He found the phone after a few seconds then stepped away to the other side of the room, holding it to his ear.

'You said that you didn't get on with Sebastian's family? How did the pair of you meet?' Monica asked, hoping for another little fragment to flesh out her portrait of him.

'At a dance. I was only fifteen. My brother set us up, said he'd be perfect for our family.'

'Were they close? Your brother—' She felt Crawford's hand on her arm. Caught the intense expression on his face as he held the phone out to her. DC Maria Khan's name was on the screen. She mumbled her own apology to Karen and held the phone to her ear.

'DI Kennedy? We've found something.'

Monica stood and turned away from Karen Sinclair. She walked out to the hall, shielding her mouth as she spoke.

'More of the body?'

'It's another one.' She could hear the shock in Khan's voice. 'Cut just like the first. Only . . .'

Chapter 16

Annabelle stared at the screen of the iPhone for a long, long time. Willing 'O2-UK' to reappear. It never did of course, and finally the voice in the back of her head piped up, *If you don't switch it off you'll drain the battery, then you'll have no chance of getting help.*

It was obviously the right thing to do. But it was only when the agony in her leg grew and became almost unbearable that she finally switched it off and lay back on the pillow. The concussive pain continued to throb behind her eyes, panic threatening to well up alongside it when she considered her situation. She had to get out of here. There had to be a way. Very slowly, taking care not to move her leg, she turned her head to the side. The first thing she noticed was the smell. The deep mustiness was still there, but she realised now there was another smell under it. A solvent smell. Glue? Looking at the room in the weak light from the lamp, she had a clue as to where this smell was coming from. The floor of the room was covered by the deep shagpile carpet that her hand had run through, and the ceiling was concrete, but the walls were covered in a strange patchwork of carpet scraps. As if someone had collected a variety of sample squares and glued them together.

'Why would anyone decorate walls with squares of carpet?' Annabelle whispered to herself. To muffle the sound of screams? But the squares only ran halfway up the walls. Above that was bare concrete. Maybe it was a kind of insulation? This seemed to make more sense. If whoever was keeping her here was genuinely worried about her making a noise wouldn't they have gagged her? Or worse put that hideous mask on her? She tried to ignore the memory of the thing and peered further into the gloom towards the door. It looked to be made of thick metal. Not unlike the door to a bank vault. Beside the door, just inside the room, was the kitchen chair the person had sat on. Next to her low bed there was a small table with the lamp. Apart from that there was nothing else. No windows, no other way in or out.

She swore under her breath, feeling the tears welling up again. She bit her index finger hard because she had to think. She had to do something.

Well, it can't be helped. She remembered Miss Albright saying the words. It was when Annabelle had told her how sad it was that the older woman couldn't accompany her and Mr Pepper out for a walk to a distant park on a particularly sunny day. The idea of her stoicism felt somehow comforting, even if it carried a sad reminder that Mr Pepper was probably waiting impatiently by the door for her now. Miss Albright had started referring to the dog as Annabelle's Little Brother. Secretly Annabelle liked the feeling of being part of a little family with the old lady and the dog.

She squeezed her eyes tight shut and tried to imagine she was back home in her flat in London. About to go downstairs, to take Mr Pepper for a walk to the cafe where she volunteered. As she pictured herself opening the front door out onto the street, another memory broke in.

Opening the door into the kitchen as a child just as Dad threw a mug, the tea splattering over the tiles behind the cooker.

74

He was shouting something at Mum. After a moment her mum turned, saw Annabelle, saw her tears. Her dad's red face as he stormed past her. The fear in her mum's eyes as she reached for Annabelle, squeezing her shoulders to suppress her daughter's upset. *Don't be silly, Annabelle, don't make a fuss! There's no need to cry!* Annabelle nodded at her mum's panicked face, forcing the upset away, forcing her eyes to dry.

She took a deep breath. Trying very hard to replace the memory with a picture of Mr Pepper, she imagined his head bobbing with excitement, pink tongue hanging out.

'I promise I'll come back,' she whispered. As if somehow, hundreds of miles away, the little creature might hear her and be soothed by the idea. 'I promise I'll come back.' There had to be some way out of here, it had to be possible.

Her leg. Maybe it wasn't as bad as she thought. She went swimming twice a week during the mid-afternoon quiet time at the pool and sometimes used the cross trainer at the gym there. Maybe she could still walk on her leg. Maybe she could find a way to make a run for it?

She stared down the bed to her right leg. *Well, it can't be helped.* It was concealed under the scratchy dark blanket. Slowly she reached down and started to pull the material to the side. She noticed first that her thigh was bare. She was wearing an old nylon nightgown. This meant someone had undressed her, taken her clothes, then put the gown on her. Normally this idea would have been monstrous in itself, but now she accepted it with barely a second thought. Encouraged by her new-found boldness she pulled harder and the blanket fell away.

Below the knee her leg was bruised purple. Swollen to almost twice its normal size. She tilted her head for a better look, and that was when she noticed the bolt. A piece of shiny metal sticking out of her leg at the ankle. She took a deep breath, her eyes glued to where the metal entered her skin, her brain scrambling to make sense of this new horror. Beside it there was a row of dark stitches. The leg was strapped between two slats of wood in a sort of splint.

Maybe it's not as bad as it looks? She tried wriggling her ankle. Screaming agony shot up her leg. She sank back on the bed, squeezing handfuls of the blanket, screwing her eyes tight shut against the pain.

She took deep sucking breaths, trying desperately to find the point where the pain would become bearable. In her distressed state the sound of the latch being drawn back barely registered. She didn't realise the door was opening until the person was standing almost right beside her.

Chapter 17

Monica smelled the man's body before she saw it. Snagged on the roots of a tree at the edge of the river. The right arm was gone at the shoulder, the left at the elbow, and the left leg at the groin. This body was further up the river, a more remote location about fifteen miles upstream from the first one, towards Glen Affric. Where the River Beauly was still called the Glass.

As she moved closer to the body, Monica reflexively switched to breathing through her mouth rather than her nose. An old trick from one of her colleagues in a forensics department in Glasgow. The idea that she might be sucking particles of death into her mouth and onto her tongue wasn't exactly appealing, but it did seem to lessen the ripe stench of decomposition.

She glanced at Fisher, who was standing a few feet away at the edge of the cordon beside Khan. The two detectives had been following up on house-to-house inquiries in the area and were the first to respond when the call had come in. Fisher had his hands on his hips, already dressed in a white Tyvek suit. The angry bruise on his right cheek edging to yellow under the frame of his glasses. He seemed in his element as he helped control access to the body until the forensics team arrived. Back to the precise and ambitious man Monica had first worked with the previous year.

She stood and zipped her own suit closed, trying to forget how absurd she must look with her arms poking out of the too-short sleeves. She pulled on the hood, then gloves. Glanced around to take the location in properly for the first time. It was close to another one of the small hydro power stations, downstream to her left across a pool of dark water. Behind her the old stone bridge crossed the river upstream. The body was hooked up among a mess of roots that had been exposed as the bank was eroded from beneath the tree.

'Who found it?' she asked Khan, remembering her own lonely early days as a young detective and feeling an impulse to include the new member of the team.

'Someone from a walking club, ma'am.'

'Man or woman?'

'It was a woman who spotted it first,' Khan said. 'But there was a group of them.'

'He must have been here at least a couple of days,' Fisher cut in, perhaps irked that Monica had been questioning Khan rather than him. 'The river level was higher until the day before yesterday, when it dropped rapidly. I called and spoke to someone at the Scottish Environmental Protection Agency – they take regular water-level measurements. He couldn't have got caught up in the roots if the water was this low.' She nodded and made a mental note of the information.

The body was in an awkward position and approaching it meant stepping down off the bank and standing on a narrow rib of rock in the fast-flowing river. The water made sloshing, gurgling sounds as it passed close to Monica's feet. She peered at the body, stained by the sediment that had stuck to it. More than anything it looked like something born of the earth returning to nature. She took another step closer on the rock, wondered for a moment how mentally unhealthy it made her: that she could view a probable murder victim's body in such a morally neutral way. The head was folded back, facing upstream and smeared with mud, hanging upside down over a branch so the chin pointed to the sky. Brown hair hung down in short, dried-out straggles, mirroring the shape of the roots the body was caught among. One of the roots had lodged the mouth open in a silent scream, the eye sockets empty. *A crow got here first*, Monica guessed with a shiver.

The stump of the left arm was stained with dirt. She crouched closer. Small pieces of gravel were embedded in the raw flesh of the wound. And her mind served up an image: someone scrambling with a bloody stump. Using it to drag themselves desperately while one leg was missing, making walking impossible.

She stepped back, edged along the rock rib to view the body from the other side. The remaining foot was cut and torn. Had he tried to escape from the river? A theory popped up: a gangland executioner slowly dismembering the two men with a saw, finally dumping them in a river. Watching as they tried to claw and drag themselves out with their remaining limbs. Probably filming it for someone's edification or as a warning.

It was possible. But something about it didn't quite fit for her.

She turned back to Fisher, who had ventured closer and was now staring gravely down at her from the bank, seemingly less perturbed by proximity to the body than Khan or Crawford.

'That's two middle-aged men in one week. We need to look into anyone who fits the same profile, anyone missing. And can you track someone down to ask about the river flow? Someone who can estimate the likelihood of the two bodies being found so far apart if they were dumped in the same place at the same time?'

He nodded. 'Seems a long way for the first one to have gone, if they went in at the same time?'

79

It did, but it didn't mean it wasn't possible. She turned back to the body, glanced around the scene again. Something about it seemed too perfect. The way the body was caught up there among the roots. She remembered the first body: it had been right by the side of the fisherman's shelter. Waiting for them. This one was clearly visible from the path across the river. The spring sky was overcast with thick grey clouds, like a lid enclosing the valley and the mountains. She felt spits of icy rain on her face and hands but also strangely calm. Maybe the first time she'd really felt so calm and focused since her last case all those months and troubled nights before. Here, staring at a dead man's face.

Were you drowned first? she wondered. *Then placed here for us to find?* She looked at that face. And those empty eyes stared back with only dark infinity as a response.

Chapter 18

When Annabelle finally registered the sound of the door and opened her eyes the person was standing over her.

Looking up, Annabelle saw only a hooded featureless head. *They don't have a face!* After a second her mind realised the person was also wearing a dark veil. Annabelle stared at that veil. Feeling the unbelievable horror of the situation blossom. *This is the part where you're raped. This is the part where you're murdered.* She clenched her hands into fists under the cover. Tried to speak, but the words wouldn't come out.

'You're probably wondering why I haven't shown you my face.' Annabelle lay frozen. 'The Doctor said you should rest so I didn't want to alarm you. I've felt a bit embarrassed . . .' The speaker paused and Annabelle waited, almost afraid to breathe. 'Should I tell you?'

'Either way,' she finally managed to croak, her voice barely audible.

'When I was young they thought I was a girl . . . up until I was twelve. It was pretty obvious then that I was a boy. I'll show you my face if you like. It's just you might find it strange.'

Annabelle took a breath then let the air leave her lungs. Whatever she had expected the person, *the man*, to say it definitely wasn't this.

'You think I'm weird, don't you?'

She shook her head quickly. 'No, no, of course not! I'm probably the weirdest out of everyone . . .'

He looked silently down at her for a long time. Then finally seemed to accept her reply and reached inside his hood, began unfastening the veil. She was transfixed. What kind of face would be horrifying enough to fit with this place? The Elephant Man? Something worse? He untucked the veil from behind his head, tugged it free.

His face was normal. Good-looking even. He was young, in his mid-twenties, slightly older than her. The kind of person who'd serve you a coffee in Starbucks and leave little mark on your day. Annabelle felt an incredible flood of momentary relief.

'I'm Marcus now. They used to call me Chloe, when they thought I was a girl.' He gave a little shrug of his shoulders, shielding his face as he spoke. With a feeling close to hysteria Annabelle recognised this as a hint of vulnerability. He wanted her to like him, to approve of him. She had imagined something from a horror movie – a psychopath, a monster – but here was someone like her, with their own insecurities.

'I think Marcus suits you,' Annabelle said quickly. Reaching for that moment of connection with both hands. 'I think it's the perfect name for you.'

'Do you really?' He dropped his eyes to the carpet as he spoke. Annabelle nodded enthusiastically and took the opportunity to look him up and down. He was wearing black boots, blue jeans, a green military-style jacket with the hood still half pulled up. He was a little under average height and slimly built. His hair was black, he had a round face and his skin was light brown.

'Thank you.' His hand hovered over his face as he cleared his throat. And for a moment the long hours Annabelle had spent alone staring at her useless phone seemed to belong only to a nightmare. Marcus seemed normal; surely her being here was a mistake? Someone would come to collect her soon, now they'd had a chance to talk?

'You should probably eat something, but I guess you'll need to use the bathroom first?' Marcus said. Suddenly his air was that of an awkward hotel employee, first day on the job. It hadn't occurred to her until that moment, but now Annabelle focused on it she realised her bladder was close to bursting. 'There's a toilet along the corridor, but the Doctor said it might be easier to use a bucket in here . . .'

'I'd really rather use the toilet,' Annabelle replied quickly, because the need to leave that room was desperate, even if just to go along the corridor. Even though she had no doubt the pain from her leg would be immense.

'Well, that's not a surprise.' He gave a throaty laugh. 'There's a wheelchair we could use? You'd have to promise not to mention it though.'

Annabelle felt the pressure on her bladder grow. She nodded quickly. 'Yes . . . I promise.'

Marcus disappeared through the door and came back moments later with a foldable wheelchair. He opened it out and Annabelle shunted herself to the edge of the bed. Trying her best to keep her leg very still and ignore the shots of pain. He flipped open the right leg rest and, with surprising strength for the size of his body, reached around her back and under her legs to lift her the few inches from the bed up onto the chair. Annabelle exhaled in discomfort as he then gently manoeuvred her injured leg onto the rest. She looked away as her eyes alighted on the bolt protruding through the skin of her ankle.

'It was a very bad break,' Marcus said, his eyes following hers. 'The bolt and some screws are holding your leg together . . .'

She nodded, the thought of those pieces of metal under her skin turning her stomach. 'I really need to go . . .'

'Of course. Full steam ahead, I suppose.' He gave a forced laugh, turned the wheelchair and pushed it out of the room.

The corridor outside was more grey concrete. Tunnel would have been a better description. It was wide and high enough for a truck and lit by a series of electric lights attached to the wall. Marcus turned to the left. The tunnel ran downhill for a long, long way into a shadowy distance. Smells of bleach and a dampness drifted in the air, shuttered by a heavy stillness. The wheelchair made a trundling noise over the tarmac floor, echoing back from the walls.

Annabelle stared down the tunnel in disbelief. Her moment of relief, her thought that that Marcus had seemed like a normal person, not a monster, evaporated. She remembered the hideous mask; in her euphoria over connecting with another human her mind had suppressed the memory of it.

The renewed panic brought a shake to her voice. 'Is it far, Marcus?'

'Not far. Just here. You must be bursting.' After another hundred feet of the same grey featureless tunnel he stopped outside a white wooden door. He pushed her a little past, unbolted the door, then backed the chair inside. The room was dark.

'Just a second.' She stared out at the tunnel through the open door as Marcus's footsteps echoed across the room. After thirty seconds the lights flicked on. 'The cord snapped; you have to use the other switch,' he explained. Annabelle nodded slowly and took in the large room. It felt more like a hotel bathroom from the 1970s than anything. Utterly incongruous after the tunnel Marcus had just wheeled her down. Covered in white tiles and with avocado-coloured bathroom fittings – sinks, urinals and several stalls.

Despite the remorseless pain from her leg and the waves of disorientation, the need to pee was overwhelming. She waited, dancing internally, as Marcus rolled her into one of the stalls. He set the brake on the wheelchair then lifted her torso carefully onto the toilet. 'It's probably better if your leg stays there,' he said, pointing at the leg rest. 'I'll wait for you outside.'

Annabelle nodded, managed to hold on until she heard the door to the corridor bang shut then hurriedly pulled the night-dress up and peed into the bowl. The physical relief swamped all her senses for a moment. But only for a moment, because her eyes registered a different quality to the light. She lifted her head. Above her was a small skylight. Not much bigger than a letter box. But through the mottled slice of dirty glass she could see the distant but unmistakable brightness of daylight.

She sank forward, recognising her error immediately. Why hadn't she brought the phone? She pushed her head into her hands. The battery would die soon. Here, close to the window, she might have been able to connect to the network.

'Is everything OK?' Marcus called with something like cheeriness in his voice. 'We should get back. We really don't want to be caught out in the corridor when the Doctor appears.'

Chapter 19

Eight hours later the memory of those empty eyes was still clawing at Monica's brain as she and Crawford went down under the ground. Into Raigmore Hospital morgue to witness the autopsy. In those eight hours they'd confirmed a likely ID on the body. Theo Gall, dismissed by DNA evidence as their first body that morning, was now back in the frame. Victim number two of just whatever kind of murderer they were dealing with. Because when Monica and Crawford had sat in the Volvo comparing an image of the dead man's face with the file photo of Theo Gall it was an obvious match. Alive, he had had greying hair, a wide, opportunistic smile on his narrow face. She turned to the picture of the body. The same narrow face, the same high hairline. She was almost certain it was him. She'd recalled Gall's long criminal record. Any experienced police officer would have put money on him coming to an unsavoury end. Not like this though, this was something different.

'What is this then? A serial murderer?' Crawford had asked, his voice low. Did he secretly hope that it was? A monster to pit himself against. Wasn't that what all men wanted on some level? Whether they knew it or not. Maybe what she secretly needed herself – an external horror to take the focus away from the horrors in her mind? Monica had shaken her head in response though, because a serial killer didn't fit for her, not in the sense that Crawford meant it – someone who killed for a personal, pathological reason, out of sexual sadism. Despite the obvious brutality of the murders, she didn't see a sexual element to these crimes.

Dr Dolohov's footsteps on the tiled floor broke Monica's chain of thought, and she looked up. He was pointing a knife at the remnants of the corpse, now lying on the slab between them.

'This one looks a real treat, Detective,' the doctor said, running a hand over his bald head. 'Two now, isn't it, Christian?' he shouted over his shoulder to his assistant at the back of the room. 'Keeping our mortgages paid.' Neither Monica nor the assistant replied, and Dolohov shook his head sadly. 'Sometimes it's better to laugh at this world,' he continued, pulling on a fresh pair of gloves and reaching for his mask and hat. 'Even in strange times,' he added theatrically. His assistant finally came to stand beside him, holding a recording device. Dolohov picked up the knife. Tapped it three times on the metal slab, the noise ringing round the morgue. A sounding bell of this dark ritual.

'I make the initial incision,' he said softly into the microphone. He laid the gloved fingers of his left hand on the chest, and with the knife in his right hand he began to apply pressure.

Monica winced but didn't look away as she watched him make the Y-cut from armpits to sternum, sternum to belly, slowly opening the body for inspection. All the time as he peeled the flesh back, reached for the saw to open the chest cavity, her thought at the riverbank niggled at her. The idea that the body had been purposely left there for them to find.

After half an hour of cutting and inspection Dolohov finally gestured at the organs inside the opened ribcage. 'The lungs have both collapsed, been torn open, the rear ribs broken. Looks to be a blunt force trauma. It's possible he went over a waterfall or hit a rock in the river—'

'Are you certain he was in the water? That he drowned?' Monica cut in, sensing that Dolohov would prolong his explanation if she didn't force him to the point. It had been a long day, and she knew Theo Gall's brother was already on his way to the hospital to formally identify the body. Lucy's bedtime was also approaching, the second in just a few days that she seemed destined to miss.

The doctor looked up at her. 'I don't suppose I can say with certainty. The lungs are ripped, there's nothing in his windpipe to indicate he inhaled any water. No leaves or other debris.'

'What was the cause of death?' Monica asked, pushing thoughts of Lucy away and thinking again of the location where the body was discovered. The bridge, the dark pool and the power station.

'Well, it wasn't blood loss.' He nodded at the amputations in turn – two arms and one leg. 'His wounds were probably closed by tourniquet during the amputations, then cauterised with a blowtorch.' He nodded to the preliminary forensic report this time, lying on a table alongside his row of surgical implements. 'Whoever did this would have needed a degree of medical knowledge to stem the blood loss and prevent him from developing sepsis. Clearly someone wanted to keep our man alive to enjoy his suffering. And oh, he would have suffered. There's been some clotting in the lungs. He was still alive when they were smashed. Ultimately he was asphyxiated. I can't say for certain if that was a result of him being injured in the water and drowning or if he received the blunt force injuries in some other way and was then in the water for some time post-mortem.'

Monica nodded, trying hard to repress an unsavoury flash of excitement. The mixture of horror and intense focus that being this close to a monster's work could elicit after her time away. Instead she turned her mind to understanding and storing the information Dolohov had relayed. And answering the obvious question: why might someone commit these crimes then stage the dump sites to look like the clearly murdered bodies had ended up there unintentionally?

Chapter 20

Annabelle stared down at the tray of food that Marcus had placed on her lap. She pushed herself further up on the bed, feeling the pain in her leg again. Though the agony was changing slowly to an ache. Deep and insistent as the snapped bones began the slow job of knitting together again. The matching ever-present thrum of anxiety that had settled in her stomach since she'd first woken in this place.

She swallowed and glanced up at the ceiling then down at the food again. Four rashers of bacon, the strip of fat still white and rubbery-looking. Beside them a row of sausages, the horrible thick kind like a fat man's fingers. Fried bread, mushrooms, beans – almost a tin of them. The plate covered in a sheen of grease. What her dad would have called *a man's portion*, and for a second she pictured his face, years ago at a restaurant table somewhere. His neat hair and suit, the smile of rapt attention he gave the person serving them. As if this stranger were the most important person in his life.

'You should eat. You should eat a lot,' Marcus said. 'The Doctor told me that your leg will heal faster if you give your body a lot of energy.'

Annabelle turned to look at him, took in his dark eyes and thick eyelashes. Eating was the last thing she felt like doing, but the memory of that metal mask was fresh. He seemed eager to please her now, but not so long ago he'd also threatened to strap that thing on her.

'Could I have a drink first?' Refusing his enthusiastic request really didn't feel like a good idea.

'Oh. I forgot the tea, didn't I?' He sounded irritated, but stood up and glanced around then realised he'd left the teapot over on the chair by the door. Annabelle watched as he splashed some into a mug then set it beside her plate on the tray. It was milky orange. She took a mouthful. Despite everything, the hot, sweet drink was comforting. It even seemed to waken her stomach.

Slowly she started with a piece of bacon, then some of the beans. Marcus watched her intently from the corner of the room. She managed another piece of bacon before the nausea rose up from her belly. She dropped the knife and fork with a clatter on the tray and held her hand over her mouth.

'I think I'm going to be sick.'

'Shhhh . . .' Marcus came over and put a hand on her shoulder. She flinched, expecting some kind of sexual suggestion in his touch, but he kept his hand high on her back. Despite her nausea, the hovering fear of sexual violence eased down a notch. She caught the smell from his green army jacket: the outdoors with a hint of something like petrol. 'You'll feel better in a second.'

After a minute he moved his hand from her back and reached into his pocket. He produced a locking knife and pulled it open, laying it in the palm of his hand. SCOTT was engraved on the dark wood of the handle. She watched, transfixed by what he might do with it. The exhausting roller coaster of adrenaline threatened to start up once more.

'Is Scott your second name?'

Marcus shook his head slowly, his eyes intent on the plate. 'No. It's Slate. Scott's a friend. He's visiting – he let me borrow this.' He spoke quietly, almost as if in a trance. Then he picked up her fork and cut into the meat with the knife. The index finger on his right hand was missing its tip. There was just a smooth piece of flesh where the nail should have been. He held the fork up for her to eat. She stared at the piece of bacon, the grease on it. Inanely she tried to remember the last time someone had fed her, probably not since she was a baby. As she took the first mouthful the thought carried her mind back to her child-hood bedroom with the shagpile carpet. There were things about that house that had been strange; it now seemed like a low-key version of the terrifying strangeness of this place. She'd spent her young life running away from the way that house made her feel only to run directly to this place instead.

Chapter 21

Monica watched as the man gazed down at the face of the corpse; the rest of the remains were concealed by a black body bag.

'That's him,' he said finally, both hands still pushed into the pockets of his grey coat. As if they had met casually in the street and he was commenting on something distasteful but of little consequence. 'That's my big brother.' He shook his head then looked up at Monica, meeting her gaze for the first time. 'If he'd turned up like this thirty years ago it would have saved everyone . . .' His voice died in his throat, another little death in the morgue.

Monica nodded to the nurse, feeling a moment of discomfort at her earlier excitement; meeting a victim's family was enough to temper any of the job's glamour. The nurse zipped the bag back over the body's face. *Over Theo Gall's face*, she corrected herself. At least this victim now had a definitive ID.

'Hell of a thing to say about your own flesh and blood. To wish a member of your own family . . .' Mark Gall's voice died again. And the voice in Monica's head spoke up in its place: *You're not alone there. You're not the only one.* The thought actually shocked her. Had she really wished her own father dead? Monica tried to ignore the question and looked hard at Mark Gall's furrowed brow – she thought he might actually cry. Instead he dug his hands deeper into his coat pockets and dropped his head forward in a gesture of resigned misery.

*

'You had a difficult relationship with your brother?' Monica asked. They were sitting at a shadowy table in the Raigmore Motel bar just across the road from the hospital. It was 8 p.m., and the hospital cafe had long since stopped serving. Besides, Mark Gall had insisted that if they wanted any further information about his brother they would only get it once he'd had a drink. Preferably more than one drink. Monica hadn't exactly felt like spending the evening in a police interview room herself.

He took a swallow of his vodka and Coke. Looked across at Crawford then Monica. Something flickered in his eyes, and for a second she thought it was recognition. Maybe he knew her from somewhere. Knew something about her, or thought he did. Instead he said, 'Anyone ever tell you that you're a funny-looking pair?'

Monica didn't respond. But irritation bubbled in her stomach at the little pang of relief she always felt when a potential spectre from her past failed to materialise.

'Sorry,' Gall said after a moment when neither Monica nor Crawford replied. 'That's not the kind of thing to say. It's the first proper drink I've had this year.' He finished the drink and set it down beside its companion, an oily double shot of vodka at the bottom of a long glass. He splashed a little Coke from a can over it, enough to make it palatable.

'You didn't seem surprised when you saw it was your brother?' Monica watched as he took a sip of the second drink. Glad to be the one asking the questions again. As a rule things always seemed to run better for her that way. 'When you saw it was Theo.'

'*That boy'll die with his boots on*. That's what my grandfather used to say about my brother,' Gall said. He looked up at Monica again from his position hunched over the table. She

94

took in his red face with the dry skin between his eyebrows, the heavy lines at the corners of his eyes. It was the face of a man who carried tension, suppressed rage even. *At what?* she wondered. At his brother? At the fates?

'You were angry with him?'

'Wouldn't you be?' His eyes darted off to the bar. 'I'm the one that holds our family together, looks after our mother when she's up and down to the hospital. He's off doing whatever, and in her eyes he's still the fucking blue-eyed boy. "Where's Theo? Where's Theo?"' Gall put on an elderly woman's voice.

'What *was* he doing?' Crawford asked.

'You're police,' Gall said. 'What wasn't he doing?'

'We only see what was on his record,' Monica said. 'Car theft, arson, falsely claiming benefits, assault, driving while under the influence. As far as we're concerned, that makes him a petty criminal. Same as a hundred other men in this city. It's a long stretch from that to turning up dead halfway up a glen in the middle of nowhere.' She let the silence hang over the lacquered tabletop, the weak yellow light reflected back off the glossy surface like it was the top of a pool of evil dark water. 'Why would Theo be up there? Why did he end up in that river?'

'I've just told you!' Gall's voice rose unexpectedly in the quiet bar. The barman glanced over, amusement across his face. 'He was bad, ever since he was wee. You know my earliest memory of my brother?' His posture had changed to alertness. For the first time since Monica had met him a couple of hours before he actually seemed fully awake. Small grey eyes lit up bright on either side of his thick nose. 'When I was four years old I saw this wooden nutcracker in a shop window. The kind that's a soldier, and there's a handle at the back that breaks the nuts open in his mouth?'

Monica and Crawford nodded in unison. Gall reached for his glass, and Monica watched his thick fingers close around it. A working man's hand, strong enough to beat another man to death. Mark Gall had told her he was a joiner. He would have the tools – saws, blowtorches – to torture then dismember a body if he wanted to. Could his resentment towards his brother have run that deep? But even if it did, it didn't explain the other body.

He took a sip, creased his face up and added another splash of Coke.

'I wanted that fucking thing for months. God knows why, it wasn't like we actually ever had nuts in the house, except monkey nuts at Halloween. My mum finally gets it for my birthday. I was delighted, put it on the windowsill beside my bed. I wake up the next morning and it's gone. I went screaming to my mum . . .' He shook his head at the memory. 'We go round looking for it and find it lying out in the back grass beside the shed, all smashed up into bits. My brother, Theo, was sitting watching us from the top of the fence. Waiting to see the look on my face when I saw it.' Gall shook his head again. 'That's my first memory of my brother. Him delighted he'd hurt me. My mum looking down at me. "Stop crying like a baby," she said. "Theo didn't mean to do it. Did you, son?"'

Monica swallowed. There was something distasteful about Gall's long-held resentment. And disquieting. If he still nursed a grudge after forty years, what resentments might her own four-year-old daughter grow up to harbour against her?

'So you're saying that he never changed?'

'I'm saying that he was born like that. Stealing, hurting people. It was just how he was. When he was fourteen he got sent down to Polmont Young Offenders for fire-starting. Stole my dad's car, my mum's purse every chance he had. He floated about when he was out of Polmont, in and out of prison. Glasgow, London. Eventually back up here, moved in with a woman up in Hilton estate, you know?'

Monica nodded impatiently, Hilton was a 1970s housing estate north of the city centre.

'He was a career criminal,' Monica said. Something she'd known before Gall had even started speaking. 'Did he still have links to anyone down the road? Glasgow? London? Did he ever mention any names?' It could fit with their original theory that the murder was gang-related.

'I steered well clear of him and his *friends*. Except Pauline, his most recent wife. I heard she kicked him out a few months ago. Since then I've got no idea where he's been. She'd know more probably. She's spent enough time clearing up his messes in her life anyway.'

Chapter 22

When Annabelle next woke, Marcus was still sitting in the chair by the door, hunched forward reading a paperback book. The cover was black and white with a close-up of a soldier's face on it, the words WORLD WAR TWO in white letters.

Marcus must have noticed she was awake because he said, 'You went out like a light after all that food. Must mean the bone's healing. The Doctor said that would happen.'

Annabelle nodded, noticing the way Marcus held a hand over his mouth as he spoke. The idea came to her fully formed: *He's lying. There's no doctor, that's the first of the secrets about this place. He operated on your leg. He's keeping you here.*

She glanced away from him, scared he would read her eyes and know what she was thinking.

'When will the Doctor come back to check on me?' It was out of her mouth before she could stop herself.

For a moment Marcus looked reticent, eyes on the floor, hand over his mouth. He picked up a piece of cardboard from the table and slid it into his book to mark his place then dropped the paperback into the pocket of his coat. 'I'm not sure.' He stood up and dusted something off his sleeve. 'He's busy with other things.'

'It's just . . .' Annabelle's voice caught in her throat. 'Do my parents know where I am? They'll be worried . . .'

'Oh. I see.' He dropped his eyes again and glanced around

the room. 'You want to go already. I thought you'd be more grateful. You might have died out there by the road.'

'No! No, it's not that,' Annabelle said, panicked. 'It's just . . .' She searched her brain for the right thing to say, words that would placate Marcus. 'I'm worried about my leg. I watched a hospital programme once where someone got an infection . . .'

Marcus shook his head and gave a dry little laugh. Then he stepped closer and touched his hand to her chin like she was a young child. She tensed but managed to avoid flinching at the contact.

'You don't need to worry about that. The Doctor gave you an antibiotic injection. There's no danger of infection.' He stared at her a moment longer as if daring her to question him. Her dad's face flickered into Annabelle's mind again. The way he would look at her when she'd displeased him somehow. The same paralysing indecision when, as a child, her mouth couldn't form the words to defend herself. Finally Marcus turned away, making it clear the conversation was over.

After a minute he said, 'Come on,' sounding relieved that she hadn't questioned him further. 'I'll take you to the toilet again. But after that it's bedtime; you really need to rest.'

She stared at his slim back as he reached for the wheelchair where it stood folded beside the door. And somehow managed to slide her hand under the pillow, felt her fingers close around the cold phone.

Chapter 23

It was just starting to rain as Monica and Crawford left Mark Gall, still nursing his second double vodka and Coke in the Raigmore Motel. Outside the grey sky and the spits of rain gave the evening a particularly muted and depressing feel. As if this mediocre world was exactly the kind of place that men like Theo Gall should inhabit. Thieves and liars who saw even their closest family members as little more than objects to be exploited.

'I'm feeling a serious dislike for our second victim,' Crawford said, chiming with Monica's own thoughts. He looked up and down the grey street before climbing into the passenger side of the Volvo. Monica got in beside him.

'You saw the state his body was in. We don't have to like Theo Gall. We just need to catch the person who killed him.'

'What's the next step then?' Crawford asked. 'Speak to Gall's ex-wife Pauline? Tomorrow?'

'If we can work out what connects Gall with the first body, I think we'll be halfway to solving this case.' Monica looked through the streaks of rain on the windscreen at the darkening sky. Not for the first time in that long winter and spring she found herself wishing for summer and the endless white nights of the north Highlands. The clock on the dashboard read 8.30 p.m.; inevitably she'd already missed Lucy's bedtime. In less than six months Lucy would be starting primary school. *It'll all be different then. This is the best time, Monica — you should enjoy it while you can.* She could hear her mum's voice in her ear. The sooner they solved these murders, the sooner she could get back to some sort of routine with her daughter. Even if the investigation seemed to be having an unsavoury but cathartic effect on her. 'What's wrong with going to find Pauline now?'

An hour later Pauline Gall looked up at the sound of her name. The woman had brown hair and a thin, tired face. She exuded the tension of a single parent who worked twelve hours a day for a pittance and lived in fear that an unexpected expense or illness might spell disaster for her and her family. Monica knew from a short phone conversation with the woman's eldest daughter that Pauline worked three jobs. Up at 5 a.m. to clean offices. From 9 a.m. to 3 p.m. she sold bread and cakes at a bakery, then came home to make dinner for her daughters. Later she left the eldest daughter in charge for three hours while she went back out to clean more offices at the Highland Council's offices on Tomnahurich Street from 7 to 10 p.m.

It was here that Monica and Crawford had tracked her down.

'That's right,' she replied, a shaky hand shooting up involuntarily to check her hair before she turned off the music on the device she was listening to and removed the headphones from her ears. Her face was alive with concern as she took in the two unexpected visitors.

'Your girls are fine,' Crawford said as he jogged down the stairs of the auditorium towards her. Monica glanced at the red hair on the back of his head and felt a flicker of affection for him, that he'd taken the woman's feelings into consideration.

'What, what is it?' Pauline laid the dusting cloth she'd been holding on the top of the lectern and folded her arms tight across her chest.

'I'm afraid we've got some bad news,' Monica started. 'It's about your husband. Theo Gall.'

'Husband in name only,' Pauline whispered finally when they'd finished telling her the grim news. She had stood with her face set hard as they explained Gall's body had been found deep in a Highland glen, that it had *shown signs of a violent death*. She was gripping either side of the lectern, knuckle bones pressing through her pale skin. As if she were about to deliver a nerve-wracking speech to the empty chamber.

'Do you have any idea who might have wanted your estranged husband dead?'

'Who wouldn't? He'd hurt enough people over the years. Hurt me and my daughters more times than you could imagine.' She shook her head at the memories. 'If there had even been a reason for it. If it had even made sense . . .'

'Are you talking about something specific?'

In reply Pauline raised an arm and pulled up the sleeve of her jumper. A scar was revealed, a patch of melted skin. Monica flinched at the sight. 'Theo gave me that last year, poured a kettle of boiling water down my arm. He didn't even seem angry when he did it. He just did things like that, for no reason. He would burn my things in the fire when I annoyed him, take things – money I tried to save mostly, but other things too. My daughters' video games even. If he'd been doing it to buy drugs or drink or something it would have at least made sense, but . . .'

Monica had met enough career offenders to recognise the profile that Gall fitted. The psychopath, the born criminal hardwired for selfishness. But this seemed to reveal something new about his character, a sadism that wasn't apparent from his criminal record. *Could he have been tortured and killed out of revenge?*

'You split up a few months ago?'

'Four months ago, just after Christmas. Happiest time of the year.' She laughed.

'You were married five years?' Crawford asked.

'Five and a half,' Pauline corrected him. 'What a waste, and putting my girls through that . . .'

'And have you had any contact? Any idea what he's been up to since you split?'

Pauline shook her head. 'I had to come off Facebook when we broke up. Everything he was posting about me . . .' She dropped her eyes to the floor. 'That I was a slut, working as a prostitute.'

'You should have come to us,' Crawford said. 'There's things we can do now.'

Pauline flicked her eyes up to his face but didn't reply. Monica recognised the expression; she'd seen it on the faces of countless abuse victims over the years: *You don't know what it's like, you don't understand what he's capable of.*

'And he didn't attempt to contact you apart from that?' Monica had no doubt that Pauline's abuse at the hands of Gall was a personal tragedy, but she needed to focus on who had killed him. Catch that person.

'At first he'd turn up outside the house, try to meet the kids when they were leaving school. We changed routines, ignored him until he finally seemed to get bored of it all. He was always like that, gets bored of everything eventually.'

'But you reported him missing? Even though you hadn't been in contact?' This didn't fit with the rest of Pauline's story, and Monica wondered if she knew more than she was telling them.

'My daughter asked me to,' Pauline said finally. 'It turned out that she'd been in touch with him on Messenger. He'd been filling her head with rubbish. About how it had been someone else who wrote all that stuff about me, how he had a new job, how he was going to buy her expensive clothes, take us all on holiday.'

Monica's ears pricked up at that. 'What did he say about his new job?'

'It was a fantasy, just another one of his fantasies. About how he had a lot of money coming his way. The kind of thing I've heard him coming away with at least a thousand bloody times.' She shook her head. 'He said that he'd got himself in with the Sinclairs – you know, the builders? Can you believe that?'

Chapter 24

Marcus helped Annabelle slide into the wheelchair again, carefully shifting her splinted leg onto the rest.

'Easy does it,' he said softly. His moment of irritation when she had asked about her parents seemed to have faded just as quickly as it flared up. And he seemed genuinely focused on ensuring her ankle hurt as little as possible. She squeezed her eyes tight shut as the pain throbbed, but kept the phone tucked tight in her hand. At least partially hidden unless Marcus happened to look closely. He pushed her out of the room and back down the sloping corridor. Then stopped outside the bathroom again, slid the bolt back and repeated the protracted procedure of backing the chair in and wandering through the room to find the light switch that actually worked. When he finally left her alone in the cubicle she held her breath and pushed the buttons to switch the phone on.

'Please, please, please,' she whispered, praying it still had battery life.

She couldn't bear to watch and looked away, up at the tiny skylight. Outside it was pitch-black. When she dropped her eyes back to the screen the white apple had appeared. Then the passcode screen. With shaking fingers she entered the digits. Finally the homepage with her apps was revealed. The icon at the top left of the screen flickered, searching for network connectivity.

'Please, please, please.'

For some reason she imagined calling one of the girls she used to know at school or university. Some of them had been nice to her. Sometimes she hearted their Instagram posts. Maybe they would remember who she was and help her?

'Annabelle? Are you OK? We should hurry.' Marcus's anxious voice carried from out in the corridor.

'I'm nearly done,' she managed to reply, trying hard to keep her voice level as she stared at the screen. For a moment she thought it might actually connect. But then they appeared again. The same uncaring words as last time: 'No Service'.

Annabelle sank forward. She knew now that there was absolutely no chance of rescue. She was Marcus's prisoner for as long as he decided to keep her.

Chapter 25

Monica paused in the corridor outside her flat. It was after 11 p.m. now; the day seemed to have stretched on interminably. She glanced up and down the quiet hallway. She could almost feel the microscopic particles of Theo Gall's body clinging to the inside of her nose and mouth. To her skin and clothes.

A noise echoed from downstairs, a door slamming shut. And for a second an absurd thought flashed in her brain: *It's the remains of Theo Gall, pushing and dragging himself through the doorway and up the stairs. The second corpse (Sebastian Sinclair, surely now) bloated and stinking alongside him, leaving a trail of decomposing flesh behind them on the carpet.* She blinked and realised she was actually watching the top of the stairwell intently, body tensed as if the stump of an arm might really appear there in front of her.

'Jesus, you should be used to this. It's only been six months,' she whispered. Patting herself down for the door key as for a second she allowed herself to imagine a *normal* life. Coming home from the office to some kind of life partner, someone to slide into bed with at the end of a long day. Someone who helped look after her and Lucy. *Well, you've got your mum at least, that's something. Better than an empty flat.* Monica tried very hard to feel grateful for everything her mum did.

She turned both locks on the door and stepped inside, pushed it closed behind her. Locked and bolted it. Relieved that her mum continued to follow Monica's demand she keep the door properly secured. Up until the case six months ago Angela had always left the door to her own house unlocked, seemingly convinced that the crimes and murders she read about obsessively could never happen to her own family and belonged squarely in the realms of fiction. The idea that the decomposing versions of Gall and Sinclair could appear outside her flat might be horrifying, but it was the living that concerned Monica. The living who had given her the nightmares.

She shook her head to dismiss the memories, strangely relieved again to have the new case to focus on, and took in the fragrant smell of Indian cooking. The flat was cosy warm. A distilled sense of home comfort and security that Angela Kennedy seemed capable of carrying with her wherever she went. An optimism that things would work out well. Monica shrugged her long Harris tweed coat off and hung it on the hook by the door. Angela looked up from where she was sitting at the kitchen table, pushed her glasses up to nestle in her hair and blinked a couple of times as if she needed to check that the person who had just walked into the flat was indeed her daughter.

'I made you curry. You must be hungry?' Her mum's hallmark was preparing hearty food then ambushing Monica with it when she came home late. Watching with satisfaction as her daughter ate, as if by keeping her well fed she was contributing in a small but vital way to the smooth running of whatever investigation she might be working on.

'How's the case going?' Angela stared gravely as Monica washed her hands at the kitchen sink then settled down at the table. Her tone was that of a fellow professional, eager to discuss different angles and potential theories gleaned from her own 'research' conducted on online news sites, detective novels and TV programmes.

Monica cleared her throat. 'It's going OK. We seem to be making progress,' she said, careful as always, knowing her mum would be thrilled to learn they'd just made a seemingly solid connection between the two bodies. Although why successful businessman Sebastian Sinclair would have associated with petty criminal Theo Gall remained a mystery.

'Sure.' Her mum nodded, face set in an intent frown. 'What does Crawford think? What's his angle on it?'

Monica cleared her throat again and tried to hide her blossoming irritation.

'We're still in the early stages,' she said without raising her eyes from the food. 'We can't rule out anything at this stage.' One of her favourite deadpan responses to nosy members of the public, to journalists, to her mum.

Angela pushed both sleeves of her jumper up. 'That's right, that's where they go wrong with investigations a lot. Just looking at the obvious solutions without taking in the bigger picture.'

Monica took a mouthful of the curry, tried to remember the last time she'd eaten, probably not since the night before.

'Nice?' Angela watched Monica's face for telltale signs. 'I made it with cauliflower for you, but me and Lucy had chicken. Bill Macdonald called. Said he'd been pleased to see you the other night.' Monica nodded but didn't reply. 'He always did like you. Wasn't one of these little boys, afraid of my Amazonian,' Angela said with a laugh. 'Your dad liked him too, believe it or not. Always had so many friends, your dad.'

Monica glanced away from her mum's smiling face. Feeling that barrier, the disconnect. They remembered John Kennedy so differently.

Angela went on: 'I think he could relate to Bill though, being a big man too. That's not easy in Scotland, all these idiots wanting to fight. Trying to prove themselves. That's why your dad got into the boxing in the first place.'

'What did Bill want?' Monica felt that familiar flicker of unease, of the past circling in on her.

'Oh I think just to catch up, take you for coffee. Though between me and you I think he's worried sick about his boy. I told you? I think maybe he wants to talk that over as well.'

Chapter 26

Back in that strange dark room, when Marcus had closed and bolted the door, Annabelle spent a long time in a state that was close to panic. No matter how often she told herself to leave her phone under her pillow and save what little of the battery was left, she couldn't resist switching it on again. Desperately hoping it would somehow connect. But 'O2-UK' resolutely refused to replace 'No Service' as the battery percentage ticked slowly down.

A sound echoed in the corridor outside, mercifully interrupting her fixation on her phone. After a moment she realised it was a shout, muffled by the thick door. She switched the iPhone off and pushed herself up on the bed, listening intently. The sound came again, indistinct but louder this time. Was it someone calling to her?

'Scott?!' she shouted back, remembering what Marcus had said about a visitor. 'Can you hear me?! My name's Annabelle!'

For a long time she listened, praying for a response, but it never came. Finally she began to doubt she'd even heard the voice in the first place, if it hadn't been a ghost of her past, come to taunt her in those haunted tunnels.

Chapter 27

When her mum had finally gathered up her iPad and gone through to bed to continue her 'research' on the case, Monica sat down on the sofa by the window. After setting her tea on the windowsill she reached to flick through her dad's old vinyls again. She had been listening to them since she'd discovered his collection up in the loft at her parents' house a couple of years previously, but had still barely scratched the surface of the collection. It was mostly country and western. Something about the genre had appealed to his macho self-image, the part of John Kennedy that saw himself as an instrument of justice in his role as a prison warden. The part her mum seemed to minimise in her recollections of him but loomed largest for Monica.

She chose another of the records at random, set it spinning on the turntable and flipped the cardboard sleeve over to check the album title: *Out of Hand*. The track was 'She's Actin' Single (I'm Drinkin' Doubles)' by Gary Stewart, possibly the most archetypal country song title ever, Monica thought as she pulled the headphones on and sank back on the sofa.

As the music started up in her ears it triggered a memory. Hearing her dad and his workmates sitting at the table in the kitchen of her parents' small house down in the Marsh. They were drinking and playing cards while she sat upstairs in the doorway of her bedroom. Half wanting to use the bathroom, but feeling a teenage shyness about crossing the landing, where she might bump into one of them if they came upstairs to use it themselves. Half listening in to the drunken conversation as it drifted up with the smell of cigarette smoke. Stories about riots they'd dealt with, difficult prisoners they'd subdued. Long John Kennedy, her dad, the big man.

She remembered them talking about another big man, a prisoner who had *tried it on. Thought he could handle himself with our Long John.* The sound of her dad's smirked laugh, then his catchphrase: *That'll be the day.* Joking but serious, like John Wayne himself. *In the infirmary for two weeks after that. Wasn't he?* Then the laughter again, her dad joining in, and Monica remembered the moment of shock.

Were they really talking about her dad? Could he really batter another man into hospital and find something to laugh about in it? And the dawning realisation that the respect she had identified as a little girl on her visit to her dad's workplace was fear: his colleagues were afraid of him. Her bare feet propped up on the wall by the door. The poster above them, Michael Hutchence leaning forward on the handlebars of a motorcycle, hair covering half his face. Her familiar teenage bedroom now tilted and strange. Her father, who she had to hide the Guns N' Roses tape from because of the PARENTAL ADVISORY: EXPLICIT CONTENT label. Boasting about hurting someone he was supposed to protect.

Monica blinked, wondered for a moment where her mum had been that evening while her dad and his cronies were drinking, then caught her reflection in the darkened window. Her pale white face and dark hair, same as her dad. And she wondered how similar they were on the inside. How much of her need to be close to crime derived from some attraction to violence? She blinked again and looked away from those shadowy eyes.

She needed to think about something else and reached for her laptop. Euston Miller's website with the story about the tunnel was still open. She clicked on another story and began to read.

The mysterious Affric Men have been spotted in numerous locations. The story of an unnamed crofter who until 1982 lived alone close to the entrance of Glen Turrit is little known. In early winter 1982 the crofter got off the late bus from Beauly and was walking the last couple of long miles on the lonely single-track road to his croft when he spotted a light in the dense birch woodland off by the side of the road. Thinking it might be a lost hillwalker in need of assistance he hailed the light and stood watching. The light immediately disappeared and the woods were plunged into darkness. The crofter shone his own torch among the silver birch trees but couldn't see anything. After a moment he decided that perhaps he'd been mistaken and continued along the lonely road.

It was then that he heard the footsteps crunching among the twigs and bracken in the forest beside the road. He stopped. The footsteps stopped in unison. He started up and the footsteps began again.

By now the crofter, who was not at all unaccustomed to being alone in these remote areas, was beginning to panic. He said afterwards that it was as if some curtain had been pulled back from his eyes, and suddenly he saw the world in a completely new and terrifying light. The fear settled across all his senses, encompassing his mind and his body. He hurried on along the road with the sound of movement in the distance echoing though the woodland in unison. Terror overtook him and he ran madly towards his croft, where he shut himself in.

Cowering in his locked cottage, he heard the first sounds through the shuttered windows. A quiet voice, just out of the range of understanding. He had no intention of responding and he stayed, hunched up with fear, in his kitchen. But an image came into his mind, as if someone else had put it there. Of two men outside. Demanding he let them into his house. When he came to from this vision he found himself standing at his front door, one hand on the key, the other on the handle. In the process of turning the lock. As those whispering voices continued.

Monica sighed and closed the laptop. She had enough to think about without adding Euston Miller's ridiculous conspiracy-theory website into the mix. Though the man's name reminded her she hadn't heard back from Fisher about his death in Glen Affric yet. She made a mental note to ask him about it in the morning. She turned to lay the laptop on the table by the sofa and caught a flicker of movement at the side of the room.

Her daughter was standing by the door to her bedroom, looking straight at her.

She pulled the headphones off. 'Lucy? Are you OK?' She unfolded herself from the couch and moved across the room towards her. Lucy didn't respond. Just kept staring at her.

Monica bent down to pick her up. The kid's body was rigid in her arms. As if Monica wasn't there at all.

'Lucy?!' Monica pushed the curly hair out of her daughter's face. Was she sleepwalking? Her eyes still fixed and staring, Lucy then collapsed forward into Monica's arms.

Chapter 28

In her dreams Annabelle was desperately trying to escape a terrifying grey world. Moving down streets and through empty buildings in an abandoned city, like London but different. Populated with characters from her life – her mum and dad, Miss Albright, Mr Pepper, girls from school and university, the other volunteers from the cafe – watching, mocking her because she couldn't walk properly. She kept trying to ask them for help, but somehow they were always just out of reach.

She opened her eyes in the murky room. The strange half-carpeted walls, the damp concrete and the stifling stillness. It took everything she had to resist reaching for her phone, switching it on and trying futilely to connect to the network again. For her sanity she needed to save that last little fragment of battery life.

Instead she stared up at the grey ceiling, lit by the bedside lamp. Her leg ached, but the pain behind her eyes had finally faded. For the first time since the crash the fog in her brain seemed to have shifted slightly too. She took a deep breath of the damp air and tried to think logically. Who might actually know where she was? Who might come looking?

Mum or Dad? The idea took her back to the past and the feeling of strangeness in her childhood house. Her parents never touched her in a harsh or inappropriate way, never hurt her, but her bedroom possessed a kind of pink-tinted emptiness.

The wallpaper with the teddy bears on it, the dolls and the little dresser. The pink clothes and being a *perfect princess.* She thought very carefully about what her mother used to whisper in her ear: *Daddy will be home soon and we're going to make everything perfect so he knows how much we care.* All the ways she'd got things wrong, disappointing her dad by not staying a perfect daughter, by getting older and becoming a strange child who couldn't smile properly and whose curly blonde hair turned dark and straight. A child who was unremarkable at school and faded into the background. So far from perfect, indeed causing her parents to split up by being a failure. Would her parents even care if she was missing?

Annabelle glanced down at her bare arms. For the first time in a long time she looked at the white marks, like plastic, where she used to cut herself when the thoughts got too much. By then she had already ruined everything for her mum through her lack of perfection, and her dad had already given up on them and left.

The scars indicated 'a history of mental health problems'. If anyone did start to worry, the police would look into her past, wouldn't they? Assume she was exactly the kind of person who would disappear? *But you haven't cut yourself in a long time or even taken medication.* Wouldn't they speak to the supervisors at the volunteer cafe? She had worked there for almost three years. Since she moved into the flat opposite Miss Albright's, although she didn't get to know her elderly neighbour until six months later when an envelope addressed to Miss Albright was wrongly pushed through Annabelle's letter box. That was after the breakdown at university, when she couldn't handle the pressure of failing to be perfect again. The supervisors at the cafe knew she hadn't cut herself since then. They knew she was doing well and wouldn't just disappear.

It doesn't matter anyway. The cruel thought came back. *Because no one even knows where you are.* How would anyone guess she'd gone down that locked road? The Instagram post at the service station was the only piece of evidence she was even in Scotland. Over a hundred miles south, no mention of where she was actually going . . . All her Internet searches about the road had been done on her phone.

'What should I do? How can I get out of here?' She heard the panic in her voice. And the unexpected answer came back almost instantly and with an unusual clarity: *You have to kill Marcus. It's your only way out.*

Chapter 29

'Kids can do strange things when they sleepwalk. You used to be the same,' Angela Kennedy whispered across the kitchen worktop. She tilted her head to glance at where Lucy was sitting on the sofa, watching breakfast TV with a bowl of Cheerios on her lap.

After Lucy had sunk into Monica's arms she'd seemed to be in a deep sleep, and for a few horrible moments Monica had thought her daughter was having some kind of fit. She was already holding her phone out, about to dial 999, when Lucy had opened her eyes and smiled up at her, seemingly completely normal.

'One morning I found you out in the coal shed.' Angela shook her head at the memory. 'Me and your dad were sure someone had come into the house and taken you. There you were, sitting chatting away to yourself as if you were talking to a friend. My gran used to say that children can just see more than adults. They're closer to what we are before we're born. For a while I thought you might have her way about you.'

Monica shook her own head. She'd heard the stories about her great-grandmother, who was supposedly able to read tea leaves and communicate with spirits, more than enough times. 'Have you mentioned any of that to Lucy?' Monica said quietly, an accusatory tone creeping into her voice.

'Of course not!' Angela snapped back defensively. 'Anyway, it's just a family story. I don't see what harm it would do . . .'

Monica sighed, feeling every one of her forty-four years after another night of broken sleep on the couch. She scraped her hair back and started looking around for something to tie it with. Her mum noticed and dug in her giant handbag, handing Monica a pack of hair ties.

'Take these. You shouldn't be using those rubber bands; they're bad for your hair roots.' Though recently Monica had noticed the posties seemed to have stopped leaving those useful red bands in the hall outside her flat anyway. Perhaps out of some new environmental concern. She unhooked one of the ties and secured her hair with it.

'Just . . . make sure Lucy's not reading anything too grown-up for her,' Monica whispered, glancing back at her daughter on the sofa. The grey spring morning was visible through the window beyond her. Lucy had always had a strangeness. The way she barely ever cried, those smoky blue-grey eyes that watched what was going on as if they'd seen other lives, other worlds. 'Or watching anything too scary. It worries me sometimes. The way she is.' The sleepwalking was a new worry. Monica wondered for a second if it was linked to her going back to work on the case. Had the change in routine disturbed Lucy somehow? Opened up everything that happened six months ago and got her wondering about evil, death again? She had asked that strange question about her grandad's funeral practically the day Monica started work on this investigation. It was probably her fault. Lucy was once again paying the price for her choices. She needed to get the case resolved quickly for Lucy's sake if nothing else.

Monica pulled the Volvo over on Union Street in the centre of Inverness, where she'd arranged to collect Crawford after he'd failed to turn up at headquarters on time that morning. She spotted him standing outside a cafe, cardboard cup in his left hand, checking his phone with the right. She sounded the horn, and he looked up, hurried along the pavement, opened the door and got into the passenger seat, the scent of his aftershave filling the car.

'Sorry . . . Sorry I'm late.' He sounded uncharacteristically flustered. Even the delicious smells he'd doused himself in couldn't divert Monica's attention from his clothes. She clocked the same suit, the same white shirt with red stitching around the buttonholes, as when she'd dropped him at his Audi the night before. No doubt he'd gone out somewhere, found himself in someone's bed. *It was already 11 p.m. when I dropped you off. How do you find the energy, Crawford?* Though on reflection she wasn't sure if she wanted to know. She shook her head and stared at the road ahead, the faded glamour of the Victorian buildings, relics of a time when the city was steeped in a romantic vision of the Highlands.

'The DNA from his son came back then? Confirmed the first body was Sebastian Sinclair?' Crawford asked, sounding distracted. Monica glanced at him; he was still jabbing at his phone.

'First thing this morning,' she said slowly. 'His sister Heather is going to meet us at her house. Same as when I called you thirty minutes ago?'

'Sure . . . I remember . . . Just . . .' His phone buzzed twice with messages, and he swore under his breath.

'Is everything OK, Crawford?' She glanced at him again, aware that she should probably tell him off. Maybe she would have, if he hadn't been so apologetic. On the drive over to collect him she'd considered some kind of reprimand for his lateness but decided against it. One of the things he excelled at was picking up information from unlikely sources, and it meant he occasionally turned up for work late or hungover.

He shook his head, his usually gelled and sculpted red hair falling into his eyes. 'Just ... I don't know. I've been seeing someone ... Then I ended up going out last night ... She tried to find me at my flat but I wasn't ...' he babbled.

'Well, make sure it doesn't affect your work,' she said softly.

'Right, boss.' He flicked the phone to silent, dropped it into his jacket pocket and took a long drink of his coffee. 'Quadruple espresso. Need it this morning,' he muttered, shaking his head. Monica put the car in gear and started down the road. There was no doubt Crawford was annoying, but he was never boring to work with. She realised that she might have even missed his company.

'So why does a respected businessman find himself dead in a glen with a career petty criminal?' Crawford asked after a minute, keen to prove his mind was back on the case. 'It just doesn't make any sense.'

'We don't know for certain that they ended up there together,' Monica reminded him as she slowed the car for the roundabout at the bottom of Chapel Street, indicating right towards the Kessock Bridge, which would take them across the Moray Firth to the Black Isle. 'It's possible the killer targeted them separately somehow,' Monica said, going back to one of the first rules of criminal investigation: assume nothing, challenge everything. Though in truth this version of events sounded unlikely after what they'd learned the night before about Gall claiming he'd found work with the Sinclairs. 'Let's hope Heather Sinclair can give us a clue as to who might have wanted to kill her brother.'

Chapter 30

Marcus laid the tray across her lap again. It was only the second time he'd done it, but somehow it already had a routine feeling. Similar to how she'd watched flight attendants deliver those little containers to a whole plane with such order. Annabelle was sure only a few days had passed since the crash, but part of her felt like she'd spent a lifetime in the room. Everything that had happened before then existed only as some kind of dream. She stared down at the plate. Another hideous-looking all-day breakfast like before, steam rising off it in the damp room, although if anything there was more food this time.

Hesitantly she picked up the fork and knife from the sides of the plate. *You need to get Scott's knife and stab Marcus in the neck.* The horrible thought came back into her head as she cut into a piece of bacon with the blunt table knife. She tried to keep her eyes fixed on the plate as she chewed. Worried he might somehow guess what she was thinking if he saw her face, the way her hands were shaking. The meat tasted like leather in her mouth as she forced it down. All the time Marcus sat on his chair by the door, watching her eat.

'I can't cut it very well.'

'Oh, should I help again?' Marcus stood up and came over to kneel by the bed. He reached into the inside pocket of his coat and produced the folding knife. Slowly he teased the blade out with the nail of his thumb. Then he took the fork from Annabelle's hand. She watched his rough hands as he cut the meat, tomatoes, eggs and mushrooms up into a mess of small pieces.

'I thought I heard Scott last night – I think he was shouting something to me,' she said, eyes on the knife.

Marcus nodded slowly but didn't reply. He skewered some of the bacon and egg on the fork and held it up to her mouth, knife tight in his other hand.

She chewed slowly, a piece at a time, washed down with mouthfuls of sweet tea. Her eyes kept drifting to the blade of the knife, part of her hoping he would lay it down on the tray so she could snatch it, part of her terrified by the idea of actually stabbing another human. What if it didn't work? What if he fought her off? He would put that metal mask on her.

'Maybe we could go outside for some fresh air?' she said impulsively.

He drew his breath in through his teeth in an exaggerated *shush*. 'There's lambing snow on the mountains. Sgurr na Lapaich is plastered again. You'd catch your death.' He stood up abruptly, picked up a paper napkin from the tray. Annabelle watched as he wiped the locking knife quickly and folded it away. Then he turned his back on her and looked at the metal door.

'There's something I have to tell you. I did what you asked yesterday,' he said slowly. 'But I'm afraid it's bad news . . . About your parents . . . I tried to contact them, to tell them where you were and ask if they'd be able to come and get you.' He paused, still facing away from Annabelle towards the door. 'I'm sorry to say this, but I'm afraid neither of them was interested in coming for you. I'm afraid they don't want you back.'

Chapter 31

The morning drive across the Kessock Bridge to Heather Sinclair's mansion on the Black Isle proved fruitless. The high metal gates that guarded the driveway were closed and there was no response to Monica's buzzing on the intercom. In the distance she could just make out the front of the house through the mature oak and beech trees scattered in front of it.

'Didn't she say she'd be here?' Crawford muttered. 'You think it's suspicious? Brother dead and she doesn't want to speak to us?'

Monica gave the buzzer a final try, then turned the Volvo back in the direction of the southbound A9. In truth she wasn't sure what to make of it. It only added to her jarringly incomplete picture of the Sinclair family. The two-dimensional Sebastian Sinclair, seemingly an old-fashioned businessman who had somehow ended up associated with a career criminal. Now his sister ducking a meeting with the police the morning her brother's body is ID'd as a murder victim.

'We'll find out,' she replied finally. Because as the last person known to have spoken to Sebastian Sinclair, his sister was currently their best lead in the case.

They drove back across the bridge to meet Fisher and Khan before they continued the search for Heather Sinclair. The spring morning had tilted towards warmth despite the fresh snow Monica could see on the distant western mountains at the head of the Beauly Firth. Framed by the pure blue sky, the postcard epitome of a majestic Highland day. *Except for the bodies*, Monica thought. Two of them, chopped up. And the locations continued to niggle at her. So conveniently situated. Why leave the bodies somewhere they would be seen, but try to make it look like they'd come to rest there accidentally? Or was it pure coincidence? Was she reading too much into it? And for the first time that day the other death came back to her – Euston Miller from four years before, the one she'd asked Fisher to look into.

It was the first thing Monica asked him about when she and Crawford crossed the busy Incident Room to where the younger detective was sitting at a desk alongside DC Khan. Fisher nodded attentively at her question. Turned to his laptop and opened a file, his hand going to his glasses in a nervous gesture. *He seems to be on top of things anyway*, Monica thought. It was reassuring after what had happened at The Clach.

'Deceased was one Euston Miller, aged seventy at the time of his death,' Fisher said. 'His body was recovered from the wreckage of his Toyota pickup truck beneath Dog Falls in Glen Affric. His blood alcohol content was up at zero point two four. Had two previous convictions for driving under the influence and was banned from driving at the time of his death. Cause of death was drowning, declared death by misadventure.' He turned the laptop round to show a picture of a green pickup, its cab underwater and tail sticking up into the air at the bottom of a thirty-foot cliff face. 'This is close to the road in Glen Affric. He crashed at night. Could have been a suicide, but the investigators weren't certain. He was so intoxicated they thought it possible he accidentally turned into the car park at Dog Falls and drove straight off.'

As Monica had discovered in the last six months, fatal car crashes like this weren't an unusual occurrence in the Scottish

Highlands. Narrow rural roads, steep-sided glens. Even if this was more dramatic than most.

'Anything from the autopsy? Other intoxicants or unusual marks on the body?'

'Nothing that stands out. He had abrasions on his forehead, but the pathologist thought they were consistent with trauma from the crash, hitting his head on the steering wheel.'

Monica nodded again, satisfied that despite Gillian Keegan's protests there was no connection between Euston Miller's death and their double murder. Better to focus resources on the solid leads in the case than chase shadows through a conspiracy theorist's website.

'You two start digging into any known associates of Sebastian Sinclair, and especially Theo Gall. Someone must know how these men ended up connected. A petty criminal and one of the owners of the biggest company in the north of Scotland.'

As the detectives nodded in unison, Fisher's phone buzzed on the table beside his laptop. He picked it up and Monica caught his expression as he looked at the screen then glanced around the office. Seemingly hunting for whoever had sent the message, although this time there was no amused-looking group of detectives pretending ignorance.

'Is everything OK?' she asked because he actually looked rattled.

'They've been doing it all week,' he said. 'This one's . . . creepy though.'

Chapter 32

Annabelle stared at Marcus's slim back, the shape of his shoulders under the army jacket. The way they were hunched slightly forward.

'But . . . what did they say? What . . .' Annabelle's objections died in her throat because for a moment it made sense. She felt the horror of abandonment in her stomach as her mind raced back to another memory from her childhood. Not long before her dad left when she was six. They were in a park somewhere in London. Her parents were arguing and Annabelle had wandered off towards the climbing frame. Two older girls were standing a little way away, close to some trees. They smiled at her. She remembered that it had felt nice, being noticed like that by much older girls. They gestured to her, and she'd gone to them. Their smiles were as wide as the world as they each took one of her hands and began to walk her away across the park.

'Your mummy asked us to come and collect you; we're friends of hers.' The voice had a tightness, and what she was saying didn't make sense, but the girl was almost an adult and Annabelle didn't speak to adults; she certainly wouldn't have contradicted one. Instead she nodded and continued to walk with them towards the trees and the row of cars by the fence beyond them.

The shouting started then, from behind them. They turned together. Annabelle's parents were visible on the other side of the climbing frame. Her father watching, her mother screaming and running towards them. The girls let go of her hands and ran. Annabelle began to cry. Her mother grabbed her tight, and moments later her dad was there too.

She stared up at him through the blur of tears, not fully understanding what had happened, what she'd done to upset her mum.

'You don't just wander off, Annabelle.' He was red-faced and angry. 'Now stop crying, both of you. You're making a scene.' He dropped to his knees and slapped Annabelle hard across the face.

She stopped crying. It was the only time she could remember her dad hitting her. Practically the only time she remembered him touching her. Her mother had stopped crying too and began to clean a stain from Annabelle's jacket, as if nothing had happened.

The curious horror of the long-forgotten memory raced through her mind in a second. Surely she was misremembering; surely it hadn't been like that?

Finally she stammered to Marcus, 'What did they say?'

He continued to look at the door, his back to her. She noticed his hands had dropped to his hips though. 'Very little, actually. I think it's better you put it behind you.'

'No!' Annabelle heard her voice rise. 'Tell me what they said!' Surely they would have wanted to know she was OK. Her father had bought her a car just months before. Even if he had seemed most excited about posting photos of himself giving her the keys on Facebook, he had at least shown some interest in her. Her mum still called sometimes, even though they hadn't spoken properly for years, since the last time Annabelle had tried to talk about her childhood. 'You didn't even speak to them, did you? You're lying!' She managed to stop herself then, and silence filled the room. It seemed an unspoken covenant had been broken. In some strange way this place had become an extension of her childhood home, with its unsaid things and all its strangeness. 'I'm sorry,' she whispered finally. 'I didn't mean . . .'

Her voice faded away, and for a long time Marcus stayed completely still, his back to her. She grabbed her phone, certain that he would confiscate it now. Her last piece of proof that she had ever even existed outside this room. Finally he turned, body tense, apparently struggling to contain a frightening rage. He reached for the wheelchair, propped against the wall, and roughly unfolded it.

'I better take you to the bathroom.' His voice was low and flat. 'After that you should rest. I can see you're tired. The Doctor might be along later to check on your progress.' Annabelle felt hot tears running down her face. *There's no doctor, Marcus. You're lying, you've been lying all along.* But she couldn't stop herself from nodding. He helped slide her across the bed, then lifted her into the chair and placed her leg carefully onto the rest.

'I'm sorry, Marcus,' she whispered, desperately trying to re-establish a connection with her captor, 'I didn't mean—'

'It doesn't matter,' he whispered back. But she could feel his anger through the chair as he pushed it down the tunnel, her leg wobbling on the rest, sending shocks of pain through her body that made her gasp.

He pushed the chair roughly past the bathroom door. Unbolted it and backed her inside. This time he stormed across the dark room to switch the light on without a word. She looked back out at the tunnel. The white icicles that hung from the cracks where water had leaked through. It made her think of *Snow White and the Seven Dwarves*. The mine. And the cackling witch. Annabelle remembered lying on her living-room floor staring at the screen and jerked in the wheelchair at the memory of her terror. As she stared at the white icicles a strange thing happened. The chair began to move towards them. It took her a moment to understand that the floor of the bathroom was on a slight incline. In his simmering fury Marcus had forgotten to put the brake on, and her movement had been enough to rock the chair into motion. She could hear Marcus's footsteps, twenty feet away at the back of the room. Almost without thinking she dropped the phone onto her lap. Her hands went to the wheels of the chair and she pushed down once. The chair rolled slowly out into the tunnel. She leaned back for the door, her fingers just reached the metal handle and the heavy wooden door began to swing closed.

'Annabelle? What—'

The door clunked shut, muffling the sound of Marcus's voice. With a shaking hand she reached up as far as she could, ignoring the pain that was screaming again from her leg. Her fingers rested on the end of the thick bolt. She slid it home, trapping Marcus in the room.

Chapter 33

Four years earlier

Euston Miller glanced at the time on the dash of the pickup. Almost 11 p.m. He sighed and took another mouthful of the Famous Grouse. Felt the whisky burn his throat and then his stomach. Shift him into a gentler version of reality. The liquid made a slopping sound inside the glass bottle. *A two-thirds-gone sound,* Euston guessed. He held the bottle up to the dim light from the moon. *Closer to three-quarters.*

He sighed again, shifted in his seat. Felt the familiar comfort of the soft fabric against his back. A thin layer of sweat on his skin from the heater. The whisky had been meant to take the edge off. Just a couple of mouthfuls, how had he gone through most of a bottle? Before he was tempted by another drink Euston managed to screw the cap on and push the bottle carefully into the door pocket. Instead he rolled a cigarette and scanned the dark lay-by. Dog Falls, halfway up Glen Affric. There were thick forests on four sides, the black sky overhead. It was a remote spot, a place that should have felt eerie and threatening. Maybe it would have if not for the whisky.

There was no sign of anyone outside, no lights approaching down the long glen. Nothing had passed in the hour he'd been there. *Another time waster?* It didn't quite fit. More likely the old man got scared. Euston shifted on the seat. Realised his hand had gone to the Grouse again, that he'd already lifted it from the pocket and unscrewed the cap. He looked down at the welcoming bottle, the smell sharp in the vehicle's interior. *Rude not to.* He took a deep pull, wiped the back of his hand across his mouth.

He'd heard the rumour about the family who lived in Glen Turrit. The Slates. People saw them coming and going sometimes in a rusted white van. Kept themselves to themselves, but that was not unusual in the rural Highlands. Especially around Little Arklow, especially in the Affric Triangle. But the name had cropped up in his research. An old newspaper article that quoted a Mr Slate as saying he'd seen strange lights in the woods around the time a man called Colin Muir had gone missing in the area. Back in 1980. Euston had spotted the link with what had happened to the crofter he'd written about online. Perhaps Slate had seen something else? Something that could finally shed some light on the mysterious Affric Men?

On the previous afternoon Euston had driven up Glen Turrit looking for the Slates' house, to see if it was really there. He'd gone almost as far as the dam but found nothing. Then, as he was leaving the glen, the white van had been by the gate, almost like it was waiting for him. The old man had climbed out and come to speak to him. He seemed friendly, interested. Asking where Euston lived, whether he was travelling alone.

'It's normally locked, you see. Not often someone comes along.'

'I came to ask about Colin Muir.'

Slate's face had changed, a tightness come into his body. He'd glanced back at the van. A teenage boy and an elderly woman were looking out at them. Him warily, her smiling. Slate said, 'Long time ago all that. In the past.'

'I think there's something strange about these mountains,' Euston had replied. 'I'm trying to find out what. You saw lights in the forest? Was there anything else there?'

Slate had met his eyes then, as if deciding. Finally he'd glanced back at the people in the van, adjusted the tweed cap he was wearing.

'Not with them.'

They'd arranged to meet the following night. At this lay-by, far from where they might be spotted. As he'd turned to walk to his van Slate had glanced back, an afterthought. 'You won't say to anyone?'

A ghost of movement in the forest on the other side of the deep ravine caught Euston's eye. A shade of black against the dark. He peered at it, but nothing clearer would form. He shrugged and took another swallow of the whisky. The bottle almost empty now, it was time to start the long drive back down the glen towards Little Arklow. Slate was obviously frightened. Had decided not to come. Euston pressed the clutch down, put the vehicle into gear. He would wait until the morning, drive down Glen Turrit again. Find out once and for all what Slate had to tell him.

The figure appeared in the pickup's headlights. Euston felt a flash of fear blossom in his chest. Numbed by the alcohol, it subsided a moment later. Slate. The old man was standing in the lights, holding his hand out to shield his eyes. With his other hand he made a spinning gesture: *Wind down the window.* Euston didn't have time to wonder how Slate had got there, without him seeing or hearing any car. He opened the window, leaned out.

Slate said, 'They're over there. They're coming. You'd better go.' His voice was flat calm. Totally at odds with the words coming from his mouth.

'What? Who are you talking about?' Euston twisted his head back over his right shoulder. There was no one there. Just the dark of the lay-by lit red by the tail lights, then the darker forest beyond.

'Who—' Euston caught a glimpse of the other person in his peripheral vision. Crouched down at the side of his pickup. Directly beside the driver's door. As he jerked his head instinctively back inside the cab, a series of thoughts rifled through his mind: *Who? Why? How?* They were cut short by the impact on his forehead. A flash of white light, then he was sitting, slumped back in the seat. He could feel a heaviness at the top of his head and tried to lift a hand to his face.

'No. They'll come looking . . . Better here.'

The words were muttered in a quiet, business-like way. The door opened and Euston realised Slate was leaning across his body. The truck must have stalled because he was moving the gearstick to neutral, then turning the key to restart the engine. Euston tried to say something. Slate didn't seem to notice him though, as he slid the seat belt across his chest and clicked it home. Then pulled hard at the strap to lock it into place.

'Old. Goes that tough, stringy way anyway.'

Euston tried again to move, to say something. But the words came out in a slurred mess. He heard the engine revving, sensed that the vehicle was moving. After a moment it began to pick up speed. The door slammed shut. Fractured images were caught in the headlights. Trees. Rocks. He realised his foot was pressed on the throttle and shifted it off. Managed to pump the brake. But the pickup was on a slope. The brakes locked out, and it bounced and skidded on down. For a moment it was airborne.

Euston stared down at the churning black water under the lights. In that long second he was taken back to his childhood. The space films he'd loved: *It Came From Outer Space, The Forbidden Planet*. As the water rushed up to meet him he pictured reality splitting open. Just like a starship going into warp speed.

The pickup seemed to hang, suspended in space. Like there might be any number of dimensions, any number of realities. But for Euston there was only this one. He squeezed his eyes tight shut as the truck hit the water.

Chapter 34

Annabelle sank back into the wheelchair and stared at the bathroom door in disbelief. A moment later it juddered and strained as Marcus tried to pull it open.

'Annabelle?' His voice was hardly audible through the thick wood. 'You'll regret this. Believe me.'

Annabelle sat almost motionless under the electric lights in the corridor. She glanced down the slope to where the tunnel disappeared into the shadows deep below. She remembered Scott, his cries, and thought about trying to find him. Maybe he could even help her to escape? The bolt rattled, then creaked as Marcus began kicking at the door.

She dropped her shaking hands to the wheels. There was no time to look for Scott. If she could phone the police they would find him. She turned the chair and started to push as hard as she could up the gentle incline of the slope. Her injured leg bounced uncontrollably on the rest. Adrenaline was coursing through her body, masking the pain. She pushed hard towards the door at the top of the corridor. The squeaking from the chair echoed down the tunnel along with the sound of her own panting breath. All the time she expected to hear the door burst open, to hear Marcus's footsteps pounding the tarmac behind her. Somehow she made it to the door at the top. Solid metal. There were two bolts pushed across, but mercifully no lock, no padlock.

'Thank you, thank you, thank you,' Annabelle murmured to

the damp tunnel. She reached up and pulled them back one after the other. The door sagged open and Annabelle was met with just a hint of breeze. Unbelievably clear and delicious after the days and nights underground.

She pulled the door further open and wheeled herself inside. By the light of two slatted windows at the far end she could see she was in a small wooden building. They were thick with cobwebs, but through the dirty glass the sky was visible. Unmistakably blue. She rolled across to the wooden door. The door was old but reinforced with horizontal slats, it was held shut by a single bolt. Annabelle reached to pull it back, began to wheel herself out.

The sound echoed up from the tunnel. A splitting sound of wood cracking under blows. Marcus was coming. Annabelle pushed the door closed behind her and desperately ran her hands over the wooden panels, searching for a bolt. There wasn't one though, just two metal hoops that you could click a padlock through.

She glanced wildly around. Taking her location in properly for the first time. The building she had emerged from was a kind of shed built against a cliff face. On either side of the shed, ferns and brambles, overhung by trees, grew thickly. To one side, through the woods, Annabelle could make out the chimney stack of a building. Beside it a flag was fluttering from a pole. Yellow background with what looked like a red monster on it. *That must be where Marcus lives*, she decided, as if referring to a casual acquaintance. Beyond the house the horizon was dominated by a row of mountains, dark and dusted with fresh snow. The same mountains that she'd seen those days before from her car. *Picture postcard.* Only now they seemed to radiate a terrifying sense of her insignificance.

She shook her head to dispel the momentary paralysis. *Block the door! You need to stop him!* The voice in her head shrieked. With what though? She glanced around again. The ground was littered with sticks – branches fallen from the trees.

Annabelle stretched her arm to pick one up, tested the wood between her hands. It snapped easily. She swore, felt tears of frustration rolling down her cheeks again. *Fucking, fucking thing!* She reached again, more quickly this time. The chair rocked and tipped worryingly, threatening to dump her on the ground. Well, if she didn't manage to stop Marcus it wouldn't matter anyway. As if to reiterate the point the sound of his footsteps carried up to her from the tunnel. Close, almost like he was right outside the metal door.

She managed to steady the chair and scoop up another branch, this one a little thicker. Before she had the chance to test its strength between her hands the sound of creaking metal screeched out to her. She reached again and pushed the branch through the metal loops. There were footsteps from behind the wooden door. After a moment the door shook.

Annabelle stared with wide eyes as the branch flexed against the movement, but held.

'Annabelle? Are you there? Let me out.'

Hardly daring to breathe, she slowly turned the chair away, then began to roll it down the slightly overgrown tarmac road.

Call the fucking police! Annabelle reached for her phone. For a moment she was certain that she had lost it somewhere in the chaos of the previous minutes. Thankfully it had slipped under her leg. With shaking fingers she held down the power buttons. Praying that the little sliver of battery life was still there. The screen jerked to life and she typed in the passcode, getting it wrong three times with her tired fingers before it was finally accepted. The battery was on four per cent.

She waited, heart almost bursting from her chest, as the phone searched for a signal. The sound came from behind her. Wood creaking under stress. The door was flimsy; he'd be through it in seconds. She stared at the screen, willing it to pick up some reception. The road sloped downhill towards the valley floor; if she went further down the chances of being able to call might diminish.

The little icon on the top left of the screen showed 'O2-UK' and one bar of reception. Annabelle punched in 999 and hit Dial. Praying silently.

Behind her the door creaked alarmingly like it might split open this time.

'Which emergency service do you require?' The sound of another voice, formal and authoritative after the days of chaos, was too much for Annabelle. She hesitated. The woman repeated, 'Which emergency service do you require?' Before she could reply the phone beeped three times and the call dropped out.

Annabelle almost screamed. The screen still showed one bar of reception. The door screeched again. She turned and saw that a metal rod had appeared through the gap between the door and the shed. Marcus was working to enlarge it, so he could fit his hand through and remove the stick.

Move! Now! You have to hide! She did what she was told and started to push the chair down the hill. The road was overgrown in places, and tufts of grass had broken through the tarmac as if it hadn't been used in a long while. The wheelchair rattled along, picking up speed on a steeper section before the road levelled out and split in two. She chose the left-hand branch, still with thick forest on either side of it, her arms aching, hands stinging every time she touched the wheels.

She forced herself to push on until she was out of sight of the fork in the road. There was a fifty-fifty chance now that Marcus would go the wrong way. She reached for the phone again, her heart pumping like it could burst. Still one bar of reception. She dialled 999. The phone beeped in her ear and cut off.

She suppressed a sob of pure frustration. Switched to the text message function. Mum never checked her phone and Miss Albright only had a landline. She searched for 'Dad', but somehow couldn't find him. *You deleted his contact details at his wedding. Don't you remember?* She squeezed her eyes tight shut. Behind her it had gone ominously quiet. Marcus was out and he would be looking for her. Why, why, why had she been so stupid as to delete him? *Because you were angry. In a weird way that's why you came here. After everything with your new stepbrother.* And the answer was right here. He lived up here. He was in the police. Ben Fisher. She pictured his face at the wedding. Dark hair, combed into a precise side parting. He had seemed as bemused as her by the wedding. His mum in a white dress and her dad in a white suit, like an eighteen-year-old footballer.

She typed out a hurried message: 'I'm being held hostage but I've escaped. I'm in the Highlands near Inverness. One of the valleys you can drive through. There's a yellow and red flag outside.'

She read back over the message. It barely made sense. What was the name of this place? *Glen Turrit.* She remembered seeing it on the sign.

A twig snapped and Annabelle looked up. The little girl was standing among a patch of ferns by the side of the road, in the shadows of the trees. A pillar of sunlight was cutting through the canopy close beside her, flecks of dust floating slowly in the golden light. The girl was thin with blonde hair. Despite the chilled mountain air she was wearing only a dirty white T-shirt and cut-off jeans. It was the girl from the road, the one who had stepped out in front of her car.

'Please be quiet,' Annabelle whispered to the little girl as she tried to operate the phone. Footsteps were drawing closer. 'Please be quiet.'

In reply the girl stared expressionlessly back at Annabelle. Then, slowly, she raised her index finger until it was pointing between Annabelle's eyes and began to scream.

Chapter 35

Fisher held the phone up for Monica and the others to see: 'I'm being held hostage but I've escaped. I'm in the Highlands near Inverness. One of the valleys you can drive through. There's a yellow and red flag outside.'

Fisher was right, Monica thought. For a joke it was creepy, particularly given the investigation they were working on. They knew the murdered men had been held hostage and tortured. She glanced around the office again, half expecting to see someone smirking over in Fisher's direction. None of the officers in the room seemed to be paying attention to them though.

'You into some kind of role play, Fisher?' Crawford asked, sliding his hands behind his head and glancing at DC Khan to check her response to his attempt at wit. 'Chase me through the Highland glens?'

'I take it there's no name? No other message?' Monica asked, joining Khan in ignoring Crawford's quips.

'No, it's not a number I recognise. This is my private phone anyway,' Fisher said sniffily. 'No one in here should even know the number.' He glanced suspiciously at Crawford as if he might be responsible for the message.

Crawford arched his back slightly in mock outrage. 'I was sitting right here.' He seemed to have recovered from his chaotic start to the day anyway. Maybe his quadruple espresso had done the trick.

'You don't know anyone . . . Anyone . . .' Monica searched around for the right words. For some reason they wouldn't come. The message just seemed so strange. 'I don't know. Anyone who has your number? Who might be in trouble?'

'Could it be someone who isn't local?' Khan chipped in. 'Otherwise they wouldn't have mentioned being in the Highlands.'

Monica nodded. It was a good point, and both women looked at Fisher. He touched a hand to the yellow bruise on his cheek then shook his head abruptly. 'I told you – it's my personal number. I'd know if it was someone who knew me.' He shook his head again, hit Delete and dropped the phone into his pocket. 'I'll keep looking into Theo Gall's previous convictions, put a list of known associates together,' he said, clearly regretting showing them the message and keen to pretend it had never happened.

Monica glanced back at him. He was probably right though. It was someone's idea of a joke. 'Well, keep me posted. Especially anyone who's got previous for serious violent crime.' She nodded to Crawford and turned to go, keen to finally track down Heather Sinclair. But as she crossed the office Monica found her mind wandering back to Lucy. To the dream the kid had mentioned, the one about the woman trapped somewhere, needing help. She cleared her throat and turned back to Fisher. 'Can you get that message back?'

He looked up at her and adjusted his glasses, suddenly wary. For a moment she couldn't help feeling sorry for him, despite his irritating pedantry. Working serious crimes could be a lonely job.

'Yes, why?' he said slowly. Like she might be about to ridicule him in some way.

'Put in a trace with the phone company.' Monica forced a reassuring smile. 'Find out where it came from.'

*

144

Monica checked her own phone for messages as Crawford pulled the Volvo across the roundabout onto the A96. The road led east from Inverness along the coast towards Nairn, and Elgin, skirting the Cairngorms before finally reaching the city of Aberdeen a hundred miles away. There were no new messages from her mum and she put the phone back into her pocket. Thinking about Lucy's dream had inevitably reminded her of the sleepwalking the previous night. The way the kid had gone so rigid in her arms. Almost like her mind wasn't there at all. It was frightening just how vulnerable Lucy made her. How could she ever go on living if something happened to her daughter? If it turned out that the kid's little idiosyncrasies somehow heralded something dark and terrifying but shockingly everyday like a brain tumour? *You'd go on living somehow*, the harsh voice at the back of her head piped up. *If not, you'd waste away and die.*

She sighed and glanced over to Crawford. It was possible he shouldn't even be driving if he'd been drinking the night before.

'Put some music on, would you?'

Crawford grunted a response and fiddled with his phone. Moments later sounds filled the car. 'Gone With The Wind Is My Love' by Rita & The Tiaras, according to the display. Seemed that Crawford was having a soul music moment. Maybe that's what the tan leather jacket's all about, she thought, glancing at him again. It did look good, she had to admit.

'You ever worry about losing people, Crawford. People close to you?' she heard herself say. 'How you might be fucking people up with the things you do?'

He shrugged, eyes fixed on the road ahead. 'I guess everyone's fucked up, aren't they?' He hit the indicator and slowed the car to take a right turn. 'That's what our job's about, isn't it?' A mist of water sprayed up on the tarmac behind them.

She glanced at him again, and her eyes landed on his wrist-watch, sure she'd never seen it before. It was on a metal bracelet, old and battered. 'You don't normally wear that?'

Crawford shrugged, glanced at the watch then held it up for her to see. 'It was my great-grandad's.' She took his wrist and looked at the manufacturer's name on the watch face. It was in the Cyrillic alphabet.

'Is it Russian?'

'He was a deep-sea diver, found it on a Russian boat. That was why I started diving a couple of years ago. It sounded terrifying and I hate the water, but I sort of wanted to see what it felt like . . .'

Monica nodded and let go of his wrist. She wondered for a moment about the need some men seemed to have to follow in the footsteps of their ancestors. To prove themselves against some imaginary ideal.

The road led away from the coast, inland towards the mountains. Finally the satnav directed Crawford to take another right and they arrived at a grand entrance archway constructed from bright yellow sandstone. A sign read SINCLAIR ENTERPRISES in solid purple lettering, a purple-and-white flag fluttering on either side of it.

'You think this could be it?' he muttered sardonically as they passed under the archway and followed the road through a section of forest before the landscape opened out. On the right there was a cul-de-sac of what looked like show homes, built in a range of styles from grey 1970s bungalows, 1980s red brick, to a modern sandstone detached house. A three-dimensional history of the company's housebuilding, Monica realised. While straight ahead on a small hill a much larger building overlooked the houses.

As Monica got out of the car she could see the beginning of

the Cairngorm plateau in the far distance, a place where the last ice age lingered in tundra-like conditions throughout the year.

'What was Sebastian Sinclair driving?' Monica asked as they crossed the car park. 'Last time he was seen?'

'A blue BMW,' Crawford said. Monica glanced around the car park at the array of expensive vehicles – Range Rovers, BMWs (none of them blue), Mercedes, a Porsche Cayenne. Clearly there was money in housebuilding, as if anyone didn't know. And she wondered for a second about the people who did the menial tasks, the cleaning, the filing. Did they drive BMWs and Mercedes too? Or was there a hidden car park at the back? One for people like her mum, who used to drive a Fiat Cinquecento to her job as a dinner lady at a private school, with the staff cars parked round the back, and space for the parents' expensive, always clean vehicles at the front. It made sense and maybe told her a little something about the culture of the company. Money up front, little secrets round the back.

The receptionist at the front desk gave them a warm smile though. As if the most exciting thing that had happened to her in this lifetime was the appearance of the strange duo at her desk. Monica saw them through this woman's eyes: the small good-looking man in his brown leather jacket and the tall thin woman who most closely resembled a ghoul in the threadbare tweed coat that hung around her like a cloak.

'Are you here to see the new Caledonian?' the woman asked, referring, Monica supposed, to the newest of the show homes they had passed. 'The reception's just down by the entrance, the house with the flag outside. I'll buzz them to say you're here.'

'Actually we're here to see Heather Sinclair.'

The woman's face changed, surprise sliding in to replace her fixed smile.

147

'Oh, let me see. Do you have an appointment?'

Monica dug in her pocket for her warrant card and laid it on the counter. 'She'll want to see us. We're here about her brother.'

The woman nodded and punched something into the phone, turned away to speak into the receiver. Monica glanced around the spacious reception area as the woman carried on her whispered conversation. The room was dominated by a series of large photographs. Pictures that appeared to be from the 1960s and 70s of housing estates, several huge dams. Monica recognised one of the Kessock Bridge. The message was clear: the Sinclair family built the modern Highlands.

'You can go up now,' the woman said, clearly surprised by this turn of events. 'Third floor. Lift's over there.'

Monica nodded, then asked her, 'What kind of car do you drive?'

'What kind of car?' She shrugged at the strange question. 'A little Vauxhall Agila. Why?'

Chapter 36

Heather Sinclair stood waiting for them when they emerged from the glass lift onto the third floor. She was small but upright with the posture of a dancer or yoga practitioner. Dressed down in loose jeans, a white shirt like Monica's own, with a thin green cardigan that looked thrown on, tatty even, but somehow seriously expensive. Her light brown hair was pulled back in a loose bun. She would have looked young for her age (forty-six, Monica knew from the company's website), but she was clearly tired, wore no make-up and her eyes were red-rimmed with grief.

Monica introduced herself and Crawford, held her warrant card out. Sinclair glanced vacantly at it and Monica could tell immediately why she hadn't met them that morning. She was visibly shocked by the news of her brother's death; probably the appointment hadn't even registered with her. It was interesting though: in her grief she'd taken herself here, to her office, rather than stay at home.

'We thought you'd rather speak to us here than at the station. We just have a few questions,' Monica said, half expecting Sinclair to brush her off, tell her to arrange a time with her solicitor.

She nodded though. 'Now's fine.' The accent was mid-Atlantic, as if she'd spent a long time living abroad. She turned to walk across the room. The flooring was reclaimed wood, a large open-plan space with huge windows towards the Cairngorms. It was an impressive view, an impressive room. Sinclair sat on a battered chesterfield sofa that faced the mountains. Monica noticed that she never glanced back to check they were following her. A hint of arrogance, an assumption that others would always follow? Monica felt a flicker of attraction towards the woman; she had always been drawn to strength. When combined with moments of unashamed vulnerability it could be a heady mix. She and Crawford sat on chairs opposite. A large wood burner heated the room; the stove's door was open, and the fire purred gently in the still space.

'I hate whisky. It's weird. When I heard this morning . . .' She nodded at the table in front of her, a bottle of fourteen-year-old Tomatin, a glass beside it. 'Is that a good one? When I lived in Japan, malt whisky was practically all they'd talk about when they heard you were Scottish. I never tasted it until my dad died. It was in his will I had to try some.' She shook her head at the memory. There was about a quarter out of the bottle, but Heather Sinclair seemed completely sober. Hard to drown grief in whisky, Monica thought. Though plenty had tried.

Crawford cleared his throat. 'They do a sherry cask one as well. It's good . . .' Sinclair glanced over at the sound of his voice. Her eyes running over his face, down his chest to his hands. What looked, to Monica, like a relatively blunt sexual appraisal. One of the instinctive responses to bereavement, like it might just be possible to fuck death into non-existence.

Monica cleared her own throat. 'Your brother . . . He came to a meeting with you here on Friday the nineteenth of April. What did you talk about?'

Sinclair let out a deep sigh. 'Money,' she finally said after a long silence.

'The business?'

Sinclair's hand went to the glass, hesitated. 'What happened to my brother? How did he end up in that glen, like that?' The horror of the situation edged into her voice despite the whisky. And Monica hoped that she wouldn't insist on seeing what was left of her big brother, that she would trust in the DNA and the dental records. Much better to remember him as he had been than as the bloated horror in Raigmore mortuary.

'We're still in the early stages of the investigation,' Monica replied slowly. Hoping that her own horror as she accessed the memory of the *thing* on the metal tray stayed hidden from her face. Just a few days had passed since then, although it seemed as if the two dismembered men had been part of her life for weeks now. 'We're following up several lines of inquiry, but at the moment it seems you were the last person Sebastian spoke with before he went missing. Other than the attendant who sold him petrol after he left here.' Crawford had followed up on the final payment from Sebastian Sinclair's credit card to a petrol station on the west side of Inverness. The attendant actually remembered serving Sebastian because of his distinctive BMW and the platinum American Express card he used to pay. Heather Sinclair took a sip of the whisky and grimaced. 'Did you receive any ransom demands? Any communications about Sebastian in the three weeks between him going missing and his body being recovered?' Monica asked. A kidnapping would explain why Heather Sinclair had apparently kept the news of his disappearance out of the press.

'There was nothing like that. Sebastian's done this before,' she replied, as if reading Monica's thoughts. 'Taken off without telling anyone. This time he came to me asking about money. The conversation didn't go well. I thought he was annoyed. I thought . . .' Her voice died away.

'What exactly was he asking about?'

Heather glanced around the room. Her eyes fell on a large framed photograph on the wall, a portrait of a man in his seventies or thereabouts. He had thick white hair, a narrow, lined face with high cheekbones, intense, staring eyes. 'That's my dad, Innes Sinclair,' she said when she noticed Monica looking at the image too. 'Built all this from nothing. Half of the Highlands too. The Big Boy, that's what his friends used to call him. He pretended not to like it . . .'

Monica felt a second of discomfort as she remembered her own father, his buffoonery and his fawning friends. *Our Long John Kennedy . . .*

'Sebastian wanted to be like him?'

Heather's eyes met Monica's, and for a moment understanding seemed to pass between them.

'Dad was always hard on Sebastian. Could never understand why my brother wasn't better, more driven, more assertive. He was softer with me. Because I was younger, because I don't have a dick. Like anything I could do competently was a minor miracle because I'm female. He was old-fashioned like that at first.' Monica nodded, despite the uncomfortable associations; she was pleased to finally be getting a more fleshed out picture of Sebastian Sinclair. 'I went off to Tokyo, then Los Angeles after university. Sebastian stayed here, groomed to take over the business, but . . . My dad asked me to come back in 2008, after the crash. When he died he left me in charge of the important parts of the company. Sebastian got the . . . well, the "leftovers", he called it – the "shit".'

'What did that refer to exactly?'

'My dad was involved in all kinds of businesses over the years. Not just building and civil engineering. He'd get up at five in the morning and start working, go to bed at midnight. He owned pubs, restaurants, garages, you name it.' Monica nodded again, pleased that what Heather was telling them chimed with what Crawford had mentioned earlier. 'Sebastian got what was left of that. My dad was an old-fashioned Highland businessman. It tells you something about how he saw Sebastian that he'd leave that lot to him, the main parts to his younger sibling, a female too . . .'

'I take it Sebastian wasn't happy about this?' This information seemed to have been kept private. The public image was of the two siblings, running the company as partners.

'No, he wasn't. He idolised my dad. Wanted to be just like him, but it's like he couldn't understand what that takes. My dad worked fourteen hours a day, 365 days a year. Not many people have got that in them. Sebastian liked to spend money, to play the role of the successful businessman, always wanted more money, to feel important, but . . .'

Monica added the new pieces of information into her picture of Sebastian Sinclair, a disappointment to the father he idolised, resentful of his younger sister. Outside the window the clouds above the Cairngorm plateau were moving quickly, hinting at a coming storm. Heather seemed forthcoming, but Monica could tell that she was also highly intelligent. What might she be holding back? What might those small business entanglements have involved?

'Do you have any idea who might have wanted your brother dead?'

Before Heather could answer, the lift doors opened and two men came out, both dressed in dark suits. She glanced over, held up a hand to show that she wouldn't be long.

'I've got to go. I have to speak to the team now.'

'You probably heard there was another body found yesterday. In the same glen as Sebastian. A man named Theo Gall. Not long before he died, Gall told his family that he'd started working for the Sinclairs.'

A series of micro expressions passed across Heather's face so fast that Monica couldn't read them. Finally she sighed, reached for the whisky again. 'Sebastian did this kind of thing. Someone meets him, thinks they're talking to a gold mine. Sebastian gets caught up in some business idea . . .' Heather went to stand up.

'Theo Gall was a career offender, a violent man. This wasn't some business idea.'

Heather stared down, her intelligent eyes scanning Monica's face. Finally she said, 'Sebastian wasn't a bad man . . . There were rumours. Things my dad had heard, that Sebastian got himself mixed up in things over the years. I never asked for details and it was absolutely nothing to do with Sinclair Enterprises.' Her eyes seemed to harden as she said this, and Monica sensed the implicit warning. 'Whatever he was doing he kept it away from me and the business.'

Chapter 37

Marcus must have heard the girl's shouts because he came running uphill through the forest and onto the road. His face was drawn tight, his lips thin. Annabelle glanced back at the phone and hit Send.

'Well, that was stupid, wasn't it?' he said.

Annabelle stared up at him. He'd taken his jacket off at some point and the grey T-shirt underneath was stained dark with sweat. The phone was still in her shaking hand. The screen had gone black now, the battery finally dead. He snatched it from her hand and pushed it into the back pocket of his jeans.

'You have to let me go, Marcus.' The tears stung her eyes and she felt them running down her cheeks. 'I want to go home.' The little girl was silent now and was standing watching them from among the trees, skinny arms hanging down by her sides, a neutral expression on her face.

Desperately Annabelle turned to her. 'My name's Annabelle,' she heard herself say. 'Please get someone to help me. I just want to go home.'

The kid's expression didn't change, but after a second she leaned forward. 'My name's Annabelle,' she said, mimicking a southern English accent. 'Please get someone to help me.'

'Just go home, Lily. This is nothing to do with you,' Marcus shouted. Then he reached for the handles of the wheelchair.

'Just forget you saw any of this.' He spoke to the child as if she were an adult rather than almost twenty years his junior.

The kid stared back. 'Get lost, weirdo. You shouldn't even be out here during the day.' She turned and ran away through the trees.

Marcus stared after her for a moment, then wheeled Annabelle back up the slope, through the doors and down the tunnel to her room. She knew that she should be frantic, kicking and screaming all the way. But it was like something had snapped. She sat frozen in the wheelchair, imagined one of the Seven Dwarves, dressed in his gown and little hat. Somehow he'd got inside her brain. He was going around the tunnels in there, unplugging the connections that led to her emotions. The throbbing from her leg was worse than ever after she'd rattled it around.

When they were back in the horrible room Marcus scooped her from the chair and laid her back on the bed. 'The Doctor's going to want to see you. After all your silliness.'

'Oh Marcus.' Annabelle found her voice finally, on the verge of hysterical laughter. 'There's no doctor. There's no fucking doctor.'

Marcus stared down at her with an expression between fear and bemusement on his face. A moment later Annabelle began to understand why, because she heard the metal door to the tunnel clank open. Then heavy footsteps on the tarmac.

'Marcus? Who is that?' In reply Marcus dropped his eyes to the floor. He shuffled back until he was standing in the corner of the room. Then he wrapped his arms around himself. The slow, heavy footsteps came closer and closer. 'Who is it, Marcus?' The sounds stopped outside.

Annabelle stared at the metal door. It swung slowly open. A man stepped into the room.

Marcus was hugging himself. Eyes fixed on the floor. The man was tall, a lot taller than Marcus. Wiry with thinning blond hair, the bottom half of his face covered with a surgical mask. He was wearing a white lab coat over dirty blue coveralls, and his long thin fingers were stained dark with engine oil.

Marcus's voice came in a whisper: 'This is the Doctor.'

But he didn't look like any doctor Annabelle had ever seen.

Chapter 38

It was almost 3 p.m. when Heather Sinclair ended their meeting with that hinted warning. Monica would have liked to question the head of Sinclair Enterprises for longer – her instincts told her there was more. Something beyond the woman's natural impulse to protect the company and her brother's reputation.

Monica now climbed out of the Volvo and went to wait for Lucy by the nursery wall. She was one of the last mothers to arrive today, but at least she was on time. She watched as her daughter trotted across the playground, today she was almost oblivious to the glances from the other mothers as they took in the tall detective. Their faces betraying the usual mix of reactions, running from intrigued to outright suspicious. Monica felt a familiar pang of guilt. *How much better off Lucy would be with a normal mum.* One who did ordinary things like volunteer on nursery trips or meet the other mums for coffee, though today she didn't have time to ponder the idea for long. Instead she focused on reading her daughter's body language, as she would a potential suspect's, watching for any hint of strangeness. Because after Lucy's sleepwalking the night before, Monica couldn't help wondering. Long-suppressed thoughts about Lucy's father, described as 'Unknown' on her birth certificate, were re-emerging. Things she'd hoped would never be important. Things she wanted to pretend had never happened. Monica sighed. Lucy looked *normal,* if you could ever say that about anyone.

Holding hands with Munyasa, her best friend at the nursery, before hugging him at the gate and skipping over to Monica. She was holding a book, inevitably the one about cats, Monica noticed, as she stooped to hug her.

'Khan called,' Crawford said as Monica leaned in to strap Lucy into the child seat. 'She says Theo Gall had lots of connections with local businesses. He'd do a bit of casual work here and there, fall out with people or do something dodgy and have to move on.'

Monica pushed the back door closed then came round to get into the passenger seat. Crawford tilted his neck to each side then reached his arms behind him to grab the headrest and stretch his back out. The effects of his long night catching up with him. He let out a groan as his back cracked, and Monica watched as his shirt rode up, revealing his stomach muscles, the line of red hair that ran from his navel to his boxer shorts. Her eyes lingered for a second before she caught herself. *Jesus, this is Crawford*, she scolded herself. He's half your age and half your height.

She climbed into the car and pulled her seat belt on. 'What did you say to her?'

'You smell nice, Crawford,' Lucy chipped in from the back seat.

'Thank you, sweetheart.' He waved in the rear-view mirror, then turned to Monica. 'Just to start looking for any businesses linked to the Sinclairs. Ones left to Sebastian Sinclair by his father. Is that OK?'

Monica nodded. Heather Sinclair had agreed to have a list of those businesses sent over. What she had told them about her brother seemed to bring the organised-crime angle firmly back into the picture as a motive for the murders. Sebastian

Sinclair, desperate for affirmation. Desperate to be respected like his father. 'Someone has to know something. What Sinclair and Gall were up to. How they met in the first place. Who they were involved with.'

'Do you have any cats, Crawford?' Lucy piped up again from the back of the car.

'No, not a cat. I used to have a dog when I was your age,' he said, glancing in the wing mirror then pulling the car into the road.

'Did it ever run away because it thought you didn't love it?' Lucy asked, and Monica wondered what she'd been reading this time.

Crawford stifled a laugh. 'No, he never ran away. He slept on my bed. We were best friends. He was an old English sheepdog called Peter. Practically used to squash me he was so big.'

'I'd like to have a cat that would sleep on my bed,' Lucy said. 'I'd let him cuddle up under the covers if he wanted to. Granny used to have a cat before Mummy was born, but Grandad said it had to go and live somewhere else because it made a mess.'

Despite herself Monica couldn't help feeling a pang of guilt when she dropped Crawford off at headquarters. Leaving him to work late with Fisher and Khan while she took Lucy home. She was the boss. She should be in there too, working through those leads with them, until late, late into the night. She should drop Lucy at her mum's, go back, that was the thing to do. But then she glanced behind her to where Lucy was quietly flicking through her cat book. How could she ever feel guilty about spending time with her daughter?

'What would you like for dinner tonight? Would you like to stop at Pizza Hut? We could go to the cinema again if you want?'

'Can we go to the Co-op restaurant?' Lucy had an inexplicable fascination with the cafe at the Co-op supermarket on Telford Street.

After an early dinner (chicken nuggets, chips and beans for Lucy, a cheese sandwich for Monica) they went for a walk to look at the boats in the harbour at Muirton Locks at the head of the Caledonian Canal. Via Loch Ness, Loch Oich and Loch Lochy, the canal connected the east and west coast of the Scottish Highlands.

'Can any grown-up live on a boat if they want to? Or are you only allowed if you're a sailor?' Lucy asked as they wandered by the side of the canal. The blustery spring day was easing down into night as far out over the dark mountains in the west the sky burned red like fire.

Much later, after Monica had put Lucy to bed, she opened up her laptop. There was still no news from Crawford and the rest of the team, and for some reason she felt drawn to Euston Miller's odd website again. Bizarrely it seemed to have become her go-to after-hours entertainment during this case, as if the investigation wasn't dark enough on its own.

She glanced up to check Lucy's bedroom door was shut tight. Tonight Monica was sitting at the opposite end of the sofa, facing the door in case her daughter sleepwalked again. She closed the story about the crofter and clicked on a picture of a car from the 1970s. In the background there was a stretch of moorland with mountains fading off into the distance.

The story was headed 'The Strange Case of Colin Muir'.

Monica began to read.

Perhaps the strangest story to come out of these glens is that of local businessman Colin Muir. In the winter of 1979–80 he was reported missing when he failed to arrive at a business meeting in Glasgow. On the weekend following his disappearance forestry workers close to the remote village of Little Arklow discovered an abandoned vehicle in a lay-by. They alerted staff at a local garage which was part of a group owned by local businessman Innes Sinclair.

Monica's mouth was hanging open. Innes Sinclair, father of Sebastian and Heather, cropping up in a missing person's case from the 1970s. Quickly she opened another tab on the screen and typed: 'Sinclair garage, Little Arklow'. The search returned an image of a battered-looking warehouse with a row of rusting vehicles outside it.

'It's still there,' Monica said to herself. For a moment she felt that old impulse to get immediately in her car and have a look there and then. To let the case take over her life and drag her down any possible rabbit hole. The perfect escape from mundane reality and her nightmares. Instead she dug in her pocket for her phone and typed out a text to Fisher: 'Could you find out if the garage in Little Arklow is still owned by the Sinclairs?' She hit Send.

She looked back at the screen.

Staff at the garage called the police, who identified the vehicle as belonging to Colin Muir. No one could understand why it had turned up in this remote glen, fifty miles off the businessman's Inverness-to-Glasgow route. Despite the harsh winter conditions a search began immediately.

No trace of the missing businessman was found in the weeks that followed. It wasn't until months later that the partial remains of his body were finally discovered by chance in an area of dense bracken about a mile from where his car was abandoned. It is believed that he perished from the cold after becoming disoriented in a white-out. Although it was never explained why he was in the glen at all. Or why he had strayed so far from his intended route of travel.

Chapter 39

January 1980

The windscreen wipers clawed frantically at the snow hitting the window. Colin Muir tilted his wrist to check the time on his watch. Almost 3 p.m. 'Almost fucking dark,' Muir muttered under his breath. The road ahead was more white than black, the snow lying thick on the tarmac. And to think it had been clear in Inverness two hours before when he'd left the office at the bottom of Church Street and headed south. He'd driven as far as Drumnadrochit, a village by the side of Loch Ness on the A82, stopped in at the hotel. Drank a cup of Nescafé and attempted to pay with a fifty-pound note. Complained about having to drive down to Glasgow for an evening appointment with his useless brother-in-law in the middle of winter. The stupid wee waitress would remember him if anyone came asking. Even though she'd barely bothered to take her face out of the magazine on the bar to serve him.

When he left the hotel, instead of turning south towards Glasgow Muir had directed the Mercedes 450 SL onto the A831, west towards Cannich. Towards Little Arklow.

Muir tapped out another Embassy Regal from the white packet with the blue stripe down the centre. Without taking his eyes from the road in front he lit it from the car's lighter. He rarely drove the SL, and the steering felt twitchy on the snow-covered road. It was the missus' car; he'd only brought it today as a little precaution. People knew him, might recognise his BMW. Reducing the chances of anyone spotting him was sensible. Probably unnecessary though, because once Slate saw the gun he'd understand. He'd know that Colin Muir wasn't someone you fucked about with. If he told you to leave a property he owned, then you moved out. No ifs or buts about what happened in the past, about who told you what twenty-five fucking years ago.

He rested his hand on the pocket of his sheepskin jacket. Felt the reassuring weight of his dad's old Enfield service revolver. Still, a hint of disquiet rose from Muir's stomach as he remembered the last time he'd met old man Slate at the pub in Little Arklow six months before. The way his eyes seemed slightly unfocused, the rumours that half his head was held together by a tin plate and screws. Hidden under that dirty tweed cap he always wore. The kid who he brought to the meeting with him, the one he claimed was training to be a doctor, blond hair and a stack of books, sat reading in the corner of the pub. Like he was on some school trip. The way Slate had smiled and nodded when Muir had told him he needed to leave his house, that he had to go soon because Muir was selling the dam. Smiled and nodded in agreement, but half a year later he'd shown no sign of abandoning that ugly house he'd built.

There was something not right with Slate, about the boy he'd brought with him. Something unsettling about the pair. Muir had even got as far as considering trying to pass the problem on to someone else. He'd heard drunken whispers at cocktail parties with the rest of the in-crowd up in the big newbuild houses at Cradlehall Park. Stories about men who would *do things* for money. Roderick Cameron, who lived somewhere out in the west, him and his boy Don. There were rumours about things they'd done for people over the years. People they'd *taken care of.*

Muir took a deep draw of the Regal and peered into the snowstorm. Probably all bullshit. The last thing he needed was to set up some half-baked scheme with a couple of west coast hillbillies. No. It was simpler this way. Over the phone he'd mentioned a sweetener to Slate. Something just between them to help with the expenses of relocating. He'd even hinted at a parcel of land he could offer in return for Slate leaving the dam quietly, without *dragging it through the courts.* The carrot and the stick. Slate had seemed receptive to the idea. Who wanted to live beside a dam at the bottom of some glen anyway, for Christ's sake? Slate was probably just holding out to see what he could get. Like all these sponging bastards you heard about now – take, take, take.

Muir wasn't weak like them. He wasn't one who waited for the state to solve his problems. Impulsively his hand went to the pistol again. If he had a problem he dealt with it himself. No chance was Innes Sinclair, the Big Boy, going to buy *his* dam, on the cheap just because a sponger and his family refused to leave it. When Slate saw the pistol he'd understand, he'd realise who he was dealing with. Moving out of the house would seem like a good deal compared to a bullet in the face.

Distracted by his thoughts and the dancing snow Muir almost missed the turn-off. He swore as the signpost for Little Arklow appeared in the car's headlamps, stood on the brakes then reversed until he could pull the car to the right. For a moment he hesitated. The trees on either side of the road seemed particularly sinister and watchful, the dense silver birch stripped of their leaves but coated in white. *What if Slate doesn't agree? What if you have to shoot him?*

Muir tried to push the thought to the back of his mind. There was no chance it would come to that. *And if it does?* Well, Muir had taken precautions, hadn't he? No one would even know he was down this glen. And his brother-in-law in Glasgow would back him up, would swear blind they'd been together from 4 p.m., once Muir explained the situation. His brother-in-law was another sponger, though sometimes that could have its uses. Once he knew it was lie or no more hand-outs, he'd understand.

Beyond the windscreen it was almost pitch-dark outside now, the thick trees blocking out what little light was still breaking through the dense snow. The road was unmarked by the tracks of any other vehicle. Muir leaned forward, close to the steering wheel. It was difficult to tell where the road ended and the pristine white forest floor began now. He eased his foot off the throttle, eyes scanning the way ahead, looking for the entrance to the lay-by where he'd agreed to meet Slate. To show him the supposed parcel of land. Muir knew he was in the right area, just a couple of miles before Little Arklow. But everything looked different in the winter, under the snow.

The figure appeared as a shadow at first, stepping from among the trees and into the middle of the road. If Muir hadn't been driving so slowly he would have had to brake hard to avoid hitting it. He eased off the throttle, let the car slow in the thick snow. He swore and, momentarily forgetting the need for discretion, leaned on the car's horn. The shadowy figure, now too close to be picked up clearly in the headlamps, showed no sign of moving though.

'Get out the fucking way!' Muir's voice echoed back to him in the car's interior. Dull and impotent. His hand dropped to the revolver again as he stared out the window. For a moment he thought it might actually be Slate, but quickly realised that the person was smaller. 'Get out the fucking way,' he repeated, but more quietly this time. Was it Slate's kid? Out here in the dark?

Muir wound the window down and felt the ice in the air for the first time. A snowflake landed on his forehead, melted and ran down his face. He glanced in the rear-view mirror. The tail lights cast the tyre tracks in a hellish red, and as he remembered the meeting with Slate at the pub he felt a mad impulse to reverse away from the figure. Instead he reached for the handbrake, pulled the revolver from his coat pocket and climbed out of the car. The snow was ankle-deep, spilling over the top of his shoes.

'Get out—'

The flicker of movement from the side of the road stopped the words in his throat. He felt the impact on the side of his head before he even had a chance to turn. There was no pain, only blackness.

And much, much later he heard the words, as if from a nightmare: 'This is my boy. He's training to be a doctor. You won't mind if he practises on you?'

Chapter 40

The Doctor glanced from Annabelle to Marcus. The bottom of his face was hidden behind the surgical mask; above, the skin of his cheeks was pitted with acne scars, and his eyes had an intent but glazed look. Annabelle felt her eyes and mouth open wide in pure terror because she could read those eyes. They told her that this man lived in his own distinct reality.

Annabelle forced her lips into a rictus parody of a smile. Desperate to establish some kind of connection. His eyes stayed cold and dead though, face expressionless. He was wiry, somehow like a spider, and exuded a feeling of repressed energy. A cocked gun. The energy of a man who never had to sleep, never had to rest. He seemed to fill the room with his wide stance and his heavy boots. He took a step closer. There was a bag in his hand, which made a clanking sound as he set it down by the bed. Then, almost as an afterthought, he danced back and swung a fist at Marcus. It connected hard above the ear, the slapping sound of knuckle on skin muffled in the small room.

Annabelle let out a gasp of shock. Marcus sank to his knees and began to cry quietly. The Doctor stood motionless for long moments, staring at her. Then, without warning, he scurried across the room to her bed. He crouched over her. Close so she could see that his eyes were a dark grey. He smelled of engine oil, and the mustiness of the human animal rose from him. He took a small notebook and pen torch from his pocket then leaned in to look at her broken leg. He ran a cold finger down her shin bone, pushing on the skin in several places as Annabelle cringed in terror. Finally he stood up to his full height and scrawled something in the notebook.

'Please.' Annabelle finally found her voice. 'Please. I can get you money? My dad will pay. Just let me call him, if I call him today it'll be done by tonight.'

But her frantic pleas didn't seem to register. He slipped the notebook back into his breast pocket and produced a marker pen instead. She felt its cold point on her skin. He was drawing something on her leg. Panicking, she sat up, but he reached for her neck and pinned her back onto the bed, forcing the breath out of her lungs.

She wanted to scream. To kick and shout and bite, but she lay still. The Doctor put the pen back in his breast pocket before crouching purposefully down to the bag. When he stood again he moved fast – like a snake. One hand whipped out to clamp onto her forehead as his other hand covered her mouth. She breathed in the chemical stink and everything began to slide away. The Doctor's dead expression. Marcus's whimpers. The whole world tilted and spiralled down onto a different plane of existence. The Doctor, Marcus, her mum and dad and all those waxwork statues from her dream, standing around her. All staring at her with cold dead eyes.

Chapter 41

Lucy ran ahead of Monica down the path among the trees. The kid ducked under a branch and leaned so far over that her blonde curls were touching the ground to inspect the first spring shoots of a fern pushing up through the earth. It was an unexpected day off nursery for Lucy. Unexpected for Monica at least, for she had neglected to mark it on the calendar that hung by the phone in the kitchen.

'I can't take her this morning, Monica,' her mum had explained over the phone, her voice rising defensively. 'I've got plans already. I've told you I'll help more when Lucy starts school in the autumn.'

'Couldn't Lucy come with you? It would just be for a few hours.' Monica had cast a guilty glance at her daughter, sitting in her favourite spot on the couch with her obligatory bowl of Cheerios.

'I'm visiting Auntie May,' her mum had replied finally. Enough said. Auntie May didn't like Lucy and always found fault with the child's supposed eccentricities and lack of *proper manners*.

So Monica had brought Lucy with her to the Little Glen. It was the section of woodland a few miles before Little Arklow where Colin Muir's car had been discovered almost forty years before. Since then the lay-by where the vehicle was left had been expanded into a small car park, with a short forestry walk laid out nearby.

She could take Lucy for a walk while still doing something potentially useful for the investigation; the fact that the path was used by walkers allayed any fears about danger to Lucy.

Monica glanced at the trees on either side of the slightly overgrown trail. Tried to imagine what might have drawn Colin Muir to this place and wondered how he might have died. Her eyes flicked ahead again to where Lucy, dressed in a blue puffer jacket and red wellies, was now poking at the fern with her chubby fingers.

'What have you got there?' Monica said, crouching until the hem of her coat touched the dank soil. Lucy stared intently at the plant, glasses balanced on her nose as she felt its shoots between her fingers. The smell of the earth and wild garlic mixed with the sound of the nearby river splashing over rocks. This glen was narrow and almost claustrophobic with dense woodland and steep slopes on either side. They had been walking for about ten minutes. Up ahead the path petered out at the head of the short valley. Monica knew from a Google search that it was here that Colin Muir's body had been discovered. An uneasy feeling ran up her back as she glanced around at the trees again. Suddenly coming here felt like a mistake.

'It feels really soft,' Lucy whispered.

Monica cleared her throat, tried to dismiss the feeling. There had been no other vehicles in the car park that morning, but the path was relatively well worn. The place seemed a popular spot for visitors. Another case of paranoia, she decided.

'Do you remember what happened the other night, honey? When you came through to the living room?'

'I don't remember,' Lucy whispered, still moving the fern between her fingers.

'Are you sure?' Monica tried to keep a lightness in her voice.

She had no idea why she'd asked the question here of all places, at the bottom of a spooky glen where a body had once been discovered. Maybe the same reason she'd felt an odd peacefulness staring at a dead man's face.

'I think I was speaking to someone in my dream. The one I told you about. He has black teeth and blue skin. He says he's called Long John. He says he used to be my grandad.'

Monica felt her breath catch in her throat.

'Where did you hear that name?' she said finally, resisting the sudden urge to reach for her daughter's head and tilt it up so she could see into her eyes.

'Sometimes he speaks to me when I'm in bed, that's all. He says he keeps bad people in prison.' Lucy stood up quickly and hurried to the burn by the path, splashing down to kick at the shallow water with her wellies.

Monica glanced around, down at Lucy. She felt her phone begin to vibrate in her coat pocket. At that moment the connection to civilisation felt incredibly welcome.

'DI Kennedy? Is that you?' DC Fisher's voice, the sounds of a busy office behind him telling her that he was back at headquarters. 'It's about the Sinclairs' garage? In Little Arklow? I got your message. I've been digging into it this morning.'

'And?'

'So, it was left to Sebastian Sinclair as part of his inheritance from his father. But it changed hands a few months ago.' Monica was listening now. 'Sold to a man named Francis MacGregor.'

'Francis MacGregor?' The name seemed to chime for her.

'He owns a few garages, a bunch of other things across the north of Scotland. Aged fifty-nine. I think you'll want to speak to him.'

'He's got previous?'

'From his youth. A string of convictions in the 1970s. He's not been in trouble since then, though.'

'What did he do?' Monica glanced over to check on Lucy, who was crouched in the shallow water poking at something with a stick.

'A lot. Robberies, serious assaults. He broke a man's legs by driving a motorcycle repeatedly over them. That was his last conviction. But we're talking about forty years ago.'

Chapter 42

The first thing Annabelle became aware of was the pain. From below her knee, up her leg. She shifted her body slightly, and the pain spasmed. It faded quickly though, lost in a strange softening of her senses. She opened her eyes and saw that the room was illuminated by candlelight. Annabelle was sure she was dreaming, then she heard the voice in her ear.

'I tried to warn you. You should have listened to me.' Slowly, through a haze of medication, she realised it was Marcus. He was sitting beside her with the hood of his coat up.

'Marcus,' Annabelle whispered. She tried to reach out a hand to him but it barely moved.

'The Doctor switched off the electricity as a punishment for what we did. He . . .' Marcus coughed. 'He had to perform an emergency surgery. The bone was going bad. From the knee down, it had to go.' Annabelle knew that what Marcus had just said should be perhaps the most horrible thing she had ever heard, but in the glow of the candlelight, with the medication in her body, the feeling of being held in the softest hands of a mothering nature, they couldn't have been less threatening if they had been the words of a lullaby.

The second time she was woken by the screaming. It echoed up the concrete tunnel from somewhere deep, deep down. Annabelle tried to sit up, and the pain immediately seared up her leg, deep and agonising. The previous gentleness was gone, and in its wake was a cold, empty horror.

The screaming redoubled, and for a moment Annabelle wondered if she was really hearing it at all. If it wasn't her agony and terror driving her own mind beyond the edges of sanity. She turned her head to the side, gritting her teeth against the pain. Marcus was still sitting by the side of her bed.

'Who is that, Marcus? Is Scott still here?' The idea came fully formed into her head. But this time Marcus was hunched forward with both ears covered by his hands. He didn't reply. He didn't even move until the screaming from the corridor had stopped. And it went on for a long, long time.

Chapter 43

After she'd dropped Lucy off at her mum's house ('I don't know why I bother visiting Auntie May. She's always the same, asking rude questions about Lucy: "Is your wee granddaughter still not quite right? Still away with the fairies in her wee heedie?" '), Monica picked up Crawford from headquarters. They drove back out on the same road that led past Cannich and on to Little Arklow.

'Sorry about yesterday morning.' Crawford sounded hesitant. Monica realised that she hadn't spoken for the first twenty minutes of the drive. Probably he was worried she was pissed off when actually her mind had run back to Lucy and *Long John*, her imaginary friend who *used to be my grandad*. Surely the kid had heard someone use the name, maybe one of Mum's friends when they were out shopping in the Marsh? But Monica couldn't recall anyone outside her dad's circle of close work friends calling him that. *She* had *to have heard someone say it*, Monica told herself. There was no alternative explanation that made any sense. She realised it might be a good idea to talk it over with one of the other mums at the nursery. Maybe they'd had similar experiences of their children sleepwalking?

'Just be careful,' Monica replied finally. It seemed like the kind of thing a boss should say.

'Sure. Won't happen again.' Crawford sounded relieved. Monica glanced over at him. Thin body spread wide in the passenger seat, obligatory can of Red Bull in his white hand. She remembered that he'd told her once he'd grown up without a father, living on the west coast with his young mother and grandparents in a strict Presbyterian family. He leaned in to the mirror and ran a hand through his red hair, back to its regulation sculpted quiff today.

'What were you like when you were a kid?' she heard herself asking. 'Did your mum worry about you? Because you didn't have a dad? I'm asking because of Lucy . . .'

Crawford cleared his throat. 'She was young. Only fourteen when she had me. I don't think she knew to worry about me at first.' He sounded matter-of-fact but Monica could see that he'd shifted on the seat.

'Sorry, Crawford. It's none—'

'She worries more now, when I'm working. When I'm not working. That I'll be like my dad probably.'

And Monica wanted to continue, drill into who Crawford's dad was, what it was about him that his mum didn't like, try to gain some insight into how other mothers dealt with worrying about their children. But she had her own secrets, her own fuck-ups that she wanted to keep buried. There was a limit to how much honesty two people should share.

It took another twenty minutes to reach Cannich and the turn-off that led them towards Glen Turrit and the scruffy village of Little Arklow. As she glanced at the silver birch forest on either side of the road Monica couldn't help bringing to mind the creepy story from the website, the one about the unnamed crofter supposedly almost driven mad somewhere near here. There was nothing about the man on file, and none of the older police officers she'd asked had ever heard of the case. Still, she couldn't shake the disquiet that this area seemed to bring with it. They passed the outlying buildings of Little Arklow, wooden shacks and abandoned caravans being slowly consumed by the scrubby woods. In another twenty years the place would be swallowed completely. And maybe for the best, Monica thought as they drove into the small village, the mountains of Glen Turrit visible beyond, dark red and melancholy in the flat afternoon light.

The pall of rottenness that the settlement seemed steeped in drifted into the car like a fog. For a moment Monica felt that it was inevitable the investigation would lead to this place, to the Affric Men, and as she looked out of the window at the dark houses, the boarded-up windows and the woodsmoke hanging in the air, a big part of her wondered again if Euston Miller had stumbled on some garbled truth about the area. That it was bad, that terrible things would always happen here.

As if to reinforce her impression, the group of men from last time, slouched smoking on plastic chairs, dressed in worn track-suit bottoms and thick plaid shirts, turned to stare.

'What a hellhole,' Crawford muttered.

Monica didn't reply but continued past the shabby Turrit Arms to the end of the street. She took a left. The satnav had given up, but after another five minutes she spotted the battered-looking white garage at the end of a track. Surrounded by the gloomy birch forest that enclosed the settlement on all sides.

The place looked abandoned. Two of the upper windows were boarded up with plywood, and the track up to it had deteriorated into a mess of potholes. An old ripped saltire flag fluttered from a rusty pole. A reminder of more prosperous times? Monica pulled the Volvo to a stop and got out. The car park in front of the garage was empty.

'How much did Fisher say Francis MacGregor paid for this place?' she asked.

'Two hundred grand. That's an absurd amount for this, isn't it?'

Monica didn't respond but went up to the front door of a small office. A shutter was pulled down over the vehicle entrance. The bell didn't seem to work so she rapped on the glass with her knuckles. Through the grimy window she could make out a desk with a pile of letters on it, some dusty old newspapers and mugs.

'Could it be a redevelopment project? Something like that?' Crawford went on.

'Or money laundering,' Monica said, thinking out loud.

Unsurprisingly there was no reply to her knock. She tried the handle but the door was locked.

'I'll have a look round the back.' Crawford stomped off along the overgrown slab path that led past the shuttered garage round the side of the building. Something troubled Monica about the place. It seemed to carry the distilled essence of the oddness of the village, the whole area. She shook her head at the thought. Her unsettled feelings no doubt lingered from Lucy's odd story that morning. She forced herself to take a deep breath and walk a little way round the opposite side of the building. Brushing past the trees that clawed at her coat, the mossy smell of the forest. The familiar tightness of high alert in her stomach, the unshakable feeling of being watched. As if her father's ghost really had followed her from Lucy's dream. At the end of the pathway a small shed stood against the garage wall.

The shed was unlocked but empty. She closed the door again and glanced up at the shed roof. Wondering if she could climb up onto it and squeeze through the boarded-up window above.

Probably a bad idea, given how rotten the roof of the shed appeared, but better than waiting for proper authorisation to enter.

'Monica!' Crawford's shout echoed through the densely packed trees, interrupting her chain of thought. She'd almost forgotten that he was there with her. She followed his voice back to the front of the garage. He was standing with his hands on his hips, brown leather jacket spread wide off his thin frame, face lit up in an inviting triumphant smile. 'You have to see this.'

Chapter 44

Much later Annabelle removed her hands from her ears and opened her eyes. The screaming had been replaced by an eerie stillness. Marcus must have gone and come back because now there was a tray on the little table beside her. The same meal as before. He was sitting quietly in the corner, watching her.

'I couldn't eat,' Annabelle said. As she did so she glanced down at the space where her leg had been. The sheet was flat. There must have been some of the painkiller, sleeping pill or anaesthetic still in her system because her horror at what she was seeing was muted. Shut off behind panes of filthy glass.

'No food, no painkillers,' Marcus said. 'Or we could put the mask on if you want to make a fuss?' His voice was dictatorial again and carried a new coldness. Clearly he hadn't forgiven her betrayal. 'It was a serious operation. You need your strength, you need to eat. And believe me when I tell you, you'll need the painkillers soon.'

Annabelle looked at the swelling on the side of his eye where the Doctor's punch had connected. 'Is your head OK? I'm sorry . . .'

Marcus ignored the question and leaned behind her to stack the pillows so she could sit up more easily.

'Where's my leg?' A question from a pantomime that should have been funny. 'I need to see it.'

'That ugly tattoo's gone now at least,' he said in reply. Holding up a forkful of food but still refusing eye contact.

'Tattoo?' With a deadened sense of shock she slowly remembered. Probably she hadn't looked at it in six months, had almost forgotten about it. There on her ankle. The little car she'd got when she was eighteen and passed her driving test at the third attempt. A symbol that she was independent, that she was free.

'Where is it?' she said again, the absurd horror of the question washing over her as her stomach tightened and she began to dry-heave.

'If you really want to know, Granny Slate took the foot. She's gone to Inverness with the family and she's carrying it in her shopping basket. She likes to imagine what people would say if they knew.' He gave a little laugh at Granny Slate's eccentricity. 'She thinks that if you don't put some part far away from the rest it'll work its way back together and come looking for you in your dreams. That's what Grandad Slate always used to say when he was alive. She might even scatter your toes at Ferry Point, just to be safe.' He cleared his throat. 'Now are you going to eat something so I can give you a painkiller, or do we need to put the mask on?'

As if in a dream, Annabelle somehow managed to chew and swallow the food that Marcus cut up for her. Finally he leaned in to wipe her mouth with a paper napkin, then produced a clutch of brown plastic medicine bottles from his pocket. He tapped out a handful of pills.

'Opioids and some sleeping pills. They'll keep the discomfort at bay.'

Annabelle swallowed the drugs with what was left of the tea and sank back onto the pillows.

'What were those noises? Last night? The screaming? I thought I heard them saying something. Was it Scott?'

Marcus flinched and looked away, put the cutlery on the plate and set the mug down beside them. 'Well,' he said finally, 'let's just say it doesn't concern you for now.'

Chapter 45

Monica followed Crawford along the path round the side of the garage, birch twigs catching in her hair and face.

'What is it?'

Crawford pretended not to hear, keen to drag out his moment of suspense for as long as possible. She shook her head and followed in silence. After thirty seconds the path, which seemed destined to end at the back of garage, turned away from the building, heading to the right. Through ever more dense foliage, her frustration mounted with every step.

'Crawford—' Before Monica could say any more he stopped abruptly in front of her and stepped to the side. The slope that the path had been following suddenly fell away to the left. Overhanging them was a cliff face, dug into the hillside.

'I think it was a quarry,' he said, pointing to a sight that would have been impossible to miss anyway. They were standing level with the quarry floor. The entire space, at least a hundred feet in width, was filled with rows of wrecked vehicles. Sometimes stacked two or three in height. Monica took in the piles of cars. Some looked new, others had been degraded by rust and vegetation to a point where they were almost unrecognisable.

'Looks like it's been used as a dump for the garage for a while,' he said. 'But look.' He pointed again, to one of the stacks, right in front of them. A blue car, the front end smashed almost flat, the result of a serious impact. 'Sebastian Sinclair was last seen driving a blue BMW M4. The plates are gone. We'll need to get someone in to move it so we can check out the registration on the chassis.'

Monica nodded, understanding his excitement now because this felt like more than coincidence. She squeezed through the trees to get closer to the car. There were deep, fresh marks in the turf behind the vehicle as if it had only recently been pushed into its resting place. She found the torch on her phone and held it through the hole where the passenger-side window should have been. Careful not to cut her face on the fragments of glass as she leaned in. In the footwell there was a small object. At first she thought it was a marker pen, then realised it was a stick of mascara. She stepped back and pulled on a plastic glove then leaned back in. Just under the seat was a touring map of northern Scotland.

Mascara and a tourist map, not the first objects you'd expect to find in Sebastian Sinclair's car, Monica thought with a hint of disappointment. Maybe the car belonged to someone else and their neat connection between Sebastian Sinclair and this garage wasn't so neat after all?

'Monica.' She heard Crawford's voice again, coming from a little further across the quarry. He'd got bored waiting for her and wandered off for another look around the densely packed vehicles. 'Boss!' His voice was louder this time and she caught the urgency.

She extricated her top half from the car and glanced around for him, the gloomy day now turning prematurely dark. Finally she saw him. Crawford had climbed up onto a vehicle and was gesturing at something.

She walked quickly over to him, pulled herself up onto the bonnet of an ancient white van so rusted it felt like her foot might well pop through the metal panel, then stepped up onto the roof of the crushed Vauxhall Astra that Crawford was standing on.

She felt the creak of the thin metal as it warped under their shared weight.

'What is . . .' But the answer was obvious. There beneath them, partially hidden by a wrecked Audi, was a second blue BMW. The plates were hidden by the car's position, wedged between vehicles to the front and back. Not that it mattered this time though because as Monica tilted her head to see what Crawford was pointing at she could read the words printed along the side of the vehicle in the familiar purple font: SINCLAIR ENTERPRISES.

Chapter 46

An hour later Monica watched the forensics team working to set up their industrial lights in the cramped area around the second BMW as the evening turned to murky night. The smell of woodsmoke drifted in the damp air from nearby Little Arklow. Monica walked over to where Gemma Gunn, the head of the team, was changing into a white forensic suit.

Gunn said, 'Looks like someone's been busy,' her overly loud voice echoing off the quarry walls as she nodded at the stacks of vehicles. For a moment Monica imagined each one of the cars was linked to a murder or disappearance, but the notion was fanciful. There hadn't been that many murders in the Highlands in the last twenty years in total. It was odd though. In that dank quarry it somehow felt like those rusting vehicles all carried the promise of death. Gunn finished pulling the suit up over her athletic body and stood. Exuding a sense of vigorousness and control.

'What's your gut sense about the place?' Monica asked, to get the sinister feeling about the stacks of cars out of her head as much as anything. Gunn glanced at her, blonde hair tied back in a tight ponytail, an expression of surprise bordering on disgust smeared across her regular features.

'We haven't even looked inside the car yet.' She sounded appalled at Monica's departure from logical thinking. And in a way her response was reassuring. Clearly the rationally minded head of the forensics team hadn't picked up on the quarry's atmosphere in the same way Monica had. Maybe to her way of thinking it was nothing more than a hole in the ground with some old cars in it.

'Well, let me know just as soon as you find anything.'

Gunn nodded in response, probably resisting the urge to reply, *Well, what else would I do?*

'DI Kennedy.'

Monica turned and walked over to where Fisher was standing at the edge of the cordon, feeling the soft ground shift under her feet. As if she might be walking over decades of forgotten things buried deep in the earth.

'There's something in the garage,' the young detective said as Monica drew close. The widening of his eyes behind his glasses, the tone of his voice, rendered the rest of his sentence obsolete. He continued anyway though. 'We think . . . well, we think it's human.'

Fisher pushed the side door into the garage open. The workshop space was illuminated by strip lights attached to the roof's beams. Monica barely noticed them though. She was staring down at the concrete floor of the garage. Crawford, wearing a forensic suit like the one she had just watched Gunn pull on, was covering his mouth and nose with his hand. In front of him was a plastic groundsheet. Eight feet square. It was a light turquoise colour at the edges, its centre dark with blood and gore.

Monica walked over the oily floor of the garage, feeling her own forensic bootees peel off the concrete with each step. The smell was overpowering, a sickening butcher's-shop stink of cut flesh. The deeper stench of purification and decay.

'It looks like it's dried, been here a while,' Crawford said as Monica came to stand beside him. She took in the sprays of blood over the plastic. The tiny scraps of flesh. Her mind went back to the remains of Sebastian Sinclair's body, Dr Dolohov's intent face. *Someone cut him up while he was still alive.*

'It could be where they were dismembered.' Fisher's voice echoed in the open space. Monica nodded. First the car linking Sinclair to this place, now this bloodbath.

'Sinclair drowned,' Monica said, staring at the blood on the sheet. 'Whoever did this kept him alive after he was tortured.' Above the groundsheet a long chain hung from one of the beams. At one time it must have served some purpose in the garage; she could easily imagine what use it had recently been put to and couldn't stop her mind from picturing the scene. A man hanging from the chain, maybe one of the victims watching while the other was tortured. The pleading and the screams then the stink of burning as the wounds were cauterised. For a moment Monica wished she was anywhere but here, doing anything but this. *How the hell did this become your life? You could have just stayed away. You could still be in London. You could have left the force and retrained, gone to university to study classics finally, like you should have done twenty-five years ago . . .*

Monica tried hard to ignore these unhelpful thoughts and glanced over to Crawford, who was looking at something on the concrete floor beside the groundsheet. She stepped closer, careful to keep her feet well away from the gore. In the harsh light from the overhead strips she quickly saw what he was looking at. Beside the groundsheet a mixed selection of tools was laid out in a careful row.

'We need to track down the man who bought the garage, Francis MacGregor. We need to do it now,' Monica said, remembering the man's last conviction was for breaking someone's legs with a motorcycle.

190

'DC Khan's already on it,' Fisher replied, his voice still shaky.

Monica surveyed the scene again. The garage was a mess – piles of greasy vehicle parts, several cars in bits – and what kind of killer would leave a victim's car barely hidden in a scrapyard they owned? Leave such unashamed evidence of the dismembering of a body in the open for anyone to find? Someone disorganised, Monica thought. Either someone in their own world who assumed the police were so stupid they wouldn't find the victim's car even though it had been concealed in the most cursory way, or someone who barely cared.

'Whoever did this is extremely dangerous, impulsive and disorganised.' As she was saying it her eyes fell again on the carefully laid out row of tools beside the plastic sheet.

It was a frightening assortment. A small hacksaw, a pair of pliers, a screwdriver, a blowtorch, some other tools that weren't familiar to her. A random collection, but laid out precisely with a uniform gap of about six inches between each one that contrasted sharply with pretty much everything else about the scene.

Monica stepped past Crawford for a closer look, and crouched forward to inspect the tools.

'What is it?' Crawford crouched alongside her.

'These look like they've been cleaned, like they've been washed,' Monica said under her breath. 'Why would someone clean the tools off and lay them out like this but leave that?' She nodded to the gory groundsheet.

'Maybe he was disturbed before he could clean the rest up?'

Monica turned the idea over in her head. It was a convenient explanation but felt wrong. 'It's like using the tools is the most important part of it for him . . .'

'So maybe something went wrong with the sale of the garage.

MacGregor lures Sinclair and Gall here. Gets his revenge then tries to dispose of the bodies? It's not far to the river from here.'

It made some kind of sense. Although Francis MacGregor was supposed to be a reformed businessman now. The garage looked like it was worth nothing, all the way out here in this dead-end glen, but he'd paid two hundred thousand for it. There had to be a reason.

The first members of the forensics team entered the garage, resigned to the long night ahead of them. Monica's eyes dropped to the groundsheet again, but her mind drifted outside to those stacks of cars. The BMWs. The stick of mascara and the touring map, abandoned in the first one. *Why were the plates missing?* None of the other cars had had their plates removed, as far as she remembered.

'Fisher,' she shouted to the younger detective as he was turning to go, 'can you make sure we get the number from the chassis on the first BMW? Get a name for whoever owns it.'

Chapter 47

It was late when Monica finally made it back to the flat. Her impulse was to ignore the couch and crawl straight into bed, under her warm blankets, but the idea of the filth and gore from the garage still clinging to her skin and hair was enough to send her to the shower. She washed her hair and body three times in an old post-crime-scene ritual. Then stuffed her black trousers and black shirt in the washing machine. When she'd dried herself Monica pulled on a pair of jeans and a fisherman's jumper she'd bought from a charity shop in Fort William on one of those tense day trips with her mum, Lucy and the hyper-critical Auntie May.

She stood and looked around the combined kitchen/living room of the flat. Took in the cosy blonde carpet, the warm lights and the sofa by the window, the photos of Lucy and her mum. One of her dad, tacked on the board by the kitchen island. Lucy's latest painting, unsurprisingly of a cat, stuck to the fridge by a magnet. Her mum was staying over at Monica's flat again to look after Lucy, but had already been in bed when Monica arrived home just before midnight.

Monica sniffed at the pan of soup her mum had left on the stove. Broccoli. Spotted the pre-crumbled Stilton cheese in a little bowl covered in cling film on the counter. She ladled the soup into a bowl, heated it for two minutes in the microwave (hoping all the time that her mum wouldn't hear and come through to remonstrate with her for 'ruining the flavour' by heating it this way) and emptied the bowl of cheese over the top of it.

She ate it sitting on the sofa, appreciating its warmth after the soul-deep cold of the scrapyard and the garage. Glanced around the flat again and wondered which was the better indicator of what life really was? This place of security or the horror at the garage? Monica wondered, not for the first time, why it always felt like she was seeing reality stripped back to its core in those dark places? In murderers' lairs and killers' dump sites? Was it simply that the primal fear of death was closer there? Or did these places reveal something true and deep about the fabric of the universe? Something waiting beneath the surface in every moment of tenderness? *Maybe that says more about you than anything?*

'That's a question for another day, for never,' Monica whispered as she finished her soup and reached for another random record from her dad's collection. Something to take her mind off the grim day. She held the sleeve up to the light. Serge Gainsbourg stared back at her, looking disreputable, bizarrely surrounded by photographs of assorted primates.

'Must be one of Mum's,' Monica murmured as she slid the vinyl from its sleeve and laid it on the turntable. Serge's voice came on singing in French, joined after a minute or so by the breathy sighs of a woman in the early stages of orgasm.

Monica lay back on the sofa and tried hard to feel some vague erotic connection to the sounds. Instead she pictured her dad's smirking hard face. *A French poof and a trollop.* She could almost hear his voice. How did one of Mum's records end up mixed in with his? He was normally so particular. As she considered this little mystery, Monica couldn't help her mind drifting back to Lucy's matter-of-fact description of her dead grandfather. His black teeth and blue skin. The fact she knew his nickname: Long John. Monica glanced at the door to her daughter's bedroom. Almost expecting to see her standing there in a trance again.

Thankfully there was no sign of her, and finally Monica drifted off down into a deep sleep. The flat was silent, save for the crackle of the needle on the vinyl. Skipping on Long John Kennedy's old record player.

Chapter 48

When Marcus finally left Annabelle alone she stared for hours at the ceiling through a haze of opioid confusion. Feeling a relentless dull throbbing from what was left of her leg, something told her she had to look at it, to check it was really gone. She couldn't make herself though, and instead she listened out for the other person she had heard screaming down the corridor.

'Scott?! Is that you?' Her voice echoed back at her in the confined space. There was no reply and for a second the idea flickered through her mind: *Maybe Scott is actually another patient, and you're in a mental hospital? Maybe you've gone insane.* This was a terrifying thought. And how would she ever know? Annabelle squeezed her hands into tight balls and stared at the grimy ceiling. Shadows danced across it from the stuttering candle by the bed. Fearfully she ran back over things: the drive to Stirling, the selfie, the drive to Inverness, opening the gate to the glen, then the crash. It seemed to hang together consistently. To make sense. *Your leg,* the voice in her head said. *If you were really in a mental hospital they wouldn't have cut your leg off.*

But maybe she had imagined her leg being taken too? Maybe that was part of the delusion.

Annabelle pushed herself up on the pillows and pulled the blanket back. Her right leg was gone from the knee down. Where her calf and ankle should have been there was only the grey of the sheet. She felt the hair stand up all over her back.

The stump was dressed in white bandages. She reached down and undid the safety pins holding the bandages in place. After laying them aside on the table she began to unwind the dressings, because she had to see what was left of her leg. She had to see what they'd done to her. It took a minute to remove the bandages, rolling them carefully so she could put them back on later. After the last one came off there was a layer of padding, taped over the wound. Slowly she peeled it back. The end of her leg stopped about an inch above where her knee used to be. It looked as if a flap of her skin had been folded over the wound and stitched in place with ugly black thread. A wave of nausea rose from her stomach, followed by a swaying dizziness as the room seemed to tilt and shift. Prickles of heat stood out across her skin and she retched. She clenched her eyes tight shut, feeling her stomach spasm violently.

But she had to look, to check it was clean. Finally she opened her eyes. By the flickering light of the candle she could see the injury, *the amputation*, was red and swollen, but there didn't seem to be any pus. Gingerly she pressed a finger onto her folded skin, close to the stitches. The skin moved slightly and pain flickered up her leg. But it was more of an ache than the raw agony of the broken leg.

The remains of her leg began to blur as the tears welled up. *He took your leg, cut it off. What will he take next?* The thought made Annabelle want to curl up on the bed, to hide somehow. Because she knew without doubt that if she wasn't crazy then Marcus and the Doctor clearly were.

They were never going to let her leave this place.

Chapter 49

Monica accepted the cup of coffee from Crawford in the Inverness Incident Room. She needed the caffeine that morning. She'd woken at 5 a.m. still on the couch, her neck cricked again. Unable to get back to sleep. The bloody sprays from the garage, the stacks of rusting cars adding fresh colour to her regular nightmares.

'Where are we up to with locating Francis MacGregor?' she asked as Khan and Fisher joined her and Crawford. The team was completely focused on apprehending MacGregor now. With his previous convictions and his connection to Sebastian Sinclair and the garage, he was their first solid suspect, and clearly potentially extremely dangerous.

'Like I said, I'd never heard of him until yesterday,' Crawford replied. 'But it turns out he used to have a big reputation. Hard to pin anything on him though.' He was leaning back in a chair, arms folded tight across his narrow chest, dark circles standing out under his green eyes as if he'd been out talking to people all night to obtain this information. 'He owns properties across the north, but he doesn't keep all of them in his name. He used to be in a biker gang.'

'I take it this gang's now defunct?' Monica asked, remembering MacGregor's last conviction was thirty-five years previously.

'Far as I can gather, they were called the Red Death. Last time I could find them mentioned was in 1985 – some kind of gang fight down in Glasgow.' He held up his phone to show a picture of a painted design on the back of a leather jacket: a pale face, the forehead smeared red with blood. 'They were quite active from the late 60s until then though. Thought they were Scotland's answer to the fucking Manson family for a while.'

'The Manson family?'

Crawford nodded to DC Khan beside him. She cleared her throat, opened a folder on her desk and pulled out a handful of prints. She laid one on the table, which showed a blood-splattered room.

'Members of the gang murdered a middle-aged couple, the MacIntoshes. August 1980. They lived out in the sticks, a place called . . . Strathconon?' Khan said, uncertain of the pronunciation of the unfamiliar name.

Monica nodded. She knew Strathconon. One of the glens that ran through the mountains to the west of Inverness, along with Glen Affric, Glen Mullardoch and Glen Turrit.

'They were a well-to-do family, members of the local church. They were protective of their only child, a daughter called Beverly. Kept her quite sheltered,' Khan said. 'One day she runs into this gang, the Red Death, at a Highland games dance, of all things. Beverly ends up going off with them—'

'On the back of a bike, like in a perfume advert,' Crawford interrupted, unable to resist the opportunity to share the dramatic picture he'd thought up. 'Except without the glamorous ending. Because in a month she's addicted to smack, living back at their castle—'

'Their castle?'

'One of the gang was landed gentry gone off the rails – had a little castle on the west coast. They've got no money though so how are they going to afford to live?'

'They decide to rob the MacIntoshes?'

Khan cleared her throat. 'It's thought that in the early hours of Saturday the ninth of August 1980 members of the gang entered the MacIntosh home. They found Mr and Mrs MacIntosh asleep upstairs and demanded money from them. They believed Mr MacIntosh had a safe on the property. He denied having a safe or any substantial sums in the house. They tortured and killed him, then his wife to keep her quiet. Afterwards they smeared blood over the walls, satanic symbols to make it appear the motivation had been an occult ritual.'

Khan reached for the photos Crawford had pulled from the file and slid them across the table. Monica looked down at the clichéd hallmarks of a supposedly occult crime: the pentagram drawn on a wooden floor, HELTER SKELTER smeared in blood on a white wall.

'The daughter, Beverly, pleaded guilty to it all, served life for it,' Crawford said. 'They could never prove who else was involved, and Beverly wasn't talking. She said she was still in love with one of the leaders of the gang. Never stopped asking him to visit her. One Francis MacGregor.' Crawford turned over a piece of paper and held it up for them to see. It showed a black-and-white photo of a man's face. The archetypal rebel. Shoulder-length hair, a thick moustache, the narrow face and high cheekbones of a Highlander.

'We already knew that MacGregor had a criminal past.' Fisher spoke up for the first time. 'Granted this is serious, but we're still talking about something from almost forty years ago. How's it going to help us find him? Or explain why a man he's just bought a business from has turned up dead?'

Crawford dropped his eyes to the table. 'Like I said, MacGregor's hard to track down. Supposedly got a string of houses as well as the businesses he owns. They're in other names though – relatives of people who were part of the gang, that sort of thing.'

'Do we have an address for any of the ex-members? Anyone who'd be able to set us in the right direction?' Fisher asked, hand going to adjust his glasses.

'I've been asking around, contacted a couple of businesses he's supposed to own,' Crawford said, 'but no one wants to talk about him. No surprise, if what happened at the garage is any indication.'

For a moment none of them spoke, as if their minds had all returned to that blood-splattered workshop.

'Do you have a list of businesses that he owns?' Monica asked finally. Khan nodded and opened up a document on her laptop, then turned it round for her to see. And as she scanned down the list of names Monica realised that the answer was right there in front of her.

Chapter 50

The cold realisation that Marcus and the Doctor were never going to let her out of there alive should have been terrifying, but it gradually seemed to galvanise Annabelle. As if her mind could accept that a certain amount of misfortune was acceptable and correct, a little corner of her mind might even have believed that she deserved to have her leg amputated. But keeping her there for ever, never letting her out . . .

Well, it can't be helped. The voice came into Annabelle's head so clearly that she actually glanced around the room. As if Miss Albright might somehow have really appeared down there with her. And with the memory of her elderly neighbour she couldn't help thinking of Mr Pepper, picture him sitting impatiently by the door, growling with anticipation ahead of his walk. He would be so bored by now, all those days (Annabelle couldn't be certain how many had passed) without a walk.

'Scott?!' Annabelle was startled by the sound of her own voice. But maybe shouting for him again really was a good idea. Maybe Scott could help her somehow? Maybe they could help each other? 'Are you there?! My name's Annabelle.' She paused, the words echoing back at her in the confined space. She listened hard, hoping to hear a response. Something that would show she wasn't entirely alone. There was nothing though. No screams, no muffled shouts, just the loneliness of emptiness at the bottom of the world.

Well, it can't be helped, the voice in her head repeated. And slowly Annabelle understood what Miss Albright was trying to tell her. If she ever wanted to see her and Mr Pepper again. If she ever wanted to breathe fresh air or see the sun again, she was going to have to make it happen herself. This was a terrifying thought. There had been times when she couldn't even imagine leaving her flat or walking down the street alone. How was she supposed to get herself out of here without even her phone to help when her last attempt had cost her leg?

She glanced around the horrible room again, at the squares of carpet on the wall and the metal door. How easily it had begun to feel like a home, like her bedroom when she was a child. Where things were turned on their head. Her parents screaming at each other meant they were in love. Smiling and not speaking meant Annabelle was perfect, while sharing what was in her mind seemed to show her parents just how selfish and rotten she was on the inside. Until all those thoughts wouldn't quite fit in her brain, like they needed to leak out. That day in the park when her dad had slapped her. She remembered the feeling of shame, the embarrassment at how much trouble she had caused, but another memory lingered. She understood for the first time how that moment had planted a seed: the shock and pain of the slap had calmed her mind. Annabelle felt a moment of excitement as another linked memory bubbled up. When she was twelve, years after Mum and Dad had finally split up, sitting in the corner of the dining hall at school on her own, trying hard to be invisible. The tip of the pencil had pierced her thumb. She hadn't even realised she was squeezing it that hard until she felt the blood, saw the black fleck of graphite embedded under her skin. When the pain started it had an unexpected effect – thoughts and feelings seemed to ebb into the background. Just like all those years before, when her father's slap had stilled her mind. Later in her bedroom that night she used one of her dad's old razor blades which she had found in the bathroom cupboard to scrape at her arm until it bled, a first spot of red on her smooth skin.

As she remembered the blood, Annabelle pictured Scott's knife again. *You already know how to cut, you already know how to stab, and if you ever want to get out of here you have to get that knife.*

Chapter 51

After looking for him at The Clach and then at his flat up in Hilton, Monica and Crawford eventually found Big Bill Macdonald in the driveway of his elderly mother's house.

It was late morning, one of those spring days in the Highlands when the huge blue skies streaked by cloud carry the promise of youth. *Or nostalgia for youth*, Monica had thought as she'd climbed out of the Volvo and looked warily up and down the row of brown semi-detached council-built houses. Less than a minute's walk round the corner from her mum's in the Marsh and far too close to home. She leaned over the same metal gate as she had thirty years before as a skinny fourteen-year-old with no clue about the world. Watching as Bill Macdonald worked at a car again. And she wondered for a moment just how the hell she'd let her life bring her right back here?

As the thought drifted up a memory rose with it. Of her father, dressed in a white shirt and his work trousers. Standing at that corner one evening at dusk. She must have forgotten the time, been late home from school. Because when she finally noticed him standing there he was watching as she laughed at something Bill had said. Pointing at the watch on his opposite wrist with his thick index finger. Watching all the time as she turned away, hurried along the road towards him.

She suppressed the uncomfortable memory, cleared her throat.

Bill turned from the car engine he was pondering, his wide face lighting up when he saw her.

'Monica! I tried phoning you at your mum's.' His initial enthusiasm fell away when his eyes landed on Crawford, a few paces along the road from her, staring over the fence himself. Bill straightened and slowly wiped his hands on a rag then dropped the bonnet closed on the Ford Focus. 'Just a fuse that had gone. Mum always assumes it's serious,' he muttered as his eyes went from Crawford to Monica.

'My mum told me you called . . . I'm here about something else though.'

'I need to get cleaned up for work.'

'It won't take long.' Monica watched as Bill ran a hand across the blond stubble on his face. 'You've managed The Clach a few years now?'

'That's right,' he replied slowly. 'Since 2010.'

'Bit of a change. Don't know how they dragged you away from under those car bonnets.' Monica tried to force some lightness into her voice.

Bill coughed and glanced over at the open front door of his mother's house. 'Rough on your body. Years working on engines.'

'Your dad liked motorbikes when he was alive. Didn't he?' This time Bill didn't reply, probably sensing where the conversation was headed. 'We're trying to get hold of someone. A suspect in a serious case we're investigating. A man called Francis MacGregor. I think you might know him.' Monica watched the pupils in Bill's blue eyes widen almost imperceptibly. 'He owns The Clach, doesn't he?'

'You tell me,' Bill said finally with a laugh. 'I just run the thing. Someone different above me every other year.' A schoolboy caught cheating, looking for the joke that will make things OK.

Monica would have felt sorry for him if the memory of the scene at the garage wasn't so fresh in her mind.

'I wouldn't be hassling you if this wasn't extremely serious, Bill.'

'I wish I could help you, but like I say I just work at the bar. I'm sorry.' He shrugged and turned to go inside.

'You called me about your son,' Monica said, raising her voice slightly. 'He's looking at jail? Could be a long stretch too.' She could feel Crawford's eyes on her face.

Bill paused. 'He was stupid. He's not—'

'It'll be tough for a sensitive boy like him. What's he looking at? Five years at least? Barlinnie first, then over to Peterhead.'

'The solicitor said he might have a chance.'

'I can try to help, but just give me an address for MacGregor. Give me something.' Monica hated making promises of this kind, but sometimes a word in a prosecutor's ear could make a difference. And owing Bill a favour would be worth it if it meant MacGregor was locked up.

Bill stared at her. Ready to turn and storm off into the house. Instead he stepped closer to the gate until his face was inches from hers and she could smell his cheap deodorant. 'There are people who would put me in a hole in the ground, just for talking about Francis MacGregor,' he whispered, then glanced up and down the street as if one of those people might be there now, watching them. 'Give me your phone.'

Monica patted herself down and pulled it out of her coat pocket, unlocked it and handed it to him. 'This is the number he calls me on.' Bill punched in a series of digits then handed it back. 'Maybe someone'll push your buttons one day. Find out where you hurt and poke a finger into it.'

'I've been there. Believe me,' she said softly, searching for eye contact. He refused the connection though and shook his head.

'You've not always been spotless yourself, Monica, from what I've heard. Not you or your dad.' He stepped back, and Monica found herself looking away along the street towards her childhood home. For a moment she almost expected to see the ghost of her father watching her, while by her side she sensed Crawford glancing away. Bill's comment must have chimed with whatever rumours he had heard about her. Monica turned back to Bill, but he was already walking into the house.

Chapter 52

To Annabelle's surprise, the next time the door swung open Marcus wasn't holding a tray. Instead he had a pair of metal crutches tucked under one arm and a plastic bag in his other hand. He set the crutches by the door and emptied the contents of the bag onto the floor. It took Annabelle a moment to recognise the alien artefacts. Her own tracksuit, pants, T-shirt and one of her white Nike trainers. The clothes had been packed up safely in the boot of the BMW on the day that she crashed.

'It's time to start on your rehabilitation. The Doctor says you need to work on using your good leg to get around before it stiffens up and you lose mobility,' he said gruffly. 'Put these on.'

He handed the clothes to her, and Annabelle experienced a moment of pure joy when she felt the soft fabric of her own T-shirt. The tracksuit that still smelled of the special eco washing liquid she used. After all that time in the horrible nylon nightie. For a moment even the terrible knowledge of what she had to do to Marcus was forgotten as she pulled the clothes on quickly while he turned away pointedly to give her privacy.

'Now your foot.' Marcus turned back and helped her to the edge of the bed. Then slid her remaining foot into a soft white sock and carefully into the trainer. It felt strange, her foot encased in fabric and rubber after being bare for so long. She glanced at the empty leg of the cotton trousers. Quickly tied it into a loose knot where her knee had been.

'It'll feel weird at first, trying to balance with only one leg, but you'll get there. The exercise will help with your healing too, pump the blood around your body more.'

Annabelle stared at the crutches he'd propped beside the chair, and for the first time the euphoria over having her own clothes back was tempered with disquiet. Why give them back? Why did they want her to use crutches? It made absolutely no sense. She knew they weren't going to let her out. Unless it was a trick? Giving her something so they can take it away again? So it hurt her twice as much?

But Marcus was already sliding the crutches up under her arms and directing her fingers around the handles. 'There you go,' he said, taking a few steps back to the opposite side of the room. 'Start walking towards me.'

'I can't . . .' Annabelle began to protest, suddenly uncertain.

'Come on,' Marcus said, holding his arms out to her. 'You can do it.'

Hesitantly Annabelle edged to the side of the bed until her weight began to settle onto the crutches. She swung her remaining leg towards the floor until her toes touched the ground, then pushed forward and straightened up, certain she would topple over, but somehow she succeeded in holding herself upright. For a few seconds she didn't move. The handles dug uncomfortably into her hands.

'Now take a step. Move one of the crutches at a time.' Marcus's voice was uncharacteristically patient, but firm.

'I can't,' Annabelle said, her anger actually flaring now at how easy he made it sound. As if he had any experience of learning to walk with only one leg. 'It's not as easy as that.'

'Just try a couple of steps and I'll catch you if you stumble. You have to exercise. It's important.'

'Fine,' she snapped, then moved one crutch forward a few inches. Felt the thing shake as she adjusted her weight and moved the other one up beside the first. Then she carefully hopped her good leg forward.

'Well done!' Marcus shouted, his voice odiously patronising, as if congratulating a three-year-old for eating a whole spoonful of breakfast cereal. 'Another one. You can do it.'

Annabelle swore under her breath but forced herself on again. Stepping carefully across the room as her hands and arms began to shake with the effort, the pain where her leg had been intensifying.

'One more!'

'My leg hurts, I can't,' Annabelle said, her voice tearing up in frustrated rage.

'Come on! I've got painkillers. We can go further once you've learned to walk properly.'

Annabelle swore again, but forced herself with shaking arms to move the crutches and swing her leg after them. This time the momentum was too much, and she toppled forward.

Marcus stepped in and caught her by the shoulders. He helped her back to bed and slipped the crutches off her arms. 'Now you've started, the Doctor said it'll only get easier.' He tapped a couple of tablets out from a container and watched as Annabelle swallowed them with a mouthful of water from a bottle he handed her.

'Who is the Doctor?' Annabelle remembered that terrifying vacancy in his eyes. 'The little girl, Lily, is she related to him?'

Marcus paused, then glanced around the room. As if he wanted to talk but was wary somebody lurking in the corner of the room might overhear him.

'We're family,' he said finally. Annabelle nodded slowly. The

Doctor and Lily looked alike, but neither of them looked anything like Marcus. She remembered the way Lily had spoken so horribly to him, calling him a weirdo, telling him he shouldn't be outside during the day. It occurred to her then that maybe Marcus didn't get on with his family. Maybe they had more in common than she thought.

'And Scott? You said he's a friend?'

Marcus didn't reply but looked down at his hands then pushed the amputated tip of his finger against his thumb. 'We're more alike than ever now – both amputees. We should start a club.' He gave a little laugh.

'What happened?'

'Let's just say you're not the only one who needed the Doctor to operate on them.'

'Were you in an accident?'

'Only of my own making. Never a good idea to try taking a piece of bread from Granny Slate's kitchen without asking. She caught it with a meat tenderiser and squashed it flat, back when they thought I was a girl.'

'That's awful.' Annabelle remembered her mum shouting at her once when she had stolen some biscuits, threatening to take her to be adopted.

'Lucky the Doctor was around to fix it,' Marcus said with a fixed smile on his face. 'These things happen in families, don't they? And in a way you're part of the family now too. The Doctor will want to get to know you much better soon.'

Chapter 53

Despite the phone number Bill Macdonald had given them, the search for Francis MacGregor became a classic example of frustrating detective work. Monica and the team were desperate to apprehend their only serious suspect, but it took time to access the records for the number. Then time, working late into the night, poring over maps of the Highlands, to find the locations of the towers the phone had connected to. Finally cross-referencing the records against properties associated with Francis MacGregor.

Monica eventually left the office at 3 a.m., frazzled by caffeine, her eyes stinging from staring at maps and lists of addresses. As she pulled the Volvo to a stop outside her flat she couldn't help feeling the self-doubt familiar to any senior investigating officer. Had she gone too far to get the number from Bill Macdonald? Was the list of possible addresses a wild goose chase? Would they have been better pursuing other associates of Gall and Sinclair? Was there something huge and obvious right in front of them they were missing?

She got out of the Volvo and took a deep breath of the chill early-morning air, colder than it had been recently. She breathed out a cloud of vapour and tried to let the self-doubt escape with it. It was funny how fragile confidence could be, even after years of working on serious crimes. The magnitude of the job, the responsibility to the victims and their families could rise like a wave, come smashing down and leave you doubting every decision. Her first boss's adage came into her mind: *You're only as good as your last case.* Not something to bring comfort when her last case still gave her nightmares.

'You're tired,' she whispered, suppressing the thought. 'You should talk to Hately again. Get some support.'

She locked the Volvo and glanced around at the other vehicles in the car park, her hyper-vigilance of the past six months kicking in again. The rows of cars put her in mind of those creepy rusting heaps at the garage out at Little Arklow, and for some reason the first BMW, the one with the mascara and the touring map abandoned in it, came back to her. Something about it just niggled. She'd checked with Fisher that afternoon but it still hadn't been moved to allow them to read the number on the chassis. *They say they've been too tied up with the garage and Sinclair's vehicle. They should get to it tomorrow.*

Monica shrugged as she walked across the car park towards her block. It was probably nothing anyway.

Chapter 54

At some point the Doctor must have decided that she and Marcus had been punished enough because when she next opened her eyes the electricity had been turned back on. Marcus was sitting in his chair, reading the World War Two paperback again. She watched his fingers as he turned a page, the way he shifted his weight. Could she really bring herself to kill him? To ram Scott's locking knife into his throat. She had already begun visualising the motion. Trying to imagine how it would feel when the knife broke through his skin. Because she really didn't want to be *part of the family*; she didn't want to get to know the Doctor.

Marcus glanced up at her, scowling. 'What are you looking at?' In her drug-addled state it didn't seem unreasonable that he might be able to read her thoughts.

'I need to use the bathroom.'

He sighed and closed the book, stood up. 'Well, I'll take you in the wheelchair this time, but next time you'll have to use the crutches.'

For some reason the electric lights out in the main tunnel were still switched off. Their path was only lit by the glow of the torch Marcus carried round his neck. As he paused to open the battered bathroom door Marcus turned the torch away and Annabelle caught sight of another light, further down the corridor. She tilted her head to peer at the flickering glow, realising that it was a candle like the one by her bed. The light itself was not actually visible, as if it came from inside a room.

'What's down there?' The medication had loosened her tongue.

'Shh . . .'

'It's Scott, isn't it? He's still here, isn't he?'

Marcus clicked the brake off and pushed the chair into the bathroom. 'There's nothing down there. Nothing that you need to think about at the moment anyway.'

'He was screaming in pain.'

'Do you want the Doctor to come and treat you again? You won't be laughing then, will you?' Marcus hissed at her. Even to Annabelle's slightly drugged mind the fear in his voice was unmistakable. He pushed the chair roughly over to the toilet. 'You'll be able to get on there yourself now, won't you?' he snapped. 'Now that you don't have a broken leg any more.'

'You're scared of him too, aren't you?' she whispered. 'I don't think you want to be here either.' The idea had the power of revelation, and Annabelle felt a new hope flicker. Maybe she didn't have to kill him; maybe she could persuade him to leave with her? Suddenly the pieces fitted together in her head: the way Lily had spoken to him with contempt, the Doctor hitting him, Granny Slate crushing his finger. In a way he and Annabelle were the same, both at odds with their families, both prisoners. If Marcus wanted her to be part of *his* family, surely she could persuade him to get her out of here.

Chapter 55

'What do you reckon?' Crawford asked as he stopped the Volvo at a passing place just ahead of a rusty gate. A mile down a remote dirt track. The huge skies of the morning before outside Bill Macdonald's house had been replaced by high grey cloud. A rare spring easterly, rolling in to chill away new life. Monica wiped her tired eyes and squinted through the greasy windscreen towards the buildings some thirty yards away. This was the seventh property Monica and Crawford had visited that day. A string of empty houses and flats so far. Fisher and Khan hadn't had any more luck on their search. Chasing shadows while the trail of their double murderer seemed to drift away with that Siberian wind. Monica was starting to have serious concerns that she had spent the best part of two days steering the investigation down a blind alley.

'We'll check it out,' she said finally, still staring down the track, which was flanked by dense stands of pine trees. Behind the red-brick farm buildings the hillside rose towards Ben Wyvis, the huge, ground-down mountain that dominated the view north from the centre of Inverness. But much nearer now, hovering ominously above as if closing in on them. This was one of the last properties on the list; MacGregor's phone had connected to a nearby tower just a handful of times.

Monica killed the music in the car. 'If I Had a Heart' by Fever Ray. Crawford had been playing it incessantly that day.

An abrupt switch from his recent soul phase. It felt somehow appropriate for the search, after what they'd uncovered in the garage. But too close to the bone now. Too sinister, here under the mountain and the dark pines. She opened the car door and got out, Crawford made to get out himself then stopped, eyes fixed on the trees by the side of the track.

She followed his gaze up. A bull's skull was attached to a tree trunk. A smear of red paint across the grey bone, reminiscent of the biker logo Crawford had pulled up in the Incident Room. There were more of the skulls, she realised, wired high among the trees every twenty feet or so up and down the track.

'The Red Death,' Monica muttered. They were close to MacGregor. Her doubts about the direction of the investigation were immediately washed away. Crawford got out and glanced warily around the trees, hands on hips. Projecting an authority that Monica herself certainly didn't feel as she remembered the sprays of blood across the groundsheet. Lucy's smiling face that morning. The pine trees and the skulls and the chill easterly sky.

'We should go back to the road,' Monica said, feeling those fingers of intuition, the ones she never ignored, tightening on her neck. 'We should get armed backup.'

Crawford glanced at her and nodded. Obviously relieved himself.

'I'll put—'

A desperate sound broke the stillness and stopped him mid-sentence. It took a second before Monica understood that it was a scream. It was coming from the farmhouse. The sound of someone out of their mind begging for help. For long moments their eyes stayed locked together in shock before they simultaneously began to move. Crawford ran to the rusty gate and jerked it open and together they dashed towards the house,

Monica glancing to either side at the farm outbuildings. Half expecting MacGregor to appear, mad eyes on fire. But there was nothing, no sign of life. Other than the screams, drifting off among the trees.

The front door was locked. Monica took a few steps back. The sounds were clearly coming from inside. The door was thick, solid oak, but to the side was a small window. Her eyes ran over the ground until they landed on the collapsed remnants of a drystone wall. She grabbed one of the stones, needing two hands to lift it, then threw it at the corner of the window. The double-glazed window cracked, a pattern of lines shooting across the pane. The screaming from inside stopped immediately and was replaced by an eerie silence. Just the sound of Crawford's breath close by and her own pulse singing in her ears. She reached for the rock again and launched it at the damaged window. Repeated the action a second and third time until the glass was mostly gone.

Silence returned.

Monica turned to Crawford, about to ask him to put in a call for backup, when in the distance a sound started up. An engine. Then another two joined it. MacGregor was coming back. The two detectives remained frozen for a second, then Crawford moved first, hoisting himself through the now empty window frame. Using his leather jacket to protect his hands from the glass. The sound of the engines drew closer as he disappeared from sight inside the house. She turned to stare at the dense forest to the south. *Quad bikes?* Monica wondered. The engines were so loud it seemed they might burst from among the trees at any moment.

She swore under her breath. Eyes scanning the treeline. How the hell had they ended up in such a vulnerable position? Just the two of them, unarmed and miles from backup. She grabbed the phone from her pocket and quickly put a call in for all nearby officers. Behind her she heard the turn of a lock and two bolts being drawn back. The door swung open.

'Jacket's ruined,' Crawford muttered, forcing a stressed half-smile onto his face. She managed to return his smile as she bustled in and pushed the door closed then bolted it. Inside the house was dark. The blinds were drawn, painting the place in a gloomy brown wash.

'Where was it coming from?'

Crawford shook his head. 'I'll try the ground floor? You go up?' Monica nodded and went for the stairs at the end of the hallway. She took them two at a time, her eyes falling on faded prints hanging on the walls. Agricultural images: cows, bulls, sheep. The upstairs landing ran off to the left and right from the stairs. Wooden floors and panelled walls. All painted in a shiny dark lacquer, lending it a curiously nightmarish quality. She caught the first hint of the smell too. A pungent earthy stink.

Her hand felt around for the switch, found it and clicked it on. Although the single bulb offered little light, Monica could now see that there were eight doorways off the corridor. All closed.

'Hello?' Her voice echoed back at her in the silent space. The engine sounds were muffled here, deep in the house. She tried again: 'I can help you.'

This time she heard the ghost of a reply. Closer to a murmur of breath leaving a body than to a comprehensible word. The hair on the back of Monica's neck stood up. The sound seemed to come from the far end of the corridor. She swallowed and stepped carefully along the passage, suddenly paranoid about potential traps. A shotgun on a tripwire or a false floorboard with a bed of nails underneath.

'Is anyone there?!' She raised her voice. Beneath her feet the floorboards creaked back at her. But there was no response to her shout. The sweat was standing out on her back when she reached the end of the corridor. The door was bolted shut with a key in the lock. She pressed her ear to the wood, holding her breath to hear. Still there was nothing though, just the smell. Much stronger now. Slowly she drew the bolt back. Then paused again to listen. Still nothing but the sound of those engines now, drawing ever closer. For a split second an image forced its way into her mind. The ghostly version of her father, on the other side of that door, his skin blue now, his teeth black as coal. Standing inches taller than her. Smiling. Monica blinked the picture away and turned the key. She pushed the door open.

The smell inside the room was overpowering. A putrid stink of decay, which someone had tried to mask with a strong floral perfume, making it only more nauseating. The room was darker than the rest of the house, almost pitch-black, its windows shuttered. Monica futilely held one hand over her nose and mouth, as she'd watched Crawford do two days before in the garage at Little Arklow, and with the other hand she reached for the light switch. Her fingers landed on the cold plastic. She caught the sound again. A murmur of breath in the enclosed space, very close to her now. She flicked the light on.

The woman was tied to the bed. Secured by straps around her arms and legs looped through metal rings on the headboard and bedposts. A blanket that must have been laid over her had fallen off into a heap on the floor. Monica stepped closer, the full horror of what she was looking at slowly dawning on her. The woman was naked, and the straps had rubbed her skin red raw. The smell was rising off her, as if her skin was slowly rotting, there where she lay.

'I'm DI Monica Kennedy, a detective. You're going to be OK,' she said softly as she forced herself to step closer. 'You're going to be OK.'

In reply the woman's head rolled to the side. The quad bikes – Monica recognised their high-pitched whine – were much closer now; they would be here any minute. Monica offered up a little prayer that backup would arrive soon.

The woman's eyes locked on to Monica's. Blue like the marbles she used to buy from the shop on the corner in the Marsh, and vacant. When she spoke her voice was cracked and dry. 'Tell us,' the woman said, clearly out of her mind. 'Tell us what you know.'

Chapter 56

The engines stopped right outside the house. Monica forced herself to take the woman's hand. It was unresponsive, hot and damp with sweat.

'I'll get you out, I promise,' Monica whispered. In response the woman stared back vacantly and began to moan, her voice rising to the demented cry Monica and Crawford had heard from the gate.

'The fuck happened here?' A voice carried up from outside the house.

'. . . better fucking not have been . . .'

Monica hurried to the door, pulled it closed on the woman and locked it. She stuffed the key into her pocket and quickly checked her phone for messages. There was still no news on their backup. She had already insisted that they needed support immediately; calling again wouldn't make it come any faster. She dropped the phone back into the pocket of her coat. Lucy's face came to mind. And her dream, a woman trapped in a room. Made real in this nightmare house. Slowly Monica made her way back along the dark corridor. Trying hard to keep the image of the two bodies on the autopsy table out of her mind. The gleefully horrible thought forced its way up in a rhyming couplet: *Lucy's dream came true, and now you're trapped here too.* Unarmed with a sadistic double murderer outside. *You should have waited. You really should have waited. Maybe they'll cut you up while you're still alive. Like the other two.*

'Crawford! Where are you?' she whispered as she reached the top of the stairs. There was no response. The voices were still outside the front door, though she couldn't catch the words.

Should she hide? She glanced around at the hallway and staircase. Go into one of the rooms? Hide from them until the backup arrived? She hesitated. For some reason it felt like a very bad idea. She moved slowly down the staircase instead, crouching after a few steps to look through the broken window. Outside she could just make out the side and part of the leg of a man dressed in camouflage clothing. Her conscious mind understood what her subconscious had been grasping at. They had been hunting. They would be armed. They would hear the backup arriving and ambush them. The thoughts spun through her head. What then? Hide? Cancel the backup? Then they would find her, kill her. Or should she try to arrest them single-handed? Her phone buzzed with a message. She reached for it. Crawford: 'I've got a gun, keep them talking.'

'Jesus, Crawford,' she whispered. But it seemed as good an idea as any. Better than hiding or blindly hoping things would turn out OK. She took a deep breath, stood up and walked downstairs. The voices from the other side of the door got louder. Slowly she drew the bolts back and pulled the door open.

Outside three men turned in unison as they heard the door opening. Monica held her warrant card out like a shield and said the first thing that came to mind: 'I'm police. Wait out here.' It sounded absurd, even to her.

The man who was closest stared up at Monica. His hair was thick and grey, the moustache had been replaced with a white beard, but his face matched the photograph she'd seen back at

224

headquarters. It was Francis MacGregor. He was wearing water-proof camouflage trousers and a jacket. Behind him a dead stag lay across the back of a quad bike, steam still rising from its mouth in the cold afternoon. A rifle strapped down beside it. The two other men, both younger, were dressed similarly.

'I've got armed backup at the end of the track,' Monica said, still holding her warrant card out. Beside the dead stag Monica noticed a small chainsaw strapped to the quad.

Slowly MacGregor reached down beside him for the rifle and began to slide it out from its straps.

'Armed backup?' He repeated the words as if they were genuinely funny. 'You think I give a fuck?'

'You've got a woman up there,' Monica said. Feeling the hair on her arms stand up as MacGregor stared intently at her. She had no doubt from those piercing blue eyes that he was capable of shooting her right there on his own doorstep regardless of the consequences.

'I'll keep a woman where I want to keep a woman,' MacGregor said. 'What business is that of yours?'

He yanked on the rifle until it was free of the strapping and held it loosely in his hands.

'You want to think about what you do just now,' Monica said, struggling to keep her voice level. 'You want to think about it carefully.'

'Fucking think about this.' MacGregor pointed the gun at the ground and pulled the bolt back, clicking a round into place. His finger went to the trigger.

'Stop there!' Crawford's voice came from the corner of the house. Monica turned to see him step round the side of the building. He was aiming a shotgun at MacGregor's head.

'Fucking hell! Like Inverness High Street here today!' MacGregor shouted, swinging his head back towards the grey sky. He straightened up and stared at Crawford, eyes narrowing into slits. 'Watch that thing, pal. Cost a couple of grand at auction. Antique conversion of a Civil War musket.' Monica could see that as he tried to distract Crawford, MacGregor was slowly inching his rifle up towards stomach level. 'Used at Gettysburg if you believe the sales pitch, and I always believe the sales pitch.'

'Put the fucking gun down, now.'

'I'm not sure about that,' MacGregor said, smiling widely at Crawford. 'I'm not sure about that at all.'

For long seconds no one moved. Then a sound came from beyond the pines. The sound of a car accelerating on the track. Time seemed to slow down, and she could take in every detail of MacGregor's face. His heavy grey eyebrows, the weather-beaten skin of his cheeks and forehead, heavy lines at the corners of his eyes. All those moments of joy this world had served up for him. And she saw his jaw clench, a muscle twitch on his face. He was going to lift the rifle, he was going to fire it at Crawford.

She knew she should do something, but he was ten feet away from her. If she moved he could fire the weapon long before she reached him.

'Just lower the gun,' Crawford said, taking a step closer.

MacGregor smiled back, said something that Monica couldn't hear because the car's siren started up. Shrieking through the grey afternoon as the white BMW burst into view then screeched to a stop yards from where they were standing. Its blue lights flickering over them. The doors burst open and two officers jumped out, pistols pointing at Francis MacGregor. 'Put the gun down!'

For what seemed an eternity MacGregor kept hold of the rifle. Staring into the shotgun Crawford was pointing at him.

Finally he dropped the rifle to the ground and raised a finger at the young detective. He smiled, nodded in a way that managed to imply all kinds of sinister intent, then slid both hands to his head and dropped forward to his knees.

'We'll see each other again, son,' he said, still smiling at Crawford. 'We'll see each other again.'

Chapter 57

'Would've been the first time I'd fired a shotgun,' Crawford said with a shaky laugh. His face still chalk white at the memory. 'I honestly thought I was going to have to shoot the bastard.'

'So did I,' Monica said. *Or that he might shoot you first.* 'Better not to think about it.'

Crawford shrugged, took a deep breath and shook his head. 'Well, it would have been one thing off the bucket list.'

Monica raised an eyebrow at his macho posturing, because she had no doubt that if he'd had to fire that shotgun he would be devastated. Regardless of whether MacGregor might have deserved it.

They were standing outside the house, just the two of them again in the gloaming light. Waiting for a patrol to arrive and secure the premises until the currently overworked forensics team could investigate the house. For the previous two hours the remote location had been a bustle of activity as Monica and Crawford helped the uniformed officers with Francis MacGregor and the two men – his sons, it turned out. MacGregor had been driven to the cells in Inverness in the back of the marked BMW, his sons in a police van that arrived from Dingwall.

As soon as the three men were secure Monica had hurried back upstairs to release the straps trussing the poor woman. Held her hand as she waited for the paramedics to arrive. After her earlier screams she now seemed almost catatonic, completely unresponsive to Monica's attempts to reassure her. When the paramedics arrived, a man and a woman in green uniforms, Monica had seen the horror written plain on their faces as they surveyed the room. And felt a strange moment of protectiveness towards the woman on the bed. As if she had been any less repulsed when she first entered the room. The paramedics were clearly experienced professionals though and overcame their initial shock to begin stabilising her. Finally, satisfied that it was safe to move her, they had shifted her onto an orange stretcher and carried her along that dark lacquered hallway, down the stairs and out to the ambulance. Monica was left with her thoughts, particularly the curious memory of Lucy's dream.

'You think MacGregor killed Gall and Sinclair?' Crawford asked, mercifully distracting Monica's attention. 'Over whatever deal they really had going on with the garage?'

'He's got questions to answer,' Monica muttered, stating the obvious somewhat. MacGregor made sense as the killer, linked to the victims through the garage and a previous conviction for a serious violent crime. But as she ran back over the scene outside the house something about it jarred with her. MacGregor had seemed relaxed, almost like he was enjoying the thrill of Crawford pointing the gun at him. Would he really have been so casual if he knew there was evidence linking him with a double murder at a garage he owned?

And the woman upstairs only added to the confusion. Monica hadn't begun to consider the implications, beyond the eerie connection to Lucy. It wasn't exactly an unusual storyline, she reassured herself. A woman trapped in a room, a monster outside who wants to eat her. How many fairy tales centred on the same basic idea? Once they identified the woman, Lucy's dream would seem less unnerving and a lot more like a coincidence. And it might bring them closer to solving the murders too.

'We need to get Fisher and Khan looking through the missing persons,' Monica said. 'Anyone fitting her description.'

'I called them while you were upstairs,' Crawford said. 'They're on it.'

In the distance at the end of the track the lights from the patrol car swept across the pines and turned down towards the house. The day had crept into a bitter evening but neither one of them had wanted to wait inside.

'Should we do something with that,' Crawford said, gesturing to the stag, which was still hanging across the back of MacGregor's quad bike. 'It'll start to rot if it's left out here for too long, won't it?'

Monica stared at its frozen dead eyes, its thick tongue hanging out like a slice of meat. She wondered again about the need some people had to control, to capture and contain. The kids with their jars of minnows. Francis MacGregor with a woman tied up in his house? *And your dad, her internal voice cut in. What about the way he needed to be in control?* She tried to ignore the unwelcome thought. Her dad had been autocratic but never actually abusive. MacGregor appeared to have taken things to a nightmarish extreme. She gestured to the approaching vehicle. 'Ask this pair to move the stag –' she began walking towards the Volvo '– or they can take it home to eat if they want. Maybe one of them knows someone who can butcher it for them.'

Chapter 58

Whenever the fear and pain eased off, Annabelle was swamped with boredom. Deprived of any stimulation, she lay staring at the concrete ceiling, imagining the layers of rock then soil and grass between her and the fresh air she'd tasted during her attempted escape. She could almost imagine floating high above the ground outside. Staring down at the mountains and the road that had brought her to this horrible place. Imagining following it all the way back down south to her comfortable flat. Where Miss Albright and Mr Pepper would be standing outside, wondering where she'd been. Maybe some of the volunteers from the cafe would be there too, waiting to welcome her back like the loving family she'd never known. Sometimes she even imagined her mum appearing, apologising for her part in all their rows, offering to talk about the past and start again. The fantasies would persist until they were punctured by fresh bursts of terror. The Doctor breaking into them, forcing his way in through her kitchen window, or crawling out from the cupboard under her bathroom sink.

The memory of those vacant dark grey eyes would drag her back to the terrible reality of the situation. Her only way out was by killing Marcus. Despite everything the thought still seemed too awful to comprehend. *You're scared of him too, aren't you?* She cringed as she remembered her words to Marcus, the day before in the bathroom. How could she have been so unsubtle? Caught up in the moment of connectivity, the idea that she and Marcus had something in common. *It's because you're afraid of doing what you really have to do*, the harsh voice in the back of her head spoke up. *You're afraid of killing him.*

Annabelle didn't try to argue, because what she'd said to Marcus certainly hadn't helped. All it had achieved was to put him in a more distant and morose mood. He'd barely spoken to her after that as he wheeled her from the bathroom back to the cell, helped her into bed, then locked the door behind her. Clearly she had annoyed him. Maybe he was even insulted. The way she would still feel if someone else criticised her parents, despite all her problems with them. She cursed herself again for being so stupid. *One minute you want to kill him, the next you're obsessing over what he might be thinking.* Like he's some fucked-up boyfriend. Annabelle shook her head at the thought and practised the stabbing motion. She turned slightly on the bed. Tensed her hand into a fist as if holding the knife and punched it repeatedly into the pile of pillows. Feeling the air *whoomph* out of them as she imagined again what it might feel like. The knife breaking his skin. Would he scream? Would there be a lot of blood? She pictured him lying on the floor in a heap. Dark blood spreading out all around him. And what then?

Her eyes fell on the crutches, propped behind the chair by the door. If she killed Marcus she would have to get a long way on those crutches. Next time she wouldn't make the same mistake of trying to phone close to the tunnel entrance. She would take Marcus's jacket for warmth. Find Scott and free him, then they would hide in the woods somewhere together. Or keep going until they found another road. This part of the plan would work itself out later, she was sure. But the crutches, they were important. She had to be able to move quickly. Marcus was right. Exercise would help her heal. She should practise. She should practise in here. It was so obvious.

She could still feel the pain in her muscles from her previous try, but somehow they already felt stronger, and doing anything had to be better than enduring the endless cycles of thoughts. She slid to the edge of the bed, leaned against the wall with her left arm for balance and hopped across the room to retrieve the crutches. She sat down in Marcus's chair, slipped the grey plastic supports over her wrists and gripped the handles. Then, pushing off on her remaining leg, she stood up.

Without Marcus watching her, it actually felt much easier. She spent a long time just walking around the small space. From the door to the bed and back again. Quickly she found that if she concentrated on her balance it wasn't necessary to grip the handles with so much force. She could sort of lean on them. The thrill of being able to move on her own rose into a kind of manic excitement and the idea resurfaced: *Maybe you can help Marcus to see that keeping you and Scott here is wrong? Maybe he was just shocked by what you said because he didn't expect it?* The fantasy gathered pace and she began to picture an alternative future – she would persuade Marcus to free her and Scott, the three of them would find a car, drive to Inverness together. They would sit in a warm and comfortable hotel room, talk about everything they'd experienced together.

With her new confidence Annabelle was suddenly sure she could pull it off. The first thing was to contact Scott somehow. She tottered over to the door and banged on the metal with the plastic of the crutch handle.

'Scott?! Can you hear me? It's Annabelle!' She banged again and waited for a long time, listening for a reply that never came. Maybe he was gone. Or maybe he'd been taken some-where else. Annabelle took a deep breath, tried to contain her disappointment. Marcus would know where Scott was; she just needed to persuade him.

Annabelle realised that her arms were hurting and sank down onto Marcus's chair, eased the crutches off and pushed them against the wall. As she did so her eyes fell on the strange patches of carpet stuck to the walls again. She leaned over and slid her finger along the edge where the top square of carpet met the concrete. The join felt tacky, as if it had been sealed with some kind of adhesive. That explained the glue smell. It felt like the silicone seal in the shower at her childhood home. Annabelle remembered peeling a strip of it off and causing water to leak onto the floor.

Impulsively she pulled at the strip of glue. It came away easily and with it the corner of the carpet tile. She swore under her breath. Not what she needed, when she had already pissed Marcus off yesterday and was relying on him more than anything for her plan to work. She hid the strip of glue down the side of the chair and pushed the carpet back against the wall. It stayed there for a moment then slumped forward.

'Bloody hell,' she muttered, pushing at it again. Again it stuck for a moment then peeled away. Increasingly frustrated, she licked the top of her finger and dabbed at the wall behind the carpet. When she was a kid this had sometimes worked for sticking pieces of paper together if she'd run out of Pritt Stick. The tip of her finger came away a dirty brown. She stared at it for a moment then raised the finger to her nose and sniffed. The familiar chemical smell of glue. Another smell beside it, like iron. Could it be blood? She reached up and pulled the square of carpet away from the wall.

Behind there was a dark patch. Smeared as if someone had wiped the concrete with a damp cloth before gluing the carpet square on top. Annabelle stared at the wall, her mouth hanging open with horror. The sound of her pulse was ringing in her ears and her hands were shaking uncontrollably.

With a knife or a piece of metal someone had scratched into the concrete in two-inch-high letters: *THEYR EATING ME.*

Chapter 59

It was 8 p.m. when Monica and Crawford finally made it back across the Kessock Bridge to Inverness. The grey clouds above the city had cleared away leaving it cold and almost frosty. They had driven virtually the whole way in silence, both exhausted from the previous long night working on the case and the events at MacGregor's house.

'I guess we'll get back on it tomorrow?' Crawford asked as Monica pulled the Volvo to a stop beside his red Audi parked outside the police headquarters opposite Raigmore Hospital, where the woman from Francis MacGregor's house was now being cared for.

Monica nodded. 'Give MacGregor a chance to stew, give us a chance to rest.' And as she said it Monica couldn't help but imagine the simple pleasure of a hot shower. Of dragging her exhausted body under a pile of cosy blankets afterwards. The pure relief that they'd caught MacGregor, that she'd made the right call in pursuing the phone records. At the bare minimum they had saved the woman. It was something, no matter whether her uncertainties over MacGregor's links to the murders were justified or not.

Crawford nodded himself, climbed slowly out of the Volvo. He went to pull his leather jacket on then remembered. He gave a tired laugh then held the ruined garment up for her to see. 'Of all the jackets I could have been wearing today . . .'

*

Lucy was still awake, past her bedtime, playing on the rug by the TV, when Monica arrived at her mum's house down in Rapinch. The lamp in the corner of the room cast a warm light, the smells of roasting potatoes and onions with rosemary and garlic, the sound of shrieks echoing across a dark pine forest. Monica blinked, shook her head and tried very hard to switch her brain from senior investigating officer to something like Mum mode.

Her daughter glanced up with pure excitement on her face. She'd been concentrating so intently on something on the carpet in front of her that she hadn't heard Monica come in.

'Look!' She held up a plastic Tupperware box between her little hands.

'What is it?' Monica asked, joining her on the floor.

'It's a nature box.' The box was filled with an assortment of dried leaves, twigs, pebbles and what looked like a desiccated woodlouse. 'Me and Granny gathered it today, when we were at the park. Granny said these leaves must have been from autumn because they're all dry. If you rub them between your hands they crumble and then make your skin go all soft.' The kid ground one of the leaves between her chubby hands and leaned to rub it on Monica's face. 'Doesn't it feel soft?'

Monica closed her eyes, smiling unconsciously as she felt Lucy's soft skin on her face. And she remembered the way the skin had been rubbed raw on the woman's wrists. There should be an ID on her soon. Monica grabbed Lucy's arm and made to bite it. The kid shrieked with excitement and jumped up laughing. Her pure happiness was such a contrast to MacGregor's house, to Monica's chill fear of her sleepwalking. She wrapped both arms tight around her mum's head, and Monica felt her hot breath in her ear as she squeezed that small body close.

Hugged her tight. She stood up, still holding Lucy. Maybe she could hold her daughter like this for ever, maybe she could keep her safe?

Later when Lucy was asleep Monica went downstairs. Her mum was curled on the sofa, reading by the glow of the corner lamp. Monica took the armchair (Dad's chair, to go with Dad's books, Dad's record collection and Dad's cupboard, still locked even five years after his death at the opposite side of the living room) and folded her long legs up underneath her. Then reached to her side to flick through his books on the shelf, almost exclusively about World War Two and true crime.

'Did Dad like his work?' Monica asked. 'Being around criminals all the time? Having to be in control of them.'

Her mum raised her chin slightly but didn't look up from her tablet. 'Oh, he never really spoke to me about his work,' she said finally. 'He kept all that separate from me. He was always such a joker about everything, I don't think he wanted me to worry about any of it.'

Monica nodded slowly, and the uncomfortable memory of standing in the corridor at MacGregor's house came back to her. The image of her father on the other side of the door.

'Lucy had another one of her stories the other day,' Monica said, trying to inject some lightness into her voice. 'About you and Dad.'

Angela Kennedy nodded again but didn't reply. She was still staring intently at her tablet. And Monica felt the stillness in the room, in the house. A stillness primed with something, something like a memory of the past. Refusing eye contact as if she could hardly hear Monica was such an alien posture for her mum, whose body language was normally so open. When they spoke about John Kennedy, it was as if they were each talking about a different man.

'She said that you had a cat when you first got married,' Monica went on, suddenly unable to stop herself. 'That you had to get rid—'

Monica's phone started ringing in the pocket of her coat, hanging on the back of the door in the kitchen. She swore under her breath, unfolded from the chair and crossed to the linoleum floor. Picked the phone out of her raggedy pocket.

'DI Monica Kennedy? Am I speaking to you?' It took her a moment to recognise the unusual accent.

'It's me.'

'I'm at the morgue. There's someone here who wants to speak with you.'

Dolohov was waiting down the stairs, holding the door open as if Monica was a new visitor who might easily miss the large black letters outside: MORTUARY.

'Is it another one?'

He looked puzzled by what she'd said, watching her face as he ran the words through his internal translator from English to Russian. Finally his face went blank and he nodded his head in a curt formal gesture. She imagined him doing the same when he was a teenager in the USSR. Somehow even in her state of exhaustion Monica knew it meant there was someone, alive, behind Dolohov in the morgue.

He turned and pushed the door open. The man was standing with his back to Monica looking down at what remained of a body. She stepped into the room and cleared her throat. The man turned to her.

'This is Mark Gall, you remember?' Dolohov said.

Monica took the man in. He was wearing the same shapeless anorak as when they'd spoken in the Raigmore Motel bar the week before, but his face looked different. Haggard with heavy lines of grief on his cheeks, bags under his eyes. Monica glanced beyond him to where the body was exposed on the pull-out refrigeration drawer.

'How have you been?'

'I've not been able to sleep,' he said, staring down at the tiled floor. 'Started to imagine my brother was following me.'

'It's difficult.' She tried to muster up some genuine empathy. 'This kind of loss can stir up all kinds of emotions.' All the time wondering just what she was doing here. Surely Gall even being in the morgue was breaching some regulation as the body hadn't yet been released to the family.

'It's not that,' Gall said firmly, his red-rimmed eyes boring into Monica's. 'I couldn't stop thinking about seeing him here.' He gestured towards the body. 'Something was different about him.'

Monica nodded him on, curious now despite her tiredness.

'We used to call him Skeletor when we were kids, he was so thin.'

She nodded again.

'I realised what was bothering me. I wanted to see him again, just to make sure. It didn't make any sense because he never ate. Hated food, he said. But his body was bigger, heavier than he'd ever been when I'd seen him alive.'

Chapter 60

For a long time Annabelle stared at the words scraped there on the concrete: *THEYR EATING ME*

'It has to be a joke,' she said under her breath. 'A nasty little joke.' But it made some sort of sense. Was this why they were keeping her?

The muffled sound of the top door echoed from the head of the tunnel. Swinging open against the cement wall. Marcus was coming.

Annabelle jerked in panic on the chair and tried pushing the carpet square back against the wall again. She needed to cover the smear of blood and the writing because the idea of them being there together, reading those words together, seemed utterly terrifying. The square peeled away, and Annabelle felt her heart in her throat as she heard the door being pushed closed, bolted and locked. Then the sound of Marcus's footsteps approaching down the tunnel. In desperation she pushed the square of carpet back against the wall then bumped the chair to the side, its back pinning the carpet to the wall as a temporary fix.

She heard the bolt draw back in the door beside her. Almost without thinking Annabelle grabbed the crutches, pushed herself off the chair and collapsed in a heap on the ground. A moment later the door swung open and Marcus stepped into the room.

'What are you doing?' He stared warily down at her.

'I was practising and I fell.' She realised she was speaking in a child's voice. 'I wanted to show you how well I could do.' She felt the tears running down her cheeks; there was absolutely no need to force them.

'Stop being stupid,' he said roughly. He crouched though, like a weary parent. She put her arms around his neck and felt her hatred for him rise. His horrible clothes, his cheap deodorant. She desperately wanted to stab him, to hurt him. Somehow those feelings mingled with something resembling love. She pressed her face into his neck, craving something. The feeling of warm skin, of being connected to another human being. It made no sense. The tears that had never seemed to matter to her mum and dad could make Marcus want to help her.

He lifted her and sat her on the edge of the bed then knelt down so his dark eyes were level with hers. 'Now, you've not to be stupid any more, OK?'

Annabelle nodded her head quickly. Doing everything she could to keep her eyes from going past his shoulder to that spot on the wall. He cleared his throat, dropped his eyes.

'What you spoke about yesterday? I need to show you something.'

Annabelle stood in the tunnel and stared down to where it seemed to drop off into dark infinity. It had the sucking, claustrophobic feeling of a deserted station on the London Underground late at night. The sense that all that tunnelled darkness must contain something when the trains weren't there, that it couldn't possibly be just a long black emptiness.

'Almost there.' Marcus was trying to open a door beside her. 'Why is it always the last key?'

Annabelle turned to him, realised she'd been in some kind

of trance. They'd walked further down the tunnel than she'd been before. Her arms were aching from the crutches but she'd barely noticed the pain as her mind wouldn't stop returning to those words on the wall.

'What is it?' Marcus had spun around and was looking at her. As if he could somehow hear her thoughts. The door behind him was open now and Annabelle could see it led into another corridor.

This passage was so tight they had to walk in single file, and had no lights. Marcus went ahead, then after every few paces he stopped to shine the torch back for Annabelle to follow. She moved slowly, fear rising with every step as she wondered just where he might be taking her.

'What happened to Scott? I haven't heard him for days.' It was out of her mouth before she could stop herself.

Marcus stopped at a door at the end of the tunnel. 'Oh, I think he left. This place wasn't for him.' He turned the light back at Annabelle so she couldn't see his face. She took another shaky few steps forward. 'He had a lot of dreams. Bad ones. It's not surprising when you think of sleeping above all those tunnels. I suppose it could give anyone nightmares.'

'What do you mean?'

But Marcus didn't reply. Instead he turned and pushed the door open onto another space. He stepped through the door and clicked the torch off. Annabelle was swallowed by the dark. She could feel it up her nose, in her throat.

'Marcus!' she cried out. A moment later lights clicked on, and she took an awkward step forward. The narrow tunnel had opened into a huge natural cavern. Dimly lit by a row of electric lights at least fifty feet above her on the ceiling.

'I'm over here.' Marcus was standing by the wall. He was

staring intently at her, his face cast in shadow. 'Did you ever feel like you didn't belong with your family?' he asked abruptly. 'Like you came from somewhere else?'

Annabelle tried to form the words that would show she understood, would show she'd felt exactly the same way. He wasn't alone, they could escape together. But before her addled brain could make her mouth utter those important sounds he started speaking again.

'What you said yesterday . . . I wanted to show you. So you'd understand. The main tunnel out there. It goes down under the mountain for more than a mile. Then there are lots of smaller tunnels leading off it. Miles and miles of them.' His voice was lower than usual, suddenly emotionless like a bored tour guide. 'It's like a fairy tale, really. A story to frighten children with.' His eyes never left her face as he spoke. 'Hard to believe it's true . . . They found this chamber back in the 1950s when they were first tunnelling here. Named it St Magnus's Chamber, after the cathedral in Orkney.'

Annabelle glanced around the cavern. She noticed for the first time that at the far end there was a pool of black water. It was fed by a trickling waterfall high on the back wall.

'You never asked about how we came to be living somewhere like this. I know it's strange, but this is the biggest privately owned dam in the Highlands. One of the first to be built too. But there was no such thing as health and safety in those days.' Marcus gave a little laugh, as if he were recalling his own memory rather than someone else's. 'The men would go down the tunnels to blast through the rock wearing tweed suits. No head protection or anything for their ears. The tunnels held up with wooden struts. It was all about speed then, how many feet of rock you could get through in one day. Some days they'd be working double, triple shifts. The lads more asleep than awake,' he went on.

Annabelle nodded, trying hard to pay attention to what Marcus was saying as images spun in her brain. 'It must have been . . . frightening.'

'Sometimes the rock was as hard as diamond – they'd be lucky to make a few feet in a shift. Other times it was as soft as wet sand and they'd be working through faster than you could shift the stuff, wondering all the time if the tunnel was going to collapse on them. Grandad Slate was working down in the tunnels. The rest of the boys, they didn't take to him. He had a sense of the mountain, you see. He could tell when something was going to happen and so he'd steer clear of trouble. Make sure he was out the way when a strut gave out or a timer fuse blew early. The other boys on the job thought it meant he was bringing bad luck.'

Annabelle watched Marcus's eyes, which had taken on a glazed quality, like the Doctor's. She could feel the crutches digging into her arms and wanted to shift but was suddenly terrified of making a sound.

Marcus seemed to stare through her. 'Men can be superstitious deep underground. They started all kinds of stories about Grandad – how he slept on his own down in the deeper exploratory tunnels, how he could see in the dark. Then one of the men who worked with Grandad took a funny turn. Thought that one of the tunnellers was trying to send thoughts into his head. Next day he brought a shotgun underground. Blew the entrance tunnel shut first with dynamite to seal them in. Then he started killing everyone. The only way to escape was by going deeper. The madman killed everyone he could, then he blew his brains out. Just out there near your room. Grandad was injured in the first blast. A piece of rock hit his head. But he was strong. Him and five others made it down into the lower tunnels. At first they stuck together. They thought the owners would be trying to dig them out. But they were narrow those tunnels. They'd gone down in a rush and found themselves all squashed in like sardines in a tin. Grandad Slate was a thin man though, like the Doctor, and careful how he stepped. At first they were all friends, but then the torches started to go out, and all there was was silence and miles and miles of mountains up above them. Crushing them down.'

Marcus glanced up as he said this, and for a moment Annabelle could feel all that weight of terrifying rock above them, as if it might crash down on them at any moment.

He went on: 'They started to say it was Grandad's fault. He'd brought them all bad luck, and they wondered how he was even still alive with his head part bashed in. Some of them began to lose their minds then. But not him. He found the weakest ones first. Separated from the group. He used them for food while he felt his way around in all those black spaces. He said they tasted better if he scared them first. Can you imagine?'

Marcus tutted and gave his strange little laugh. 'He explored every inch of the tunnels with his hands and using his sense of smell. It was six months before he found his way out. In the end he came up right over there.' Marcus gestured towards the pool of dark water.

Annabelle's heart beat in her chest as though she expected Grandad Slate to come slithering right out of the water there and then.

'And you know, he said that eating those people had been what kept him alive with that hole in his head. And it had made him better. Made him so much stronger. He never needed the light on to see at night after that; he said his hearing was so good he could tell someone's weight from their footstep. Tell if it was a male or female, how old someone was from their smell. When he went to the hospital to repair the hole in his skull they said it was a miracle he was still alive. He definitely wouldn't live past another five years. They fixed a piece of metal over the hole and screwed it in place. But Grandad knew better than them at the hospital. It was him who trained the Doctor. Taught him to do surgeries. He used to drain the fluid off Grandad's head when he took one of his turns. Grandad only died last year, aged one hundred and three.'

The handles of the crutches were excruciating and her injured leg was throbbing, but she still couldn't bring herself to move, to break whatever spell seemed to have settled over Marcus.

'Of course the owners weren't pleased about him wriggling out with his story of how they'd been trapped and left for dead. That's why he was given the house up there. He said he'd be the caretaker and he'd never tell the story of what really happened.' He continued to stare at Annabelle. 'When Grandad was around he was always careful. One person a year maybe. Someone he picked up in Inverness, or someone walking alone. The kind of person no one would miss. It was just to keep him strong. He needed it, with that hole in his head. It's been different since Granny Slate and the Doctor have been in charge. The Doctor's wanted to use more of his training. More of what Grandad taught him.' Marcus shook his head. 'Now do you understand? About whether I want to be here or if I'm afraid of the Doctor?'

For a long time Annabelle didn't reply. There was no sound in that dark cavern save for the distant trickling of the waterfall. 'I think I want to go home, Marcus,' she finally managed to say. 'I want to go home.'

Marcus blinked at her as if coming out of a trance. 'Yes. Well, you'll be tired after the walk, won't you?' He stepped towards Annabelle and dusted himself off. 'I'll take you home. The Doctor will be along tomorrow. He'll want to check on how your leg's healing.'

Chapter 61

It was pitch-dark when Monica opened her eyes, still more asleep than awake. The fabric on her cheek felt unfamiliar and for a nightmarish half-second she was in a house that was a lot like Francis MacGregor's. She was strapped to that bed but somehow overhead was open to the stars. She blinked, frantically tried to move her hand and felt her arm pinned behind her against the sofa, the sweat across her back. She took a deep breath and tried to slow her pulse. *You're in your mum's living room. You came back from the morgue. You double-checked the doors and windows. Lucy and Mum are both safely in bed.* Monica took another deep breath, went to look at the time on her phone, but stopped when she heard the sound.

A rustling. A moment later she understood that this sound was what had woken her. She froze. Somewhere deep in her psyche she knew the sounds were being made by a human. She felt the panic rising in her throat but stayed very still and listened, eyes open in the dark, gradually adjusting to the orange tint of the street lights outside seeping through the thick curtains. Monica whispered, 'Mum?'

There was no reply, just the sound coming from the corner of the room. Her parents' old dresser. *Dad's cupboard.* Monica blinked again until she began to make something out. A black shape moving in the dark hours of the night, something small and malevolent, busying itself.

Monica stared at the shape for several seconds then reached for the lamp by the sofa, felt her fingers close around the plastic switch and clicked it on.

She could see the small back, the blue teddy bear pyjamas, the wild blonde hair.

'Lucy?' She sat up on the sofa. Her daughter was sitting on the floor at the far end of the living room, the cupboard door open. From Monica's position it seemed she was holding something. The rustling sound was her sliding it along the floor. 'Lucy?!' Monica repeated her daughter's name, louder this time. Fear washed over her as the little girl in the corner showed no sign of responding or even of hearing Monica's voice. She stood and crossed the floor.

The cupboard door was open. *Dad's cupboard.* How had Lucy unlocked it? Slowly she reached out and laid a hand on her daughter's small shoulder. Felt the familiar warmth of her body through her cotton pyjamas.

'Are you awake, honey?' She heard the shake in her own voice as she crouched to look at her. Lucy's blue eyes were glazed, still asleep. Monica glanced down. Clenched between Lucy's small hands was an old address book about the size of an iPhone. Monica realised that it belonged to her mother. She hadn't seen it in years. With her own hand shaking, Monica reached and took it. Lucy lifted her head, her glazed eyes on Monica again, then she fell forward into Monica's arms. Completely asleep.

Chapter 62

The morning smells of an office returning to life – brewing coffee and bacon rolls in this case – met Monica as she pushed the Major Incident Room door open. Her hair was still damp from the rushed shower she'd taken before leaving her mum's. Lucy had only stirred when Monica laid her back down in bed. 'Where did you find the key, honey?' The key to her dad's old cupboard that she and her mother had thought lost for years.

Lucy had shaken her head. 'I don't remember. I must have found it when I was playing . . .'

Monica blinked and caught a glimpse of herself in the glass panel of the door. Her reflection looked exactly like someone who'd had about four hours' sleep in the last two days. She pulled her hair back into a ponytail, glanced around the office looking for Crawford. Hoping he'd picked her up a coffee when he'd bought his own from his favourite place – Coffee Affair in the centre of Inverness.

There was no sign of him, but her eyes stopped on DC Ben Fisher instead. Noticing something unusual: the way he was strangely motionless, staring straight ahead at the screen in front of him. Monica took a step towards him. Glad to have something to focus on for a moment that wasn't Lucy and her sleepwalking. Fisher was dressed in his usual smart suit, his dark hair as neat as always, but he looked ill. His face painted white with shock. She looked around the office for a second time.

Was she missing something? But the other officers in the room appeared to be acting normally.

'Fisher?' He didn't seem to hear her. She flapped a hand in front of his eyes.

He blinked and finally turned to look at her. 'Monica?' She was sure it was the first time he'd ever used her first name, always preferring DI Kennedy or, worse, ma'am. He gestured at the screen. 'The cars,' he mumbled. 'From the garage.'

'What about them?' Registration details were on the screen. Blue 2017 BMW M4. She stopped on the name of the registered keeper. 'Annabelle Whittaker?'

'I know her.' Monica heard the catch in his voice. 'She's . . . well, I suppose you'd say she's my stepsister.'

'Your stepsister?' She couldn't quite believe what he'd said.

'It's her name.'

'But . . .' It took Monica about half a second to remember the strange text message. After that she had absolutely no doubt that Annabelle Whittaker was part of their investigation, that if she wasn't already dead then she was in terrible danger.

'Have you heard where that text message came from?'

'Text message?' In his shocked state Fisher obviously had no idea what she was talking about.

'Fisher!' She raised her voice and the whole room stopped. 'The text message? We thought it was a wind-up, a few days ago?'

'I haven't chased it up. I assumed it was a prank, then everything yesterday with MacGregor . . . It just went out of my mind.'

An hour later Hately and Monica were sitting with Fisher in the detective superintendent's office as they tried to make sense of exactly what was going on with their investigation. To be certain the text really was from Annabelle they had logged on to Fisher's Facebook account and checked the number against Annabelle's, rarely updated, profile. The numbers matched.

'How do we know Annabelle isn't our woman from MacGregor's?' Hately asked, face set in a frown.

'It was the first thing I checked,' Monica said with a sigh, rubbing her face. *What a fucking mess.* 'She's at least thirty years older than Annabelle.'

Hately took a deep breath. 'What steps have you taken so far? You've contacted the family?' He glanced at Fisher, and Monica caught Hately's expression, which mirrored her own thoughts: *This is strange, this whole thing is strange.* 'The rest of the family?'

Fisher was staring at a framed photograph of Hately's own smiling family on his desk – wife, two teenage sons. 'I'm trying to contact my . . .' Fisher struggled with the word, as if he couldn't bring himself to say it. 'My stepfather,' he said finally. 'Joel Whittaker. He's always busy, difficult to get hold of.'

Monica couldn't miss the hint of bitterness in Fisher's voice. She watched as he took his glasses off, put them on again with shaking hands. He seemed almost beside himself, as the reality of the situation – the danger Annabelle was in – began to sink in.

'DC Khan's tracking down Annabelle's bank details to find out when she last used her cards, and Crawford's chasing the phone records right now,' Monica said. 'I thought we might be able to find her intended destination from the car's satnav, but it was smashed in the impact.'

Hately nodded. 'Do you know where Annabelle lives, Fisher? Why she was up here?'

A flash of uncharacteristic anger crossed Fisher's face. The same suppressed rage that led to the night at The Clach, Monica guessed. 'I don't know her,' he said quietly, jaw tight as he battled to control his emotions. 'I've only met her once, briefly.'

Monica stared hard at Fisher because what he was saying didn't add up. 'But she came up here, sent the message to you?' Did Fisher know more than he was letting on? Was he involved somehow? But why would he have shown them the message if so?

Fisher took a deep breath, face red now, eyes locked to the floor. Probably running through the same thought processes as she was. Aware of how suspicious his position could look.

'We met a few months ago, the first and only time. At a wedding. My mum was marrying Annabelle's dad.'

'You weren't happy about this?' This seemed obvious to Monica from his tone of voice.

'I liked Joel at first. I knew Mum had been lonely. He seemed . . . perfect for her, almost too good to be true. He worked as a management consultant, had his own business, was financially secure. He proposed to her after less than three months together. It just . . . started to feel wrong.'

This was a story Monica had heard before. 'What happened?'

'Little things. He was supposed to come to my grandparents' anniversary party but never showed up. Mum was worried, phoning hospitals. Afterwards it all got swept under the carpet – he was busy with work, he said. Then a couple of months before the wedding he finally told my mum that he had a daughter from a previous marriage. Annabelle. Supposedly she's a *night-mare* who had caused all sorts of problems for him over the years, but now he wants her to come to the wedding . . .' Fisher glanced up at Monica, then at Hately.

'You were worried for your mum?' Monica asked.

'It was a difficult time. While I was working on the case, last year. I told my mum she shouldn't marry him, I said I wouldn't come to the wedding . . .'

'But you ended up going, and that's where you met Annabelle?' Monica asked.

'We were sitting next to each other at the meal. It was strange, I can tell you. Meeting your new stepsister who you didn't know existed until a few weeks ago.'

'What's she like?'

'I don't know – slim, dark hair . . . She was always on her phone . . .'

'But is there anything that could actually help us find her?' Hately barked, tapping his finger on the desk now, clearly impatient.

'My mum told me that she'd . . . had difficulties, was vulnerable.' Fisher's eyes dropped back to the floor.

'Vulnerable how?' Monica asked.

'She used to self-harm, when she was a teenager. I think she had to leave university – some kind of breakdown.'

'What did you talk about?'

'She said she liked driving,' Fisher offered. 'I told her the Highlands were good for touring. Maybe that's why she came up here.'

Monica nodded. 'Do you think her father could be involved in Annabelle's disappearance?' First rule of serious crime: look to the family, and if Fisher's descriptions were reliable, Joel Whittaker clearly exhibited narcissistic traits.

'I don't see how. He was working in Paris. He said he hates Scotland, made a point of telling me it's not worth visiting. He doesn't know anyone up here.' Monica felt a flutter of disappointment. A neat connection between Joel Whittaker, MacGregor and Sinclair would have been convenient at this point.

'There was no animosity between them at the wedding?'

'Joel and Annabelle? I don't think so . . . I can't remember it too well . . . I drank a lot. I'm afraid I made a bit of a scene. Tried to have a *quiet* word with him, which didn't exactly go down well . . . I ended up sitting on my own in the side bar. Annabelle came over. I thought she was going to have a go, but it was like she was thinking the same things about her dad . . .' Monica nodded Fisher on, her detective's instinct sensing some kind of confession. 'We drank a lot. I told her I was having a hard time at work, and we ended up going back to her room. I woke up beside her the next morning. I couldn't believe I could be so stupid.' Fisher was speaking in a monotone now. 'I just left and started walking. The hotel was in the country, and I just walked on until I got to a train station, then I came back up here. I don't do things like that . . . I don't break the rules: never used to drink, don't smoke, keep things in order. It was like I was just as bad as Joel. I warn my mum off him then act like that at their wedding . . . It was like the case last year had changed things – society's rules just seemed like . . . inventions.' Fisher ran a shaking hand down the dark wool of his perfectly cut suit, seeming to find comfort in his pristine exterior, such a contrast to his internal turmoil. 'I knew Annabelle was vulnerable. I just complicated everything . . . Afterwards I think I sort of blanked it all out.'

'You need to unblank it, Fisher,' Monica said softly. 'Do you know anything about this? You're telling us you slept with her. Now she's turned up in a double murder investigation. Did she come up here to see you? Had you planned to meet her?'

'I must have given her my number when we were drunk. It's the only explanation.' His eyes went from Monica to Hately. 'But I've never heard from her. Honestly.'

Chapter 63

Monica entered the interview room and sat down opposite Francis MacGregor. The murders that had just yesterday been the main focus of the investigation had now almost been side-lined by the news about Annabelle. Her head was still reeling from the implications. *I'm being held hostage but I've escaped.* The parallel with what they'd discovered upstairs in MacGregor's house was obvious. Was Annabelle still alive? Was the person who took her sitting right across from her?

She raised her head to look at MacGregor. Took in his thick grey hair and white beard. His eyes were blue, laughter lines carved in deep on either side of his face. Someone who had spent his life mocking the world and enjoying every minute of it. Her eyes ran down to his hands, marked with small scars, the skin toughened to leather. Up close he had aged remarkably well. If it hadn't been for his hair and beard he might have passed as two decades younger than his fifty-nine years.

DC Khan came into the room a moment later. Monica clocked MacGregor's eyes following the younger detective and felt momentarily protective of her. It was the first time they'd conducted an interview together, and in truth Monica would have been more comfortable with the familiarity of having Crawford beside her. But she needed him, a more experienced investigator than Khan even though he was a few years younger, to start figuring out just exactly where Annabelle might be.

'Tell us about the woman, Francis,' Monica said after the formal introductions for the recording.

'Do I have to?' he replied in a lazy drawl, leaning back in his chair with his hands behind his head, addressing Khan rather than Monica.

'Here or in court,' Monica said. 'We can keep you on remand for that rifle you were carrying, unlicensed.'

MacGregor raised an eyebrow but didn't move his hands. He was wearing faded blue jeans and a white T-shirt. His arms were tanned brown and the muscles stood out on them. He looked strong across the chest too. For a moment Monica wondered if his youthful appearance might be explained by some kind of hormone supplementation.

'Do you know Theo Gall?'

'Not familiar.'

'What about Sebastian Sinclair? Sinclair Enterprises.'

'The famous Sinclairs! I've heard of them, but . . .' He shrugged and pursed his lips. 'Not really my kind of people.'

'Who are your kind of people?'

'Not them.'

'Do you know a young woman called Annabelle Whittaker?'

MacGregor shook his head.

'No? You like people you can manipulate, don't you?' MacGregor stared back at her but didn't reply. 'People like Beverly MacIntosh?' Monica said, referring to the historical case Crawford had described. The teenager whose parents were allegedly killed by MacGregor's gang.

A little smirk ran across his face, and he waved his hand as if he were wafting away a bad smell. 'The MacIntoshes. People talk about that like . . .'

'Like what?'

'Like it was a big deal. The MacIntoshes were an unpleasant couple from what I gather.' He broke into a wide smile, and Monica caught the glint of a gold tooth from the back of his mouth.

'How so?'

'They kept that poor girl on a tight leash. Never let her evolve into the best version of herself.'

'She was a teenager when they were murdered. They didn't get much of a chance to help her *evolve*.'

'No?' MacGregor finally dropped his hands to his lap, tilted his face up as if he were posing for a portrait. 'Well. Things were different then. For us young people. It was a time for freeing ourselves. From all those old ideas.'

'By killing people?'

MacGregor put his hands on the table and leaned forward so his blue eyes were close to Monica's. 'Beverly MacIntosh did what she did. She evolved. Served her time. You want to know where she is now?'

The lines at the corner of his eyes were creased up with satisfaction at what he was about to tell her.

'You met her yesterday,' he said softly. As if he were delivering the last line in a bedtime story. 'Her love never died. She came back to me, voluntarily.' Monica tried very hard not to let the horror she was feeling show on her face. 'She came home five years ago. Not long after she was released from prison. That's a love story for the ages, isn't it?'

'No,' Monica said after a moment of stunned silence. 'If what you're saying is the truth, I'd say she's a very sick woman.'

MacGregor's face fell slightly at that. 'I can see you're no romantic, Detective. What about you?' He turned to DC Khan. 'You understand. Even though you try to hide it. From all the rest of them. The way you're trying to hide it from me now. I can see it though. It shines out of you, no matter how hard you try to contain it.' His voice was low and had a strangely unsettling quality. Before either of the women could reply, he was standing up. 'I take it we're finished here? You'll need to clear things up about Beverly, I suppose? Maybe it would be better if she stayed in hospital for a while.'

Monica slowly stood up herself and stared down at MacGregor – she was about four inches taller than him. 'No. We're not finished. Not by a long way.'

He stared back at her for long moments, then sank down, spreading himself across the chair. His eyes drilled into Monica's like they might be the only two people in the world.

'You're different, Detective. DI Kennedy. I think we'd get on well together.' He ran a hand through his long hair, leaned back, arms spread wide on the seat. Looking completely relaxed and comfortable.

Let's see how long that holds up for, Monica thought. Quietly relishing the opportunity to present MacGregor with the evidence they'd so far gathered from the garage. She made a show of taking some pages from a file and placing them on the table between them, face down.

'You've been successful in your businesses, Francis? Haven't you?'

'Buying at the right time. Spotting an opportunity. People up here are too cautious. It's the Highland way, I suppose. The heirlooms of defeat, of being a subjugated people.'

'You're a nationalist then?'

'I'm a Highlander,' MacGregor said softly. 'Last of the free.' His smile spreading wide across his face again.

'Free to run a bunch of businesses,' Monica said dryly. 'To be a sort of shopkeeper?'

'We all have to eat, don't we?'

Monica turned one of the pages over and began reading names from the long list: 'Mountain Bar in Aviemore, Braemore Petrol Station in Ullapool, Cairngorm Hotel in Grantown . . .' He stared back but didn't reply. 'It's one of your newer acquisitions I'm interested in though.' MacGregor's eyes didn't move from her face but something shifted in his body language and she sensed he was surprised by the turn the questioning had taken. 'A few months ago. You purchased a garage from Sebastian Sinclair. Do you remember him now?'

MacGregor didn't respond.

'Several days ago we visited your garage as part of our investigation into the murders of the same Sebastian Sinclair and Theo Gall. What do you think we found?'

Still MacGregor didn't respond. Monica nodded to Khan, who slid two pictures of the blue BMW out of the file. 'This car belonged to Sebastian Sinclair. Do you have any idea why it ended up at your garage?'

MacGregor's face had tightened. Monica waited a long thirty seconds then nodded to Khan again. She placed three photographs of the inside of the garage down on the table. Sprays of gore across the groundsheet. Tools carefully set down, each a few inches apart from its neighbour.

'These were taken inside your garage. We should have the DNA back any time.'

She let what she'd said sink in then stood up and cleared the photos from the table.

'I'll leave you to have a think about that. When I come back I'm going to be asking you questions about Annabelle Whittaker. She's a young woman who recently went missing. We found her car at your garage too.'

Chapter 64

On a normal day Monica could rely on Crawford to look for any opportunity to niggle at Fisher, who he seemed to regard as a rival in some status contest playing out exclusively in his own mind. *Today is not a normal day,* Monica thought as she walked back into the Incident Room, still feeling a desire to scrub herself clean after being in that confined space with Francis MacGregor. Crawford even seemed to have taken pity on his colleague and had donated Monica's untouched coffee to him. Fisher was gripping the cup of tepid liquid like it was some kind of life raft. The two detectives were sitting side by side, similar neat suits and precise hairstyles. Monica was reminded of playing cards. A jack of hearts and a jack of clubs. Though Fisher's encounter with Annabelle seemed more typical of a situation she'd imagine Crawford would find himself in.

'Where are we up to?'

Crawford leaned back in his chair and glanced at DC Khan, then Monica.

'I gave the mobile provider a bollocking,' he said, in his element with an audience. 'Told them Fisher sent the request through last week and if it had gone missing it was their problem.' Monica clocked the second quick glance in Khan's direction. Clearly Crawford was after her attention.

'And what did they say?' Monica dropped her coat over the back of a chair and sat down beside him. She looked at her long legs, her thigh muscles visible beneath the tight black material of her trousers. For a moment her mind flickered back to Theo Gall's brother the previous evening at the morgue. Could Gall really have put on a significant amount of weight while he was missing? It seemed unlikely.

'The phone definitely belonged to Annabelle,' Crawford said, bringing Monica's mind back to the present. 'I got a hit on the location. It's not exactly conclusive though.'

'How so?'

'Out in the sticks. Near Little Arklow. The mast covers a wide area though. Could be coming from anywhere down there.' *Little Arklow again*, Monica thought. *Of course.*

'Does Francis MacGregor own property there,' Monica asked, 'other than the garage?'

Crawford shook his head. 'Just the garage, and the land around it has been thoroughly searched this morning. If she's close to the garage then she's really well hidden.'

He swung his laptop round for the others to see and ran the cursor over the map on the screen. The browny colour of contour lines, dense where they indicated steep hills, the blue of rivers and the green of forestry plantations. 'The mast's here,' he said, pointing to a spot on the map in among a forest. Monica could see immediately that the area of their focus was into the hundreds of square miles. She knew from previous investigations that theoretically a mobile phone could ping a tower from as much as forty-five miles away. Even the more realistic maximum of twenty miles gave them a massive area to cover.

'Khan, dig into any reports from this area from the last month. It could be something small, something that seems insignificant. Someone might have seen Annabelle by the road, might have—'

'She's dead, isn't she?' Fisher said. His voice cracking, the composed facade he'd struggled to maintain finally breaking completely. 'It's my fault.'

Monica glanced up and nodded to Crawford and Khan. She needed a moment with Fisher. They nodded back and walked off across the office to the coffee maker. Earlier she had persuaded Hately to let her keep Fisher on the case in a strictly office-based capacity. She turned to face him. 'It's not your fault. You haven't done anything to her.'

'I've tried to do things differently, but it's like I'm destined to screw everything up, just like the rest of my family. I thought things would be different when I joined the police, like I had something I could be a part of . . . I can't believe what happened with Annabelle, and now it's part of a double murder investigation . . . bringing my stepfather who I can't stand right into my work life . . .'

'Everyone has problems with their family.' If she took a mental step back Monica could even see dark comedy in the situation, although it was anything but funny when looking at Fisher's distraught face or remembering the flesh and blood on the floor of the garage. 'If you knew half of how things were with my family . . .' She glanced around to check no one was in earshot. 'My dad was a controlling man – with me, with my mum. He was a prison officer.' As she spoke Monica realised she'd wanted to say these things out loud to someone for a long time. 'He . . . he broke the rules. Put me in a situation when I was a young detective. Your age. I've regretted it every day since. This job isn't easy. We all fuck things up, Fisher. Focusing on the worst possible outcome with Annabelle isn't going to help anyone. We need to focus on finding out where she is and who took her there. Can you do that?'

Fisher met her eyes. She could see a mixture of relief and hope in them. 'I managed to get hold of . . . I found her Instagram account and there was a—'

'Fisher, take a breath,' Monica said. 'You found her Instagram account?'

He picked up his phone, clicked open an app. 'I don't use it, but I was searching through to see where she'd last posted. I found this.' He held the screen up so Monica could see it.

The image showed a slim woman in her early to mid-twenties. Her hair was brown and she was dressed in black leggings and a tight long-sleeved T-shirt that exposed her flat stomach. The garment had *BRAT* written on it in red letters. Her scarlet lips were set in an exaggerated pout. Over her shoulder Monica could see the blue BMW, the same one they had found at the junkyard. The words under the photo read, 'Look ugly today but who cares! Heading beyond the wall!! Road trip to the frozen north xx.'

Monica felt her skin tingle with the eerie sense of being close to something like death. Something like tragedy.

'Is the location tagged?'

'Stirling,' Fisher said. 'Almost a week ago. After that nothing.'

'And you said that you got hold of someone?'

'Well, yes . . . I still haven't got Joel or Annabelle's mum yet, but a bunch of Annabelle's pictures on Instagram are tagged to a cafe in Bethnal Green in London, a volunteer-run sort of place. I called them up, and they said that she does the odd day in there, helping out as some kind of recovery thing.'

'OK,' Monica said softly. 'Was there any connection between Annabelle and the Sinclairs? Francis MacGregor?'

'I don't see how there could be. She told me at the wedding that she'd never been up here.'

'Anything else from the cafe? Anything that might be useful to us?'

'Nothing,' Fisher said. 'Just that she said she'd be away for a while. They thought maybe she'd gone on a road trip. They said Annabelle liked to drive.'

'DI Kennedy? Ma'am.' Monica heard her name and turned to see a uniformed officer standing in the doorway. 'It's Francis MacGregor, ma'am,' the woman said. 'He wants to talk. He says you'll want to hear it. He knows who's responsible for the murders at the garage.'

Chapter 65

For a long time after the visit to the St Magnus cavern Annabelle lay still on her bed. It seemed that her mind had lost all ability to judge its position in space or time. Her body felt like it belonged to someone else, and she had risen gently out of it, like a ghost. She had become something very small and separate, watching the meat and bones called Annabelle from the corner of the room.

As if through a dream she felt a hand on her cheek and was back in her body.

It was Marcus. 'Shhh . . .' She hadn't even realised he was in the room. 'It's time for your examination.' She lay rigid until he nudged her again. Then he started to pull her good leg over the side of the bed. 'Come on, Annabelle. It's your chance to show the Doctor how well you're doing.' The tension in his voice cut through her dissociated state, and she let him help her to sit up at the edge of the bed and slide the crutches onto her arms. Finally she made herself raise her head.

The Doctor was standing out in the tunnel, arms folded impassively across his stomach. His body language was something like that of a busy hospital consultant, keen to get on with his rounds. Although this doctor was wearing filthy overalls under his white lab coat. Smeared in black grease and stained dark with what looked like dried blood. His face was mostly covered by the surgical mask. With a feeling of pure horror

Annabelle saw a gym bag on the ground beside him. It was open. She could see it was filled with tools.

'He just wants to see how well you're recovering. That's all,' Marcus whispered. Annabelle was shaking, jaw locked with fright. Somehow she managed to put her weight on the crutches. Under his breath Marcus said, 'Come on, don't be silly now.'

She clamped her teeth as hard as she could and managed to take the few steps out of the room into the corridor. Focusing all her effort on the crutches, eyes on the floor, the Doctor's worn black boots at the edge of her vision.

'Well done,' Marcus said from over her shoulder. 'Now try walking a little down the tunnel.'

Annabelle did what she was told and managed a few steps down the slope. She raised her head slightly and saw that further down the candlelight was flickering again. Could Scott really still be in there, despite what Marcus had said? Maybe he would understand how she felt? *Scott?! It's Annabelle!* The words were almost out of her mouth and she had an overwhelming impulse to hobble towards the light. To at least try to escape, however pitiable the attempt. What if there was no reply though? What if Scott was gone? What if she really was alone down here? The idea was somehow more frightening even than the thought of what the Doctor might do if she tried to escape.

'Now turn and come back, Annabelle,' Marcus called. She stared down into that dark abyss, further down the tunnel. Remembering Marcus's story about Grandad Slate and how he'd crawled among those tunnels for six months. Surely it wasn't true, surely it had been a story to scare her? But even crawling through those tunnels would be better than being stuck in the cell.

'Come on. The Doctor's in a hurry.'

She turned back. It was no good; she wouldn't make it ten feet before they caught her. And who knew what they would do to her then? She stopped outside the door. Still with her head down. The Doctor took a step towards her, so close she could smell the oil and blood. He leaned into her and then she felt his hands on her arms, on her remaining leg. She was shaking but didn't lift her head. *Please, make him stop touching me.* Maybe if she could get back into her room and under the covers it would all be different in the morning.

Finally he stepped away from her.

'On you go now,' Marcus murmured, directing her into the room. He stayed out in the corridor with the Doctor. They were talking, but so quietly that Annabelle couldn't even make out the occasional word. She sat down on the edge of the bed, propped the crutches against the wall, careful not to make a sound as she did so. Silently she rolled into the foetal position and dragged the blanket over her.

Much later she finally opened her eyes. Marcus was sitting by the side of the bed. She could read the concern in his eyes.

'I'm afraid I have some bad news.'

Annabelle's mouth was dry as sandpaper.

'I'm afraid it's your arms,' he said gravely.

'My arms are fine,' Annabelle managed to whisper.

Marcus shook his head sadly. 'The Doctor says that they're infected. That they need to be treated . . .'

Chapter 66

MacGregor hadn't been lying when he said he wanted to talk. He started up almost as soon as Monica and Khan were sitting back down across the table from him in the interview room.

'You might not believe it but there was a time when the Highlands were an interesting place. Had a bit of class. The big clan houses would have the whole extended family out for the parties. Hundreds of people, going at it for days. Bastards made on both sides—'

'I don't see what this has to do with the garage.'

'You wouldn't, would you? Too tied up in your brain. She might get it though.' He tilted his head to look at Khan. 'I think you'd get on the back of my motorcycle, wouldn't you? I think you'd—'

Monica slapped her hand down hard on the table. 'Listen, if you're just going to waste our time trying to cover your—'

'I met the Big Boy, the old Sinclair, at one of those ceilidhs. That's what I was getting at.'

He had Monica's attention now. 'Go on.'

He let that wide smile spread across his face. 'Told you you'd want to hear.' He shrugged his shoulders and ran a hand through his hair. 'This is the Highlands – supposed to be a fucking tradition of storytelling.'

'Tell me your fucking story then,' Monica replied, and for a moment, despite everything she knew about the man, Monica couldn't help feeling a ghost of attraction. His endless enthusiasm was bizarrely appealing. She glanced away, reminded herself of the smell of Beverly MacIntosh. Just what was behind his wide smile.

'The late 1970s, back when I was just a sprat. Believe it or not but they'd do business at those things, back then. Last of the clan culture it was. Before the communists finally killed it off with their inheritance taxes. No sense of aesthetics. Just resentment and a desire to destroy. I was there with my own little clan. The Red Death. There were all kinds of people there for those parties – rock stars, actors, Jimmy Page, Mick, Marianne. All sorts.' MacGregor paused, clearly expecting some kind of reaction to the name-dropping, but Monica stared expressionlessly back at him. 'Well,' he went on. 'The Big Boy Sinclair – not that he was called that then, you understand – he was having some difficulties at the time.'

'What kind of difficulties?'

'The Traveller kind. You know?'

Monica nodded. Traveller communities, 'Tinks', were a feature of Highland life. First in line to blame for petty crimes and acts of vandalism. Sometimes justifiably, more often not. 'What happened?'

'He'd bought a plot of land for his first big housing development outside Inverness. Only thing was is he'd got it cheap 'cause there was Travellers on it.'

'They weren't keen on moving?'

'That's right. You should be a detective.' That wide grin again. 'They liked it, so why should they move? This was your old-fashioned Tinks, selling fucking clothes pegs they'd made by hand, dishcloths, that kind of thing. Dirt poor. Sinclair didn't

271

have the know-how to negotiate with them, so I agreed to step in and help with his problem.'

'You moved them on?' Monica dimly remembered Crawford mentioning Khan was from a mixed Pakistani and Traveller background. She resisted the urge to check her face for any response to MacGregor's unpleasant implications.

'With the help of my lads,' MacGregor said. 'The Big Boy took care of me after that. And I was able to help him take care of problems when they arose with his businesses. Win–win.'

'What kind of problems?' Monica asked, wondering briefly why this connection had never been picked up by CID. Then reminded herself that they were talking about forty years ago. Probably the information was lost as detectives retired. Or was buried somewhere down in the basement files.

'This and that,' MacGregor said, his eyes deadpan. And Monica wondered what myriad dark activities were covered by his clipped phrase. 'But that was a long time ago.'

'Why the garage then?'

'I mourned for him in my way, when he died. End of an era really. But then out the blue I get a call from his girl.'

'His girl?'

'The one back from America.'

'Heather Sinclair?'

'Bingo.'

'When was this?'

'A few months back.'

'What did she want?' Monica remembered Heather Sinclair in her office, the panorama of the Cairngorm Mountains.

'Advice.'

'Be specific.'

'Her brother was a waste of time. The Big Boy had been

272

good at handling him, Heather had less patience. I met her down at the Coylumbridge Hotel. I thought we were going to have a nice dinner, a nice chat about her dad. It wasn't long before Christmas and the place was done out like it was Santa's own gaff. I love Christmas me – teddy bears, candy sticks, weep every time I see *It's a Wonderful Life*. Had the feeling that old Innes Sinclair would have wanted me to go. Turns out I was wrong.'

'You still haven't told me what she wanted.'

'She wanted her brother to stop being a problem.' MacGregor let the words hang in the room. 'She wanted *advice* on how to make that happen.'

That word again. 'You're saying she wanted you to kill Sebastian Sinclair?'

'She wasn't that stupid. She just fished to see what I'd come back with. She was subtle. I never even noticed at the time, thought she genuinely wanted my business advice.' He shook his head at the memory, still smiling. 'It was only the other day, when I heard about Sebastian on the radio . . .'

'Why did she want her brother out of the picture?'

'He was angry about the situation, his baby sister getting the bulk of the business. He was always asking for more money, causing trouble with the business.'

Monica nodded. This chimed with what she knew about Sebastian Sinclair from Heather. Although she still struggled to imagine the slick businesswoman attempting to set up a hit on her brother. Or understand where Annabelle Whittaker fitted into all this.

'This still doesn't explain why you end up buying the garage?'

'She's got a brain, the girl, knew how to cover herself. This was later, a month or so later. She calls me up again. Tells me about this garage. She knows I'm in the auto trade. Her brother's got this garage out in Little Arklow. A piece of shit. Heather wants me to buy it for well over what it's worth. Two hundred grand. I told her it wasn't worth ten per cent of that; she said it was worth that and more.' MacGregor shrugged. 'You know the Beauly to Denny power line?' Monica nodded. This was a famously contentious project, a line of huge pylons that ran from Beauly near Inverness to Denny in central Scotland, through some of the most beautiful scenery in the country. It carried the electricity generated by the huge wind and hydro projects across the sparsely populated Highlands down to the cities in the Central Lowlands. 'She told me she had inside information. A second line would run through Glen Turrit. The garage was right in the path of it. Could end up being worth a lot, lot more . . . I said, *Yeah, yeah, whatever*, not expecting anything to come from it, but two days later I get a call from Sebastian Sinclair – it's all finalised. Heather transferred the money to me and I bought it from him.'

This made very little sense to Monica and seemed to raise more questions than answers. 'Why did you put the garage in your own name?'

'Getting sloppy in my old age . . . Same reason men have been doing stupid things since the dawn of time, I suppose.' His eyes lingering again for a moment on Khan. 'And who doesn't like money?' He shook his head again. 'I remember Heather from when she was a girl. Who'd have thought she'd grow up to be the kind of woman who would cheat her own brother then have him killed?'

Chapter 67

Through the plate glass Monica could see Heather Sinclair sitting alone at the head of the boardroom table leaning over a stack of papers. Behind her out of the windows the panorama of the Cairngorm Mountains was visible. The reds, browns and golds, the spring snow still frosting the plateau higher up.

The receptionist gestured for them to wait and walked in ahead of her and Crawford. Monica watched the expression on Sinclair's face change quickly from surprise to irritation, then back to a forced composure. In Monica's opinion this was close to what you'd expect to see on the face of a psychopath who'd ordered the killing of an inconvenient brother. Maybe because Sebastian discovered Heather had cheated him out of a valuable piece of land?

Heather Sinclair's eyes landed on Monica. She straightened the papers, then strode round the side of the table. This time she was wearing a dark grey three-piece tweed suit over a white linen shirt. Unsurprisingly she looked much more composed than when they'd visited her on the day her brother's body was identified.

Monica shook her outstretched hand. 'Why do you think we're here?' Heather tilted her head back slightly to look up at Monica but didn't reply. Finally Monica went on: 'Do you know a man called Francis MacGregor?'

Recognition flickered across Heather's face, and Monica could tell immediately that at least something of what MacGregor had told them two hours earlier in the interview room was true.

'You gave him money to buy a garage at Little Arklow from Sebastian?'

'To Francis?' Heather Sinclair glanced quickly around the room as if the impulse to run was threatening to overwhelm her. Instead she turned away from Monica and Crawford, went to sit back at the head of the long table. She took a deep breath. 'I told you my brother wanted money?' Monica nodded. 'It was more than that . . . There's more to it than that.'

Monica pulled out a seat and sat down facing her. 'I'm listening.'

'Look, Sebastian was a nightmare, OK? He had this fantasy about himself, that he was some great businessman. He'd try to set up *deals* that made no sense, practically commit fraud half the time. Spend money like it was water. Meanwhile we're trying to maintain this facade . . . I've fired people before, but how do you fire your own brother?'

'Was it easier to get rid of him?' Monica whispered. 'Easier to have someone kill him?'

'No! I was looking for . . .' She shook his head. 'It was a mistake. My brother wouldn't listen to me because I'm a woman. It's that simple. I'm not his fantasy of an old-school Highland businessman. He respected Francis. I thought he might be able to frighten Sebastian or something.'

'Francis doesn't remember it like that.'

'Have you actually met Francis MacGregor?' She sighed. 'Look, you probably think I'm some sort of corporate sociopath, but believe me I don't care that much about this business. If my dad hadn't asked me to come back I would've stayed far far away from this godforsaken place. I was happier when I was poor . . .' Her voice faded away.

'So you're at the end of your tether with Sebastian,' Monica said. 'You speak to Francis for advice, then a few months later you give him the two hundred thousand to buy Sebastian's garage, so you can make money out of the power line project?'

Sinclair sighed again, 'There's no second power line. I told Francis MacGregor I had inside information so he'd go along with it.' She raised her eyes to the ceiling then pointed to the stack of papers by her elbow. 'I'm in the process of trying to sell the business. Have I made it clear what Sebastian was like?' Monica nodded and she could feel something of Heather Sinclair's sense of desperation. Shackled to an out-of-control family member. 'I'm trying to run the business with Sebastian like a millstone around my neck, continually interfering. Look, if I could have clicked my fingers and been rid of him I probably would have done it. But that's a long way from killing him.' She shook her head, glancing round the room with an expression on her face that Monica knew well: *I can't believe I'm having this conversation. I can't believe I'm sharing this with these strangers, these detectives.*

'About a year ago Sebastian started talking about relocating to Vietnam, setting up a hotel and golf course out there. I assumed it was another one of his bullshit schemes, but he kept talking about it and even bought a place out there. Then he actually started putting his own businesses on the market. The garage was the first one.'

'And you thought you'd buy them up through a third party so he didn't know the money was coming from you? Brother out the way. Problem solved,' Monica said. It actually sounded crazy enough to be true.

'I don't know many people up here, and my dad always trusted Francis MacGregor, more importantly I knew Sebastian would love the idea of doing business with him. I know it was a terrible idea, but I was desperate.'

Monica tried to work out the implications. Even if what she was saying was true, it didn't seem to bring them any closer to who killed Sinclair and Gall. Could there be someone else linked to the garage? Someone they were missing? And where did Annabelle fit in? Could she have turned up at the garage somehow? Stumbled onto something?

'Do you know someone called Annabelle? Annabelle Whittaker?' Crawford interrupted Monica's thoughts. Heather glanced at the detective, then at the ceiling, turning the name over in her mind. Finally she shook her head. 'I don't think so. I speak to so many people in this job, but . . .'

As she was speaking, Monica's mind flickered back to another woman. Sebastian Sinclair's wife, Karen. Her perfect house high above Inverness. The one she was so concerned about losing. 'What did Sebastian's wife make of all this? Selling up and moving to east Asia?' To Monica this looked a lot like a potential motive for murder.

'Karen?' Heather looked surprised. 'You know, I don't remember her saying very much about anything. Sebastian was the kind of man who took up enough space for both of them.'

Monica nodded, remembered her sense of Karen's helplessness. The fact she didn't seem to know what a text message was, didn't own a phone. And as the memory bubbled up Monica found her hand going to the little address book in the pocket of her coat. The dry, aged paper under her fingers. Locked in her dad's cupboard. Why had he kept it locked away from her mum?

'Was your brother controlling?' Monica heard herself asking. 'Did he try to prevent Karen from contacting her friends and family?'

Heather Sinclair raised her eyebrows, then actually gave a little snorted laugh. 'Sebastian? Control someone else? He couldn't even control himself from minute to minute. Jesus, that would be . . . Karen was on a tight leash, but if someone else was holding the other end of it, it sure as hell wasn't my brother.'

Monica felt the address book in her pocket again, and a watery, long-suppressed memory surfaced for her. The phone ringing through their small house when she'd come back to visit from her first job down in Glasgow. Forgetting the rules, reaching to answer it. *No, Monica, your father answers the phone.* Looking down at her mother's worried face. She was frightened of him, the way his colleagues at the prison had been frightened of him. Suddenly it seemed so obvious, something that been a family eccentricity, a little joke. *Mum hates the phone; Dad always answers it.* Her address book locked away, and Monica remembered now how the phonebook would vanish every year as soon as it was delivered. Of course she was frightened of him, of course she was controlled by him. He decided who she could see, he decided who she could speak to.

Monica blinked and realised that Heather Sinclair and Crawford were both staring at her. How could she not have realised this, when she could so clearly remember how he'd tried to control her as a teenager? When she was a fucking detective and it was right there in front of her her whole life. She had seen her parents as a single indivisible unit right up until his death.

'Do you know anything else about Karen?' she heard Crawford ask. A clumsy question, obviously the first thing he could come up with since Monica had been struck dumb.

'Who else was important in her life?' Monica managed to say before Heather had a chance to reply.

'I'm . . . not sure.'

'What about her family? How did your brother meet Karen?'

'Karen?' Sinclair repeated her sister-in-law's name as if she were so forgettable she had to remind himself who the woman was. 'I don't know exactly. We thought Sebastian was going to end up a bachelor . . . I think he met her at a disco – out in the sticks somewhere? I think Sebastian knew her brother?'

'Any idea where?'

'I want to say somewhere down Glen Affric way, though God knows how Sebastian ended up there. Little Arklow, that would have been the place.' She gave a dry little laugh. 'Where that bloody garage is.'

'What was Karen's maiden name?'

'Her maiden name?' Heather Sinclair ran her eyes over the ceiling. 'Slate,' she said finally. 'I think she was a Slate.'

Chapter 68

Marcus repeated what he'd said: 'Your arms need to be treated.' Then he added, 'The same way your leg was treated.'

No! Annabelle realised that she should be screaming, but the room was silent. *No!* Still curled up in the foetal position, she was frozen with terror.

'I knew you'd understand. The Doctor thought we'd have to use the mask to calm you down.'

Not my arms, not my arms.

'This'll help you to sleep. Everything will feel better later.' She watched from the corner of her eye, unable to move, as Marcus reached into the inside pocket of his jacket. *Now! Scott's knife. Grab it!* This was her chance, what she'd planned for.

He moved quickly though. She felt a dull pain, as if through a dream. The needle went into her shoulder; the cold liquid spread through her arm, and her vision began to blur. After a while she moved her cheek against the pillow. The skin brushed against a cold spot and it felt so fresh. She realised how cosy the room was, and it all began to make sense. The Doctor was right. Maybe she did need treatment? The Doctor knew exactly what she needed. A peaceful space, just like being held in the arms of the world, the arms of the perfect mother she'd never known. Of course he knew what was best for her.

She felt her tongue, damp and sensuous in her damp mouth. 'Hold me, Marcus.' This time the words came out. 'Hold me tight.'

Chapter 69

Back out in the car park the icy wind was coming down off the mountains, whipping through the wool of Monica's coat and sapping the warmth from her body. At first she hardly noticed it as she reflected on the way something from the past could open like a trapdoor. Drop you into a strange new version of reality. She stopped beside the car, aware that Crawford was saying something to her but unable to take it in. As she searched for the Volvo's keys the mountain wind chilled the skin on her wrist. How quickly heat, and life, could be spirited away. If Annabelle was out in the open she wouldn't survive for long. Monica clenched the key in her hand, used the feeling of discomfort as the metal dug into her palm as an anchor to the present. Resolved to force the thoughts about her family out of her mind for now, to focus everything on the case. It had always worked as an escape route from reality in the past.

'Monica?! Are you OK?'

She glanced at Crawford, nodded, shivered and climbed into the car, pleased to be out of the cold. Hopefully Annabelle was somewhere warm, somewhere safe.

'Can you call Khan for an update?' she said as Crawford opened the car door to let in a fresh blast of freezing air. Monica was pleased to have Khan on the case, especially given everything with Fisher. He got in beside her as she started the car. Watched her for a moment then shrugged and nodded, reached into his pocket for his phone.

Monica glanced at the time on the dash. Almost 3 p.m. She was supposed to collect Lucy from her play date on the other side of Inverness in half an hour. Right when she really needed to be focusing everything on this complex investigation. Karen Sinclair's possible motive for wanting her husband dead was a new angle added to the mass of unanswered questions jostling in her brain. Wouldn't Annabelle have made it to a road by now if she'd escaped? How did Annabelle connect with Sinclair and Gall? The only clear link seemed to be the matching cars.

For a moment Monica felt the prickle of a new perspective on the case. *It was mistaken identity.* Someone looking for Sinclair's car had gone after Annabelle by accident. Her excitement was short-lived though. Quickly she remembered that Sinclair and Gall were both already missing before Annabelle was even in Scotland.

She sighed. 'We need to find out more about Karen Sinclair.' Crawford nodded, phone clamped to his face. 'We should go and speak to her now,' Monica whispered to herself this time.

For a moment her thumb hovered over the Call button on her own phone as she contemplated ringing her mum. Asking her to take a taxi over and collect Lucy. Then she pictured her daughter's face, disappointment more ingrained with every new let-down. She really needed to spend some time with her, especially after the latest sleepwalking episode the night before and the nagging sense it could have been triggered by Monica's return to work on this demanding case.

'The mountain rescue volunteers have started looking for Annabelle,' Crawford said to Monica, still with the phone to his ear. 'Her car was badly damaged. We're working on the basis that whatever happened to her began with a road collision of some kind.'

Monica nodded as she felt the heat from the Volvo's engine finally begin to warm her chilled hands.

'The Glen Turrit road turns into a private track just after Little Arklow. It's shut off by a gate, so they've ruled that out for now,' Crawford went on. 'She wouldn't have been able to get down there. The teams are looking at Glen Affric first, then Glen Mullardoch. They're going to keep the search going through the night, as long as the weather holds.'

Monica felt an opposing little flash of guilt about Annabelle. How important was it really that she collect Lucy, rather than her mum doing it? When they were talking about a woman's life possibly being at stake? She swallowed and ignored the unhelpful thought. There would always be something that felt vital associated with her work. It was her choice to do this job, not Lucy's.

'MacGregor's story checks out,' Crawford said, 'about Beverly MacIntosh being there voluntarily. Her probation officer knew she was staying at that address, albeit not that she was in that state.' He shook his head. Monica had almost forgotten about the woman in all the sudden drama around Annabelle. 'They're going to keep her in Raigmore until they can fully assess her, but she says she wants to go back with him.' He put a hand over his ear, listening again, then he turned back to Monica. 'Turns out the rifle he was carrying belongs to MacGregor's son, so it might be difficult to make anything stick. Given that we were in plain clothes and in the house when he arrived, Hately wants to let him go.'

Monica nodded. Although she would have preferred to see MacGregor locked up, he was currently low on her list of priorities.

Crawford went back to the phone. 'What did you say?' Monica caught the change of tone in his voice. He turned to her, covered the phone's receiver. 'The DNA results from the garage have just come in this minute, finally.' Then back to the phone again: 'No, I'll wait.'

For thirty seconds neither of them spoke. Monica turned left at the archway that marked the exit from Sinclair Enterprises property, back towards Inverness. Crawford was tapping the fingers of his free hand impatiently on his knee.

'Yeah, I'm still here,' he said, eventually. 'Really?' She heard the deflation in his voice. He turned back to Monica. 'No match with Sinclair or Gall from the groundsheet.'

'So it was Annabelle?' Monica felt a drop of pure horror. Were they were too late? Was she already dead?

Crawford shook his head, still with the phone to his ear. 'No, it wasn't her either. The DNA all came from one person. A male.'

Monica tried very hard not to show her growing impatience as Lydia, the mother of Munyasa, Lucy's friend, made small talk. After dropping Crawford back at headquarters she had raced across town to the house at Clachnaharry, at the head of the Caledonian Canal, to collect Lucy. Lydia had somehow sat her down and thrust a mug of coffee into her hand before Monica had the chance to muster a meaningful excuse.

'. . . and I just think it's terrible,' Lydia continued. 'They come speeding through like it's a racetrack. Someone's going to be killed sooner or later.'

Monica nodded and glanced through to where Lucy was still sitting on the carpet beside Munyasa. Shoes off and no sign of her jacket or little bag with the cat pictures on it. She looked fine, happy even, the way she was smiling. Glasses perched on her nose. Focused on the toy cars they were pushing around on the carpet. Monica's mind drifted back to those stacks of rusting cars at the dump. The two blue BMWs. She was sure that what had happened to Sinclair and Gall was not random. They were chosen specifically for some reason. But how could Annabelle have been targeted when she seemed to have driven up from London impulsively and was unknown in the area? And the DNA in the garage, male but not belonging to Gall or Sinclair. Not matching anyone on the database. Just who was it then?

She cleared her throat. 'It's a dangerous road,' she offered, hoping Lydia hadn't changed the topic in between. She glanced down at her mug. *Here you are*, she thought. *Look, you're doing it: having coffee with one of the other mums, being normal.*

'Well, that's what I said,' Lydia replied. 'They should at least have a crossing up there – it's dangerous, for the wee ones especially.'

Finally Monica succeeded in catching Lucy's eye and gestured outside. 'We'd better be making a move, Lucy. Granny's made dinner.'

'Oh, you must think I'm a right bore. Bending your ear like that,' Lydia said, standing up and dusting the front of her jumper down for crumbs from the biscuits she'd been nibbling. 'It's just that road up there. The speed some of these boy racers go along it. Like they want their own personal racetrack.'

Chapter 70

All the coldness of the world had returned to that small room when Annabelle came back to consciousness. Slowly she remembered: *Your arms need to be treated.* The words carried the weight of a butcher's block as she lay motionless. Stripped of the opiate softening. Not daring to move. *The same way your leg was treated.* Not to even twitch a finger in case there was no response from her body. In case she no longer had any hands.

The tears flowed though. Hot and slow down her face.

The tingling started in her left arm. Could it be a ghost pain? Like her missing leg? Still she was too afraid to move. What if there was no response? What if she lifted her arm and there was only emptiness? The discomfort grew though, like a muscle cramping. Finally she couldn't bear it any longer and opened her eyes. A candle was burning by the side of her bed. *When you look down you'll see bandages.* You'll see two shortened limbs. Two stumps above the elbow. She lifted her head, and by the flickering light she could see a pair of arms. Lying still on the blanket in front of her. Pale white, like wax where they stuck out from the vest top she was wearing. She turned the strange things over, saw the familiar mass of scars she always tried so hard to ignore.

Annabelle began to cry harder, her body racked with sobs. She hugged herself tight using her newly discovered body parts.

'Not my arms, not my arms,' she whispered to the uncaring walls and to the dark void surrounding her. The only reply came from inside her head in a shaky, disjointed voice. *Well, it can't be helped. You need to do something. You need to do something. You need to do something. You need to do something. You need to do something.*

'That's easy for you to say!' Annabelle shrieked. The words seemed to pummel at her brain. 'So easy for you to say!' The room seemed to expand and then to contract. A moment later Annabelle was lying on the floor. A guttural screaming echoed in the room, she saw the square of carpet, reached up and tore it from the wall. THEYR EATING ME. She ripped and clawed at the next square. More concrete, more dark stains ·revealed.

She realised the screams were hers. *You're losing your mind,* the voice inside her head chipped in sardonically. *If you ever had one to begin with.*

She screamed again and tore at more carpet. At some point she must have stopped, because when she looked around, panting for breath, Annabelle could see the lights had come back on, and she was surrounded by a mess of squares and patches of dried glue. Her hands were coated in blood from her torn fingernails. The door into the room was already opening.

Marcus stepped in, holding the familiar dinner tray. His mouth fell open in a comical expression of horror. 'What have you done? The Doctor—'

Annabelle heard the laughter and realised it was coming from her mouth. He stared at her with a look of sheer hatred and set the tray down on the table. Annabelle braced herself against the wall and managed to push up onto her single leg.

Marcus's eyes flicked around the room at the mess of carpet, then settled on the writing scratched into the wall. 'The Doctor's just coming. You've only made things worse.' He shook his head quickly and stooped to start tidying the squares of carpet into a pile. 'For both of us.'

Annabelle's eyes dropped to the tray. The pile of beige food on the plate. The heavy ceramic mug beside it.

Do it. Do it right now.

She reached for the mug. Felt it hot and smooth in her hand. The crown of Marcus's head was right in front of her.

'He'll be arriving any minute . . .'

Not there. The temple.

'Did you hear what I said, Annabelle?' Marcus paused what he was doing.

Before he could look up, Annabelle had gripped the body of the mug tight in her hand. Then she swung it, just like she'd practised with the imaginary knife, as hard as she could at the side of his head. The rim of the mug connected with his temple. It made a thunking sound. A spray of hot tea splashed against the wall. Marcus dropped to his hands and knees. Annabelle fell beside him, the momentum of the swing unbalancing her. She grabbed his far shoulder and desperately swung the mug again. This time it hit behind the ear, and Marcus's face dropped into the pile of carpets. He groaned, his body horribly still.

Again.

She swung it again, and it made a squelching sound like stepping in mud.

Again.

She looked at the mug in her hand. The white ceramic at the rim was smeared with blood.

Again.

She looked at Marcus, the back of his faded camouflage jacket, the shapes of his rounded shoulders. He had wet himself, and the stain was spreading across the carpet beside his prone body.

Annabelle dropped the mug and with shaking hands she went through the pockets of his jacket. Her fingers closed around the cold metal of Scott's folding knife. She pulled it out and pushed it into the pocket of her tracksuit bottoms. Then she took the torch from around his neck and put the loop of string over her own head. *Now you need a phone. Then you can lock Marcus in here, look for Scott, sneak outside and call the police.* She glanced over to the crutches, propped by the chair. For a moment she allowed herself to imagine opening the door to Miss Albright's flat. Seeing Mr Pepper growling up at her with excitement.

But no matter how hard she tried, she couldn't find a phone in any of Marcus's pockets. *Forget the phone. All you have to do is walk to a road. Someone—*

A sound echoed down the tunnel and Annabelle froze. A sound she had never heard before because her cell door was usually closed. After a moment she realised it was wood on wood. The outside door into the shed, squeaking as it was opened.

Chapter 71

Monica watched as Lucy dug into the plate of cauliflower cheese her mum had placed on the table for her. It smelled delicious, and Monica knew she should have been hungry herself, but for some reason her appetite often deserted her when she was engrossed in a complex investigation. It wasn't unusual for her to go without food for forty-eight hours at a stretch. The detached sense of otherworldliness this fasting provoked had even led her to useful insights in more than one murder investigation.

'Crawford called,' Angela said. 'He's going to the gym now, but he'll be back at the office soon.' Monica nodded, not really hearing what her mum had said at first as she watched Lucy struggling to balance a piece of cauliflower on her fork. The vegetable tottered, threatening for a moment to fall on the floor.

'He called here?' Monica finally took on board what she'd said. Felt herself bristling at the ongoing leakage between her work and home lives. She took a breath and recalled her emotional response to the memory of her father's controlling behaviour during the interview with Heather Sinclair. The sense of sadness and outrage on her mum's behalf so easily slipping over into misplaced anger.

'That's right,' Angela said, either missing or pretending to miss, Monica's tone. 'He said he tried your mobile but there was no answer. Thought you might be dropping Lucy off here,' she added primly. Monica nodded slowly, tapped the pockets of her coat and realised she had indeed left her phone out in the car.

'I like Crawford,' Lucy piped up from the table. She was now lining the piece of cauliflower up with her mouth. 'He used to have a dog that slept on his bed when he was my age. It was so big that he couldn't move and sometimes he wondered if he'd ever be able to get out from under it.'

Monica watched her daughter as she put the forkful of food into her mouth, wondering for a moment if she should suggest to Lucy that she stop exaggerating things. Surely there came a time when it was better for her to differentiate reality from what was going on in her head?

'He's nice, isn't he, Lucy?' Angela chipped in. 'Your mummy's lucky to have him as a partner. So they can look after each other when they're out helping people at work.'

Monica sighed. At least Lucy seemed to have forgotten about Long John for the time being; she hadn't even mentioned him the night before when Monica had asked about the key. The kid had probably found it at the back of a wardrobe or in a chest of drawers when she was playing. Monica felt in her pocket for the address book and for a moment thought about giving it to her mum. Asking her why she had allowed John Kennedy to exert such control over her life, stopping her from seeing friends, family, keeping her address book locked away from her. Monica could barely remember her mum's friends or extended family ever visiting the house, and certainly never without her dad being there. Had she really been frightened of John Kennedy? Had he ever threatened her? Had he ever hit her?

Instead she stood up and glanced at the clock above the cooker: 5 p.m. A fresh stab of guilt when she thought about Annabelle. If only they had taken the text message more seriously . . . If only they'd chased it sooner . . . Was Annabelle still alive? Surely the chances were slim.

It was almost completely dark when Monica pulled the car up outside the warehouse down in the Carsegate Industrial Estate, the other side of Rapinch from the metal bridge that led over the River Ness close to the port. She recalled that the warehouse used to house a fish-handling facility back when she was a kid. The stink from the place had hung over the nearby housing scheme, and seagulls would gather on the roof, waiting for the fish heads to be dumped outside.

There was no signage on the building, and for a moment Monica thought she might have the wrong place, but then the door swung open. Crawford came marching out, carrying a duffel bag almost as large as he was over one shoulder. He spotted the Volvo and held up a hand before making a detour to sling the gym bag into his own Audi. Then he jogged back and got in beside Monica.

He had just showered and smelled of shampoo and cologne. Despite the evening chill he was wearing just a white shirt and trousers, carrying a grey wool coat folded over his arm.

'Still roasting hot from training,' he said by way of explanation. He pulled down the passenger mirror for his habitual hair check. *He does look good*, Monica thought. Maybe exercise really was beneficial? 'Boxing then wrestling,' he added when Monica showed no signs of asking. 'Two most important disciplines for the street. Bruce Lee said someone with six months' training in boxing and wrestling could beat a life-long traditional martial artist. Can you believe that? Bruce Lee?'

Monica said that she wasn't sure she believed it, and she felt a little surge of affection for her colleague. Maybe it wasn't the worst thing if he came around sometimes? It cheered her mum up, and Lucy obviously liked him. Kids were supposed to have some kind of male figure around, weren't they?

'Have you heard anything?' Crawford asked finally. Seeming to conclude from her silence that Monica wasn't interested in discussing the street effectiveness of the martial arts.

'Still nothing,' Monica said as she pulled the car into the road. Pleased they could focus on the case again. Everything else could wait. 'Right now we need to speak to Karen Sinclair. From what Heather said earlier, it sounds like she has family down near Little Arklow. I want to know what she thought about her husband's plans for selling up and moving to Vietnam.' *About who was coercively controlling her – if it wasn't her husband,* she thought to herself.

From outside the Sinclairs' house above Inverness the city spread out below them. Just as impressive as their last visit, but this time like a bed of embers in a fire burned low. The red lights on Kessock Bridge stood out against the black sky. The gate was open, and Monica pulled into the empty driveway. In front of them the large house was completely dark.

'Doesn't look like anyone's home,' Crawford said as he got out of the passenger side of the car then pulled his coat on.

You think so? Monica thought, getting out herself. She strode up to the front door anyway, the motion-sensing lights clicking on and illuminating the grass of the front garden. The cul-de-sac of newbuild mansions were surprisingly close together, given the size of the houses.

'Places like this give me the creeps,' Crawford said. 'Like they're trying too hard, like they're hiding something.'

Monica pushed the bell and heard it ring inside the house.

There was no response, no lights coming on, no sign of movement. She leaned in closer to look through the glass in the
door. Trying to see the shadowy lobby inside. In the light from
the porch Monica could just make out the interior of the
house.

'Do you—'

'Can I help you?!' Monica jumped at the voice, loud and
close. She turned towards the row of trees beside the fence that
separated the Sinclairs' garden from their neighbours'. The
speaker was on the other side, a female voice that carried the
weight of middle-class respectability.

'We're police,' Monica shouted back. Funny how after all
these years a posh accent could still make her feel like a child.
'We're trying to track down your neighbour, Karen Sinclair. Do
you know her?'

'I'd like to see some proof of ID first,' the woman replied.

Of course you would, Monica thought as she walked off
the porch, back out past the Volvo, into the street and down the
neighbour's driveway. The woman had retreated inside and was
now standing with the door chain on, the wide porch of her
house illuminated.

Monica glanced at the nameplate beside the door – MR &
MRS TEY – held her warrant card out at arm's length.

'"Detective Inspector Monica Kennedy",' the woman read
out loud. 'There were journalists here earlier, you see. Asking
about Sebastian . . .'

Crawford had walked up behind Monica now, holding his own
ID open. The woman glanced at him then back up to Monica.

'It's actually his wife, Karen Sinclair, we're trying to trace.
Do you have any idea where she might be?'

The woman shook her head. She had brown hair cut into a

bob and was probably in her early seventies. 'They keep themselves to themselves, generally.'

'Do you remember when you last saw Karen?'

'I went to the door the day after I heard about Sebastian going missing.' Her eyes flicked to the right, towards the Sinclairs' looming house, and she lowered her voice. 'I was a midwife. I've seen a lot of death, a lot of tragedy . . .'

Monica could hear her uncertainty. 'Karen's reaction was unusual?' Mrs Tey shifted uncomfortably and pulled her cardigan tighter. 'Something disturbed you?'

When she met Monica's eyes there was something very close to fear on her face.

'I'd never seen Karen's family before. When I went over they were in a sort of old minibus, loading things from the house into it. This was just after Sebastian had gone missing.' Involuntarily her eyes went back to the hedge and the dark house beyond it. 'I couldn't understand it. Clearing the house out like that.'

'What were they taking?'

'I just saw some furniture, some antique chairs, I think they were Georgian . . .'

'Who was there?'

'An older woman – Karen called her Granny. There was a boy. Wearing a khaki jacket, he kept his head down, always holding his hand up to his face, like he was shy. He was playing with the little girl. She was blonde, a pretty girl. They seemed . . .'

'Go on.'

'They just seemed odd. It's hard to explain exactly, but there was something disturbing about them.'

'Why do you say that?'

Mrs Tey's brow creased beneath her hair. 'It sounds stupid . . .'

'Stupid things can be important.'

'There was a man, tall with blond hair. He kept his face covered with a scarf too, didn't speak. He was in Sebastian's garage. Look, I'll be honest with you. Sebastian was a loud-mouth, always playing it large. But when my husband was alive, occasionally they'd get chatting, and Sebastian would invite him over for a beer. His garage was done out inside like a little bar on one side, a workshop on the other. It sounds unkind, but we laughed about it a bit. He had peanut packets on the wall behind the bar, a fridge with a glass door so you could see the bottles inside.' Monica nodded her on, impatient. 'Anyway, that man came striding out of the garage. It's stupid, but it upset me . . . My husband told me that Sebastian had a collection of tools, sort of on display – hammers, saws, chisels in an old toolbox. Sebastian said he'd inherited them from his father, who founded the family business. His dad's first set of tools, from when he started out as a joiner. Sebastian seemed so proud that his father had passed them on to him. I saw that man coming out of there with the toolbox. It just felt wrong. Taking them like that when they meant so much to Sebastian.'

Chapter 72

'Still nothing about Annabelle,' Crawford said as Monica joined him back in the car. He had taken a call from Fisher while Monica was questioning Mrs Tey.

Monica was pondering what the woman had told her. The coincidence of the tools seemed to offer a potential connection between the Slates and whatever had happened at the garage. But Mrs Tey said she'd have no chance of recognising the tools. It would take time that Annabelle didn't have to find someone else who might be able to tell if the tools recovered from the garage originally belonged to Innes Sinclair. More importantly, Monica had no idea where the Slates lived.

'Fisher's finally got hold of his stepfather, Joel Whittaker, Annabelle's dad,' Crawford continued. 'Apparently he's on his way up, freaking out about it as you might expect. Annabelle's mum's going to be here tomorrow too.'

'How does Fisher sound?' Monica wondered for a moment if she should drive down and see him. But what could she say? *Sorry we can't find your stepsister? Sorry this seems to be at least partly your fault?* So far only she and Hately knew what had happened between Fisher and Annabelle at the wedding. It would be better for the young detective and his family if it stayed that way.

'Like he's still in shock about it all. It's weird . . . him drinking like that the other day, so out of character. Then this. Like something was bothering him.' Crawford wasn't stupid. But the fewer people who knew the details the better. Monica nodded but didn't reply, turned the Volvo in the street and pulled out onto the long road that led back downhill towards the centre of Inverness.

'I take it nothing came back about the Slates' address?'

'Khan hasn't been able to find any record of them,' Crawford said. 'It's as if they don't exist. Not on any database anyway.'

'So Karen's family supposedly live out somewhere close to Little Arklow, near where Sinclair and Gall were discovered.' *And near where the body of one of Innes Sinclair's business associates was discovered forty years ago*, Monica thought but didn't add. This piece of information only seemed to add to the complexity of the case. 'And for some unknown reason, Annabelle drove down that way too and was taken hostage but escaped.' She thought about the cars again, matching BMWs. Trying to find some new clue she hadn't considered so far.

'Karen Sinclair clearly had a motive. The fact he wanted to sell their businesses. The house was practically the first thing she mentioned to us,' Crawford said. 'But how does Annabelle fit into that? Sinclair and Gall were both already dead before she was even in Scotland. I just don't get it.'

Monica swore and slapped the dashboard. Hating the feeling of impotence, knowing Annabelle was out there somewhere. If she could only work out where.

'We need to find the Slates, it's as simple as that,' she said, turning the car to the left at the bottom of the hill. West, towards those mountains and glens that lay shrouded in darkness.

Through the window Monica could see shadows cast by flames from an open fire dancing over the walls, the only light inside the small house in Little Arklow. She got out of the car and caught the mix of smells. Chilled air from the mountains and the cloying scent of woodsmoke, hanging low over the dark village. Crawford came and stood beside her at the gate, taking in the birch woods that surrounded the house on three sides.

A hundred feet away a group of men standing smoking outside the pub turned to stare. Crawford and Monica looked back at the figures, only visible as dark silhouettes against the shifting smoke.

'Feels strange here,' Crawford muttered. 'Almost like a different country . . .'

There was no reply when Monica rapped on the door. She tried again and finally heard the sound of rustling from inside. 'Go away! There's nothing for you here.'

'Gillian? It's DI Monica Kennedy.'

'I don't care who you are. You can get lost.'

Monica cleared her throat. 'It's about the Affric Men.'

Silence. Then slowly the door opened a crack until Monica could see a grimy face peering back at her.

'The big policewoman? Is that really you?'

Monica realised with a start that the woman was pointing a knife at her. She took a step back and held her ID up, shone the light from her phone onto it. Gillian reached a grubby hand through and poked at Monica's face as if checking she was really there. Monica caught the smell of unwashed human steeped in alcohol and jerked her head away reflexively.

'Jesus,' Crawford whispered from behind her.

Gillian seemed convinced and after a moment she pulled the door all the way open.

'I thought you were them lot, coming back to play tricks on me again.'

'Who are you talking about?'

Without answering, the woman turned and walked through into the earth-floored room Monica had visited before.

'Slide that bolt back across, they'll just try sneaking in otherwise,' she shouted over her shoulder to Crawford. Who shrugged but did as he was told.

Gillian crashed back down into her chair by the fire. Laid the knife on the hearth and picked up a bottle of vodka, splashed some into a mug.

'There were lights over the mountains earlier. Usually means something bad's going to happen.'

'Why do you say that?' Monica glanced around for somewhere to sit, remembered there was only the one seat and crouched by the hearth instead. Appreciating the fire's warmth after the cold night outside. 'The Rescue are out looking for a girl who's missing. It'll be their lights.'

'People disappear in these mountains, and good luck finding them.' Gillian raised the mug as if in toast to Annabelle then took a mouthful of the vodka. Her face twisted up at the sting of the spirit.

'Her name's Annabelle Whittaker. Does that mean anything to you?' Crawford asked hopefully.

'Drive you mad,' Gillian continued as if Crawford hadn't spoken. 'A surveyor came up here in the 1960s. Mapping the place. He had these two clocks that had to be synchronised. One he kept at his office down the street, one he brought with him into the hills. Every day when he took the one from the mountains back with him it would be out by a fraction of a second. Running slower. At first he was convinced it was a problem with one of the clocks, so he replaced them. Same thing though. Out by fractions of a second at the end of each day. He couldn't work out what was going on with these bloody clocks. He became obsessed with the idea that time ran differently up in these mountains.'

'I'm guessing he didn't win a Nobel Prize for this work?' Crawford chipped in.

Monica looked at him in irritation, and Gillian set the mug of vodka down on the hearth. Reached for a ratty-looking roll-up.

'What are you here for if you think what I've got to say is a bloody big joke?' The tip of the cigarette flared as she lit it with a match. Monica glanced at the window where a branch was poking through. Since her last visit Gillian had stuffed scraps of cardboard around the hole to keep the cold air out.

'I'm sorry. I shouldn't have said that.'

'Well . . . he did end up in Craig Dunain nut house. Wandering about in those mountains will do that to you.' Gillian seemed delighted by this part of the story and creased up with laughter for a full minute.

Monica glanced at Crawford, who was still standing by the door. He raised his eyebrows and opened his hands: *Why did you bring me here again?*

She turned back to Gillian. 'Tell me about the Slates.'

Abruptly she stopped laughing.

'I don't know anything about them.'

'But you know the name?'

Gillian didn't answer, just stared into her mug. Monica surveyed the room, taking in the smoke from the open fire as it snaked up among the row of unlit candles on the mantelpiece. 'You knew the surveyor, didn't you?'

Gillian didn't raise her eyes. 'He wasn't the only one in the nut house. I'd had my problems too. That was where I met Euston. I told him I had a mission to save the world through

302

unconditional love; he told me he was close to being able to control time.' She smiled at the memory. 'Eventually they kicked us out and we moved here. Euston started his work in the mountains again—'

'And it led him to the Slates?'

'I heard him mention a man called Slate, once. Euston thought he knew what happened to Colin Muir back in 1980. That was just one of his stories though.'

'Why do you say that?'

'Because he said Doc Slate lived up in Glen Turrit. And everyone knows there's been no one living up there since they flooded the old village to build the dam. Back in the 1950s.'

Chapter 73

The sound of the door echoed down the corridor. Annabelle stared at Marcus's prone body as if waking from a trance, suddenly flushed with a new kind of horror. What had she done? He was dead, and she had killed him. She was a murderer. The flash of guilt at that word was almost overwhelming. In one moment the world was a completely different place.

He deserved it. Her harsh internal voice spoke up. *Not that it'll matter either way because the Doctor's coming to take your arms. You need to move.* Annabelle tried to respond, but she couldn't wrench her eyes from Marcus's body. How could she leave him lying like that? She had to cover him with something.

No! The voice inside her head seemed to explode with frustration this time. *You need to move now!*

Somehow she forced herself to turn away from what she'd done, grab the crutches from where they'd fallen to the floor. She managed to stand and staggered out into the tunnel. She glanced up at the metal door. Half expecting to see the Doctor standing there, staring down at her. It was still closed. Was he really out there? Maybe she had imagined the sound of the shed door opening? Surely she wouldn't have been able to hear it through the metal? Maybe he wasn't coming at all. If she could just get out of the tunnel she would be free.

She hesitated then turned to the right, facing up the slope. Another sound echoed down the corridor. The wooden door squeaking closed. She hadn't been mistaken, and Marcus hadn't been lying. Any moment now the top door would open and the Doctor would see her.

She looked around frantically. Just the electric lights of the tunnel and the damp smell of the rock. All those tons and tons of the mountain, weighing down on her. With the Doctor blocking her only way out.

Not the only way out, the voice piped up again. She had to go deeper. Down into the old tunnels, just like Grandad Slate had in Marcus's creepy story. Annabelle turned and looked at the row of lights that dropped down into the darkness.

She desperately didn't want to go down there, but the top door would open any moment. The Doctor would take her arms. And who knew what else he would do to her when he saw the terrible thing she'd done to Marcus?

Chapter 74

Monica glanced in the rear-view mirror at the figures outside the pub. They had wandered closer and were now standing in the middle of the road. Almost as if preparing to block the way back down the glen towards Inverness. Crawford stared at the men as he adjusted the collar on his coat, making a show of not being intimidated, then he climbed in beside her. They were going in the other direction anyway, the road west to Glen Turrit.

'Fisher said one of the patrols checked. The gate on the road's still locked up at the head of the glen,' he said as she accelerated down the gloomy street out of the village and into the birch forest that enclosed the road on either side. 'There's no way Annabelle could have gone down there.'

Monica didn't reply. Gillian's story sounded crazy, and Fisher had already looked into Euston Miller's death and found nothing obviously suspicious. But these little fragments – the Slates' link to Sebastian Sinclair through Karen, that connection to the garage. Now Gillian's ghost of a link between the Slates and the death of Colin Muir.

'I just want to have a look,' she replied finally as she pulled the Volvo through a tight bend in the single-track road, exactly the kind of place where she had attended several accidents in her recent traffic stint. Over-exuberant teenagers who had gone too hard at a corner and wrapped themselves round a tree. Cautious Sunday drivers swerving for a deer and ending their days at the bottom of a gully. She took heed of the memories and eased off the throttle after thirty seconds.

After another five minutes their path was blocked by a gate. Beyond it the road was black and foreboding, crowded by yet more birch trees.

'I told you,' Crawford said from beside her. She looked at the sign picked out in the Volvo's headlights: STRICTLY PRIVATE.

Monica glanced at the time on the dashboard: 9.30 p.m. 'We know she messaged from somewhere in this area,' Monica said almost to herself as much as to Crawford.

'But it could have been from anywhere within a twenty-five-mile radius of the tower.'

Without replying Monica got out of the car and walked over to the gate. The mountain air already felt colder; it was just that little bit higher than Little Arklow. She shone the light from her phone onto the padlock. She tried pulling it open, but it was secure.

'Why would she have come out this way anyway?' Crawford had got out of the car and was standing beside her. High above the black shape of the mountains the moon was almost full, the shadows of the trees dense around them. 'The tourists all go down Glen Affric; that's the place for sightseeing.'

'What if she wasn't sightseeing?' Monica said, and she lifted her head to gaze at the road beyond the gate. Smooth and black in the moonlight. So alluring to someone who wanted to drive fast.

'What was—' Crawford stopped. 'She was driving an M4.' As if it was suddenly the most obvious thing in the world. 'She wanted somewhere to race. This road goes all the way through to the west coast. Like the one in her message.'

'There should be a set of bolt cutters in the boot of the car,' Monica said, still gazing at the black road. 'Can you get them?'

Chapter 75

Annabelle forced herself to turn and began hobbling down the tunnel. She was uncoordinated and felt much slower than when she'd practised with the crutches in the cell. Twice she almost fell. Any second the door would swing open, and the Doctor would see her straight away. He would walk quickly towards her, faster than she could move. If she was lucky he'd inject her so she was asleep when he took her arms. *If* she was lucky . . . because he'd see what she'd done to Marcus. This time he might make her watch.

The thought was too much. She lost concentration for a moment; the crutches tangled, and she landed hard on her side. She jerked her head back over her shoulder. Not even registering the pain where her hip had smacked the ground. He still hadn't opened the door. 'Please, please, please,' she whispered under her breath. Willing some magical force to keep the door closed as she scrabbled frantically for the crutches. It was hopeless though. It would take her ages to make it far enough down the tunnel to where he couldn't see her. The tears stung her eyes as she finally heard the metal handle clank. *He'll see you. Use those tools on you.*

Her eyes fell on a door in the side of the tunnel. She'd already passed the bathroom and the locked door that led to St Magnus's Chamber. This was Scott's old room, the one she'd heard the screaming from. She'd completely forgotten about finding him. It was only closed by a bolt, the same as her room.

Over her shoulder she could hear the top door creaking open now. Horrified, she looked back. He was there. Clearly illuminated under the electric lights, he was crouching over something in the open doorway.

Hardly daring to breathe, Annabelle pulled herself towards the door. Slid the bolt back as quietly as she could, pushed the door open and crawled into the dark space inside.

Chapter 76

After twenty minutes of driving they emerged from the birch forest. The valley opened out ahead of them, cast in archaic shades of grey by the bright moonlight.

'Different world out here.' Crawford's voice was tight. He sounded genuinely disturbed by the eerie landscape. 'You really think the Slates might live down here?'

Monica scanned the wide horizon. He had a point. There were no signs of life, no house lights, no cars. In the distance she could make out the shape of a black wall blocking the valley, a string of lights running along the top of it. She realised it was a dam. Tonight the huge dark structure seemed to carry a mythical, nightmarish quality. And the story came back to her: the madman running amok in the tunnels, deep under the mountain.

She shivered and gripped the steering wheel a little tighter as they continued down the road. Crawford kept up a commentary on the status of his mobile phone reception: 'Still one bar, but it keeps cutting out. Oh, two bars now.' As if this fragile link to the civilised world buffered him against the deep unease the landscape seemed to evoke in him. She reached to hit Play on the stereo, thinking music might ease the tension, but the sound of 'If I Had a Heart' filled the car again. *Not exactly relaxing.* The road had become a long straight. Monica glanced down at the stereo. Glanced up again. The tarmac stretched like a black canal ahead of them. A single large tree off to the left-hand side.

'Was that . . .' Crawford's voice died away.

Monica eased off the throttle a little and hit the Mode button. Fever Ray was replaced by jazz music – cheesy, but more upbeat at least.

'What is it?' She lifted her head as they passed the tree.

'It's nothing.'

'Do you want me to stop?'

'No, it's fine.'

For another five minutes neither of them spoke. Each scanning the hills off to either side as they drew closer to the dam. The road had started to wind up the right side of the valley, climbing towards the top of the dam. They had been on the road for almost half an hour now and still seen no sign of life. What were the chances they would just stumble on some evidence that would lead them to Annabelle in a valley this size? The idea that the Slates even lived down here was fanciful in itself.

The dam triggered an idea though. 'Can you call Fisher? Ask him to find out who owns the dam.'

'You think it could be a link to Sinclair?' Crawford reached for his phone, but swore in frustration. 'Reception's cut out again.'

Up ahead the road curved to the right then straightened and went left over the top of the dam. Monica stopped the car. There was a gate blocking the road. She got out and went to inspect it. It was six feet high and closed with a heavy-duty pin code lock. There was no chance of getting through it with a bolt cutter, Monica decided. Even if she was minded to cause hundreds more pounds' worth of damage on what felt increasingly like a misguided hunch.

She glanced up and down the dark valley, looking for some

little spark of light, but there was nothing save the bright lights of the dam. No sign of human habitation.

'Come on.' She turned to Crawford, who was standing beside her hugging himself against the cold. 'We're wasting our time out here.'

Chapter 77

With her heart almost between her teeth, Annabelle dragged the crutches into the room and pushed the door closed behind her. It was pitch-black.

The sound of the door at the top of the tunnel clanking shut carried down the corridor to her. Followed by the noise of the bolts being drawn shut. A moment later the Doctor's footsteps echoed off the concrete, moving slowly down the tunnel towards Annabelle's room. Where he'd find Marcus's body . . .

A sound broke Annabelle's chain of thought. A noise from behind her, like an arm sweeping softly across the covers on a bed.

She froze, shoulders hunched. The terrifying thought came to her: *It's Grandad Slate. He's been waiting here for you. He knows what you did to Marcus.* With a shaking hand Annabelle felt for the torch that she'd slung round her neck. *Or was it . . . ?*

'Scott?'

The sound came again. This time followed by a faint moan. Somehow Annabelle forced herself to turn and, feeling like she was deep inside a nightmare, she clicked Marcus's torch on.

Chapter 78

They drove silently back down the glen towards Little Arklow and Inverness, Monica's brain rattling back over the facts of the case, still trying to find a clue in the mix. Something that would somehow help them find Annabelle. They only spoke once, when they hit a spot with good mobile reception and Crawford got Monica to pull over so he could call Fisher.

Crawford's phone pinged. 'From Fisher,' he said as he opened the message to read it.

Monica glanced over, hoping it would be good news: *It's Annabelle, she's alive.*

' "Glen Turrit hydroelectric dam. Opened in 1956, earliest wholly private power station," ' Crawford read. 'Why does he have to include so much . . .' he muttered as he read further down the message. ' "Originally funded by a group of investors. In 1980 a fifty per cent stake in the company was purchased by Sinclair Enterprises." '

Monica glanced over to him again and their eyes met. 'So what? Sebastian Sinclair came here to visit the dam?'

'Watch!'

The stag had wandered from the moorland onto the road. For a second it stared back at Monica as she stepped on the brake. Adrenaline flooded her system, and time seemed to slow down as she took in the beast's brown eyes. The white tint to its brown fur. The car juddered to a stop, and the stag looked at them a moment longer then lumbered on its way.

'Jesus.' Monica let out a sigh and felt the moment of tension drop from her body. 'Are you OK?' She realised that she had placed her left hand on Crawford's chest when she'd thought they were about to crash. As if that would have made any difference had a 250-pound stag come through the windscreen.

He didn't reply.

'Crawford?' She removed her hand from his chest and turned to look at him. He was staring straight ahead, as if transfixed.

Without replying he unbuckled his seat belt and got out of the car. In front of them a single oak tree was illuminated in the headlamps of the Volvo. It was standing in the middle of the valley, alone among acres of wild grass.

'What is it?'

But Crawford was already jogging over to it.

'I saw it in the headlights,' he shouted back.

'What—' The question stopped in her throat when she saw what he was pointing at.

A section of the thick, folded oak bark had been stripped away. On the exposed brown wood behind was a smear of blue paint.

'Looks fresh,' Crawford called.

Monica came to stand beside him. She remembered the BMW at the garage. The front concertinaed like a crushed can of Coke. She glanced around, took in the deep gouges cut through the grass, a smattering of glass fragments.

'So someone found her here, took her?'

'That, or they caused her to crash somehow,' Monica replied. She heard the breath catch in Crawford's throat. 'What is it?'

He was looking warily around at the shadowy spaces surrounding them.

'I thought I saw something just here. On the way up,' he whispered. 'A light by the road. For a second I thought it was a torch.' Together they glanced around the wide darkness. Anyone could have been there, watching from a fold in the terrain.

'Do you have reception?'

Crawford leaned over, jabbing at his phone. 'It's dropped out again.'

Monica looked at her own screen: 'No Signal'.

'Should we drive back to Little Arklow?' As Crawford was saying this, Monica caught sight of a light in the distance. The flash of a torch in among a copse of trees beneath the dam.

'Did you see that?' But before Crawford could turn to look it was gone. Monica stared into the darkness, willing the light to reappear. Could Annabelle really be here? Alone and praying someone would rescue her?

Chapter 79

The weak light from the torch showed a low metal-framed bed. There was a body lying on it. Annabelle clamped a hand over her mouth to stifle the screams that had risen from the pit of her stomach. Illuminated by the yellow light, she saw both of its legs had been taken all the way back close to the hip joint. The right arm was gone, and all that remained of the left was the part from the shoulder to the elbow. Annabelle couldn't move. Her skin crawled with terror. Here was calamity. Annabelle stared, hand glued over her mouth. She could see pubic hair, a penis and testicles. The man gestured to her with what remained of his arm. He couldn't speak. *Had his tongue been removed?* There were marks and rough black stitches all over his body. She caught the smell now too. Blood and fresh meat.

He made a gurgling sound. Annabelle felt her stomach turn but forced herself to keep looking. After a moment she understood and made herself crawl closer. He was tied around the waist, a length of blue cord digging into his belly.

He made the sound again, and despite her own fear Annabelle moved closer still. She took what was left of the man in her arms and held him to her chest. 'It's OK, Scott,' she whispered in his ear. She could hear the terror in her own voice. 'I'll get help. Don't worry. Everything's going to be OK.'

Chapter 80

After pulling on a protective vest and insisting Crawford did the same Monica carefully turned the car on the single-track road, aware that if she went too far off the side they would end up stuck in the ditch.

'It's searching again . . .' Crawford was staring at his phone.

She dipped the headlights and began to drive slowly back towards the dam. Towards the copse of trees where she had glimpsed the light. Staring into those dark shadows, images of Gall's and Sinclair's mutilated bodies came drifting into her mind. She imagined them hovering there among the trees somehow, the light coming from candles in their open dead mouths. She blinked the image away, but the memory of those bodies made her question what she was doing. Was she walking into a trap? She glanced at Crawford by her side as he tried again to put a call through to headquarters, then towards the black mass of the dam.

If there was a chance Annabelle was here they had to at least check it out. She knew Crawford would feel the same without even having to ask him.

'Stop! I've got reception.' They were on a slight rise in the road. Monica squeezed the brakes.

In the close confines of the car she could hear the sound of a phone ringing from Crawford's earpiece. 'Fisher?' The call must have dropped out because Crawford swore then brought the phone down to stare at the screen. 'I'll text instead.'

Monica dug for her own phone and opened an app that gave a precise map coordinate regardless of mobile coverage. The app took a moment to load before the numbers appeared onscreen. She read them out to Crawford, who nodded as he was typing. She watched as he hit Send. The green bar sliding along above the message as it uploaded.

Monica glanced again towards the dam. The forest in front of it was black and foreboding. A light flickered among the trees. She watched, almost expecting it to disappear, but it remained as a glow, muted by the trees. She killed the Volvo's headlights completely.

'Could it really be her?' Crawford had spotted it too and was leaning forward in his seat, face close to the windscreen. 'All the way out here . . .'

Monica lifted the clutch and allowed the car to roll down the other side of the rise. Eyes fixed on the light.

'It's someone. We have to find out who.'

Chapter 81

Annabelle held Scott in her arms. In the tunnel outside she could still hear the Doctor's footsteps coming closer as he approached her cell. Finally he stopped and she pictured those vacant eyes as he looked at the closed door. Perhaps wondering why the door wasn't propped open like it usually was when Marcus was inside.

'You have to trust me,' Annabelle whispered into Scott's ear. 'I'll come back for you.'

She let go of him and crawled back to the door. After an excruciating moment a squeaking sound echoed down to her. *He's opening the door. He'll see Marcus now.* Hardly daring to breathe, she reached up and pulled the door to Scott's room open. Willing it to stay silent as she scrabbled with her other hand for the crutches.

Agonisingly slowly she stood up on her one leg, the pain beginning to pulse harder in her stump, pushed her arms through the cuffs on the crutches and gripped the handles. Finally she bit her lip and stepped out into the tunnel. *He's standing there above you, waiting for you to come out.*

She forced herself to look up the slope. The tunnel was empty. Annabelle stared up at the top door. Beyond was the outside world. The road south to her flat, to Miss Albright and Mr Pepper. She could get help for Scott. For a moment she even thought about trying to sneak past the Doctor.

You have to go deeper. A strange new voice inside her head interrupted her thoughts. *You have to go down into those tunnels.* The dread was alive in her veins, but for some reason she knew immediately that she had to listen. As quickly as she could, Annabelle turned and hobbled down the tunnel. Into the belly of the mountain.

Chapter 82

As Monica and Crawford drew slowly closer, the light danced among the trees like a will-o'-the-wisp. A supernatural flicker from the fairy world in that strange landscape. Caledonian pines were mixed in with the dense birch, usually their shapes made Monica think of Japan somehow. In this place a horror seemed to lurk among their body-like trunks and arm-like branches.

She shook her head at the idea and peered into the gloom. Slowly she made out shapes in the moonlight, saw that as the road turned to the right there was a lay-by off to the left, the same direction as the light. Impulsively she pulled the steering wheel, feeling her too-small vest ride up uncomfortably under her chin as the car bumped blindly onto the uneven ground. She bit her lip and rolled the car forward carefully, waiting for a wheel to crunch into a pothole at any moment.

The tension rose up her back as the light ahead of them continued to flicker, much closer now. The lay-by actually led to a rough track. Running parallel with the dam towards the mountain slopes on the left of the valley. Stone chips skipped under the car tyres as she drove uphill towards the light flitting among the trees directly ahead of them.

'It's still there,' Crawford whispered beside her. Obviously wanting a moment of human connection in this lonely place. 'Should we stop here? Investigate on foot?' Before they could even discuss it, the light clicked off. The forest returned to darkness and the chalk light of the moon.

Monica swore under her breath, glancing at the trees on either side of the car. Could they really be heading into a trap? She swore again and drove further up the track, her body tensed as if for a sudden impact.

The shape was black. It was in the middle of the track, directly ahead of them. Monica pressed the brake. Screwing up her eyes in an attempt to make out what she was looking at. If it was even there?

'Are you seeing that, Crawford?'

She sensed rather than saw him nodding beside her. Her hand hovered over the headlight switch. She blinked, tilted her head to better make out the edges of the shape in the fractured moonlight.

'Is that . . .' She shifted the gearstick to neutral and pulled on the handbrake then slowly opened her door. Feeling the chill of the night as she got out. The shape was about twenty feet in front of the car. Was it human?

'Annabelle?' Monica pushed the car door gently closed behind her, then took a step towards the figure.

Chapter 83

Annabelle made her way down the tunnel, praying the Doctor would stay in the cell with Marcus for just a few minutes longer. Her movements cast long dark shadows on the opposite wall. The horror of what they'd done to Scott had almost fractured her mind: her every fear about the world had been confirmed. It really was hell, and its demons were called humans.

She didn't even notice the pain as the cuffs and handles of the crutches pounded at her arms and hands. Descending the slope quickly was awkward though. In her haste Annabelle never noticed the patch of damp tarmac. Her foot slipped. Reflexively she went to steady herself on a leg that wasn't there, fell and landed hard on her shoulder, knocking the air from her lungs. She swore, already reaching for the crutches because she had to keep moving.

When she raised her head Annabelle realised she had rolled over during the fall. She was facing back up the slope to where the Doctor was now standing, watching her. He was in the middle of the tunnel with his long arms hanging loosely by his sides. His legs spread wide in a spidery stance. Almost crouched as if ready to sprint at her. He wasn't more than two hundred feet away. She knew immediately there was no escape. The Doctor began to move towards her using a strange shuffling motion. It was fast and unlike anything she'd seen before. In what seemed like seconds he was passing the door to St Magnus's

Chamber, then Scott's room. This time his feet made no sound. As if he'd only been playing when he made those clunky steps on the tarmac. Now he was halfway to her. Annabelle realised he was carrying a stubby saw in his right hand. The floor seemed to shift. She screwed her eyes tight shut and began to pray.

Chapter 84

'Annabelle? Is that you?' Monica glanced into the shadowy woods on either side of the track as she moved closer. Feeling the velvet night all around. The stones shifted under the soles of her boots. 'We're here to help.'

She stepped closer again and squinted. The person's hair was long, longer than Annabelle's had looked in the Instagram picture. It looked lighter too. She took another step and realised that the figure was small – a child surely? She moved even closer. The child had long blonde hair. It was a little girl. Despite the cold she was dressed in just a sweatshirt. For a second she imagined it was Lucy, alone and frightened out here. Forgetting any caution, Monica stooped to take the child in her arms.

'It's OK, you're safe,' she whispered. Breathing in the slightly mossy smell of the forest that clung to the girl's hair. She was freezing and seemed to weigh nothing. Monica held her tight, anticipating a screaming struggle, but the girl went limp.

She opened the back door, slid the child onto the seat and bundled a tartan travel rug over her before climbing into the driver's seat herself.

Crawford's eyes mirrored her own thoughts: *What the fuck?* He was talking on the phone. 'I sent the coordinates before . . .'

Monica put the heating up high and turned to look properly at the little girl in the back. She was pretty, wearing a dirty old sweatshirt with *FRANCE 1998* printed on it in block capitals with a Scottish saltire background. Grubby hands folded in her lap, smears of grime across her cheeks. Monica resisted a motherly urge to dig in the glove compartment and start cleaning the girl's face with a wet wipe. Instead she smiled. 'What are you doing out here? Are your mummy or daddy nearby?'

The girl didn't seem to hear.

'My name's Monica. This is Crawford. Do you live near here?'

'You're big,' the girl whispered, finally. Still staring straight ahead and refusing all eye contact. 'You'd have a lot of bones to make soup with.'

Monica leaned in to the girl, convinced that she'd misheard. 'What—'

'Are you here to collect Annabelle?' the girl said, staring down at her small hands. Monica froze. 'She's not very well, and we've been looking after her. She's with my uncle and Marcus, the weird-looking one. Would you like me to show you where they are?'

Chapter 85

When Annabelle's eyes flicked open the Doctor was crouched into a squat. Stock-still, watching her from thirty feet away. So close that she could see the dark stains on his lab coat. Holding the stubby saw. For some reason he'd removed his surgical mask, and he was smiling at her.

Annabelle began to hyperventilate. His crooked smile widened at the sound of her gasps. His dark grey eyes locked on to hers. She understood then that he was enjoying himself. He wanted to take his time.

Slowly she reached for the crutches, never taking her eyes from his. Somehow she managed to fit them back onto her arms. Stood up on her remaining foot, turned and began to make her way down towards the darkness that lay at the end of the tunnel.

She hobbled along for what seemed like an age, always expecting the Doctor's hand to land on her shoulder, to pull her to the ground and begin cutting her there and then. Finally she couldn't bear it and had to glance back. There was no sign of him, and she noticed that the lights on the wall were more widely spaced and the tunnel had levelled off, was almost flat now. *He must still be up there, waiting. He wants you to go into the tunnels. He wants to catch you down there like Grandad Slate caught those people.* Annabelle's hand went to the pocket of her tracksuit bottoms, remembering Scott's knife for the first time.

It was still there. Maybe she could stab the Doctor in the narrow tunnels? Maybe there was a chance? Before she could expand on the thought a noise started. Up the tunnel. A slapping sound. His footsteps on the tarmac were loud again. He wanted her to know he was coming. He wanted her to play his game.

Chapter 86

Monica couldn't quite believe what the kid had just said. Offering to take them to Annabelle?!

'Where are they?' Monica said slowly. The girl looked back at her for a second and seemed about to speak, but then she was moving. She lunged for the door handle. In a second it was open and the girl was running. Monica was quickly out of the car herself, but the child had cut off into the trees and was immediately lost in the dark undergrowth.

Monica had forgotten the child lock. *Fucking hell! How could you be so stupid?*

'Fisher has spoken to Niall Souter. The armed response unit's on its way,' Crawford said softly. He was standing beside her now, staring into the forest.

'If she gets to Annabelle first they might kill her. How long?' she asked, already knowing the answer: *Too long.*

'As fast as possible, but it'll be at least thirty minutes.'

Monica swore again.

'Where could . . .' She glanced around as she was speaking and caught the edge of a shape through the trees. She wiped a hand over her face and moved further up the track. It was a building. Right beside the dam, so close that the glare of the floodlights on the road above made it difficult to see. 'I think we've found the Slates.'

Without speaking they began to move towards it, hugging

the cover of the trees. As they drew closer they could better make out the building. It was an architectural mess, built in ramshackle sections from a variety of materials. At least three storeys high, heaped up like it might collapse at any minute.

A fresh thrill of horror ran down Monica's neck when she spotted the flag. Hanging limp above the highest window, a yellow-and-red lion rampant. Annabelle had mentioned such a flag in her desperate text message to Fisher.

'She's here, I'm sure of it,' Monica whispered to Crawford.

He nodded, the sound of his breathing close by her side as they moved closer still. There was no sign of the little girl. The place was eerily quiet. Monica could see now that the far end of the house actually butted up against the side of the dam like a cancerous growth.

'Do you think we should split up?' Crawford's hesitant whisper broke through her thoughts. 'Cover more ground?'

'No. We definitely shouldn't.' A light glowed from one of the windows at the very top of the house. She checked around again. It was unclear which entrance to the house was their best bet. There were at least four possibilities to choose from, each door looking like it had been salvaged from a rubbish dump. A cast-iron sign hung above one of them: SLATES.

'Come on.'

They crossed the few feet of bare ground from the track to the door beneath the sign. Monica pushed on it and it swung open.

'Here.' Crawford passed the torch he'd taken from the boot of the car to Monica. She clicked it on. The light picked out a corridor that was almost impassable, stacked with an assortment of objects. Heaps of old books and magazines, cardboard and wooden boxes, car parts, even an old fridge freezer half buried among the mess. The place stank of mould and the ammonia of cat's piss. At the end of the corridor there was a staircase. Monica moved carefully towards it. From deeper in the house she heard music. After a moment she realised that, of all things, it was 'Agadoo' by Black Lace.

'For Christ's sake.'

'Get the disco started,' Crawford muttered, trying for some dark bravado.

Monica forced a smile and stepped closer to the staircase, glanced down at the stained carpet, her feet sticking to it every time she planted a shoe, the smells of fried meat and cigarette smoke rising from it. There was a glow at the top of the stairs. Monica moved towards it, glancing back to check that Crawford was still behind her. The music was louder as she reached the first-floor landing. Half expecting an ambush, the sound of gunfire at any moment. And then Lucy would be . . . what? An orphan? Just as good as. Monica forced the thought away into a deep dark hole. Whatever the personal cost, she couldn't abandon Annabelle. Instead she needlessly checked she was still wearing her protective vest and felt behind her to check Crawford had his on too.

She could hear the ridiculous lyrics now – about pushing pineapples, shaking trees. They lent an utterly surreal atmosphere to the situation. A strange image from *Top of The Pops* flashed into her head. Gary Glitter and Jimmy Savile on stage, in glittery outfits. She shook her head and squeezed past a load of tea chests stacked down one side of the landing.

'You think the kid ran up here?'

Monica shook her head: *I don't know.* She kept on though, up the next flight of stairs. These were narrower and ended at a door. She could see random coloured lights flashing from under it. Without giving herself a chance to think, she moved quickly up the remaining steps to the door and grabbed for the handle.

Chapter 87

Annabelle kept moving. The idea that the Doctor was enjoying her terror, was somehow feeding off it, was horrific, but if all those tunnels Marcus had told her about really existed, maybe she could hide from him? Maybe she could even escape and get someone to help Scott?

In her panic she didn't realise at first that the tarmac beneath her foot had been replaced by roughly hewn rock. The ceiling was much lower too, so low she could have stretched to touch it. And up ahead tunnels branched off the main route. Dark entrances cut in the rock. Marcus hadn't just been trying to frighten her; these were the beginnings of the old passages. She could see that further down the line of electric lights finally ran out. Beyond that there was only blackness.

Down here the tunnel seemed drier, and so silent. As if she could feel all the weight of the mountains above, pushing her down. Deep underground where any kind of thing could be hiding. Waiting for decades to whisper into the ear of someone. Lost and alone in such a lonely place.

Then she heard the sound of feet again. The Doctor, much closer now. She hesitated for a moment then forced herself to step past the very last of the electric lights into the darkness. She fumbled with the torch. The light was swallowed in the dark, barely illuminating more than a couple of feet in front of her, but she could see the tunnel had become narrower and lower. She could have touched both walls at the same time now and the roof was only inches above her head. She felt the ache in her arms from the crutches, the pain in her wounded leg finally registering even through the adrenaline. In the faint light from the torch she could see a split in the passageway. Both tunnels seemed of equal size. Which to take?

This is the labyrinth. This is where Grandad Slate ate those men. An impulse told her to go left. She heard the Doctor's heavy feet echo off the rock behind her. She knew he was enjoying every moment of this slow chase. She bit her tongue and chose the right-hand tunnel.

Chapter 88

Monica turned the handle and pushed the door. It scraped across carpet. She held her breath and stepped into the room. It was long and narrow. Disco lights flashed from the ceiling, the music blared. The people were dark shapes against the flashing lights. They seemed completely unaware of her presence. Without turning her head Monica felt at the side of the door. Her fingers settled on a switch and she flicked the light on.

Four people turned towards her simultaneously. Startled by the interruption. She glanced between them. Her eyes settled on the familiar face of Karen Sinclair first. The same anachronistic Princess Diana hairstyle as when they'd interviewed her just days before. She was sitting on an armchair among piles of tattered fabrics. Beside her, face pushed into Karen's side, was the little girl. In the middle of the floor, staring dumbly at Monica, was a woman. It was hard to gauge her age, but Monica guessed she was in her early sixties. She had grey hair and was wearing a plaid skirt and a stained beige cardigan. Behind her was a man. An inch or two shorter than Monica but wider, with a heavy stomach sagging over the top of a blue-and-red kilt. The kilt was stained with splashes of filth down the front, likewise his red tracksuit top. Beside him was a large stereo system with a mountain of records and CDs heaped around it.

The older of the women stared at Monica, eyes narrowed. Finally she seemed to make a decision and turned to the man, shouting something. His wide face was splattered with acne and he wore a gormless expression. Monica could see flecks of white spittle at the corners of his mouth. Finally he seemed to understand because he reached out a hand, and mercifully the music stopped.

The woman glared at Monica, then her thin lips turned up in a grin. Monica stared back but didn't smile.

'Who'll you be then?' the woman asked.

Monica glanced around the room for a second time, checking for weapons. The family seemed to be unarmed though and genuinely surprised by the appearance of two visitors.

'I'm here for Annabelle.' She watched the woman's face for cracks in that smiling facade.

'Annabelle,' the woman repeated dumbly. Then she started to laugh. 'It won't be hard to find her, will it, Lily?' She turned to the little girl, who was now watching Monica suspiciously. 'Lily, show this lady where Annabelle is.' The girl didn't move. 'Come on, show her.' There was a malicious edge to her voice now.

Monica's eyes flickered between them. 'You know where Annabelle Whittaker is?'

The girl pushed her face into Karen's side.

'Come on, tell the lady,' the woman repeated. The little girl shook her head. 'Not got anything to say, have you?'

The woman stepped towards Monica. Up close there were dark grey circles under her cold eyes. Her nose was large and sharp as a knife, hair hanging around her face in scraggly bunches.

'Lily has problems with her wee heedie, she likes to make up wee stories to herself. Don't you, Lily?' The woman turned to the child, then back to Monica. 'She's been talking about poor Annabelle since we heard about her being missing on the radio.'

336

'I'm sorry, what's your name?' Monica asked, to buy a moment to think as much as anything.

'Slate,' the woman said. 'Marjory Slate, but everyone calls me Granny. And I must say, I'm surprised to see you and your wee man here.' She nodded up at Monica then over to Crawford. 'Up here at this time of the night. You maybe shouldn't have come here. Not without getting some permission. It's not always a safe place.'

'Why not?' Monica said as the woman stared straight up at her.

'Oh, there are things that happen out in that glen. Tinks who come in and steal things. Strange lights sometimes. We seal the road over at nights. It's a private road, you see. It's a wonder you made it up here.' The woman smiled and ran her thick grey tongue quickly over yellowing teeth. 'And we've more family coming over soon.'

Chapter 89

The passageway became narrower and narrower. Annabelle moved along as quickly as she could. Panic rising. She was sure she could hear the Doctor's breathing growing nearer. The smells of blood and oil running ahead of him like a fog. Her shoulder hit the rock wall and knocked her off balance. Instinctively she tried again to steady herself with her missing foot and toppled over. This time her head met the stone of the tunnel wall. A bright light flashed behind her eyes. Pins and needles ran all the way down her neck to her chest. She tried to get back up, but the floor seemed to tilt away at a steep angle. She slumped forward, her leg and arms tangled with the crutches.

The Doctor's slow slapping footsteps filled the tunnel. Desperately Annabelle kicked the crutches away and dragged herself on. The torch bounced around her neck, sending yellow beams dancing against the walls.

Her shoulders brushed either side of the tunnel as she crawled. There was a throbbing heat at the side of her head, something running down her face. She realised it was blood and for a second she wondered how bad the injury was. *As if it matters. He's going to catch you. Then he's going to cut you up.*

She had no choice but to keep moving. The dust from the floor was in her mouth and nose, in her eyes, the torch as good as useless now as she crawled awkwardly on her belly.

Annabelle felt fingers close loosely around her ankle. She

screamed and kicked free. A strange sound followed her down the tunnel. It took her a moment to realise that it was laughter. He was enjoying this. Every moment of it. Through the waves of terror she forced herself on. Focusing on each movement of her hands, each time her leg slid forward. She only realised how tight the tunnel had become when she felt the walls on both sides. Touching her shoulders. Her body beginning to fill the narrow space, trapping her. Somehow she understood she needed to tilt her shoulders to the side. More sideways than straight ahead now. The tunnel walls were so close on either side of her face that she could taste the dry rock. She could hear her own heaving breath, the scrabbling sound as he followed.

'Stop it!' Annabelle screamed. 'Leave me alone!'

Her head hit the roof. The tunnel was more like a pipe now. Low and narrow. She screamed again. Wedged in that deep dark hole. So tight she couldn't move. The horror of the place, crushed and hyperventilating. Buried alive under mountains.

Chapter 90

Marjory Slate's eyes were cold. Monica repeated the woman's words back to her. 'You've got more family coming?'

'They'll be along soon. Don't worry about that.'

Monica cleared her throat, willing Niall Souter and his armed response team to arrive. 'We're going to need to have a look around. In case you hadn't worked it out for yourself, we're police.' She pulled her warrant card from her pocket and held it out.

Slate ignored the ID and continued to stare at Monica. 'There's no police up here,' she said finally with a crooked smile. 'This is private land.' She edged a little closer to Monica. 'And I don't think you should be up here.' Her eyes flickered to Crawford and back. 'I don't think either of you should be up here.'

For long moments their eyes stayed locked together. The room was silent, the coloured lights flickered over the carpeted floor, over the walls. Monica could hear the man's heavy breathing from beside the stereo.

Slowly Marjory Slate turned round to the man. 'I think these two—'

A distant noise stopped her. From far down the valley, the sound of a siren.

Chapter 91

Annabelle tried again to wriggle forward, but her shoulder was now locked up tight against the rock. She stretched her arms out ahead of her to try and squeeze through. She was able to move forward by a few inches. Her face scraped the dry rock, hot blood from her head wound ran down her neck. She pushed again, then tried to bring her arms back past her head to lever herself forward, but they were jammed, stuck out ahead of her. Lodged tight with no way forward or back. Fresh panic juddered over her in claustrophobic waves. She tried to scream, but her diaphragm was compressed, and the sound came out as a gasp. Instinctively she tried to stand, felt her head and back pressed tight against the rock. Her chest could barely expand as she panted in terror, her mind threatening to break apart.

You have to slow down, you have to breathe gently. Somehow she managed to do what the voice said. *Try tilting your head to the side.* Annabelle did as she was told, and there was a fraction of an inch of give. She was able to slide her arms back by an inch then brace her hands against the tunnel walls to slide her hips forward along the floor.

After another minute of desperate wriggling the tunnel began to open out slightly. Annabelle found she could move more freely. She reached down for the torch, suddenly fearful that it had broken. Thankfully the light shone up in her face and she felt a moment of pure relief. She realised that there had been no sound from the Doctor behind her for a few minutes. *Maybe he went down a different tunnel?* She paused, listening carefully, still trying to slow her breathing. Maybe she could escape after all? Maybe she could wait here for a while then creep back to the surface? For the first time she actually started to believe it.

It was then she felt the Doctor's hand close around her ankle again. This time his grip was solid as iron. No matter how hard she screamed and kicked, Annabelle couldn't break free.

Chapter 92

The sirens drew closer down the long glen. Monica took a breath and felt a fraction of the tension ebb from her body. It seemed that whatever else happened, at least she and Crawford weren't going to be killed in this lonely place. Not tonight. She sensed that it had been close; she'd seen the look in Marjory Slate's eyes. Monica knew murderousness. She'd spent her life around it. And she was sure the woman in front of her had too. If she and Crawford had come to that door on a different night. A night when they were unsuspecting, unguarded . . .

'Where's Annabelle?' Monica resisted the urge to grip Marjory Slate's neck and pull her close. To lean forward and grab her and find a way to make her speak. 'Where is she?'

The woman stared back into Monica's eyes. The sirens drew ever closer. 'Well, I just hope they find her,' she replied finally. A smile flickered around her eyes. 'But if you ask me, I don't think they ever will.'

'Why do you say that?'

'Oh, once they're gone a few days, these kinds of girls don't ever come back. Better to forget about them. Better to leave them in peace.'

The sirens screamed outside. The blue lights skipped around the room, joining the flashing colours of the disco lights. Crawford shouted something over the din and ran downstairs.

Monica's eyes didn't move from Marjory Slate's. She knew Annabelle was close. And that they would never find her.

Monica heard a muffled sob. Karen Sinclair, curled up on the chair, had a hand over her face. The little girl, Lily, was beside her, face pushed into her side.

'Karen feels for the girl. Imagines what it would be like it was her wee one,' Slate whispered with just the shadow of amusement in her voice. 'All we have is family, isn't it? We lost my husband just last year. Things have been harder since then.'

Monica could hear other sounds under the sirens now. Shouts from the armed response team outside. They would search the house and they would find no trace of Annabelle. She was sure of it, could read it right there in Slate's eyes. Monica felt her anger flicker and rise.

'Where is she?' Outrage crept into her voice, and Slate's smile grew perceptibly wider. Taking pleasure in the detective's impotent rage. Monica felt her blood stirring. *One of Monica's turns*, in her mum's parlance. She pushed both her hands down into her coat pockets. Not quite trusting what she might do with them.

'You're the detective,' Slate said finally. Taking a step away from Monica as the shouts of the armed response team carried up the stairs. 'Shouldn't that be your job, *detecting* her?'

Monica wished she could have just a minute alone in a room with her. Karen Slate let out another little sob and Monica turned to look. Tried to catch her eye, appeal to the mother in her, but she now had both hands over her face. Lily was still beside her. The little girl was young, maybe just a couple of years older than Lucy, or small for her age. Monica stepped away from Marjory Slate, walked over and crouched beside the girl.

'You said you were going to take me to Annabelle. Where is she?' she asked quietly. Lily kept her face in Karen's side, didn't reply. 'You need to show me where Annabelle is.' Monica reached for the girl, grabbed her by the waist and hoisted her up onto her hip. In one movement she turned and started out of the room.

'Marcus is away!' Marjory Slate shouted, reaching for Monica's elbow. 'It was all in her head!'

Monica shrugged her off and hurried down the flights of stairs. 'Leave her alone!' Marjory Slate was shouting after her. 'She's not yours, she's mine!'

Monica emerged into the darkness of the early morning. She squeezed Lily tight against her chest, caught the mossy smell of the forest from the little girl's hair.

'Where's Annabelle?' she whispered. Feeling the heat of that skinny little body against her arm. So like Lucy. 'You need to show me where she is right now. If you don't, you'll never get to see your family again. They'll take you away. They'll all go to prison and it'll be all your fault.'

She felt the kid tense.

'You need to tell me. You need to tell me now or I'll put you in that van, and they'll drive you to a police station,' Monica whispered into the kid's ear. Even as she spoke Lucy's face came to mind and with it a deep pang of instant remorse. She could feel the child's tears on her cheek. Running down her neck. Her hot breath as the little girl hyperventilated.

'She's hiding over there. She's playing a game. Hiding in the secret place.' Lily gestured to a corner of the fence that surrounded the house. Close to where the steepening hillside became a cliff face. The fence was the temporary type used around construction sites, consisting of linked panels of tube-framed metal mesh slotted into concrete-block bases.

Monica felt a hand grabbing at her arm. 'What is it? What are you doing?'

345

She glanced down at Crawford's concerned face and pushed Lily into his arms. Ignoring his shouts she ran towards the battered fencing. Monica knew from her uniformed days working at public events that the panels were secured together by small metal clamps. Only here the clamp wasn't properly tightened. She turned the bolt to loosen it further, twisted it off, then lifted one end of the panel out of its base and swung it back, then pulled the torch out of her pocket.

The path was narrow, cut through the dense undergrowth close to the cliff face. She hurried along it, ducking as branches and thorns from the brambles caught at her hair and coat. After fifty metres she could make out a bulge in the cliff face. The path skirted round it. On the other side there was a ramshackle shed. Tight up against the cliff.

'Annabelle?!' Monica shouted as she tried the handle then hammered on the locked shed door. Praying for an answering cry. There was nothing though, just voices from outside the house, carrying through the dark of the forest.

Was she in there?

It took Monica minutes to pry the wooden door open. Inside there was no sign of Annabelle, but another door. Wide and metal this time, it seemed to lead directly into the mountain. For some reason her mind served up an image of a Renaissance painting from an exhibition an old boyfriend had dragged her to see. A saint or pilgrim going down into limbo.

She shook her head at the strange recollection then turned at the sound of feet on the dirt floor behind her. Crawford stepped past and tried the handle on the door. It clanked but seemed to be bolted from the inside.

'Can you get Souter?' Monica said quietly. 'I think Annabelle's in here.'

Chapter 93

Annabelle screamed. She shook her leg as hard as she could, but it barely moved in that fist. She tried to kick out at the Doctor's fingers, momentarily forgetting her other leg was gone. What was left of her leg kicked thin air.

She screamed again and sat up. She tried to bite the hand, close her teeth on it and rip one of the fingers off, but couldn't bring her mouth close enough. Her ankle bone threatened to snap as the Doctor twisted it and began to drag her slowly back towards him. She slapped ineffectively at his hand, the light from the torch bouncing wildly.

She kicked and tried rolling to her left to lessen the pressure of his grip, felt the spasm of pain as something hard connected with her already bruised hip. Something in her pocket. It took half a second to remember Scott's knife. *Could it still be in there?* Annabelle dug in her pocket and felt the cold metal, squeezed it tight in her right hand. Teased the blade open the way she'd seen Marcus do when he was about to cut her food up. It made a clicking sound when it locked into place.

The Doctor jerked her closer and she fumbled the knife. Dropped it on the ground. He was reaching up to her waist now. She screamed and slapped madly around on the rock floor. Her fingers touched metal and she grabbed it a second time. It felt smaller in her fist than she'd imagined when she'd practised swinging it.

She sat half up. With her left hand she grabbed the Doctor's wrist on her hip. Then swung the blade. His screams filled the tunnel. She felt the knife sink into his flesh and twisted it hard to the right. There was a snapping sound. He jerked his arm away. Annabelle kicked out, and her foot connected with what she thought was his face. She twisted and crawled blindly away down the tunnel.

After a long, long time she realised that there was no sound behind her. She stopped moving and held her breath to listen. Still there was nothing, just the sound of her own breath. *The same as last time, just before he grabbed your leg.* Pain from her leg and tiredness washed over her. She was too exhausted to move any further, even if he had been only inches away in the dark. Annabelle laid her cheek down on the rock floor. And in that dark place, miles from the light of day, she somehow dropped off into a deep sleep.

Chapter 94

The angle grinder squealed then finally quietened. The first sound of a rescue effort that would become one of the most famous in Scottish police history. The officer operating the power tool stepped back from the metal door, reticence in his movements. And much later, when she recalled those tunnels, Monica sometimes wondered if he'd somehow sensed what was waiting for them behind that door. She certainly didn't, as fixated on finding Annabelle, she hurried down the tunnel. It was the smell that struck her first, the damp stone, like the vaults below a cathedral. And a medieval stink, the wretchedness of a condemned human animal.

'This is one of the hydro tunnels Fisher was talking about?'

Monica didn't reply to Crawford's question. She had already spotted the door on the left of the corridor, and despite the shouted protests of the armed officers she was heading straight towards it. It was open, and Monica saw the body on the floor, the face smeared dark with blood. *Annabelle?* She took in the shoulders, the body shape and weight of the jaw. It seemed more likely to be a man. She crouched beside the figure and felt for a pulse. 'We're going to need a helicopter evacuation.'

Monica heard Crawford relay the message.

'Marcus?' She leaned in close. A shallow breath dusted her cheek. If this was Annabelle's captor then had she escaped? She

349

raised her head to shout for the medic and her eyes landed on the wall. The words carved into it: THEYR EATING ME

Lucy's dream, the girl held captive and the monster waiting to eat her.

'Fuck! Jesus!' The words, laden with primal horror, echoed up the tunnel, immediately pushing the dream from Monica's mind and simultaneously obliterating the brief moment of hope for Annabelle. *They've found her body, of course they have. You were too late.*

Slowly Monica stood, pulled her eyes away from the hideous words on the wall as the team's medic pushed in beside her to attend to the casualty – Marcus, or Lily's unnamed uncle, presumably. She paused for a moment in the tunnel to compose herself. She glanced back into the room for a second and took in the grimy bed, the concrete walls marked with strips of glue. In that moment she hoped Annabelle had done it, hurt the man who had shut her up in there, smashed his head in somehow, gone down fighting. But then what difference would that make? If Annabelle had been cut up like those other two?

There was another door further down the tunnel. An armed officer was holding it open with the barrel of his gun. As she approached, Monica could see the shock plain on his face. A glimpse into hell that would last his lifetime.

As if in a dream she raised the torch that was still in her hand, clicked it on and wordlessly stepped past the officer. The stink was almost overwhelming. With one hand she covered her nose and mouth. In the torch beam it took a moment before she could fathom just what she was looking at. The body was naked. A man. All four of his limbs had been crudely amputated. There were several fresh scars on his torso, roughly stitched with dark thread. He had been secured with a blue cord which cut into his deathly pale stomach.

Monica felt the bile rise in her throat. The man moved. He was still alive. She let out an involuntary gasp of horror. It took every ounce of the mental strength she had to meet his eyes. The horror of his physical mutilation was nothing compared to seeing into the man's soul. Seeing the spark of intelligence there, the shame at what had been done to him. She tried to speak, to communicate something other than the utter horror and disgust coursing through her body.

'You're safe,' she managed to say. 'You're safe.' She forced herself to shrug her long coat off and covered what was left of him. She crouched down. 'You're safe now.' She touched a hand to his bare shoulder and felt the fevered heat of his skin.

'We need that helicopter right now,' she shouted to Crawford, as if she hadn't said almost the same thing less than five minutes before. There was no reply. She turned to look at where he was standing in the doorway. His hand had involuntarily gone up to his mouth and his hair seemed to be standing on end.

'It's . . . o-on its way,' he finally managed to stammer. 'It's on its way.'

Chapter 95

It was rare that Monica drank alcohol. Even rarer that she'd ever gone out to drink with a colleague, but tonight was one of those times. By the time they'd finally driven back down Glen Turrit, through Little Arklow and on to Inverness almost twenty-four hours had passed since they'd chopped the lock on that gate. It was long after Lucy's bedtime already. And after seeing the man in the room, discovering just what the Slates had done to him, she and Crawford both needed something to take the edge off. Particularly as it had quickly become apparent that Annabelle was gone. Either she was already dead, or she had escaped or been taken down into the complex of tunnels under the mountain.

After the helicopter arrived to evacuate the two casualties Monica had gone back to the waiting police cars to ask Karen Sinclair for help in finding Annabelle. Practically begged her. She'd stared blankly away as if unable to hear the woman in front of her. Finally Monica and Crawford had followed the armed response team deeper down the main corridor to where the electric lights gradually faded into gloomy infinity.

'I can't believe this is real,' Crawford had whispered from beside her. 'This place is hell.'

It wasn't a statement she felt like disputing as the darkness slowly swallowed the team. The lights became more intermittent. Eventually they ended altogether and there was only the glow of their torches. Little comfort against the darkness and their belief that someone was deep down there, terrified and desperate for help.

'Annabelle?! Annabelle!'

Their shouts were claustrophobic, fathom after fathom down. So deep down. The tunnel had become narrower, then side passages began to split off, and it became impossible to tell which way she might have gone.

'We're not finding her today, are we?' Monica had said to Souter as they'd stood together glancing between the maze of passageways arrayed ahead of them. Moments later the radio on Souter's vest crackled. He had contacted the surface, requesting expert assistance when they had begun to appreciate the extent of the tunnel system.

'I'm just off the phone to Cave Rescue.' The voice was patchy, distorted by the poor connection. 'They don't have any record of tunnelling down there, other than the main hydro excavations.'

'How long do you think it'll take them to work through all the tunnels?' Crawford's question brought Monica back to the present. A pub in Inverness at the bottom of Church Street.

Automatically she checked her phone. Frustration prickled her skin again at having to wait impotently for news on Annabelle, news on the poor man they'd found. He was still unidentified. Placed in a medically induced coma while the doctors tried to save him from the trauma of the amputations and the infections coursing through his blood. The other man, presumably Marcus Slate, was still unconscious too. Skull fractured but likely to make a full recovery in time. *Probably not in time to help us find Annabelle though*, Monica thought. Another frustration. Surely he knew what had happened to her.

And the memory inevitably led on to those words on the cell wall. *THEYR EATING ME*. Like in Lucy's dream, as if her daughter was somehow at the centre of this case in a curious way that Monica didn't understand, bound together with those dismembered bodies and Fisher's out-of-character behaviour that night at The Clach.

Instinctively it had all felt connected at the start, and turned out that in a strange way it was. *Well, Fisher's behaviour and the bodies are connected in a coincidental way through Annabelle*, her internal voice chipped in. *Probably you're simply projecting your worries about Lucy and her sleepwalking onto the case though?* It seemed a far more likely explanation than the alternative: Lucy had genuinely had a dream insight into Annabelle's plight. Monica didn't have to remind herself of what a familiar trope of fairy tales the story was.

Finally she said, 'It's out of our hands. Our job is to focus on the Slates for now. Find out who knew what. What the hell happened with Sinclair and Gall.' Word of what had been done to the man in the tunnel had inevitably leaked from Raigmore Hospital. Sparking rumours that the Slates were a family of cannibals. 'The media are going to be all over this.' Once again she felt pleased to have had DC Maria Khan on the team; she had so far proved adept at handling the swell of media interest.

Crawford took a long pull on his second bottle of lager. He'd finished his first before Monica had even touched her own vodka and orange juice.

'I still don't get it,' he said, wiping his lips with the back of his hand. 'Why leave Gall and Sinclair where they could be found?'

Monica sipped her own drink, looking around the noisy bar. The alcohol was soothing. Softening at least some of the rough edges off the long day. A day of horror mixed with the boredom of waiting for news. She glanced back at Crawford. His bright green eyes, the red stubble across his face. His hands were on the table, one on either side of his beer. For a moment she had the impulse to reach over and lay one of her hands on top of his. Maybe they could go back to his flat. What difference would one night in bed make when that day they'd already walked down into hell together?

Crawford cleared his throat. 'Can't stop thinking of her down there. Not being able to do anything ...' His voice faded. 'Fisher said that Annabelle's mum and dad are both in town now. Her dad wants to go up to the dam tomorrow. Seems to think he can take charge of the search himself ...'

'I'll speak to them in the morning.' Monica shrugged and slid her hand back across the table to her glass. *You just almost propositioned Crawford.* That would not have been a sensible idea.

'Why are you still up here?' she asked, keen to change the subject from the case. 'You could transfer to Glasgow or London, easily.'

He leaned back in his chair. 'Are you trying to get rid of me?'

'Just curious.'

'What about you? Why did you come back? You were on track for senior management in the Met, I heard.' He tilted his head to look at her. She could tell he was already a little drunk. 'You know, you could be a model.'

Monica laughed. Almost choking on the mouthful of vodka and orange she'd just taken. Sensing the hysteria that proximity to death seemed to encourage. Sex, anger, laughter – anything to keep the reaper at bay.

'What?' Crawford screwed his forehead up. 'You're statuesque. It was compliment.'

'You're funny, Crawford.' She finished her drink and stood up to leave, but lingered for a second, glancing around the bar. The sounds of casual drunken conversation were a comforting reminder of normality. 'Don't stay out too late; we've got a world of shit coming our way tomorrow.'

Chapter 96

According to the faded birth certificate that the investigating team had recovered from the house, Marjory 'Granny' Slate was born Marjory Foster on Thursday 5 May 1938. Despite her unkempt appearance, she looked at least two decades younger than her eighty years when she sat down opposite Monica and Crawford in the interview room at Inverness police headquarters.

Monica had the opportunity to take her in more closely this time. Her untidy grey hair hung around her face in ropey straggles. The whites of her eyes had a yellowish tinge to them, but when their eyes met Monica could see her defiance from the previous night remained. There was a slight smirk at one corner of her mouth, but her face was otherwise expressionless.

'We just want to clear a few things up,' Monica said finally. 'Can you tell us who the permanent residents of your house in Glen Turrit are?'

She stared silently back.

'We know there's yourself, Marcus, Hamish, Lily and Karen there at the moment. But Lily mentioned someone else – her uncle. Is that Doc? We haven't found any trace of him so far.' Despite working through the day and night the Cave Rescue team were making slow progress. Reporting that many of the small tunnels were dug into loose rock, making them extremely unstable and dangerous. The team of rescuers had to work on the assumption that Annabelle's captor, presumably 'Doc' Slate, might also be down there. This meant having armed officers with them throughout.

'No comment,' Marjory Slate whispered with the ghost of a smile.

'Marcus is critically ill in hospital. His skull was fractured in an attack. Is there anything you can tell us about who might be responsible?'

'The weird-looking one? Belongs underground, that does.'

'Is Marcus related to you?' Monica asked, pleased that she seemed to be opening up. Her pleasure was short-lived.

'No comment.' Slate was clearly unwilling to elaborate on *the weird-looking one*.

'You've lived in Glen Turrit since you married into the Slate family in 1958?'

'Nothing to say.'

'You know the area around the house well? The dam?'

She looked straight through Monica.

'Are you aware of a tunnel, two hundred metres to the south of your house?'

Again she didn't reply.

'Do you know what the tunnel was being used for? That at least two people were being held captive there?'

'Nothing to say.'

'We've got a forensic team going through your house and those tunnels,' Monica said, leaning across the table and letting the frustration she was feeling seep into her voice. 'They're going to find something, something that links you with the people in those tunnels.'

Slate still didn't reply.

'I'm going to say some names, and you can tell me if you

recognise them,' Crawford said after Monica had nodded to him. 'Annabelle Whittaker?'

No reply.

'Theo Gall?'

Again no response.

'What about Sebastian Sinclair? Do you know him?'

'Nothing to say.'

'He was married to your daughter, Karen. Before someone dismembered him. Cut his arms and legs off, tortured him and dumped him in a river a dozen miles from Glen Turrit.'

'No comment.'

'The same thing happened to his associate, Theo Gall. You sure you don't remember him either?'

'No comment.'

'You've got nothing to say?' Monica asked. Slate didn't reply. 'In that case I'm concluding this interview.' She completed the formalities and stopped the recording, then stood up to leave.

'We ate them,' Slate whispered between her yellow teeth. So low Monica doubted what she'd heard.

'What did you say?' She turned back and crouched so her eyes were level with Marjory Slate's. She caught the smirk of dark pleasure crossing her face. As if she'd just uttered the funniest one-liner and would be repeating it to friends for years to come. But before Monica could press her further the door to the interview room was opening. She turned and saw DC Khan standing in the doorway. Her face was tense.

Annabelle, they've found her body.

Monica braced herself and pulled the door closed behind them as she and Crawford stepped into the corridor. The last thing she wanted was Marjory Slate watching when Khan delivered the news.

Chapter 97

One month earlier

Sebastian Sinclair glanced across the interior of the BMW to the man sitting beside him. The gate at the entrance to Glen Turrit was closed but Theo Gall showed no sign of getting out to open it. Sinclair squeezed the steering wheel just a little tighter. Who was paying who around here?

'You getting the gate?' he said finally. He felt the pressure in his chest. Annoyed at himself that he'd asked rather than told Gall to open it.

Gall shrugged and reached lazily for a stick of chewing gum in his pocket. Clearly demonstrating that he moved at his own pace, that no one was his boss. Finally he reached into the back of the car for the bolt cutters, opened the door and got out. He was wearing a red tracksuit, his greying hair combed and gelled in a centre parting. Once he'd chopped the lock Gall swung the gate open then stood waiting for Sinclair to drive through. His face set in that permanent half-smirk. The expression that had unconsciously drawn Sinclair to him in the first place. The way it seemed to suggest he'd seen it all before. That he knew just exactly what he was doing, where he was going. A wolf in a world of sheep.

Sinclair wanted to be like that, to look like he was in control. That there was nothing that could surprise him. The way his father used to suck his teeth and narrow his eyes when he was weighing up a proposal. Somehow he could fill a room just with his presence without even saying a word. The memory of his father ramping up his anger, Sinclair gunned the engine on the BMW. Blasted through the now-opened gate and skidded the car to a stop on the other side. Twenty metres up the road so Theo was forced to walk further than necessary.

Sinclair glanced in the far wing mirror, took in the way Theo Gall swaggered slowly along the side of the road, lit a cigarette, blew smoke into the air then dropped his lighter back into his tracksuit pocket, like he hadn't even noticed that Sinclair was annoyed. Sebastian glanced away, doubly angry. Ahead the road disappeared into the dense silver birch forests. Beyond them the mountains, white with snow. Somewhere up there was a dam he owned. His property. His wife's family lived up there. Rent-free since God knew when. Well, the party was over – time to move on, family or not. His wife Karen had gone into one of her moods about it, acting like it was a bad idea. Like it was wrong to make a bit of money.

'Clutch control, mate. Should get an automatic next time – better for women drivers.' Gall pulled the door open and flashed that wide smile. As if he knew exactly what was going on in Sinclair's head. Knew exactly how spiteful and pathetic he was.

'Yeah? Watch your fucking mouth,' Sinclair replied. Staring straight ahead so he wouldn't have to meet Gall's mocking eyes.

'Joke, boss man.' Gall's words made it sound like Sinclair was anything but the *boss*.

For a long moment Sebastian regretted bringing Gall, regretted even trying to move the Slates on. Karen was right about one thing: technically they were family. Another mess he'd got himself into. For a moment his mind ran back over twenty years to when he'd first met Karen. He remembered being impressed by Doc, her brother, the way he seemed so ambitious and in control. The stories he told about studying medicine at Oxford, graduating a year early, how he still went down occasionally to help with particularly difficult operations. The notebooks he'd carried around full of his anatomical sketches. It was Doc who had introduced them.

Karen had made him feel like he was a real man for once, deferring to his opinions, asking him to make decisions for her. She seemed delighted to be around him, right up until the night of their wedding, when he'd found her crying in the hotel bathroom. The sacrificial bride, playing him from day one, used by the Slates so they could keep their place rent-free all these years.

Sinclair clenched his fist tight into a ball. And now Karen's mum, *Granny Slate*, would persuade him out of selling the dam if he gave her a chance. Like she'd persuaded him to buy that big house above Inverness when he'd wanted to live further south in Aviemore. Persuaded him to hand over thousands of pounds to Doc Slate back when they were first married. Granny Slate seemed to like him at first. 'Sebastian knows. He's a smart one,' she used to say. Face set in a crooked smile. 'He knows how to run his family.'

Well, those days were long in the past. The fawning gradually turning to open contempt on the Slates' part when they realised he wasn't about to hand over money every time they asked. Quiet hatred on his when he saw that contempt. He hadn't spoken more than a few words to any of Karen's family in over five years. Even at the funeral the year before for Grandad Slate that *he'd* paid for. So much for Doc's supposed university degree and his trips to Oxford. So much for the piles of money he supposedly earned from them. Sebastian remembered the digging he'd had done several years before. No record of a Slate attending or graduating from Oxford for decades. No Dr Slate listed on the General Medical Council register.

Sebastian couldn't help shivering because truthfully he had always been intimidated by Doc. Maybe even more so since he'd uncovered the lies about his medical training. Not that it mattered now. The time for talk was long past anyway. And that was where Gall came in.

Sebastian glanced in the rear-view mirror, craning to check the green plastic petrol containers on the back seat of the BMW. There would be no discussion. The house was on his land. He would burn it down if he wanted. But as he imagined the conflagration, the first licks of smoke rising up from the windows, he couldn't help his mind from returning to the doubts. The ones he'd had since he first explained the plan to Gall. Seen the wicked smile on the man's face. Understood that he was enthralled by the notion of being paid to burn down a house.

A couple of times he'd even resolved to call Gall and tell him the plan was off. He'd overcome this weakness. The weakness that had held him back his whole life. The indecisiveness, the lack of the killer instinct his father had identified in him at a young age. Shame flickered in his stomach at the memories, at the incidental humiliations and put-downs. The worst of them all 'The Last Will & Testament of Innes Sinclair'. His baby sister left the family business, while he got the scraps his father had accumulated over the years almost without even trying.

He'd gone to Heather that morning. Left Gall in the BMW and stormed into the meeting with his sister. It was about some bullshit, another one of her *ideas* their dad had been so impressed by. Impulsively he'd asked her for money. More money. For some reason it felt good to see that disappointment and discomfort in her eyes. To see his own worthlessness reflected back precisely on her face, in the way she held her body. If he could have mustered up the energy he would have sunk down on the carpet in front of her and cried. That would have felt good. Really humiliating himself and letting her know that it was her fault. That she and her father had ruined him. Led him to this point of degradation. Instead he'd turned and left without a word.

Back out at the BMW he'd hesitated before getting into the driver's seat. Glanced at those petrol containers Gall had loaded into the car that morning to fill on their way to Glen Turrit. Glanced back to the impressive company headquarters his father had built. Maybe he should have burned that down, preferably with his sister still in it. Maybe he could have paid Gall to do it, then burst in at the last minute and saved her. Carried her out with her arms around his neck. Everyone would have seen him differently then. Would have known who he really was.

'What is this? Fucking coffee break?' Gall's mocking eyes were on Sebastian's face. 'Thought we were here on business?'

'Yeah. I said watch your fucking mouth.'

Sinclair gunned the engine again and started down the road. He'd never visited the Slates' house in all his years of marriage to Karen. Never even come down this horrible glen. But Karen had reassured him the family were away this week. On one of their trips to the south. Well, there would be a surprise for them when they got back. Lock changed on the gate at the top of the glen. House burned black at the bottom. He allowed himself a moment of glee as he pictured Doc and Granny Slate. The moment they realised how wrong they'd got him. And when he finally spoke to them, he'd shrug. *It's my land, and I'm not bothered anyway. I'm going to be spending most of my time in Vietnam and I told you it was time for you to move on. You probably left a hob on or something.* They would know the truth, but what could they do? For once he would be the one in control.

He took the bend in the road fast. Blasted the BMW out the other side. The road straightened. A wide flat section like a series of football pitches with the mountains white and foreboding on three sides. The black shape of the dam visible in the distance.

'They really live down here? Ten miles from a pub or a shop? We're doing them a favour.'

Sinclair didn't reply. Up ahead there was a single tree by the side of the road. Somehow watchful and sinister. There was movement at the side of the road. A moment later a figure appeared; it must have been crouched behind one of the tussocks of heather. He swore and slowed the car as the person came to a stop in the middle of the single-track road. Then, impulsively, he accelerated again. As he would if a pedestrian was slow in crossing a road in the centre of Inverness. A warning to get the fuck out of his way.

But the person showed no sign of moving, and Sinclair was forced to stand on the brakes, bringing the car to a juddering halt less than ten feet away. He realised that it was a child. A girl with blonde hair. A strangely familiar face, though he was sure he had never seen her before.

'Fucking shite dri—' A sound interrupted Gall's tirade. A flash of movement in the wing mirror. A bang then a hissing sound as the car lurched to the side. It took Sinclair a moment to understand that a rear tyre had burst. He stared transfixed at the girl in the road. She was holding something, something dark. Slowly she raised it until it was pointing at his face.

Sinclair heard the car door open beside him. Doc Slate, that vacant look on his face. Sebastian tried to jerk away as he saw the hammer in his hand. But his seat belt locked tight, held him in place. 'Wait! Wait!'

With his left hand Doc Slate blocked Sinclair's arms. When he swung the hammer in a short, choppy blow it connected with the top of Sinclair's forehead. Sebastian's world turned strange, soft and fuzzy. He watched as if from behind a veil as beside him Gall unfastened his seat belt and threw the passenger-side door open. Doc Slate must have moved much faster than any human Sebastian had ever seen because as Gall exited the vehicle Doc was already swinging the hammer from the roof of the car. It was only a glancing blow but enough to stagger Gall, whose legs went. He hit the ground. Doc landed hard on him with two feet. Sinclair watched, still too dazed to move, as Doc Slate slipped a wiry arm around Gall's neck then strangled him to unconsciousness.

Sinclair blinked. Time must have passed because when he tried to move his arms they were tied tight behind him; his feet were bound too. He realised that he was in the back of the BMW. Gall was beside him. Bound and gagged with a thin trickle of blood running down his face. His mocking eyes reduced to those of a child, shocked and frightened. The car was moving slowly along the road on its burst tyre. Doc Slate was in the passenger seat, half turned, watching them with an expression of distant amusement, while the little girl, barely able to see over the dashboard, was driving.

Time moved in strange fragments, and a moment later he was being dragged into a hole in the mountain. More fragments. Down a tunnel, into a room. Tied to a bed. He screamed. Screamed and screamed. A hand covered his mouth; something was pulled roughly over his head. When Sebastian screamed again the sound echoed back into his ears. He tried to move his head and felt the cold metal against his cheek.

'Are you going to stop being silly?' The voice was difficult to gauge. Male or female? Young or old? 'The Doctor says we'll have to keep that thing on you if you don't stop screaming.'

Sebastian stopped screaming.

'You've made a fucking big mistake.' He tried to make his voice intimidating, inject more of the Scottish accent he used when he was negotiating. The words echoed with a metallic edge to them. He tilted his head and caught a glimpse of light. As if through a small hole. With a sense of horror he realised that he was wearing some sort of metal helmet. He felt the condensation forming on his face. 'I know people. They'll be looking for me.'

The person didn't reply, but Sebastian felt a hand on his wrist. He tried to jerk it away, but his arms and legs were still tied. He felt the sleeve of his shirt being rolled up to above the bicep, then something being tightened around his upper arm.

'What are you doing?' Sebastian hated the weakness in his voice. 'What are you doing?'

'The Doctor thinks you're going to need an operation.' Sebastian felt the needle slide into his arm, the cold spread of the liquid. Felt his consciousness begin to slide. 'You might need more than one operation . . .'

Chapter 98

When Annabelle woke up the cold seemed to have risen from the rock floor and through her thin tracksuit top into her flesh and bones. She blinked rapidly, trying to adjust her eyes to the darkness before slowly, with dawning horror, she remembered. Marcus, Scott, the Doctor, the chase through the tunnels. His grip on her ankle. How she had stabbed his arm. She lay very still and tried her best to breathe silently as the pain throbbed incessantly from her leg. Listening, because surely the Doctor was nearby. Maybe he was waiting? Maybe he was listening too? There was only silence though and the pulse in her ears, the pristine blackness lying heavy all around her.

He could be there in the dark waiting for the fun to begin again. She remembered what Marcus had told her. The Doctor could see in the dark practically, could smell the difference between a man and a woman, could hear how heavy someone was.

Annabelle listened and listened to the silence. How long had it been now? How long since she found Scott in that room? She had promised to help him, promised to go back for him. And what about Mr Pepper? It seemed like months since she'd taken him out. He would be so bored now, stuck in the flat with nothing to do. For a second Annabelle couldn't stop herself from imagining that the little dog was there with her. She would have given anything to feel that soft warm fur on her face and up her nose as he made that little growling sound of proud contentment.

The thought was too sad though as the ache from her missing leg intensified and the cold spread through her body. Imagining herself anywhere else, imagining she could be anyone but someone alone and forgotten at the bottom of the world, was too much.

Finally she had to shift, and felt the torch press painfully into her chest. After a minute the temptation was overwhelming. Despite her fear of the Doctor she switched it on. The bulb was dim, batteries running low, but just that moment of light was a comfort. The roof in this section of the tunnel was about five feet from the floor. The space had more of the feeling of a natural cave than the cut tunnels she had crawled through and was far wider too. The light from the torch was swallowed up in every direction. For just a moment she allowed herself to accept the reality of her situation: deep underground, lost in a labyrinth of caves and tunnels. *First the light will fail. And then you'll slowly go mad.*

Annabelle somehow managed to push away the thought. 'You need to switch the light off to save the battery, and you need to move,' she whispered. 'Even if there's nowhere to go, you have to try.'

Chapter 99

Monica and Crawford sat down in the interview room opposite Karen Sinclair. DC Khan's news hadn't been about Annabelle but the man they'd found mutilated in the tunnels, so far still unidentified. He'd died that morning, his body unable to cope with the massive trauma, blood loss and infections. Monica had watched Khan's lips as she relayed the information, struggling to feel something. But numbness seemed to be the only response her body and mind could summon up.

'At least he didn't die down there. At least he was with people who cared,' Khan had offered. Still young enough, new enough in the job to take comfort from such sentiments. Still certain that existence tilted towards the good.

Monica tried to put the man out of her mind. Annabelle might still be alive. While there was even the tiniest chance of finding her she had to focus all her efforts on her. Whatever had happened to Annabelle and the other victims seemed to be tied to the whole of the Slate family, not just one member. Marcus was still unconscious and Marjory Slate clearly wasn't about to share anything. While Karen's brother Hamish, the man in the kilt at the Slates' house, had a very limited vocabulary and struggled to communicate in the most basic way. Karen seemed like their only chance.

Monica looked at the woman opposite her in the interview room. Karen Sinclair showed none of Granny Slate's self-assurance.

Her face was pinched, eyes rimmed red and arms folded around herself pathetically. *Well, you won't be getting any sympathy in this room,* Monica's inner voice suggested as she remembered Karen's blank face when she had virtually begged her for help in finding Annabelle. Another memory came with it: Lily, pushing her face into Karen's side in the room at the Slates' house.

'Lily's your daughter, isn't she?' They hadn't been able to find any record of Lily Slate's birth ever having been officially recorded, and as far as they could tell she'd never been enrolled in school.

Karen didn't reply but dipped her head in a barely perceptible nod. Monica remembered the Sinclairs' mansion above Inverness. There had been a recent photograph. A portrait of the perfect family: Karen, Sebastian and their teenage son, who was away at boarding school. No sign of Lily, so where did she fit in? 'Sebastian didn't know about Lily, did he? He wasn't her father, was he?' Monica guessed.

This time Karen shook her head. 'It was nine years ago. I told Sebastian that my parents were ill, and I had to stay in Glen Turrit for a few months to help the family . . .'

'And Sebastian didn't miss you? Didn't want to come and visit?'

Karen shook her head. 'He'd stopped speaking to my family by then, didn't want anything to do with them. He was busy with work anyway, probably hardly noticed I was gone. My son had just started boarding school. Sebastian's sister had just come back from America, she looked after our son at weekends and during the holidays.'

'Did you meet someone? Have an affair? You were worried Sebastian would find out?' Monica asked, softening her tone. Pleased just to have Karen talking.

'No, it wasn't like that. I never meant . . . I never wanted . . .' Her eyes met Monica's with some kind of desperation. And Monica realised her own hand had gone to the address book in the pocket of her coat. She could feel the dry paper under her fingers. The phone numbers of her mum's friends and family. John Kennedy's way of symbolically and practically cutting her off from them.

'Someone forced you?'

'My dad, my brother Doc, they said we needed another one for the family to survive and carry on.' Karen stared down at the table as she spoke.

'Where was your mum when all this was going on?' The words were out of Monica's mouth before she remembered Marjory Slate's cold, mocking grey eyes. Clearly there would have been no support against the family system from her.

Karen shook her head. 'She told me I shouldn't be selfish,' she whispered. 'That I should shut up and get on with it. Doc drove me to some bars – in Aberdeen so Sebastian wouldn't find out. I hoped I wouldn't get pregnant . . . It isn't always right for a family to go on how it is . . . Doc delivered Lily at the house. They wouldn't let me go to hospital, even though I asked. He said he'd studied how to do it in his textbooks.'

'Tell me about Doc, about your family,' Monica said softly, starting to feel some empathy with Karen. 'Why wasn't it right that it went on? What was wrong with the family?' As if everything Karen had just told her wasn't wrong enough, Monica thought. But Karen shook her head again, stared at the desk.

Monica tried a different question. 'You sent your son to boarding school to keep him away from your family?'

Karen nodded quickly.

'You said Doc Slate's your brother?'

'That's right, older.'

'What about Marcus? Is he your son too? Another brother?'

'Marcus was a foundling.'

'A foundling?'

'Dad brought him home when he was about two. Said he found him by the side of the road, that most likely Gypsies left him there. Mum said they might come looking for him, so she dressed him as a girl at first.'

Monica couldn't quite believe what she was hearing.

'Does Marcus know this?'

Karen shook her head quickly. 'Bad luck, Dad said. Telling him. It would only bring trouble. They kept him down in the tunnels mostly – to help with the dam, all the work Doc had to do to maintain it.'

'There was a man,' Monica said slowly, 'in the tunnel beside your house. He'd been badly mutilated. Half an hour ago one of my colleagues told me he'd died. We still don't know his name.' She let the silence lie for almost a full minute. 'I can't believe what was done to him.' She leaned a little closer across the table and Karen quietly began to cry.

'The media are calling Turrit the "Glen of Horrors" already,' Crawford said from Monica's elbow. 'Whatever your family were doing down there, it's over.'

Monica continued: 'If you talk to us now you might get out of this with some kind of life. You might even get to live with Lily again. I've got a daughter a few years younger than her. I'd do almost anything to keep her out of social services.'

'It was the dam,' Karen whispered. 'Sebastian wanted to sell it, went down there with Theo, some tough guy he'd met and got working for him. I tried to tell him. Hints about what Dad had done to Colin Muir all those years ago when he wanted them to leave . . . But Sebastian wouldn't listen. Said he needed the money.'

And there it was: Sebastian Sinclair and Theo Gall's murders as good as solved. Monica wished she could feel a moment of satisfaction.

'What happened?'

'I never . . . I never knew about any of it. It was Doc.'

'What's his real name?'

'It's Doc. Dad chose it for him. When he was born he said he was going to teach him to be his wee doctor. My dad had a metal plate in his skull. He'd have these turns. Doc would drain fluid from him, do other procedures. He has a whole library of textbooks, all these tools and surgical instruments he keeps – they became sort of an obsession. He'd buy them, steal them, spend hours playing with them, arranging them in his room before deciding which ones he liked best and wanted to keep.'

Monica shivered as she remembered the neat row of tools laid out on the bloody groundsheet in the garage. Wished she could feel a moment of professional satisfaction that her detective's instinct about the importance of the tools had proved correct.

Karen went on, mercifully interrupting the thoughts, 'Once I moved to live with Sebastian I could see my dad was a strange man . . . Doc stayed down there and ended up almost stranger. He got much worse after Dad died last year . . .'

'What did Doc do to Sebastian?'

'He said that if we didn't do something they'd take the dam and the house. The Sinclairs would take it all. That's why he put the bodies in the river.'

'He put the bodies in the river so the Sinclairs wouldn't take the dam?' Monica said back to her, trying to make sense of what Karen was saying.

'The dam and our house in Inverness were both in Sebastian's name. Doc said that once he was dead they would come to me. That's why he left the bodies out. So the police would know Sebastian was dead, and there wouldn't be any confusion about who owned the dam. We'll still have the house in Inverness at least? Won't we? For when Lily's older?'

Monica was aghast. Even after a lifetime of hearing the stupid and banal reasons people committed murder, Karen's matter-of-fact explanation was shocking. And still none of it explained where Annabelle or the other unnamed male victim came in.

'I don't know,' she replied finally. The absurdity of giving housing advice to a woman who had a good chance of spending the best part of the next decade in Cornton Vale prison for conspiring to commit murder was almost overwhelming.

'Where's Doc now?'

'I don't know. He works on his own mostly, occasionally with Marcus. Fixing things in the dam. Sometimes he doesn't come out for days at a time.'

'What happened to Annabelle?' Monica asked. The details of the other victim could wait for now.

'It was a mistake. Doc got Lily to stop Sebastian's car . . . She wasn't meant to do it again with Annabelle. It was a mistake. It wasn't meant to happen with her.'

'Lily stopped Annabelle?' Monica remembered the lone tree in the middle of the open glen. Marked with blue from the impact with the car.

'She saw the car and thought it was Sebastian again.'

'And then you decided to keep Annabelle captive?'

'No! I thought they'd taken her to the hospital. I only found out later. Lily saw her outside . . .'

Monica remembered Annabelle's hurried text message to

Fisher. Had she tried to escape from the tunnel? Been caught and taken back? What then? Was she killed? Had she really managed to escape from Marcus down into the tunnels?

'Tell me where Annabelle is. Tell me how to find her.'

'She must be down in the tunnels. Doc and Marcus know them better than me,' Karen whispered. 'That's the only place Doc would keep her. But no one ever comes back from down there.'

Chapter 100

Annabelle moved slowly through the darkness. Without crutches her technique was to feel the ground in front of her with the palms of both hands, before laying them flat and hopping her remaining leg forward. It was slow and exhausting. The tunnel seemed to incline gradually upwards, making her progress even more tiring. The skin on her hands stung constantly. Her leg and back were cramped and aching, and there was a deep throbbing pain from her amputation. She could feel a dampness in the dressing as if the stitches had begun to open up.

Despite the discomfort it was good to focus on the challenges of moving because all around her the darkness seemed infinite and terrifying. All that was real was the pain. And increasingly her thirst. What had started as a dry discomfort in her mouth soon evolved into a furious craving.

Repeatedly her mind ran back over the previous days. She tried to recall her last drink. The moment of the tea spraying against the wall when she'd hit Marcus with the mug. How could she have wasted that precious liquid? Couldn't she have drunk the tea before hitting Marcus?! Then she became aware of the smell of fresh water. Maddeningly it seemed to come from all around – from under her hands on the rock floor, from above her in the cave roof. She swung her head side to side, trying to home in on it. Finally she stopped and clicked the torch on. Shone the weak light around, convinced it would land on a trickle of water somewhere. There was nothing though. Just dry rock and the darkness beyond.

For what seemed like hours she repeated the same routine, her desperate thirst even overriding her fear of the Doctor as she sniffed the cool air for water. Moving on, praying for the blessed relief when her hand would touch a puddle and she could lean in to drink. Switching the ever-weakening torch on to see dry rock in every direction, finally forcing herself to click the torch off again. Her mind began to play tricks too. She would feel the cool damp of a puddle on her hand, think that she had found water. Joyfully she'd collapse forward to drink, only to taste the familiar dry rock.

The voices started soon after. Calling to her from distant corners. People she'd known years before. Her parents. Her classmates from school, shouting to her, laughing and calling her towards a Soda Stream dispenser they'd set up. Only to move it when she drew close and send her off in the opposite direction until she bumped up against the wall of the cave. They seemed to enjoy mocking her. Sniggering at her missing leg, chuckling at her begging.

Finally she collapsed into a heap, too exhausted and ground down by pain to force herself on. Her hand went to the torch around her neck for a moment's comfort against the dark and the cruel laughter. But when she pressed the switch Annabelle realised that it was already on. She had forgotten to switch it off. The battery was dead, and now the darkness was absolute.

Chapter 101

Twenty minutes after the interview with Karen, Monica was standing with her hands on her hips in the Major Incident Room. The frustration was almost overwhelming as she listened to what Hately was telling her.

'The rescue team are having a really tough time. Most of the tunnels are unsupported and sections of them could collapse at any moment.'

'Sir, we already know this.'

Hately dropped his eyes. She could sense what was coming. 'They're saying they've never seen anything like it. There are literally miles of tunnel. It could take them months . . .'

'If she's not already dead, then she will be in a couple of days,' Monica said quietly. 'There has to be something . . .' She glanced around at Crawford, Khan and Fisher. None of them would meet her gaze and she knew they were experiencing the same sense of impotence. They had as good as solved their double murder case that morning, but it felt as if they'd suffered the worst defeat.

'They're talking about bringing in robotic equipment and cameras to help with the search, but it's still going to take time.'

'We don't have time.' Monica took a deep breath and for a moment couldn't stop herself from imagining what Annabelle might be experiencing. Miles underground with no idea that anyone was looking for her. *Jesus.* Even thinking about it was enough to make the hair on Monica's arms stand on end. *We're never going to find her.*

'The DNA from the man in the tunnel came back. It's a match with the blood at the garage,' Fisher said, obviously keen to have something to talk about. She nodded, tried to smile. It had to be hardest for him. His stepfather, Joel Whittaker, had been waiting for Monica that morning when she'd arrived at the office. The impression of narcissism she'd gained from Fisher's descriptions had been confirmed. Whittaker had demanded he personally take charge of the rescue. *I'm hearing about tunnels under a mountain? Never heard such rubbish. It's absolutely ridiculous.* He was threatening to sell his story to the press as two uniformed officers arrived to shepherd him outside. Fisher had stood dumbly beside him in Hately's office throughout, staring at a square of carpet on the floor. Clearly wishing he was anywhere but in that room with his stepfather and two of his bosses. Annabelle's mum had seemed more straightforwardly terrified and upset when Monica had met her briefly before interviewing Marjory Slate. The horror of what had happened to her daughter seemed to crowd out any impulse to blame or accuse.

'Do we have any ideas for an ID?' Monica asked.

'One came through this morning,' Khan said. 'Half an hour ago. It looks promising. A Canadian national, Scott MacConnell. He was hiking in Scotland, been out of contact with his family for a couple of weeks now.' She held up a picture of a smiling man with longish blond hair, snowy mountains in the background. He was good-looking, healthy. Nothing like what was left of the man in the tunnel, although the shape of the face was similar.

'I think it's him,' Monica said, feeling that numbness return as she spoke. 'We better contact his local police department in Canada.'

The day dragged on for Monica. Hoping for news from the Cave Rescue team. Having to resist the urge to drive back out to Glen Turrit and head down into those tunnels looking for Annabelle herself. As if it would achieve anything. She forced herself to focus on the case. The team was beginning to collate the evidence so at least they could be confident of getting a conviction for the murders of Gall and Sinclair. Probably Scott MacConnell now too, she reminded herself grimly.

At 2.30 p.m. she went to collect Lucy from nursery and drop her at her mum's.

'Freddy at nursery said there's monsters in the glens near Inverness. His daddy told him,' Lucy piped up from the back seat as Monica pulled out into the road. 'Is there really monsters there? I liked the trees in that glen. I don't think you would get anything like a crocodile out there, do you?'

'I don't either, honey,' Monica replied as she took the turn-off across the metal bridge into Rapinch. Her phone began to ring. Monica answered and heard DC Khan's excited voice on the other end of the line.

'Ma'am? It's Marcus Slate. He's woken up.'

Marcus was propped up in bed when she entered the room. The doctor Monica had spoken to out in the corridor told her he had a niece about Annabelle's age himself. He would let her talk to Marcus for five minutes, *but only if the patient agrees, I still have a duty of care, no matter what happened to that poor girl . . .* Marcus's head was wrapped in white bandages, his eyes still looked sharp though as they met Monica's for a second before he quickly dropped his head. She introduced herself and took a seat beside his bed.

'You won't remember, but I was there when we found you. In the tunnel.' She watched his face. 'How are you feeling?'

'I think it's safe to say I've felt better,' he said with a dry little laugh, his hand hovering over his face as he spoke. As if trying to shield himself from Monica's eyes, from the world. *The weird-looking one.* Monica remembered Marjory Slate's description and what Karen Sinclair had said about him spending most of his life underground. Although his tone was friendly, Monica sensed immediately that getting him to open up might be impossible. He was intelligent, and he'd spent a life hiding in tunnels of half-truths and lies. 'I'm afraid I'm not sure how much help I'll be to you. I can't remember much.'

'I don't need you to,' Monica said. Struggling to keep her voice level as she remembered Scott's cell. The stink in those rooms. 'I just want to find Annabelle.'

'Annabelle?' He frowned as if the name was unfamiliar. 'Oh, Annabelle. I remember. She's a friend of the family. My family are like that, always collecting friends, new people.'

'Like Scott?'

'I think he was ill. The Doctor was trying his best—'

'Where is she?' If anyone knew where she was and how to find her, it had to be Marcus.

'As far as I know she left. She . . . went off somewhere.'

'The tunnel was locked from the inside.' Unconsciously Monica had lowered her voice into a threatening growl. She had to suppress the urge to reach a hand out and take hold of Marcus by the neck. 'Annabelle hit you, then she escaped down into the lower tunnels, didn't she? How do we find her? There must be a way?'

'I'm sorry, but I can't talk about the tunnels. My family would never forgive me. It sounds silly, but they're sort of sacred to us.' He shook his head at his family's little eccentricities.

Monica felt her hand tense into a fist. 'Annabelle will die if we don't find her.'

Marcus snorted as if to laugh. 'I think you're being melodramatic. She's been well fed and well looked after by the Doctor. I'm starting to feel tired.'

Monica glanced over her shoulder to where the doctor was now hovering in the doorway. 'You need to tell me where Annabelle is,' she whispered.

For the first time Marcus met her eyes, still holding his hand up to cover his mouth. 'You can choose your friends, but you can't choose your family, Detective.'

The doctor stepped into the room.

'Your family?'

Marcus tilted his head in query.

'I think that's enough for now,' the doctor said, taking a step towards Monica.

'They're not your family. They took you when you were just a baby, from God knows where!' She was almost shouting now, finally losing her cool after the long days of tension.

She felt the doctor's hand on her arm. He said, 'I'm sorry, you have to go.'

'You could have had a different family.' With difficulty she lowered her voice. 'You could have had a different life!'

Chapter 102

For a long, long time Annabelle lay still in a heap on the cold ground. Her throat was swollen, and it felt like razor blades even to swallow. *You'd look hot in a selfie right now.* The odd thought flickered into her head and Annabelle pictured herself pouting with cracked lips and a bloody wound on her temple. She almost smiled at the image, despite her aching thirst.

Then a voice penetrated the darkness. She realised that someone was whispering her name, over and over. Could it be the Doctor? She blinked and with her tired hands tried again to click the torch on. Hoping it would light up and she could find out who was there. The skin on her hands was worn raw, her remaining knee rubbed to a bloody mess. The torch was dead.

'Hello?' she shouted finally. 'I'm over here.' Her voice echoed back to her, shaky and pathetic, frighteningly weak. The whispering stopped.

For a long time there was only silence. Annabelle blinked and blinked. Then she caught sight of a figure somewhere off in the darkness. Someone hunched, bent almost double under the low roof, but somehow able to move remarkably quickly, shuffling along in the darkness. Strangely Annabelle could hear the sound of the person's footsteps as if they were directly beside her. They continued for what seemed interminably long time. At some point the person disappeared, the whispering and shuffling replaced by a humming sound.

Slowly Annabelle recognised the tune. 'Somewhere Over the Rainbow' from *The Wizard of Oz*. She couldn't remember what the dog in the film – Toto – looked like. Instead she pictured Mr Pepper, imagined him running through the caves looking for her, desperate to nuzzle up to her face and lick her cheek. Then she heard his barks echoing through the caves, and the song became louder. Clearly someone was looking for her. 'Annabelle! Annabelle!'

'I'm here!' she shouted, throat burning, 'I'm here!'

Everything stopped. Annabelle realised she had made a terrible mistake. She became aware of a presence close beside her. She turned and saw the face, grey and terrifying. Smiling at her with crooked yellow teeth.

Annabelle screamed.

And then there was darkness. Silence. As if someone had turned off a switch. None of it was real. The truth was worse though. She was alone, forgotten and abandoned. Her mind had rebelled against the darkness, the silence, the utter emptiness. Her dried-out body began to heave with dry sobs. No one was coming, no one was even looking for her.

Chapter 103

Marcus didn't respond, and the doctor's hand on Monica's arm became firmer.

'I can't allow this. I told you.'

Monica glanced at the doctor, tried very hard to contain her overwhelming rage. Without trusting herself to speak again or even to look at Marcus, she turned to go.

'Wait.' Marcus's voice was barely a whisper but when Monica looked back his hand had dropped from his face and he met her eyes. 'You're lying.'

Slowly Monica turned to the doctor, who hesitated then nodded. She dug into her pocket for her phone and opened the voice memo function then skipped through until she found the correct part of the recording. She laid it on the crisp white sheet, watched as Marcus folded his small hands together on his lap. Monica noticed that the very tip of his right index finger was missing. He was staring straight ahead, his body now tensed as he listened. She felt the sweat pooling in the small of her back, her shoulders locked tight.

Karen Sinclair's voice came through the slightly tinny speaker: 'Marcus was a foundling.'

'A foundling?'

'Dad brought him home when he was about two. Said he found him by the side of the road, that most likely Gypsies left him there. Mum said they might come looking for him, so she dressed him as a girl at first.'

'Does Marcus know this?'

'Bad luck, Dad said. Telling him. It would only bring trouble.'

Monica switched the recording off and watched Marcus's face. For a long time he stared straight ahead, eyes fixed on the wall.

'You don't have to let them define the rest of your life,' Monica said softly, almost afraid to speak, because surely if Marcus turned away now then their hopes of finding Annabelle alive were over. 'You can choose right now. To be someone different.'

'I don't . . .' His voice was a whisper. 'I don't think . . .'

'Just tell me what happened. Tell me how to find Annabelle.'

'It got worse last year, when Grandad died. He told us that he'd been trapped down in the mines when he was young, that he had eaten people to survive. Occasionally he'd give us meat that he said came from people and told us it would make us strong like it had made him strong. It had helped him to live with a metal plate in his skull for sixty years. I never really believed him, about where it came from . . . But my uncle – I thought he was my uncle – Doc, the Doctor, he was much closer to Grandad Slate. He believed it all. Wanted to carry on. Granny Slate too, she said we had to, she said it would keep us young. Sebastian and his friend came to burn the house down and take the dam, but the Doctor caught them. We kept them in those rooms. The Doctor . . . cut them up. He told them we were eating them so they'd be more frightened. When they died I hoped it would be over. But then he brought Scott . . . Annabelle . . .'

'You know those tunnels, Marcus,' Monica whispered, trying very hard to keep her voice level. 'You're Annabelle's only chance.'

'I don't know them . . . The Doctor knows them . . .'

'What did he tell you about them? There has to be something?'

For a long time Marcus didn't speak, then finally he glanced up.

When she'd finished passing on Marcus's information to Hately, Monica rushed out to the Volvo in the Raigmore Hospital car park. She almost ran straight into Crawford, who was on his way to meet her, carrying two paper cups of coffee. She knew he'd spent a frantic but futile day trying to contact anyone who had worked on the tunnels back in the 1950s.

'I think I know how to find her.'

Crawford gave her a sceptical look but was intrigued enough to hurry across the car park after her. Trying to hold the cups steady while simultaneously doing his best to maintain his cool. In the Volvo she reached across and shoved the door open for him, virtually at the same time turning the key to start the engine with her other hand.

'What did he say?' Crawford shuffled into the seat. 'I got hold of a couple of old boys from the 1950s, but no one who'd worked on the tunnels or knew anything,' he said, trying to balance the cups and fasten his seat belt as Monica accelerated impatiently towards the junction. She hit the indicator to turn right and drummed her fingers on the steering wheel as she waited for the lights to change.

'Karen said he knew the tunnels.'

'I was there, remember?'

'I played him part of the tape. He told me the tunnels are like a labyrinth but they eventually lead to a cave system. The cave system isn't anything like as complex as the tunnels, and there's no obvious way in or out, except through the mined tunnels.'

'No obvious way?'

'Marcus says there's a flooded chamber.'

'A sump?'

'I guess so . . . if a sump's a name for a section of flooded cave,' Monica said impatiently, annoyed by his insistence on the technical term. The lights changed and she gunned the engine, pulled the car hard right through the junction. She took another right at the roundabout then headed straight down towards Carsegate Industrial Estate.

'Where's the sump then?' It was his turn to sound impatient as Monica had gone quiet, concentrating on the road ahead as she overtook a string of slow-moving cars.

'In a cave he called St Magnus's Chamber. He told me how to find it.'

Monica's phone rang as they were approaching Little Arklow, the afternoon slowly fading to a hazy evening, the skies directly to the west beyond the mountains burning down into flaming reds and oranges.

It was Hately. 'They've explored the pool. Marcus Slate wasn't lying. There's definitely a deep sump. They're going through it now.'

Chapter 104

When the noises started up again Annabelle knew not to respond to them. How could her mind cope with another horror like the last one? This time they began with the distant sound of water, moving very gently at first. As if someone was gently stirring a bath, and the water was lapping at its sides. Such a comforting sound, and yet so terrible when her body was dry like a desert corpse, and water was a myth. Something so perfect that it had surely never existed.

But the noises grew louder until they became splashes, the sound of someone breaking the surface of a pool. The noises were so clear, so believable, although distant. So obviously real that she turned her head to stare into the darkness and had to resist the overwhelming impulse to begin crawling towards them.

She dug her fingernails hard into the scraped and cut palms of her hands. Desperate to stop the maddening hallucinations. It was better to be dead than tortured like this. Finally low voices were added to the splashes. Murmured conversations echoing off the cave ceiling.

When Annabelle opened her eyes there were distant lights, white and ghostly this time from somewhere far off in the cave. But they seemed to be moving closer and were so real that it seemed impossible they could be from her mind. But she'd thought the same the last time.

The voices came closer, and she heard her name being called, echoing softly from the ceiling above her, from the walls.

'Annabelle?! Annabelle!'

Could it really be someone? She clenched her eyes tight shut and clasped her hand over her mouth. 'Please go away,' she whispered. 'Please go away.'

Chapter 105

It was almost completely dark when Monica and Crawford reached the gate that blocked the road into Glen Turrit. Two nights before, the place couldn't have felt more lonely; this time it was alive with activity. A pair of marked police cars blocked the road, and journalists sat in cars parked on the verge on either side, waiting for more news from the bottom of the glen.

They passed through the gate. The drive to the dam seemed to take forever. The winding sections, then the open straight with the single oak tree where it had all begun for Annabelle, finally the black line of the dam appearing on the horizon beneath the pink sky.

'Do you think they found her?' Crawford murmured as Monica turned left onto the track at the back of the lay-by, guarded by another marked police car. She shook her head and continued up through the dark forest towards the Slates' house. They parked outside, beside the two forensics team vans. Monica glanced at her phone again. Still no news. Anxiety twisted at her stomach. The feeling before an exam or when waiting for results at a doctor's office.

'Come on,' she said, climbing out of the Volvo. She followed Crawford's slight figure through the gloaming along the narrow path towards the tunnel entrance. This was lit by a pair of industrial floodlights running off a generator. A uniformed officer was standing to the side of the wooden door, staring suspiciously out at the gloom beyond the lights. He gave Monica and Crawford a once-over, held out the clipboard for them to sign in. They hurried inside and down the strange underground road. Much further down a pair of armed officers was guarding the bottom of the tunnel in case Doc Slate came stumbling out of the darkness. They passed Scott's room and took the right turn down the narrow tunnel to St Magnus's Chamber. Monica had to stoop to avoid the low roof. She pushed the door open and stepped into the cavern.

The place was illuminated by banks of floodlights as if the searchers were fearful of what might be lurking in the dark corners. Divers were emerging from the pool at the far end of the cavern. She could see that it was fed by a constant trickle of water from high on the back wall. She followed Crawford across the uneven ground, straightening under the ceiling, which was now far above. Her stomach tightened again as she took in the divers' slumped shoulders, their lowered heads.

Souter was standing with his hands on his hips. 'The sump leads to a cave system. But there's no sign of her. They spent twenty minutes looking around, shouting for her, but there was no response.'

'How big is the cave? Did they explore it properly? Twenty minutes doesn't seem . . .'

Souter lowered his voice. 'They're close to exhaustion. One of the guys started hallucinating, thought he saw something in the dark. He nearly lost it. They had to come out.'

Monica swore under her breath.

'What now?'

'Only those three are dive-trained and they've been working flat out for pretty much thirty-six hours searching the tunnels. I can't ask them to go back under after what happened . . . It's not—'

'She might—'

'I'll go.' Monica and Souter turned at the sound of Crawford's voice. 'I'll go. I've got a Technical Two qualification. I've dived down to sixty-metre shipwrecks. I can go under a sump.' Monica could hear the catch in his voice though. She remembered what he'd told her back at the first dump site, his fear of the dark mountain water.

'No, Crawford. You can't go on your own anyway.'

'I'll go with you.' One of the divers had overheard and stood up. 'I can do one more dive.'

Monica started to protest, but Souter had already turned to start hunting through the rescue team's bags to find equipment for Crawford.

Chapter 106

Monica sat staring at the dark pool of water. The other divers were hunched beside her, still kitted out in their suits.

'They've been too long,' one of the men whispered. 'If they'd found her they'd be back by now.'

Monica tried to ignore him and the feeling that letting Crawford dive had been a mistake; he was exhausted himself. They should have waited. She was aware of just how dangerous cave diving could be. Pitch-black, underwater in a restricted space. A mistake could mean lungfuls of frigid water, a terrible death . . . She tried to ignore the tightness in her throat as she couldn't help but imagine that water filling her own lungs, and joined the others staring into the dark water. Willing something to happen. A hand to appear, something that would mean Crawford and the other diver were safe.

'No.' The man beside her stood up and began to adjust his suit. 'We're going—'

An explosion of bubbles erupted from the water. Followed a moment later by a masked head, shoulders, arms and the rest of a body as a diver broke the surface. With the help of two other team members he heaved himself out of the pool and stood, water sloshing from him as he set his oxygen cylinder down, and finally, after what seemed like an eternity, reached up and pulled his mask off.

'We've found her!' The man took another lungful of air, his voice echoing in the cavernous space. 'She's in a hell of a mess. But she's alive.'

Chapter 107

It was almost eight hours before the team was able to bring Annabelle out of the cave through the sump. Initially they'd been reluctant even to attempt the risky evacuation. The flooded section was relatively short, just over fifty feet, and a confident caver might even have been able to pass through simply by holding their breath and following a guide line. But Annabelle was badly dehydrated, close to hypothermic and had suffered a traumatic amputation to one of her legs. Consideration was given to drilling a tunnel to reach her before it was finally decided that the risk of her being down there any longer outweighed something going wrong in the flooded section. In the end she was dressed in a drysuit and oxygen mask. When a fresh team of rescue divers arrived, they went in and brought her back through the sump.

Monica watched as the young woman emerged from the black water, was lifted out of the pool, taken out of the drysuit and wrapped in blankets. Her dark hair hanging around her face in wet streaks. Quickly she was loaded onto a stretcher for the trip to the surface. Monica hung back from the bustle, letting the paramedics and rescue team do their work.

'What she must have been through . . .' Monica whispered. Crawford had come back through the sump minutes before and was now standing beside her with his arms folded across his narrow chest.

'She kept asking about a dog – Mr Pepper.' Crawford shook his head, then glanced warily around the cavern. 'Terrifying down there . . . She said Doc Slate, the Doctor, went down there after her. That she stabbed him in the arm. He must still be down there, mustn't he?'

Much later that night Monica finally made it home to her flat. After she'd checked on Lucy, showered and eaten the lentil soup her mum had left out for her on the hob, she finally undressed and crawled into bed. When she woke the next morning she had the novel feeling of being refreshed. Of having had a night without nightmares.

Chapter 108

Annabelle didn't really believe it was true. The pure relief of the water on her cracked lips, the comforting voice saying her name. Even though the man stayed beside her for a long time, she wasn't really sure if it was real until they finally carried her out to the tunnel. She stared up at the familiar string of electric lights overhead until they were replaced by the cold air off the mountains and the icy sky with a billion stars. She had never seen anything more beautiful, and she tried to ask the people who were carrying the stretcher to stop. Just for a second, to wait so she could look at that fresh infinity for a moment.

They were hurrying though, and before she could frame the words she was in the back of an ambulance. She closed her eyes and let the smells wash over her: detergent, fresh bandages and ointments. A female paramedic looked over her battered body and said calming, authoritative things. Finally, when she felt the ambulance moving over the rough track, when she heard the sound of the siren, she sighed and let her eyes drift closed.

When she opened them again Annabelle was in a room. There was a smell of disinfectant and the sound of distant voices. She understood then that it had been a dream. The tunnels, her rescue. Marcus and the Doctor had moved her, that was all. They were still going to eat her. Piece by piece.

'You slept for twelve hours.' A woman's voice. Slightly husky with a Scottish accent, but there was something reassuring about it. Annabelle tilted her head towards the sound. The woman had dark hair tied back in a ponytail and grey circles under her eyes. Her intense expression should have been frightening, but Annabelle noticed the little laughter lines at the corner of her eyes. 'My name's Monica Kennedy. I'm a detective.' Annabelle glanced quickly past her and saw a hospital ward through the open doorway.

'Where's Scott?' Annabelle felt a flash of panic wash over her. How could she have forgotten? She saw the woman's expression change.

'They couldn't save him. I'm sorry.'

'I promised I'd come back for him.' She felt the horror. It was part of her now, the way the tunnels and the Doctor were part of her. And what she'd done to Marcus . . . Probably that was why the detective was here.

'I killed Marcus.' There was a tremble in her voice. 'I murdered him.'

'No.' The detective almost sounded surprised. 'You didn't. He's OK. He told us how to find you.' Annabelle nodded slowly, unsure of what to make of this information. The detective stood up, and Annabelle realised just how tall she was. 'I'll leave you to sleep.'

'Please don't,' Annabelle whispered.

Monica nodded slowly and sat back down again. 'Well, do you feel like talking?' She pulled her phone from her coat pocket.

Annabelle wasn't sure if she did, but she really didn't want to be alone. 'Definitely.'

'Can you tell me what happened? From the start? Don't leave anything out.' She pressed the red button on the phone's voice recording function and laid it on the bed between them.

Annabelle started to talk. About leaving Mr Pepper (Monica reassured her that Crawford had already contacted Miss Albright), the drive up from England, the fateful decision to take the road into Glen Turrit. Sometimes the detective nodded along with her, as if she already knew what Annabelle was telling her. Like when she spoke about the little girl suddenly appearing in the road in front of her. At other times she furrowed her brow and listened intently, like when Annabelle told her that the only members of the Slate family she'd actually met were Marcus, the Doctor and Lily.

She kept talking, even when her throat ached and the cuts at the corner of her mouth stung. She talked about when the Doctor had taken her leg. Still matter-of-fact, though she could see the horror in Monica's eyes. The overwhelming terror when she'd pulled the carpet square off the cell wall and seen those terrible words: THEYR EATING ME. The moment she'd hit Marcus. The terrifying race through the tunnels, and her certainty that she would die down there.

At some point she must have stopped talking because when she woke up again she was alone in the room. It was dark outside, and the glow of the city's lights had dyed the sky orange. And there was someone in the shadows in the corner of the room. Long and thin with strange staring eyes.

Annabelle looked back at him for a long time. Neither of them moved until finally the dawn light drifted in through the window and the figure faded away into the nothingness of memory.

Chapter 109

The search for Doc Slate carried on in the tunnels for a further three weeks. The police eventually employed remotely controlled cameras to survey the miles of unsafe passages, but it was slow going and expensive. Finally it was decided that if he was still down there, there was no chance he had survived in the dry tunnels without food or water, and the search was suspended. Some on the team, however, believed there was another, deeper network of tunnels with water from the sump section of the caves, where it might be possible for someone to survive for longer.

There were those who argued it was inhumane to leave a man to die in the tunnels. No matter how heinous his crimes. Once the entrance doors into the network were sealed an old phone line from the tunnel to a control room in the dam was reactivated. If by some miracle the Doctor had survived, he would at least have the option of summoning help.

Doc Slate never called in the months after the line was reactivated, but a rumour swept the schools of Inverness. That the phone in the control room would occasionally ring. Always late at night, always when a lone engineer had been called out to the bottom of that lonely glen to work on one of the frequent leaks or turbine breakdowns that the increasingly decrepit dam was prone to. There was never anyone on the other end of the line, but if you listened hard, you might just catch the ghost of a voice. Echoing up from the rooms where the Doctor used to operate on his victims.

Monica had been correct in her assessment that the forensics team would find no trace of Annabelle in the Slates' house. However, there was other evidence. Slowly uncovered as the team spent weeks sifting through three generations of junk. Clothing that belonged to Scott MacConnell, a watch and rings that matched objects owned by Sebastian Sinclair. Theo Gall's wallet. There was also DNA blood evidence from all three men in the filthy kitchen of the house. Doc Slate's room, in contrast to the chaos of the rest of the house, was kept in perfect order. Rows of medical textbooks and papers, notebooks filled with anatomical sketches. And boxes of surgical implements and tools, several of which were eventually identified as taken from Sebastian Sinclair's garage.

The evidence from the house combined with Annabelle's testimony was enough to convict Karen, Marcus and Marjory Slate of abduction and conspiracy to commit murder. Doc Slate (tried in his absence) was convicted of abduction and three counts of murder. Hamish Slate was found not to have any knowledge of the crimes. Various other small personal belongings and items of clothing discovered in the house, some dating back to the 1960s, led to speculation about the Slates' involvement in other disappearances, though none of this evidence was strong enough to link them to a specific case.

Despite the evidence and what Marcus, Marjory and Lily had separately said or hinted at to Monica, none of the Slates ever confessed in court or under formal interview to cannibalism.

Chapter 110

Annabelle's insurance actually paid out on the written-off BMW M4, even though she had been on a private road. She replaced it with something a little roomier, a Mercedes-Benz GLC crossover – 'More Space. More Fun. More Comfort', according to the Mercedes website. Actually it cost more than the insurance money, but her dad had offered to pay the difference. Suddenly he was interested in her now that she was famous.

She ignored his calls. She didn't want to see him, or even speak to him. Not after all those memories she'd unearthed down in the tunnels, and once she'd opened that closet she'd discovered other dusty bones and fragments. The times he'd forgotten to pick her up from school, cancelled plans at the last minute without explanation, not even acknowledged her messages and emails. She understood that she barely existed in his mind. For him she was little more than one of those waxwork models from her fevered nightmares. She understood that this was never going to change. It was different with her mum. When they spoke at the hospital she'd agreed to talk about the past, to try to patch things up. It was a start at least.

Since the tunnels she'd begun to understand other things about friendship and family too: that your family didn't have to be the one you were born into. Because in her darkest moments it hadn't been her parents she'd looked to for comfort but Miss Albright and Mr Pepper, the volunteers at the cafe,

Scott, even her stepbrother Ben Fisher. She had accumulated online friends too on Instagram. Ten times as many as before *everything* had happened, without even posting a picture.

She still wanted to go on driving trips and she had found the extra money for the Mercedes by selling her story to a newspaper. She wanted the bigger car because of Mr Pepper and Miss Albright. Taking them with her seemed like a good thing to do so they weren't shut up inside all the time. She also offered to take one person from the cafe with her on each trip. Sometimes no one wanted to come, but other times she had to write the names on scraps of paper and put them in a mixing bowl in the kitchen to decide.

Her new stepbrother even came down to visit her in hospital. Ben. They didn't exactly talk about any of it – what had happened at her dad's wedding or even the Slates – but having a kind of connection felt like something. He actually suggested she came back to finish her tour of the Highlands. 'But with a police escort this time,' he had said with a slightly arrogant tone that somehow made her think of Marcus, of those long days in that cell underground.

So far Marcus hadn't responded to any of her messages. Maybe that was a good thing, but she planned to keep trying. Maybe she would even visit him in prison, where it would be the opposite of before. Him locked up and her allowed to leave. In a way she felt sorry for him. Monica had told Annabelle about his child-hood. He wasn't a Slate and could have had a different life. In a weird way she felt like she was the closest thing he had to family now. And only he could understand the time she'd experienced underground. The way it had changed her into a different person.

When she thought about it like that, Annabelle even considered doing what Ben had suggested. She was strong enough, of course she was. When the weather was warm and she'd taken Miss Albright, Mr Pepper and one of the people from the cafe down to Lyme Regis. Or even on to Dartmoor and Plymouth. When it was a hot day and they'd had an ice cream and laughed about how they all wanted another one. On those warm days she could imagine driving along those open Highland roads. Visiting picturesque, deserted beaches, admiring sculpted mountains. Sometimes it felt like she might actually do it.

There were other times though. When the days were gloomy and the cold hinted at the far north-west. The Atlantic chill that made her shiver and hug herself. Feel the ache where her leg had been. On those days she would go quiet on the drive home. The shadows in the rear-view mirror would even take on a human shape. Someone with strange disconnected eyes. The words would come back to her. The ones she'd whisper to herself when she woke from the nightmares.

'I will never, ever, ever, go back to the Highlands.'

Chapter III

The doorbell rang and Monica glanced over to where Lucy was lying on the rug by the TV. She was staring resolutely at the book open in front of her, face set in a stern pout, attempting to contain her excitement. Monica could see the way her little hands were clenched tight in anticipation and tilted her head to watch her for a moment longer. Her daughter seemed fine, although Monica still couldn't shake the memory of her crouched by Long John's cupboard.

In the two months since that night she hadn't sleepwalked or reported any more strange dreams. One rainy afternoon at her mum's house Monica had found Lucy poring over a stack of old books. Small Ladybird hardbacks from the 1970s that had been Monica's as a child. *Beauty and the Beast, Rumpelstiltskin, Journey to the Centre of the Earth, Sleeping Beauty*. She had crouched beside Lucy, felt the dry paper between her fingers as she turned the pages, remembered the distantly familiar stories – as if from another life. And taken in the frightening illustrations: hard-faced witches, monsters, talking animals. It was a clue. *Perhaps this was where Lucy's dream had come from.*

'Have you looked at these before, honey?'

'I think so. I think I like *Puss in Boots* the best. He's a cat who walks on two legs and wears boots like a person.'

It was a good enough explanation for Monica, and an online search had reassured her that sleepwalking was particularly common among children around Lucy's age. Changes in routine, such as Monica's return to irregular working hours, could also trigger episodes, apparently. When Lucy had finished looking at the books Monica had quietly put them away in a box and put the box up into the attic. So a reasonable explanation for the dreams and the sleepwalking, but where Lucy had found the key to her dad's long-locked cupboard or heard his nickname remained a mystery. Although since the day out in the glen Lucy hadn't mentioned Long John. It was as if finding the address book had somehow put the name out of her mind. Even as it had forced it harder into Monica's. *Long John Kennedy*, the ghost hanging over the family.

She had shown the address book to her mum the week after they'd found Annabelle. They were in her mum's kitchen while Lucy was safely at Munyasa's. Just the two of them. They'd had a conversation they should have had twenty, thirty years before.

Monica laid the address book down on the counter. 'Lucy found this in Dad's cupboard.'

'Oh!' Her mum tilted her head towards the book, avoiding eye contact. 'I hadn't seen that . . .' Her voice faded away.

'Dad took it from you? Didn't he? He used to control who you could see – he stopped you from contacting friends and family, didn't he?' Monica still couldn't quite believe what had been there in front of her for her whole life. Her sociable mum who never did anything with friends or family without her husband. Her competent and outgoing mum who never answered the phone, who didn't have access to the family bank account. 'That's coercive control, Mum,' she said more softly, 'did he hit you? Did he hurt you?'

Angela Kennedy kept her eyes fixed on that address book for a long time. 'Your dad wasn't perfect,' she said finally, her voice barely a whisper. 'Who is? But he tried his best. I know you didn't think much of him –' Monica heard the catch in her mum's voice, could sense that her upset was tilting towards anger '– but I can't believe you would even ask if he hurt me. Of course he didn't . . . You left like that then never wanted to speak to him. How do you think that made him feel? You never even explained—'

Unexpectedly Monica felt her own anger begin to rise: a pressure in her temples, a tightening of her jaw. 'You really want to know? After all this time?' Her emotions were still running high after the horror of the case, and for a moment those years of hurt took control of her mouth. 'I was twenty-six years old when I went!' She was almost shouting. 'You never thought to ask then? You never thought I might need *you*?'

'Well, you used to get on with him so well when you were wee, then as a teenager you were always so secretive! You never told us anything.'

'Me?! Dad isolates you from your family and friends, doesn't let you answer the phone, and *I'm* secretive? You really want to know what happened?' Monica let the awful silence fill the room, felt the hot blood pumping in her head as she thought back to the case all those years before. Driving across the bridge into Carselang to investigate the death of a prisoner. The horrifying discovery that her father had turned a blind eye to bullying and even violence in the prison. Had covered it up, chosen to safeguard his own position, his reputation, even if it meant lying to the police, to his own daughter, tainting her in the process. She thought of Lucy, of what had happened to her in the case six months before, how she would do anything to change the past, anything to protect her daughter. Yet when her father had the same choice, the chance to protect Monica, he had left her exposed in order to stay in control himself. Even though it meant Monica could never look at him with admiration again.

Mercifully there had been a knock at the front door. The distraction was enough for her to regain control. To remind herself why she'd never told her mum. Did she really need to know her husband had been corrupt? Had permitted violence in the prison he was so bloody proud of? That he had put his daughter in an impossible situation as a junior detective on one of her first investigations? Dragged her into a web of lies and violence, until she was almost complicit in the corruption? That she had felt it as a stain on her conscience and regretted it every day since? The lies that had undermined any love, any sense of respect for her father or his role as a husband to her mum. His choices had removed any chance of them being happy together as a family in a simple, ordinary way. Monica felt the heat flare in her chest at the thought of how things might have been different. But would it really do her mum or Lucy any good to talk about it now, after all these years?

The knock came again, louder this time. Through the kitchen window Monica saw Lydia's red Citroën parked outside. Dropping Lucy off early. She glanced back at her mum. Soon Lucy would be starting school. Wasn't it better she and her mum enjoyed watching her grow up, made the best of life, than dig up the unchangeable past?

Crawford looked up from where he was leaning on the breakfast bar in Monica's flat. He was standing beside Angela. Monica realised that she had been staring at him, forced a smile and pushed the memories back down. He'd arrived five minutes earlier wearing a pristine new tan leather jacket. A replacement for the one shredded at Francis MacGregor's house.

'It must be him; he said he'd be here any time,' Crawford whispered, sounding almost as excited as Lucy.

Monica went to open the door. Michael Bach was outside in the hall, crouched over a cat basket. He stood up when he heard the door opening. He was almost as tall as Monica and seemed somehow larger than the last time they'd met, months before. Michael was a social worker Monica and Crawford had previously collaborated with on a case. More important on this occasion was the fact that a number of semi-feral cats had moved in with him at his remote croft house. A young tom had recently attempted to join the others but was being bullied by the three older cats.

'I think he's a bit stressed. Colonel Mustard tried to attack him earlier.'

Monica nodded, trying again to dislodge the lingering memory of the conversation with her mum. Then crouched down to the basket and peered through the grille in the door. The cat stared back at her with wide green eyes. He was large and had creamy-coloured fur.

'I was looking into getting a kitten, but Lucy had it in her head about giving a home to a stray,' Monica said as Michael stooped to pick up the basket and carry it inside.

Lucy was standing now, almost dancing with excitement. Hands pressed together in front of her.

'Is he really going to stay with us?' she finally blurted, unable to contain herself.

'If you'll have him?' Michael opened the front of the basket. The cat resisted leaving the safety of the container until Michael tilted it a little, then he crept out, belly close to the floor, glanced cautiously around and settled on the rug. 'Try stroking him.'

Lucy moved closer. Face set in grave concentration, she held her hand out. Monica, Michael, Crawford and Angela all watched on as the cat raised his head a little and nuzzled Lucy's hand. 'What's his name?' she asked.

Michael cleared his throat. 'Well . . . I've been calling him Doughball. You can change it to something nicer.' He watched Lucy stroking the cat a moment longer then bent to pick up the basket. 'I should go. I've got a lot on.'

'How's Lily?' Monica couldn't resist asking. She knew that Michael's department was handling Lily Slate's case.

'Lily was around some horrendous things,' he whispered, glancing down at Lucy to be sure she didn't hear. 'She thinks it's her fault that the family was broken up . . .'

Monica nodded. Feeling a spasm of guilt in her stomach as she remembered the scene at the Slates' house and what she'd said to Lily. Hopefully she would understand some day. And while Monica hated the memory of Lily's small body going tense in her arms with fright, of the awful things she'd said to her, she knew they had saved Annabelle's life. She glanced at her own mother, who was fussing over the kettle. At Crawford on a stool, who was watching Lucy stroke the cat, poised to intervene if it scratched her. 'We're born to love our families. No matter how bad they are.'

Michael nodded, but his expression wasn't hopeful. 'The Slates were beyond . . .'

'I spoke to the psychologist who was evaluating Karen Sinclair and Marcus Slate,' Monica said, 'about the degree of control Doc and Marjory Slate exerted over them. Hopefully it'll be reflected in their sentencing. Hopefully Karen will still have a chance to be a mother to Lily and to her son.'

'The other brother, Hamish, Lily's been spending some time with him. He's in supported accommodation.' Monica nodded this time, Hamish Slate hadn't been involved in any of the crimes as far as anyone could tell. And Karen and Sebastian's son was now living with Heather Sinclair.

An awkward silence fell over the room. Michael rubbed a hand over the stubble on his face. Monica thought he was going to turn and leave, instead he said, 'What about Annabelle Whittaker? Have you heard how she is?'

'She was trying to contact Marcus,' Monica replied. 'Apparently she wanted to meet him . . . Apart from that I've not heard.' She shrugged then smiled as she remembered. 'The last time she messaged me she'd just got a new car. An automatic so she can drive with one leg. She says she still loves to drive.'

Acknowledgements

Two books were incredibly useful when I was researching the history of the Scottish hydro-electric projects: *Tunnel Tigers* by Patrick Campbell, and *The Hydro Boys* by Emma Wood. I recommend them both.

Neither Little Arklow nor Glen Turrit exist outside this book. I based Glen Turrit on beautiful Glen Strathfarrar, the closest glen to where I live near Inverness in the Scottish Highlands. Like Glen Turrit in the book, the road down Glen Strathfarrar is closed, but during the summer months friendly gatekeepers will let you in on certain days.

Big thanks to my sister Tanya Baron for answering my random text messages about amputations and blood poisoning. Thanks to Gregor Matheson for feedback on an early version of the novel, and for years of chat about cannibals in dark corners of the Scottish Highlands. Thanks to Lulu Woodcock for feedback on an early draft of the novel. And huge thanks to my amazing partner Sarah Woodcock for massive support when I was feeling the pressure of the second novel, for giving me so much expert psychological input on the characters and help with the storyline, and for reading multiple versions of the book and somehow maintaining enthusiasm despite being twice as busy as me.

Huge, huge thanks to Sara Nisha Adams, my editor on this novel, for providing such detailed and creative editorial input that had a massive impact on shaping the feel, storyline and characters of *Dark Waters*. Also big thanks to my agent Camilla Bolton, Jade Chandler and Liz Foley at Harvill Secker for feedback and editorial input, I really appreciate all your creativity and support. Thanks to the rest of the teams at Darley Anderson agency, Harvill Secker and Vintage. I can't thank you all enough for everything. I feel incredibly lucky to work with so many talented and creative people.

I probably wouldn't have written this book if it hadn't been for all the adventures in the Scottish mountains over the years. Thanks to all my climbing and walking partners. Especially Alisa Hughes, Ben Kylie, Duncan Lang, Ranald Macdonald, Graeme Marsden, Michael Mullender, Andrew Park, Alex Runciman (RIP), Sarah Woodcock, Harry Thompson, and Graeme Young.

Also thanks to Graham Hanks, Rita Farragher-Hanks, Nikki Milne, Paul Mathur and all my other amazing colleagues from over the years at ICA Inverness. Really appreciate all your support.

G. R. Halliday was born in Edinburgh and grew up near Stirling in Scotland. He spent his childhood obsessing over the unexplained mysteries his father investigated, which proved excellent inspiration for his crime writing. His debut novel *From the Shadows* was shortlisted for the McIlvanney Debut Prize 2019. G. R. Halliday now lives in the rural Highlands outside of Inverness, where he is able to pursue his favourite pastimes of mountain climbing and swimming in the sea, before returning home to his band of semi-feral cats. *Dark Waters* is his second novel.

Follow G. R. Halliday on Twitter @gr_halliday.